"Say you love me forever, whether we are wed or nay."

"I swear it. You are my true husband now and forever."

David gazed down at her. How beautiful she looked, her face silvered by the light of the rising moon. Catrin lay helpless beneath him in the heather like some pagan captive. And a primitive part of him was highly aroused by the thought. Though David was many generations removed from his ancestors the Gaels, that same love of plunder, the wild, primitive arousal of taking captive flickered in him still.

The strange expression on David's face made Catrin tremble as she gazed up at him. She listened to the gentle lap of water and his harsh breathing, aware that she would never forget this magical night on the shore of the loch...

MORE PRECIOUS THAN GOLD

by Patricia Phillips
author of
TOUCH ME WITH FIRE and **JENNY**

MORE PRECIOUS THAN GOLD

PATRICIA PHILLIPS

A JOVE BOOK

MORE PRECIOUS THAN GOLD

A Jove Book/published by arrangement with
the author

PRINTING HISTORY
Jove edition/April 1985

ISBN: 0-515-08037-3

Jove books are published by The Berkley Publishing Group,
200 Madison Avenue, New York, N.Y. 10016.
The words "A JOVE BOOK" and the "J" with sunburst
are trademarks belonging to Jove Publications, Inc.

PRINTED IN THE UNITED STATES OF AMERICA

Chapter 1

The broad ribbon of the Thames shimmered in the sultry afternoon heat. Congested with watermen and goods-laden barges, this main thoroughfare of Georgian London bisected the city's heart, lapping both warehouse and mansion with its dark, flotsam-strewn waters.

Upstream the surroundings grew pleasantly bucolic, with black-and-white cattle grazing the riverbanks and fishermen lazily dipping rods into the murky, reed-choked shallows. Grand houses lined the way, their flower-bright gardens stretching to the water's edge. The commercial river traffic gradually gave way to pleasure craft bound for the delights of Hampton Court and Richmond Park.

Outside the tree-shaded Black Bull, Catrin Blair and her brother Ness reined in their horses and dismounted. The picturesque half-timbered inn, known for its dark ale and moderately priced meals, was a favorite resting place of travelers on the river road. The fresh breeze that had stirred the heavy-leaved trees on their journey from Chiswick suddenly dropped, turning the July afternoon oppressive.

"It'll storm before the day's out," Ness predicted, glancing to the east, where heavy clouds had formed a canopy over the city. "Are you sure you won't ride back with me?"

"No. I told Papa I was going to paint and he might get suspicious if I've nothing to show for my time. Besides, I'm looking forward to a few hours to myself. Go to your rendezvous alone—Drury Lane actresses aren't to my taste."

1

Ness grinned, self-consciously straightening his stock. Though he was not actually ashamed of his liaison with Doll, whenever his sister mentioned her he grew vastly uncomfortable. "I intended to take you home first."

Catrin smiled and gave him a playful push. "Go. She'll think you're not coming."

"I'll set up your easel, then I'll be off—after I've downed a couple of pints to quench my thirst."

Catrin frowned at Ness's words. Lately drink had become a sore subject between them. Glancing critically at her handsome brother in his expensive green cloth coat and fawn breeches, she could see that so far his "failing," as the servants termed Ness's excessive drinking, had not destroyed his good looks. Yet if Catrin studied his face, which was almost a reflection of her own, she could see the early signs of debauchery. Beneath a fading tan Ness's complexion bore a grayish cast; his large gray eyes were bloodshot, his eyes puffy from lack of sleep and overindulgence. Thrusting aside her depressing observations, Catrin gave Ness a sisterly peck on the cheek.

"Don't forget Papa's important dinner. You will be home in time?"

He shrugged. "I'll try, but I'm making no promises. It all depends on how generous Doll becomes. Don't worry about me," he added sharply as he saw his sister's face tighten. "Surely I'm old enough to take care of myself. Even when I quarrel with old Millbank, it's just between the two of us. You mustn't fret over every outburst."

"I'll try not to," Catrin agreed, aware that such detachment was beyond her. She loved Ness dearly and it distressed her to see him destroying himself. Though her brother had always hated his stepfather, Humphrey Millbank's efforts to settle his stepson's future arose out of concern, not meddling as Ness supposed. And much to her stepfather's annoyance, despite Ness's many failings, Catrin usually rose loyally to her brother's defense.

Catrin bit her lower lip as she watched Ness lead his horse toward the inn. He stopped a passing barmaid, took a brimming flagon of ale from her tray, and rapidly quaffed it. He returned the empty flagon with a peck on the girl's cheek and surreptitiously slid several coins inside her ample bodice. His laughter, mingling with the barmaid's false screams of modesty, grated on Catrin's nerves, and she turned away.

Impatiently Catrin brushed the thick chestnut hair from her

smooth brow. She adjusted the green satin ribbon securing the bunch of glossy ringlets at the nape of her slender neck. The fashionable riding habit of spring green silk faced with pink fitted Catrin's small-waisted figure like a second skin, its military-style braided bodice accentuating her ample bosom. Her oval face, its wide-set gray eyes framed beneath dark winged brows, became melancholy as she considered Ness's dismal future.

Preoccupied though she was with her thoughts, Catrin could not fail to notice the approving glances of a group of fashionable gentlemen who had paused for refreshment at the riverside inn. The men were naturally intrigued by her presence there, since it was highly unusual for a lady of quality to travel alone. But, knowing their attentions would not be welcome to a young woman of her class, the rakes refrained from making romantic overtures and contented themselves with staring at the devastatingly lovely creature.

A rising breeze stirred the leaves overhead as Catrin seated herself on her folding stool and deftly began to mix shades of green. Tension slowly ebbed from her body as she concentrated on the canvas and concern over her brother's disastrous mode of living, her stepfather's rage should Ness absent himself from the dinner table once again, even the possibility of her own deception's being discovered, all faded. This scene of shimmering water framed by low-hanging trees, of riverbanks wild with lush foliage and aflame with patches of fragrant rosebay willow herb, brought her a deep sense of peace.

As she painted, Catrin's thoughts followed a train of thought started by her morning visit with Easter and Comyn Stewart, childhood friends recently arrived from Rome. Like the Stewarts, Catrin and her brother had been raised in genteel poverty on the fringe of Rome's exiled Jacobite court. Their father, "Mad Alisdair" Blair, slowly drank himself to death, forcing their mother to turn to portrait painting to support them. Though in Rome they were impoverished nobodies, the Blair children were always aware of their exiled parents' rightful rank in Scotland as kin of the Grahams of Monteith. "Mad Alisdair" had forfeited both title and estates when he supported the Stuarts in the unsuccessful Jacobite rising of 1715.

It was this same deeply instilled sense of roots in their beloved homeland which had brought Easter Stewart across the Channel to give her expected child Scottish birth. The taxing voyage had induced premature labor, and instead of riding north, the young couple had been forced to take lodgings in Chiswick for the impending birth.

"At least he wasn't born Italian," Easter had said, her pale face proud as she admired her puny month-old infant. Not born Italian. Catrin found Easter's statement strange. She, like they, had been born in Rome, but though Italy was the country of her birth, Catrin had never felt Italian. Like many of the younger generation of exiles, she and Ness were more devoutly Scottish than their parents. Those embittered men who "came out" in the '15, forfeiting lands for a lost cause, had primed their children well, making them aware of their rightful heritage in deliberate preparation for "next time."

Neither Catrin's visit to the Stewarts nor her brother's company on the journey had been sanctioned by Humphrey Millbank. Her stepfather disapproved of impoverished Jacobites and, in his opinion, the less Catrin saw of Ness, the better. She had told him she would ride into the countryside to paint, and now felt guilty about the lie. Since painting was one of the few indulgences Catrin was allowed, her stepfather had readily agreed. Humphrey Millbank's uncharacteristic charity on this issue arose from his deep love for Catrin's mother, who had been a gifted artist; in his stepdaughter he hoped to nurture inherited talent. Milly, Catrin's maid, was supposed to accompany her mistress. It had taken little persuasion to convince Milly to visit her family, thereby leaving Catrin free to enjoy a blissful day to herself—a freedom she enjoyed seldom of late, since Catrin's impending marriage to the Cavendish heir was of great importance to Humphrey Millbank and he feared that any unseemliness on her part might cancel the arrangements. As a result, he generally kept his stepdaughter under close supervision. Having risen from poverty himself, her stepfather had become obsessed with being accepted as quality in recent years. His beautiful stepdaughter's betrothal to the scion of a great family would assure this distinction for Millbank's descendants, and it was a treasure he guarded more fiercely than gold.

The ominous rumble of thunder echoed in the distance and Catrin's young mare whickered, straining at her tether.

"Hush, Puppet, it's all right," Catrin soothed, glancing toward the gathering clouds, steel gray against a sullen sky. Her brush moved rapidly as she strove to capture the threatening mood that had turned the summer's day majestically somber. The inn's patrons had already retired inside the Black Bull to escape the oncoming downpour. Just a few minutes more, thought Catrin, as she feverishly mixed paints, hoping to produce the perfect shade of ocher-tinged gray that would mimic the rapidly building thunderhead.

The wind suddenly picked up, whipping leaves and debris along the towpath and churning the peaceful Thames into frothing whitecaps. Catrin ignored the ominous change as she swiftly reproduced the turbulent cloud. Lightning cut a fiery swath through the murk and, screaming in fright, the young mare reared, threshing her forelegs in an effort to pull free.

Alarmed by the animal's frenzy, Catrin put down her palette and tried to soothe the frightened bay, whose eyes rolled back into her head, gleaming white against her dark face. Though the mare still snorted and pawed the ground, she was responding to her mistress's touch when a second jagged spear of lightning split the heavens. The mare reared again. Catrin grabbed the reins, soothing Puppet while she unlooped the leather, but as she was leading the animal to shelter, penny-sized raindrops spattered the dusty towpath. Catrin gasped with alarm and raced back to rescue her painting and supplies, dragging the mare with her. Cold raindrops pelted her skin through the thin habit as Catrin struggled one-handed to collapse the easel. Her brush fell in the dirt while the rising wind whipped her skirts against the wet oils. Deepening thunder drove the mare to new frenzies until she pulled so hard that Catrin had to abandon her half-collapsed easel to attend to her.

"You seem to be having trouble. Let me help you," shouted a masculine voice.

"Oh, thank you," Catrin gasped, turning to view her rescuer through the strands of wet hair plastered over her face.

The young man seized the mare's reins and quickly calmed her. By now the rain was pouring down on them, pocking the river and releasing heady perfume from the tangled bankside grasses. He quickly collapsed the easel and stool; then, thrusting them under his arm, he shouted for Catrin to follow before he raced for the Black Bull, taking the mare with him.

Catrin sheltered beneath the stone archway leading to the stableyard while her rescuer summoned a groom, instructing him to rub down the mare before repacking the painting supplies for her return journey. Catrin was amazed at how fast the man had come to her rescue; when the rain began, she had been alone on the towpath. She debated whether to pay him for his assistance. By his dress he appeared to be a gentleman and, afraid of insulting him, she decided against the offer.

He was walking toward her now, his dark hair sticking in rain-wet curls to his brow. "Not too wet, I hope," he inquired cheerfully as he ducked beneath the broad stone arch.

"No, thanks to you. I really can't thank you enough for coming to my rescue."

"You're most welcome, milady. I can't bear to see a lovely lady in distress."

Catrin smiled at his compliment, surprised to find her stomach pitching when their eyes met. At such close quarters he was very handsome. In fact, she found him so fascinating it was hard to take her eyes off him. His deeply sun-bronzed skin and an occasional un-English inflection to his speech made her wonder if he came from a hotter clime. Thick black lashes made a sooty frame for luminous green eyes, which regarded her with approval. When their gaze locked a second time, Catrin shuddered, enjoying this delicious new sensation.

"Come, you're shivering with cold. I'd never forgive myself if you took a chill. We'll make a run for it. Ready?"

She nodded, laughing as he seized her hand and raced with her through rapidly forming puddles to the inn's side entrance. They burst into the gloomy oak-paneled passageway leading to the common taproom.

"Landlord, a warming meal for milady," the man ordered, catching the stocky innkeeper's arm as he hurried toward the kitchen. "And mulled ale—no, on second thoughts, make that claret, more warming by far. Here, this should be sufficient for your pains."

The landlord accepted a handful of coins and respectfully touched his forelock. "Aye, sir, take the lady inside to the fire. She'll soon be dry."

Catrin found herself bustled to a padded settle before the roaring hearth in the low-beamed taproom. Firelight glinted off copper and brass utensils hanging on the oak-paneled walls. Despite the fact that a maid in a frilled mobcap was hovering in the background, anxious to set the table, Catrin's rescuer made sure she was comfortably settled before he allowed the woman to accomplish her task.

"I must reimburse you, sir."

"No, thank you, it's my pleasure."

"I insist."

"No." Catrin's hand was gently thrust aside as he refused her money.

This abrupt end to their conversation puzzled Catrin until she noticed a well-dressed gentleman with a sour expression at the corner table impatiently summoning her rescuer back to his meal.

"Thank you again, sir, you've been most kind."

"Please, don't mention it, milady. I told you, I can't bear to see a lovely lady in distress." Delivering this final compliment, the man bowed politely before rejoining his companion.

Catrin grew uncomfortably conscious of her heart pounding beneath her tight-buttoned bodice as she spread her skirts before the fire. Considering the man's evident interest in her, she found it strange that he had not introduced himself. Though admittedly she had no experience with men, having been constantly under her stepfather's watchful eye, Catrin's woman's instinct assured her that he found her most attractive.

Presently the maid reappeared bearing a pewter tray on which steamed a bowl of pea soup, a platter of roast beef swimming in gravy, a dish of spicy, raisin-studded plum pudding and a brimming cup of mulled claret.

While she ate with a most unladylike appetite Catrin could feel the stranger's penetrating gaze; her cheeks flushed. Yet when she glanced in his direction he seemed to be engrossed in his companion's conversation. His apparent attraction to her made Catrin shiver in anticipation. Did thoughts of a wicked dalliance excite her? Or was she merely flattered? she pondered, as she sipped from the mug of warm, spiced claret. When again she glanced his way, the man openly returned her interest, until she was forced to look away from his appraising gaze.

The message she read in his large, dark-lashed green eyes was plain enough. Catrin was shocked by her own eager acceptance of his invitation. What was the matter with her? So attracted was she to this dark-haired stranger, for a moment she even contemplated going to his table to thank him again for his assistance, fully aware of the likely consequences should she encourage him. Anticipation of their probable romantic encounter was so pleasurable, she gasped. The claret must have addled her wits!

Eyes closed, Catrin recaptured in her mind his handsome, high-cheekboned face with its aquiline nose and sensual, well-shaped mouth. The unmistakable invitation in his eyes she found the most stirring of all. The man's broad-shouldered, athletic body, attired in a well-cut claret camlet coat, skintight doeskin britches, and tall black riding boots turned down with scarlet, vastly enhanced his romantic appearance. Like someone from a magnificent dream he had come to her rescue, almost too attractive to be real...

But he was real. Catrin opened her eyes and her cheeks flushed hotly as he winked. There was no mistaking his silent suggestion. Catrin sighed as she imagined herself in his arms, his sensual mouth closing over hers, his long-fingered, olive-skinned hands caressing her shoulders...

She sat up straighter, her face warm. The combination of the fire, food, and wine imparted a drowsy sensuality unlike anything she had experienced before. Why had he set her senses reeling? Could inner rebellion against her arranged marriage to Bryce Cavendish be partly to blame? Undeniably the man was handsome, yet Bryce too was considered handsome. Though they had been betrothed since she was thirteen, her future husband was practically a stranger. On the few occasions Catrin had been alone with Bryce, his nearness had stirred no flicker of excitement. Whereas this handsome stranger, who watched her intently across the crowded taproom, kindled the deepest responses, both pleasant and disturbing.

She was tipsy! Yes, that must be the reason behind this unusual reaction. Catrin smiled at the idea, deciding light-heartedly if being tipsy felt like this, it was a most pleasurable state. Growing bolder, she ventured another glance in the man's direction. This time he acknowledged her with a smile, his even white teeth flashing against his tanned skin. Now he inclined his head toward the door, his meaning unmistakable. Catrin's heart raced and the breath choked in her throat. What a fool she was being! She did not even know his name. Besides, following when a man beckoned was for tavern maids, not ladies. Just for once she suddenly longed to be a nameless tavern maid instead of Humphrey Millbank's stepdaughter, destined for a grand marriage.

As this point their communication was broken by a passing barmaid. Catrin wound her hands together in agitation beneath the scarred oak table. Why shouldn't she go to him? She need carry the flirtation no further than she wished, and she assumed him to be gentleman enough not to force her to his will. At the very least she would learn his name and could give him hers. They would converse, and afterward... thrilling sensations of his kisses, of his strong body pressed against hers in passionate embrace, sped through Catrin's mind. The breath-taking fantasy stirred her to such an extent that she was convinced her emotion was apparent to everyone in the room. She could stand the suspense no longer—she would go to him!

"Catrin! 'Pon my word, it is you!"

Catrin froze. Gingerly she lowered herself back onto the settle. To her horror she recognized the elderly couple who were shouldering their way to the fireside, their rich clothing damp from the rain outside.

"'Pon my word," repeated Daniel Fisher, "I didn't believe my eyes, but Dorcas insisted it was you. What are you doing here alone, my dear?" In vain the elderly gentleman glanced about the room for Catrin's companions.

"Why, Mr. Fisher, what a pleasant surprise," Catrin mumbled foolishly, searching for a plausible explanation of her presence. She had no idea how long the Fishers had been watching her. She hoped fiercely that they had not seen her talking to that man, for if they had she knew they would tell her stepfather.

"I'll grant you it's a surprise," Dorcas Fisher agreed grimly as she lowered her vast bulk onto the settle beside Catrin. "Does Humphrey know you're here, mixing with this riffraff? He doesn't, I'll be bound," she pronounced, without giving Catrin a chance to reply. "What are you young people thinking about these days? I suppose that disreputable brother of yours is at the back of this."

"Dorcas," her husband warned as he balanced on a wooden stool before the hearth, stretching his damp hose to the flames, "let the child explain herself."

The "child" gulped, longing to slap Mrs. Fisher's puffy face. "I was painting beside the river and got caught in the storm. I assure you, Papa's aware of my outing."

"Really! Well, I am surprised—surprised he'd sanction your presence in a place like this," Mrs. Fisher commented sourly. "And where, might I ask, is your abigail? A young lady of quality most definitely does not appear alone in public."

"Milly was taken ill. My being at this inn is not out of choice, it merely happened to be the closest shelter from the rain. When the storm broke a kind gentleman came to my assistance—"

"Yes, we watched the gallant rescue," rumbled Daniel Fisher, exchanging meaningful glances with his wife. "That young fellow was bold as brass. Disgraceful, I say, but what else can be expected at a common inn."

Their swift exchange of glances told Catrin that the Fishers had also observed her interest in the stranger and had drawn their own conclusions. Given the thousands of people populating London, why had she the ill fortune to meet her father's friends under such damning circumstances?

"I'm sure Papa will be most grateful that the gentleman came to my aid," Catrin retorted coldly, fixing Mrs. Fisher with an icy stare. "I'm perfectly capable of looking after myself."

"That's a matter of opinion, Catrin. Anyway, we'll see you safely home. Our coach should be ready by now. Got caught strolling beside the river. Dreadful downpour. A fine how-do-you-do. We've probably taken our deaths of cold."

"I can already feel my throat scratching," complained Dorcas Fisher, clasping her puffy neck.

"You should've taken a preventive glass of mulled ale, Dorcas, my love."

"You know I never touch spirits," Mrs. Fisher pronounced piously, fixing Catrin's empty claret cup with a beady gaze.

Catrin smarted in silence, knowing it was pointless to defend herself further. The Fishers' conclusions were already drawn, and a splendid version of them would undoubtedly be presented at tonight's supper table. Belatedly she recalled that the elderly couple were to be among her stepfather's guests on this, the eve of his departure for Bristol.

"You really mustn't bother. See, the rain's already stopped," Catrin declared brightly as she glimpsed the clearing skies through the diamond-paned window. "I can ride home by myself."

"Never!" exploded Daniel Fisher. "I wouldn't want it on my conscience to allow a well-bred young lady to ride alone through the London streets. One of my men can lead your horse. You, my dear, will ride in the coach with us. I certainly owe Humphrey that much, 'pon my soul, I do."

Catrin made her way through the crowded taproom, her full pink mouth in a pout, her face almost crimson with embarrassment as she met the dark-haired man's eyes again. He had been watching the unfolding scene with interest. As she passed his table he flashed her a sympathetic grin. Catrin felt extremely foolish as she realized he must assume the elderly couple to be her parents, she their errant daughter caught misbehaving.

Head high, Catrin stepped into the rain-cooled air. She could have refused—as indeed she longed to do—to accompany the Fishers to Bloomsbury. But if she openly defied them they would undoubtedly assume an even worse reason for her presence at the Black Bull. Far better to appear meekly obliging in hope they would be kind when relaying her indiscretion.

Catrin's prayers for leniency were futile. When her stepfather's heavy jowls turned purple during Mrs. Fisher's suggestive account of her waywardness, she prepared herself for the worst. Anxious to maintain family dignity—a virtue of the quality he aspired to, if not of his own class—Humphrey Millbank did not rebuke Catrin before their guests. The accusing expression in his bulbous brown eyes and his angrily distended nostrils warned of future discord.

When finally the guests had departed, their fine coaches rumbling along the deserted Bloomsbury street in the gathering dusk, Catrin stood beside the open windows of the parlor overlooking the narrow garden at the rear of their elegant four-story townhouse. The cool breeze was a welcome relief from the close atmosphere in the dining room. The pool of light from the silver candelabra on the walnut sidetable shed a soft glow over the yellow-walled room with its lush velvet draperies embroidered with birds of paradise.

A steady, ominous tread ascending the stair warned Catrin of her stepfather's approach. Ness had not come home, and his absence was probably a further irritant, for a solicitor friend had been invited to dinner to discuss taking Ness into the firm in an effort to settle him respectably before his twenty-fifth birthday.

"So there you are, Catrin," thundered her stepfather as he stumped into the room, his squat, ungainly body glaringly out of place amid the elegant furnishings.

"Yes, Papa, here I am," Catrin repeated unnecessarily as she stared out the window at the fading shrubbery.

"What have you to say for yourself?"

"There's little left to say. Mrs. Fisher's already covered the afternoon's events most thoroughly."

"There's no need for sarcasm. What excuse have you to make? That's what I want to know."

With a sigh, Catrin turned to face him. Humphrey Millbank stood squarely in the center of the room, his expanding paunch raising the front of his snuff-stained brown suit and white silk embroidered waistcoat. He stared at her, awaiting her explanation. Though her stepfather was harsh in his treatment of his stepchildren, Catrin knew that at heart he was not a cruel man.

Whatever rules he imposed were generally in their best interests, yet when crossed he could be stubbornly unyielding. If she extolled the virtues of her handsome rescuer she could expect little sympathy. A bare recounting of fact should be sufficient to satisfy Humphrey Millbank's unimaginative nature.

"I was painting beside the river when a storm blew up. You know how highly strung Puppet is. I couldn't handle her alone. A man came to my rescue. That's all. There was no secret tryst, no unseemly behavior..."

"Even being in a place like that was unseemly," he bellowed impatiently. "Don't you know that? What if Bryce or one of his friends had seen you, eh? Do you think he'd sanction his betrothed supping alone in a common taproom? And making calf's eyes at some blade into the bargain."

"Whatever Mrs. Fisher may have implied, I was not making calf eyes at him," she retorted hotly.

"That's not what she says. Can't I let you out of me sight for a few hours? I thought you had more sense than to go to an inn. And another thing—where was that simple-minded Milly? And why were you out so late? You left well before eight. Now, I want some explanations. There's more here than meets the eye."

Huffing angrily, Humphrey Millbank sank into the nearest chair and assumed a threatening pose, chin sunk on his chest, mouth hard.

It was tempting to feign innocence, but Catrin realized he would not be fobbed off with half-truths. Her own guilt made her eager to avoid a head-on confrontation over the handsome stranger, so instead she decided to confess her deception, in hopes of eclipsing the other incident.

"I did intend to paint, Papa, *after* I'd visited some old friends," Catrin confessed, ignoring his snort of indignation. "I knew you wouldn't approve of them, or I'd have told you, though in truth they're most respectable. Friends from Rome—" though she raised her voice, Catrin was unable to drown his explosive response.

"Bloody Jacobites, I'll be bound! Am I right, lass, am I?"

"Yes, the Stewarts are children of exiles. But Papa, listen, there's nothing wicked about them. They didn't want their child to be born in Italy, that's all. I went to see their baby."

"And where, might I ask, are these respectable people lodging?"

"Chiswick."

"Chiswick! You fool lass, you mean you rode to Chiswick by yourself? As devious as you've been, I'm not daft enough to think you took that soft-headed Milly along."

"I wasn't alone . . . I was with . . . Ness."

"Ness! Oh, well now, that makes everything right. I suppose he was half drunk, or maybe he took along a couple of his fancy pieces to liven up the journey . . ."

"Papa," Catrin reproached sharply and he huffed into silence. "Ness was not drunk, nor did he bring any women with him. We merely went for a pleasant ride to Chiswick. The Stewarts are his friends also."

"And I don't suppose it matters that I've forbidden you his company. Your behavior's got to be beyond reproach for young Cavendish to follow through with the marriage," he shouted, his blood pressure rising. "I've no time for impoverished Jacobites and you know it. Them with a barrel full of fancy airs and not a penny for rent. When I married your mother she'd been left penniless with two young bairns to raise. That fancy father of yours was nowt but a drunkard! What good did his title and fine upbringing do for you? It never put food on the table."

Catrin shook her head, nervously shifting her feet on the dove-gray carpet. This was familiar territory and she knew the speech by heart. When she was much younger she had wondered why her mother had chosen to marry this uncouth north-countryman instead of a handsome nobleman from their own circle. Only as an adult had Catrin understood the reason: a wealthy shipowner, Humphrey Millbank could amply provide for their comfort. Arabella Blair was no fool. Noblemen with forfeited estates and empty titles made poor marriage prospects.

"Papa, nothing I did was to annoy you. Had I thought you'd have given me permission to visit my friends, I'd have asked. I did intend to paint later, so it was not really a deception."

Still huffing and puffing, he pulled at his squat fingers, on one of which a huge ruby ring looked out of place. "You know I've only got your best interests at heart," he defended gruffly, his thick lips jutting forward. "You're a young lass, you don't know the ways of the world. I learned soon enough—you don't stay innocent long on Liverpool dock. I know what happens to a lass alone. That's why I don't let you have your own way, not out of spite. We've got to protect our interests. You know how much this Cavendish marriage means to us."

"To you, Papa, not me."

"You? What do you know about it? A young lass hasn't sense enough to make a good match."

"I'm not in love with Bryce Cavendish, I know that much."

"Not in love! What's love to do with it? Marriage isn't for love, it's for betterment. And don't you forget it."

Angry herself now, Catrin glared back at him, finding it hard to keep her temper in check. Tonight, more than ever before, she felt the deepest reluctance to become Bryce Cavendish's bride. The man she had met at the Black Bull had been constantly in her thoughts ever since. Marriage to him seemed as if it would be a thrilling proposition, whereas marriage to Bryce Cavendish was no more than the fulfillment of an unwelcome contract.

"You'll marry Cavendish and the sooner the better. And if I have any more larking about, you're off to your Aunt Isobel. A spell in Liverpool will do wonders for you. If ever anyone could teach a lass how to act respectable, it's our Isobel."

"Oh, Papa, don't threaten me with that!"

The distress in her voice made him relent slightly. "Aye, well, I suppose that would be a bitter pill to swallow. Isobel can be a trial and no mistake. I know she's my own sister, but she can act as if she's been dipped in vinegar. Comes from marrying a preacher, I suppose."

"Surely visiting old friends and getting caught in a rainstorm doesn't deserve punishment as severe as that."

Humphrey Millbank's brown eyes began to twinkle and Catrin breathed a sigh of relief. "Nay, I reckon not. But, mark my words, lass, I want no more wantonness. And no more of Ness's company. That brother of yours is a rakehell who'll blacken your reputation. Talking about Ness," he rumbled, his good humor dissolving, "where is he? Come on now, you're always ready with alibis for him. What's the excuse tonight?"

"No excuse. Ness was visiting friends. He must have been delayed," Catrin offered lamely, though in truth she had no idea where he was. Surely his rendezvous with Doll had ended hours ago.

"Delayed, is he? Drunk, more likely! Let's call a spade a spade." Gradually Millbank's belligerent expression softened as he looked at Catrin, radiantly beautiful in the candlelight. "You're a grand lass to look at. Any man'd be proud to have you for his wife. Set a date for the wedding. It's a fool's game to play about. We don't want young Cavendish changing his mind, do we?"

Catrin swallowed uneasily. She had no desire to set a wedding date. For years she had known she was obligated to marry Bryce, yet it had always been comfortably in the future. Now that future loomed unpleasantly close. It was the custom for women of her class to enter arranged marriages. It was only since this afternoon, when her heart had been turned upside down by that handsome stranger at the Black Bull, that she had begun bitterly to resent the sealed paper committing her to a future as Lady Cavendish.

"Last week in September. How's that?"

Her stomach pitched. "Oh, Papa, that's so soon!"

"Soon!" Humphrey Millbank exploded, his quixotic temper roused. "You've kept the lad dangling since you were thirteen. I shouldn't have listened to your mother. I knew lasses who were birthing at that age. You should have been wed years ago. Anyroad, we'll have no more dallying about. Last week in September it is. Surely it's a small thing to do for me. The Cavendishes are a good, noble family, loyal King George's men all. Just think, someday relatives of Humphrey Millbank will be lords—my ancestors'll be spinning in their graves. If there's much more of a to-do, you'll be off to Isobel's! There's young Ruth there to set a good example. A right proper lass she is too."

Catrin frowned. Cousin Ruth was a younger version of her primly virtuous mother. Catrin despised her. "Ruth's a trial, but Adam's all right," she ventured, banking on Millbank's soft spot for his nephew.

"Oh, Adam's a likely lad, all right. Too bad he's set on the ministry. I could've given him a place in the shipping office. Liverpool's a grand place for a man to start. When my mother apprenticed me to Perkins Tallow Chandlers, she set me on the road to fortune. There's some as thinks my money's dirty, seeing as I took slave cargoes, but brass is brass. It all spends the same. Anyroad, Adam will get plenty of brass of his own when I'm gone."

Her stepfather's final statement was an unpleasant reminder of his new will. Much had been made of excluding Ness from the document in favor of Adam, his sister's son. Hard feelings had deepened, placing Catrin in a difficult position, for she was still to benefit from the will. Ness was to be supported until his twenty-fifth birthday, according to an agreement made with their mother. After that he got not one penny of the Millbank fortune.

She could not blame her stepfather for his mounting disgust with Ness, Catrin said to herself later as she undressed for bed. Their unpleasant discussion was thankfully behind her, her lapse temporarily forgiven. Her stepfather's angry warning that Ness would catch it when he finally showed his face had left an unpleasant aftertaste. Though she loved her brother dearly, Catrin understood that she could not continue to make excuses for him. Ness had been sent down from university, cashiered from the army, and generally bailed out of one scrape after another, Humphrey Millbank's money buying him freedom from prosecution. Ever on the defensive about Ness, she had to admit his heavy drinking had subtly altered the person she knew. Ness despised his stepfather's lowly origins, his uncouth ways and north-country accent. So heated had the arguments between the two men become that Catrin had contemplated running away from the turmoil. Yet she would never do that. She was far too sensible. Running away could solve nothing.

The reckless side of her nature was ever at war with the more practical Catrin. She assumed this reckless tendency to be inherited from their father—charming, noble, dissolute Alisdair Blair. It was from him also that Ness had inherited his fondness for drink. More distressing than her brother's excessive drinking was his growing instability, an even more ominous inheritance from their father. Sometimes, when Catrin compared the adult Ness to her memories of their handsome father, the likeness sickened her.

Unknown to their stepfather, during his absence Ness entertained mysteriously cloaked men and women who drank and talked long into the night before slipping out of the side entrance as stealthily as they had come. Though she thought she understood the purpose behind the women's visits, Catrin had no idea why the men maintained such secrecy. Could Ness be involved with criminals?

Yet, dissolute wastrel though he was, Ness was still her beloved brother. They shared the luxuriant chestnut hair and distinctive features of the Blairs. Catrin's face was on a more dainty scale, as befitted a woman, while Ness bore the prominent nose and hard jaw of the male Blairs.

Catrin sighed, deliberately thrusting aside her concern over Ness. She blew out her candle and crossed barefoot to the uncurtained windows. The sky was heavy with rainclouds and a fresh dampness blew in the wind. While she gazed at the churning heavens, she indulged in a delightful fantasy wherein she pictured the man from the Black Bull coming to her door.

A foolish pastime, the practical Catrin admonished, as she resolutely turned her back on the window. That man at the Black Bull, though admittedly attractive, was gone from her life forever. They were ships that had passed in the night. Come September, when she became the bride of Captain the Hon. Bryce Cavendish, she must banish her romantic daydreams.

The prospect was depressing. Angrily Catrin dragged the thin coverlet over her body and lay tense, trying instead to picture herself as lady of Bryce's vast estate. Undoubtedly that would be pleasant, for she could ride and walk freely in the grounds. Her father had schooled her well in the administration of a household, so managing the servants and the household accounts would not be too difficult. Her most formidable task was going to be Bryce himself. And on that disconcerting thought, she resigned herself to sleep.

Chapter 2

In the early hours of the morning Catrin was awakened by Ness as he bumped drunkenly along the corridor.

"Ness, where in heaven's name have you been?" Catrin demanded, wrenching open her door.

"What are you doing awake?" Ness muttered thickly, swaying where he stood. In the pool of light shed by her candle, Catrin looked like an avenging angel in her voluminous white nightgown, a mobcap atop her chestnut curls. Her pretty mouth was set in a tight, disapproving line.

"Where've you been till this hour? You know Papa wanted you home for dinner. He was going to ask Sir William to take you into the firm."

"Listen, Catrin, you don't know—" Ness hesitated, glancing about the darkened hall in case someone was listening.

"Oh, don't I? I know you've been drinking again. My God, you must be one of the biggest sots in London."

Her temper was sorely strained as he blinked owlishly, oblivious to the stale brandy fumes, tobacco smoke, and cloying perfume wafting about them. When he opened his mouth, presumably to protest his innocence, she angrily grabbed his sleeve, damp from the rain, and yanked him across the threshold.

"Look, Catrin, you've got it all wrong," Ness muttered angrily. In an attempt to salvage his dignity, he brushed off his crumpled coat and twisted his soiled stock into a more appropriate position.

"Oh, no, I haven't. You never fail to sabotage every good thing Papa tries to do for you."

"I don't give a tinker's damn for Millbank's likes and dislikes. He'll accept me as I am, or not at all."

"Then it will be not at all."

"So be it."

Brother and sister glared at each other. Ness swayed a moment and hastily sat on the edge of the bed. He reached for a pitcher of water and poured himself a glassful.

"Look at you. You're barely able to negotiate—"

"Wrong, sister dear, absolutely wrong," Ness said, interrupting indignantly. "I'll have you know I've just ridden post haste from Chiswick, and damned near got a soaking into the bargain."

"Chiswick? You're surely not trying to tell me you got this way at Easter's?"

"Well, not exactly . . . left a party to help the gel . . . don't say it, I'm sober enough. Eacy's in a damnable spot of trouble."

"Trouble? What sort of trouble?"

"Money. Seems the lout of a landlord's demanding back rent . . . threatening to clap her in debtor's prison. Made his move, the scoundrel, when he found Comyn was away on business."

"He can't do that! The baby's barely a month old. We must help her. There's no point in asking how much cash you've got," she added bitterly, aware Ness was always out of funds. "How much does she need?"

"Well, damn me, but I forgot to ask," Ness mumbled contritely, wincing at his sister's explosion of anger. "Take what we've got, how about that? Should cover it admirably. Can't owe a mint on that hovel, surely."

"Probably not. I've only got about thirty guineas. Papa's allowances are never generous."

"Don't tell me," moaned Ness, pulling out his empty pockets. "By the by, there's a relative of hers staying at the Black Bull. Eacy wants us to contact him. I suppose she's hoping he can bail her out . . . forgot to mention that."

Catrin snorted impatiently at this oversight as she struggled with the lock of the small chest where she kept her modest funds. "And when's the landlord coming back?"

Ness shrugged. "They do say those leeches delight in tipping people out of bed. I'd say there's no time to lose. I'd hate to see the little gel clapped in jail."

"Your horse is faster than mine. You take the cash to Easter. Now! Go on, the landlord may bring the bailiffs."

"In that case we'd best have reinforcements. What about contacting the relative first. Black Bull's on the way," Ness offered hastily, not anxious in his current state to tangle with a party of armed bailiffs.

"Poor Easter hasn't another friend in the world. It's up to us to save her," Catrin cried angrily. She was shushed by her brother. "All right," she whispered hoarsely, as she pulled on a serviceable blue gown over her nightdress. "We can't afford to lose time. You take the money and I'll go to the Black Bull. What's this relative's name?"

"Name?" Ness blinked, running his hand over his stubbled chin as he concentrated on the problem. "I have it—Stewart— blind me if that's not it. Mr. Stewart. Not too difficult to remember. But, Catrin, love, you can't go gallivanting about at this hour of night. I can't let you ride to the Black Bull . . . woman of your class shouldn't be at a place like that. It can't be done. Eacy will just have to wait."

"You had no objections to me being there this afternoon when you wanted to keep an appointment with Doll," Catrin pointed out sharply. "Easter's safety's more important than worrying about propriety. I'll bring Mr. Stewart back with me."

Muttering and protesting even as his sister yanked him to his feet, Ness stumbled and righted himself against a side table, setting a potted plant swaying.

"Are you sure you're not too drunk to stay in the saddle? Maybe I should take the money."

Straightening himself, with great effort Ness mustered his fading senses. "Dammit all, Catrin, that was a cruel cut. I'll stay in the saddle all right. Just give me the money."

"You're sure?"

"Positive. And if the scurvy bastard starts any nonsense, I'll run him through," Ness pronounced with relish, patting his sword hilt.

This last statement made Catrin uneasy. Ness drunk at the business end of a sword could get Easter in even greater trouble. "Perhaps you should leave your sword at home," she suggested hesitantly, aware that Ness considered himself a swordsman par excellence. The dark look he cast her was answer enough.

"Never heard such damned nonsense . . . a gentleman go out

without his sword . . . ridiculous. Come on, no more brainless suggestions. Let's be off."

Catrin drew a dark cloak about her shoulders and led the way, hoping Ness could manage the stairs without tumbling headlong and alerting the household. If their stepfather ever learned of this escapade, she could expect to spend the rest of the summer at Aunt Isobel's, being purged of her waywardness.

Through the sleeping city they rode, avoiding those more lively quarters where entertainment of sorts flourished till dawn. Soon London's smelly streets were left behind and the horses picked up speed as they entered open country. There was a hint of rain in the cool wind as they cantered along the highway. Though Ness slumped in the saddle, he seemed sober enough to manage the journey. Catrin was reluctant to turn off the road to the river and let him continue alone to Chiswick. At the time she had not really considered it, but her suggestion that Ness ride to Chiswick instead of to the inviting taproom of the Black Bull had been wise.

At the crossroads they parted, Ness urging Catrin to hurry and promising to do likewise. If only he would reform of his own accord, she thought as she watched him gallop into the night. Life would be so much calmer if the two hardheaded males in her life could agree.

She turned and headed down a leafy lane toward the Black Bull. The scent of farm animals blew in the rising wind which tossed branches overhead, spattering her with rain. Before Catrin had gone much further, the rainstorm began in earnest. Thunder rolled in the distance and, recalling the mare's terror that afternoon, she urged Puppet on, praying she would not balk at the threatening conditions.

She drew close to the timbered inn, where pools of light shimmered invitingly over the wet ground. At the welcoming sight Catrin unconsciously urged her horse on, eager to reach civilization. She marveled at her own daring in undertaking this night ride; most women would have been too afraid to travel alone at night on England's notoriously unsafe roads. She had given little thought to her own danger, thinking only of frail Easter alone with her baby, expecting every knock on the door to be the landlord come to evict her.

The sight of the inn turned Catrin's thoughts to the handsome stranger who had rescued her this afternoon. He would be miles away by now. Yet what if he was staying at the inn? Catrin experienced a warm thrill of pleasure at the thought of meeting him again before she sternly dismissed the idea. Easter was in danger and there was no time for flirtation.

When Catrin finally reined in her mount in the inn yard, the rain had stopped. She shook the beads of moisture from her heavy cloak and, handing Puppet to an ostler, walked purposefully into the inn. Though the taproom was brightly lit, at this late hour the Black Bull's patrons were few. Barely sparing a glance for the lolling drunkards slumped over their ale cups, Catrin addressed the aproned landlord with as much authority as she could muster.

"I'm seeking a man lodging at the inn. A Mr. Stewart. Will you take me to him? It's a matter of great urgency."

"Stewart? Naw, dunno who he might be."

"Yes, you do. I have it on the best authority that he's staying here. I assure you, there's nothing indelicate about my visit. One of the gentleman's relations is in trouble."

"Well now, mighty sure of yourself, ain't yer," retorted the landlord. His mouth set belligerently as he looked closely at her pretty face, partially obscured by the dark hood. "And what exactly is this trouble?"

"That's for Mr. Stewart's ears alone," Catrin retorted, with mounting annoyance.

"And what's in it for me if I takes you to 'im?"

"If you expect money, I'm afraid you'll be disappointed. All my ready cash has gone to help a friend in need, the very matter about which I must speak to Mr. Stewart."

"A handout! So that's it. Not on your life, Mrs. My guests aren't going to be bothered by the likes of you! Be off with you."

Catrin gritted her teeth and persisted. "I've tried to be both patient and polite. But I warn you, if you don't take me to Mr. Stewart at once, you're going to be extremely sorry."

"All right, all right. No need to make a scene," muttered the landlord as Catrin's voice rose in anger. "You'd best 'ope he welcomes you, Mrs., or you're the one who's going to be sorry."

Having delivered this pronouncement, the landlord beckoned her to follow and stumped off down the corridor. They stopped before a closed door and the landlord rapped sharply on the wooden panel.

"Mr. Stewart, sir, begging your pardon. There's a lady 'ere as wants to see you. Asked for you by name, she did."

The door opened and the landlord disappeared inside the room. Catrin fumed inwardly as she counted the elapsing minutes. She thrust back her hood, allowing her damp, undressed hair to fall in loose ringlets over her shoulders.

The door finally reopened and the landlord beckoned. "All right, Mrs., the gentleman says he'll see you."

"Thank you, landlord, you've been most helpful," Catrin snapped sarcastically as she walked through the doorway.

The warm, softly lit room was inviting. A well-dressed man stood before the hearth, his back to the door. Lighted candles in silver sconces shed soft pools of light over the supper table, revealing that it was set for two.

"Mr. Stewart?"

"Yes, I am he."

Catrin gasped as the man turned to greet her. Though his handsome face lay in mysterious shadow cast by the leaping fire, Catrin could not mistake the fascinating stranger from this afternoon. Her heartbeat quickened as he stepped toward her, his hand extended in greeting.

"I hear you bring me news of a relative."

She knew he had not recognized her. Swallowing nervously, Catrin stepped into the light to confront Mr. Stewart, his curiosity aroused by this uninvited female. Immediately his expression changed, his eyes lighting up eagerly, his mouth forming a lazy smile of greeting.

"What a pleasant surprise!"

Curiously, instead of exciting her, his rekindled interest confused Catrin. She longed to continue that exciting flirtation they had shared this afternoon, yet she was far too aware of her purpose here. Even the fact the handsome stranger was related to Easter had taken the luster off their flirtation. She was somewhat shocked to discover her fantasies had been vastly enhanced because he was a stranger and his open admiration had been their special secret.

"David Stewart at your service, milady," he said, bowing to her. "How did you learn my name?"

"I come from Easter. She's in grave danger."

The expression of lazy sensuality faded from his face and his jaw tensed. He let go of her hand, which he had been about to press to his lips. "Easter in danger! What type of danger?"

"The landlord's demanding back rent. He's threatening to put her in debtor's prison."

At her words he visibly relaxed. "Don't worry. That's

an old ploy. But Easter shall certainly have my help. And you are . . . ?"

"Catrin Blair."

"Blair! Not related to Ness Blair, surely?"

"I'm his sister. I didn't know you knew Ness."

"Slightly, milady. We are . . . what shall I say . . . business acquaintances."

His entire attitude had undergone a subtle change; Catrin did not know if it was the news of Easter's danger or the revelation of her own identity that had brought it about. The intimacy of his smile, the invitation in his eyes, disappeared; even his body movements were more formal. He bowed stiffly.

"Will you come back to Chiswick with me?" she asked quickly.

But he was not listening. "I must apologize for my unseemly behavior this afternoon. I'd no idea you were Ness's sister. I thought you were . . . well, never mind what I thought. It was most unmannerly of me to stare and I deeply regret my rudeness. I hope you weren't offended."

His obvious discomfort further shattered the delicious communication between them. Catrin knew she should accept his apology, though in truth his bold stares had not offended her. Quite the contrary. Yet she could not reveal how much she had enjoyed his attention. "There's no need to apologize, Mr. Stewart. I'm most grateful for your assistance. I'll always be in your debt," she replied in a tight voice. Then, suddenly coming back to the present, she remembered her reason for being here. "Mr. Stewart, we mustn't delay. I'm not as convinced as you that the landlord's threats are empty."

"I'd love to be able to leave at once, milady, but my departure depends on my guest. Perhaps I can dispense with the meal . . . that would speed matters along. Kindly wait for me beside the hearth in the other room and I'll join you as soon as possible."

One glance at the carefully laid table, with its snowy linen and crystal centerpiece of salmon roses, aroused Catrin's suspicions. David Stewart was impeccably dressed in embroidered buff satin, heavy lace at his throat and wrists; his dark hair, though unpowdered, was carefully combed and fastened at the nape of his neck with a black velvet ribbon. There could be only one explanation of this important supper—he was expecting a woman!

The sudden realization was like a slap in the face. She certainly did not own him—this afternoon she had not even known his name—yet, foolishly, as their secret communication deepened, Catrin had considered him her own. The discovery that he was waiting for his mistress roused her to unreasonable anger. She felt spurned and betrayed.

"How dare you consider entertaining a woman more important than rescuing Easter? I suppose your pleasure always comes first."

"I'm afraid I can't break this engagement. If I could, I'd already have left. Please be so kind as to wait while I try to be brief . . ."

"Brief? Oh, don't insult my intelligence! I know well enough the intimate little evening you've planned. I shall go by myself. This supper's obviously far more important than rescuing Easter. I've misjudged you, Mr. David Stewart."

"You little she-cat, have done," he admonished, roughly seizing her arm. "You haven't the first idea whom I'm waiting for."

"Nor do I care," Catrin cried, dangerously close to tears. She pulled free of his demanding grasp. "I'm only glad I discovered your true nature before I made a complete fool of myself."

"Wait!"

Not heeding his sharp command, Catrin rushed from the room.

A few minutes late she stood trembling in the inn yard, the cold wind cutting through her garments. An ostler trotted out her mare and Catrin thanked him, belatedly remembering she had no money.

"Mr. Stewart will be responsible for the bill," she assured the man airily, aware of a flicker of pleasure at the thought of exacting this small revenge.

Her satisfaction was short lived. As Catrin rode around the front of the inn a cloaked figure, apparently taking great pains not to be seen, melted back into the shadows. A surge of emotion gripped Catrin's stomach as she looked at the dark shape hugging the wall, wary of the beams of light spilling through the inn's mullioned windows. David Stewart's light of love must not want to be recognized. Fury raced through Catrin's body as she dwelled on the disturbing thought, and she blinked back hot angry tears. Wheeling about, she headed for the highway.

The thudding hooves kept time with the emotion pounding in her veins. Anger, disappointment, jealousy, she could not put a name to the source of her distress. She cursed David Stewart for deceiving her into thinking . . . what?

Catrin slackened her pace and straightened her sagging shoulders. David Stewart had promised her nothing. She was behaving like a fool. What did it matter if he had one mistress or twenty? Besides, when he refused to accompany her to help Easter, he had shown his true colors. If she was wise she would put him out of her mind.

In a short time Catrin had reached the village of Chiswick and made her way to the Stewarts' house. But she approached the ramshackle cottage, one of two set in a former cornfield, only to find the buildings in darkness. Swinging from the saddle, she was appalled to find a padlock on the cottage door. She had arrived too late! The landlord had already evicted Easter. But where was Ness? Catrin glanced about the wind-blown field and saw a chink of light glinting through the ill-fitting boards of a barn at the rear of the cottage. Perhaps someone there could help her.

Catrin pushed open the rickety door and was startled to see Easter and the baby on a bed of straw under a blanket.

"Catrin! Oh, thank heavens it's you."

"Easter! Where's Ness? Hasn't he arrived yet?" Catrin ran to her friend's side.

"Ness brought me the money. I can't thank you enough, Catrin. I never expected it. You were always such a good friend to me. When you didn't come, Ness was worried. He's gone in search of you."

"I didn't pass him on the road."

"He mentioned a shortcut."

"I didn't mean to take so long. Your relative was . . . er . . . too busy to come," she explained hesitantly, careful to keep her annoyance from her voice. "He had an engagement he could not break."

To Catrin's surprise, Easter merely nodded understandingly. "I shouldn't have disturbed him with my troubles. He's much too important for that. Cheer up, don't look so downcast. You did your best, Catrin, that's what counts."

The baby stirred and Easter turned her attention to her son, leaving Catrin to wonder in surprise at her statement. It was strange that Easter should forgive David Stewart so readily.

She had expected at least a glimmer of anger over his refusal to aid her.

"Is David Stewart a relative?"

"Yes, a very distant one. He's the son of my father's laird. So you see, he's far too important to come running at my beck and call."

It was on the tip of Catrin's tongue to say she did not consider entertaining a woman that important, but she declined to reveal the truth. It was bad enough for Easter to have been evicted while her husband was away, without revealing her revered laird's indifference.

"Never mind, we'll soon have you back inside," Catrin pronounced cheerfully as she tucked the wool blanket more securely around Easter's thin body. A cold wind blew draftily through the building, stirring the straw and the creaking pieces of old harness hanging from the beams.

Easter squeezed Catrin's hand. "I hope thirty guineas will satisfy the landlord until Comyn returns."

"How long will that be?"

"Oh, probably before the week's out," Easter assured without conviction. "Surely no longer. Do you suppose he'll wait that long?"

"That long . . . I intend to have you indoors tonight. Where does this landlord live? Thirty guineas should buy a property like this, let alone rent it."

Easter's pale face looked increasingly woebegone. "It isn't just rent we owe, Catrin, it's other things too. A horse, a saddle, furniture, food, supplies for Comyn's journey . . . we owe well over a hundred pounds."

Catrin gulped. "A hundred pounds! I'd no idea. True to form, Ness forgot to ask the amount. I'll have to raise more money." Catrin considered where, at such short notice, she could put her hands on the sum. Perhaps she could convince her stepfather she needed money for clothes. Humphrey Millbank handled the accounts, keeping track of every expenditure, yet he had never begrudged her dressmaker's bill, aware Catrin must be suitably attired to remain an attractive marriage prospect.

"Don't worry about us. At least we've a roof over our heads, though admittedly it isn't much."

Catrin smiled at her friend's cheerful words and she patted Easter's thin, transparent hand. Blue shadows circled Easter's eyes and her cheekbones almost seemed to protrude through her pale flesh. The baby began to wail and Easter clasped him to her meager breast, whispering endearments, her mouth pressed against his downy head.

While they awaited Ness's return, Easter's strength waned. The cold wind raking the dilapidated building grew stronger and Easter shivered beneath her old blanket. Catrin covered her with her own cloak and presently the young mother slept.

Smiling affectionately at her friend, Catrin recalled how, as daughters of fellow Jacobite exiles, they had played together during those hot dusty Roman summers, cheering every misfortune of the fat German king, ever awaiting that glorious day when the Stuarts would be restored to their rightful throne. That day never came. Men grew old and dispirited in exile, living out their days on the quixotic charity of foreigners.

Clattering hooves on the flint road disturbed her thoughts. That would be Ness.

Catrin ran to the barn door to greet him. To her dismay, not her brother, but a party of five strangers loomed out of the rainy darkness.

"Who might you be, woman?"

"She must be one of them. Bloody scoundrels, the lot of 'em, taking me goods and never intending to pay for 'em. Prison's too good for the likes of them, too good by far, I says."

A cloaked man brought his horse forward at a trot, his heavy face set in a scowl. Catrin jumped back in alarm, for he threatened to ride her down.

"How dare you! I'll have you know my father's Humphrey Millbank, the shipowner..."

"Oh, aye, and I'm King Peter... now get out of me bloody way, Mrs., before you're sorry. I want me goods, or me money. Well over a hundred quid that scoundrel owes me."

The men swung from their saddles, grunting with exertion. Ignoring Catrin, they pushed their way inside the barn. Easter struggled to sit, her face pinched with fright.

"All right, you, now where's your man? I want me money, or it's off to the Fleet with you. I'm not a charity. I've got me own debts to pay. What with the other house empty too..."

The landlord broke off his speech, his small dark eyes probing the shadowed barn as if he expected to see Comyn lurking there.

"I've already told you my husband's away on business. And

I've no way to pay you until he returns," Easter explained, trying to keep the tremor out of her voice. "Surely you can wait till weekend. I'm out of the house now."

"Aye, and into me bloody barn! Oh, the cheek of it!" Grinding his teeth in rage, the landlord turned to the bailiffs. "Search the place. Likely he's skulking about trying to weasel out of paying. Damned foreigners are all alike. Give me some cock-and-bull story about 'is wife's sudden confinement. Took 'em in good faith, I did, and now he's scarpered with me goods. Probably fencing them while we stand 'ere."

The landlord left with the bailiffs. When they found nothing, the men moved outdoors, taking a lighted lantern to search the surrounding fields.

There was little Catrin could say to comfort Easter. She held her close, glad to be able to offer that much. The baby cried, disturbed by the angry voices.

After a while the men returned empty-handed. "You're bloody well right when you say he's gone. I'll not be bested. I'll 'ave you put where he can find you well enough, you and the little nipper. One hundred pounds is what I want. You say nothing's been stole . . . well, when I gets me money I'll believe it. I could 'ave the lot of you up for thieving. As it is, being a charitable man, I'm only charging you with debt."

Gathering her wits, Catrin suddenly remembered the thirty guineas Easter had beneath the blanket. "Here's part of your money. Surely it'll suffice until the end of the week. When Mr. Stewart returns you'll get the rest."

The man's stubby hand shot out to greedily snatch the gold. "Thirty guineas! That's a drop in the bucket. But it's better than a kick in the arse. Here, Jem, get them out of here before I lose me temper."

To Catrin's horror the bailiffs rushed forward. Despite her shrill protests, they pinioned her arms and manhandled her toward the waiting horses. She cried out in anger as they yanked Easter from the straw. The baby wailed loudly with fear and his mother almost dropped him as she was shoved out of the door. Giving her captors a withering glare, Catrin broke free and rescued the infant. Easter flashed her a weak smile of gratitude, finding her way easier now that she was relieved of her precious burden.

"How dare you? Take your hands off her! I'm Catrin Blair and this lady's my friend . . ."

"Stow it, Mrs.," growled one of the men as he raised his

arm to strike her. "You can babble till doomsday but you're bound for the Fleet. If your father's rich *he* can pay your debts."

The bailiffs chuckled derisively at the suggestion. Catrin prayed for Ness to magically appear, accompanied by several friends who would prove more than a match for these bailiffs. But the road remained empty. It was raining harder than ever and she made poor frail Easter put on her cloak. Once Easter was safely on horseback, she handed up the baby to her.

"If we'd 'ad more time you doxies'd be walking," grumbled the head bailiff, annoyed at having to carry the women on their horses.

Thunder rolled ominously in the distance and the men cursed the elements as they grasped their captives with rough hands. Easter had ceased to resist long ago; Catrin, her pride getting the better of her, had put up a bit of a fight, quickly subdued by a well-placed cuff across the ear.

Bound for the Fleet prison! Catrin tried to be brave, but tears pricked her eyes. She had expected Ness to rescue them. As they traversed this stinking quarter, seething with the human flotsam of Georgian London, she finally abandoned herself to her fate. Ness was not coming. No one would inform her stepfather of her predicament. She would be trapped forever in that hideous cesspool known as the Fleet prison.

The next few hours were a nightmare of filth and degradation. The early hours of the morning were not a popular time for admitting prisoners, and the guards, annoyed at being roused from their sleep, took out their hostility on their captives. In vain Catrin tried to protect Easter, kicking a guard in retaliation when he sent the frail woman sprawling against the slimy wall.

"Wait till tomorrer, you bitch," hissed the man as he shoved Catrin inside a dark, fetid room. "Tomorrer I'll get me own back."

The last flicker of hope sustaining Catrin died as the door clanged shut behind them. Tears trickled down her cheeks as she hugged Easter, deriving comfort from the presence of her friend.

"Get over there and be quiet. Folks want to sleep." Arms reached out of the darkness to thrust them away. Stumbling over recumbent bodies, Catrin fell against a wooden bench next to the wall. To her disappointment she found it packed with smelly bodies; a rickety table was likewise covered with sleeping forms. The only place unclaimed was a section of straw-covered floor oozing with slime and stinking like a filthy stable.

"Here, spread out the cloak."

Catrin kicked aside the matted straw and put down her cloak for Easter to lie on. Squeaks and rustling in the corner warned her that the debtors were not the cell's only occupants.

Easter crumpled against Catrin in despair. "What if Comyn doesn't come? What if he can't raise the money? We'll have to stay here forever."

"Don't be afraid. As soon as Ness finds we're gone he'll go to Papa for help," Catrin reassured her, wishing she was as convinced as she pretended. Since Ness had taken to the bottle, his will could be a feeble thing. Would her brother find the courage to face their angry stepfather, to admit he was partly to blame for her imprisonment?

Tears of self-pity squeezed between her closed lids and Catrin angrily blinked them away. Ness would help her. She had to believe that. Her brother would seek aid; he owed her that much for past loyalties when she had sided with him against their stepfather. Even stronger than loyalty was their bond as brother and sister. Catrin knew she would risk much to save her brother's life; she had to believe the bottle had not robbed Ness of the capacity to feel that same deep emotion.

Chapter 3

Catrin awoke to see feeble bars of murky daylight creeping across the stone wall. Beyond the cell door clanging pails announced the arrival of breakfast. Hours dragged by as, time and again, their cell was passed by. Even the unappetizing aroma of prison gruel made the others salivate. Catrin and Easter were not hungry, yet they supposed, given time, that they too would fall victim to this refined torture. The baby was screaming in protest over his soiled clothing and Easter, who had no way to clean him, wept for their plight.

Finally the jailer appeared, jangling his keys. As he stood in the doorway, surveying the prisoners, weeping men and women stretched out pleading hands to him. Several debtors boldly approached him only to be brutally cuffed aside. Catrin cried out in outrage at his cruelty, attracting unwelcome attention to herself.

"Yer new, ain't yer? Name?"

"Catrin Blair."

"Naw, they said your name was Stewie..."

"Stewart," Easter corrected proudly.

"That's it, Stewart. Got an 'usband out there asking fer you."

Tears of joy filled Easter's eyes. "Oh, God be praised! Comyn's home safe!"

"Are we free to go?" Catrin asked, hardly able to endure to watch the collective torment in this room. The starving inmates were mesmerized by the vat of unappetizing gruel cooling, just beyond the open door, yet so broken in spirit were they that none dared claim his ration without permission.

"Come on. We'll see."

"Can I 'ave your share?" begged a hopeful woman with sunken eyes.

"Take both our shares."

"Coo, generous bitch, ain't yer?" scoffed the jailer, boldly slipping his hands over Catrin's hips, ignoring her warning to leave her alone. "I 'opes yer man don't 'ave enough cash to spring yer, that's what I 'opes. You'd make a nice armful these long summer nights."

Catrin shuddered in disgust over the hideous prospect, trying to keep away from the man's wandering hands, which seemed to be everywhere at once. Behind them she heard someone dragging the vat of gruel inside the cell, evoking a chorus of delight. Those piteous wails of joy brought bile to her throat.

They were taken inside a small room where the stale air was so thick it must have been trapped inside the walls for years. Several other women were waiting, one of whom was accompanied by three unbelievably filthy children, who stared wide-eyed at the newcomers. Catrin was shocked by the children's appearance. Vermin visibly hopped from their hair and clothing, and she drew back, guiding Easter to the farthest corner of the room. At last, after what seemed like hours, someone shouted, "Stewart."

Easter gasped, her eyes shining with tears of delight. "I'll make sure Comyn frees you too, Catrin dear."

A man bobbed his head inside the room when Catrin hung back. "You too, Mrs., look lively."

No longer trying to explain her relationship to Easter, Catrin obediently followed her friend inside an anteroom containing a huge desk stacked high with papers. The room was so gloomy, she wondered how the man seated there could see what he was writing.

"Lucky devils, you two," the man said with a gap-toothed grin. "This is probably the quickest anyone's been in and out of here. Course, your man slipped us a few extra quid to speed things up. Knows 'ow it's done, all right, 'e does. Sorry for the mistake. Could've happened to anyone."

Catrin accepted the document he proffered. "Are we free?"

"Mrs. Easter Stewart, one infant, name of Douglas Stewart,

and one spinster, name of Catrin Stewart, to be released into the custody of one Comyn Stewart, 'usband, father and brother of said," he pronounced officiously.

A door opened into an equally gloomy side chamber where stark wooden benches lined the stone wall. A couple of jailers lounged on a bench, surveying the proceedings. Four men were waiting for released prisoners. It was so dark in the corner where the men were huddled that Catrin could not make out their features, but she knew Comyn was not among them, for despite the murk she would have spotted his thick, corn-colored hair.

At their entrance and following a grunt from one of the jailers, the man furthest away from them rose. As he stepped forward, Catrin's stomach pitched. That lean, sun-bronzed face, the dark, gleaming hair were painfully familiar—David Stewart, not Comyn, had come to their rescue.

"Easter, sweetheart, how can I apologize for having caused you such grief?"

Easter and her baby were enfolded in his strong arms. Tearfully Easter handed him their release papers, mumbling her thanks as he led her to the outside door.

When Easter was safely outside, David Stewart returned for Catrin. "My dearest sister," he said, his voice suitably emotional for the jailer's benefit. When Catrin resisted his embrace, he exerted more force while he hissed, "Don't be a fool. Play along."

Stunned, she allowed him to bestow a brotherly peck on her cheek before she too was taken through the door into a chilly corridor.

A few minutes later Catrin was standing outside in the blessed sunshine of a hot July morning. She was free!

Easter leaned against the building trying to catch her breath, squinting against the bright sunlight. "The saints be praised," she whispered tearfully.

David Stewart's eyes lit up with amusement when he beheld Catrin's grim expression. "And you, sister dear, were you not pleased to see me?"

"Naturally. Only a fool would prefer the Fleet to freedom," she snapped at him. When he cocked a dark eyebrow toward Easter in silent warning, she swallowed uncomfortably and forced a smile. "Yes, I was very pleased to see you. I trust you did not have to shorten your important engagement to accommodate us?"

"Not at all. You'll be happy to learn everything went according to plan."

Catrin's mouth tightened as she encountered his mocking gaze. Naturally, where a woman was concerned, everything would go as planned. "How gratifying," she remarked with forced sweetness. "You must forgive me, Mr. Stewart, for my rudeness. I had thought we were abandoned."

"Of course you are forgiven. It would be most surly of me to take offense at such a beautiful lady."

Color rose in her cheeks as he made her a sweeping court bow out there on the filthy street, where ragged traders trundled handcarts and gawping mutton-pie sellers paused to watch this unusual tableau.

"I don't believe we were ever properly introduced, Miss Blair. Allow me. I am David Stewart of Garth, your most obedient servant."

Their eyes met and Catrin gasped, caught unawares by the naked appraisal in that unusual shade of green ablaze with amber lights. The heady rush of emotion she had known in the Black Bull's taproom engulfed her. For an instant she felt cast adrift on the ocean with only David Stewart for company...

"Thank God you're safe. Damned if I expected this outcome, Catrin, and I apologize for me own foolishness."

Ness's drawl broke the spell and David Stewart straightened, turning about to greet Catrin's brother.

"Ness! I thought you'd deserted us. Did you get the bloodsuckers paid off?"

"To the penny, though I'm damned if they deserve it," Ness grumbled as he embraced Catrin and kissed her cheek. "Lud, you smell like a sewer."

Though she tended to agree with him, she shot him an angry glance. Ness was the perfect person to shatter a budding romantic mood. "Thank you, brother dear. What a charming observation."

"No offense meant," Ness mumbled, not understanding her anger. "It's just damned true. Now, are we for home?"

"First we have to find lodgings for Easter," she reminded him in an undertone, glancing to where Easter was sitting on a low windowsill, clutching her wailing baby to her chest.

"I can take her to my lodgings," suggested David Stewart.

"Why don't I put Easter up at home? Papa was supposed to leave for Bristol this morning. She'll be much more comfortable there."

"An excellent suggestion, Miss Blair. My rooms are far from palatial."

The decision made, David Stewart strode down the street to summon and pay a hackney to take the women home.

After they had helped Easter inside the rented conveyance, Catrin bid her brother and his companion goodbye.

"Goodbye, Ness. Mr. Stewart, thank you for coming to our rescue. I'd begun to give up hope," she added with a genuine smile, relenting slightly in her annoyance. "All I want now is to go home, burn these clothes, and wash away the stink of the Fleet."

David Stewart bowed politely over her outstretched hand, barely brushing her fingertips with his warm mouth.

"To have been able to help two ladies in distress has been my utmost pleasure," he said gallantly. When he straightened, their eyes met and a bolt of excitement shot through Catrin. Aware of her heightened interest, his mouth quirked slightly as he said, "I trust we'll meet again. Ness never told me he had such a lovely sister."

"Thank you, Mr. Stewart." Catrin lowered her gaze, fascinated and at the same time made vastly uncomfortable by his penetrating stare.

The door closed; the hackney driver clicked to the horses and they lurched forward. "Today I truly believe in the power of prayer," Easter said, catching Catrin's arm.

Catrin looked through the murky hackney window, but David Stewart was lost to view. "We'll soon be home," she assured her friend as she stifled her disappointment. It was a shock to realize she would have been content to watch the handsome Mr. Stewart all the way to Bloomsbury.

Easter soon began to nod against the dingy upholstery, and Catrin was free to return to her absorbing thoughts of David Stewart. He had rescued her once again, yet this time her danger had been far more acute. The remaining anger she felt toward him evaporated as she contemplated the risk he had taken by posing as Comyn to obtain their release. In all fairness she could not condemn him for entertaining a woman—she did condemn him, however, for considering his pleasure more important than Easter's safety. Yet the rage she had felt when she learned he was awaiting his mistress had faded. Sense told her she was not the only woman who found him attractive. From now on she must be a little fairer in her judgment of him, for though he had delayed, he had eventually responded to her call for help. Had he been truly as self-centered as she supposed, he would never have endangered himself to obtain their release from the Fleet.

Catrin closed her eyes, her mouth softening as she again remembered how she had felt when she looked into his green eyes that morning. She longed to know more about him, but cautioned herself to refrain from questioning Easter about her handsome laird. Her current infatuation with Mr. David Stewart must remain her own secret.

They drew up outside the Millbank residence. In the bright morning sunlight the tall narrow brick house was quietly impressive yet indistinguishable from its neighbors marching in strict precision about the broad square. Orange girls sauntered beneath the trees and piemen and yoked watermen crossed the open expanse bound for the crowded city quarters.

The downstairs maid answered the door, her eyes round with shock when she saw Miss Catrin accompanied by a strange woman holding a dirty, crying baby. "Oh, my lord, Miss Catrin! What happened?" she cried, her hands going to her face.

"It's a long story, Jessie. Be an angel and have two baths prepared. Is the master home?" Catrin asked as an afterthought, hoping her stepfather had gone about his journey as planned, unaware of her absence.

"No, Miss Catrin, he left at dawn for Bristol."

"Jessie, see if one of the servants can find some baby clothes."

Jessie nodded, wrinkling her nose at the offensive odor as the two women walked inside the cool hallway. "At once, Miss Catrin. We'll burn those terrible rags straight away."

"Have cook prepare some food—something suitable for an invalid, if possible."

Then taking Easter's arm, Catrin slowly led her upstairs. A pop-eyed Jessie stood in the hall watching them before charging away to the servants' hall to deliver the startling news that Miss Catrin had come home looking like a tramp and brought some filthy pauper's woman with her.

The following hours reinforced Catrin's belief in miracles. A maid took charge of Easter's baby, promising to bathe and outfit him. The two women then luxuriated in warm, scented baths, dozing in the heavenly warmth, reluctant to leave the bliss of the water until it grew unpleasantly cool.

Catrin sighed with pleasure as she glanced about the room. Though plain by current standards, after the Fleet this bedchamber seemed the height of luxury. The plain green velvet bed hangings and draperies devoid of lace, the white satin Holland quilt, the drab rose gros-point rug were the most beautiful furnishings she had ever seen. Humphrey Millbank's conservatively furnished home, which at times she had considered ugly, had suddenly become a thing of beauty. Never again would she criticize him for his miserly expenditures.

Presently her maid, Milly, and two other girls came upstairs to towel the women dry and rub their bodies with perfumed oil. Easter Stewart was introduced as an old friend from Rome. The maids curtsied, accepting her as gentry, though at first they had had serious doubts she was anything other than a tramp's woman picked up off the London streets.

By the time Catrin and Easter were dressed in clean linen and their hair had been washed, brushed, and coiffed, memories of that hideous nightmare inside the Fleet had begun to recede. It was hard to believe that only this morning they had shared a cell with fifty other miserable souls.

Catrin had not thought to ask David Stewart the cost of obtaining their release and now she regretted her bad manners. As soon as she could she would reimburse him for his trouble.

Easter stretched out on the soft bed and began to doze, leaving Catrin to her own resources. After she had drawn a light quilt over her sleeping friend, Catrin walked to the broad windows and seated herself on a pink satin upholstered chair facing the street.

At this time of day orange sellers and lavender girls strolled beneath the shady plane trees, calling their wares. An occasional carriage clattered across the square. Liveried servants carried a gilded sedan chair inside the chair porch of number twenty-nine, while across the way a small boy sped a hoop over the cobbles, a couple of spaniels yapping at his heels. Catrin sighed in contentment at the pleasant view. Never again would she be dissatisfied with her lot. One night in the Fleet had made her appreciate her surroundings as never before.

Heavy footsteps on the stair attracted her attention. Turning, she saw Ness stumbling against the banister. She was incensed by the sight of him so visibly intoxicated at this early hour.

Grimly Catrin rose and left the room, quietly closing the door behind her so as not to disturb Easter.

"Ness."

He turned in surprise, aware of the tension in her voice. "Looking like your old self again, Catrin. Vast improvement— damned if it's not."

"We must talk."

"Like to, but I'm already late for an appointment. Some other time. I can't stop now."

"You will talk to me now! I've turned a blind eye to your way of life for the last time."

Ness blinked, taken back by her determined tone. He wiped his brow, which was beaded with sweat. "What do you mean, Catrin? Damned if I know what you're..."

Not waiting for further protests, Catrin took his arm and propelled him down the gray-walled corridor to his room. Malleable, even affable in his current mood, Ness meekly obeyed. Inside his bedchamber, he turned to face her, his smile indulgent.

"Now, sister, what nonsense is this? I can give you ten minutes. No more. I must be at the Temple by four."

"I've tried patience. I've tried ignoring the problem. I've supported you even though I wasn't sure you deserved the favor ... this is the final straw! It's not three in the afternoon and you're already weaving. Where have you been?"

Ness grinned in amusement at her angry recital. "Well, not that you've any damned right to know, but seeing as you're me sister, Catrin, I'll tell you. I've been at the Cocoa Tree in St. James's..."

"Coffee doesn't turn your legs to porridge."

"Very observant." Ness rose, apparently considering their conversation at an end. "I must admit I did stop at a few other places—definitely not for your ears."

"I can imagine." They glared at each other. "You're going to be just like Father in another five years. You're throwing your life away just as he did. And you don't even seem to care."

"To be 'just like Father' is my greatest desire."

"Father was a reckless fool who sacrificed everything for a dream."

"A man without a dream might as well be dead."

Catrin's smoke-gray eyes flashed with anger and she gulped rapidly in an effort to control her temper. As always, Ness was unremorseful. He did not even see the disastrous pattern emerging, or, if he saw it, he did not care. "Are you going to drink yourself to death like he did?" she demanded angrily.

"That's enough, Catrin! You're right, it's high time we talked."

Her brother's even tone surprised her. In fact, his calm

demeanor was somewhat deflating. Catrin perched on the moss-green daybed beside the open window. "Oh, can't you see what you're doing to me . . . to us . . . to Papa?" she asked, fighting to contain her anger.

"I've told you before, Millbank's wishes mean nothing to me. But your distress is something I can't overlook. I realize you've been through a hellish night and perhaps that's behind this outburst . . . whatever the reason, you have to know sooner or later. You must give me your word you won't go tattling to 'Papa dear' or you can damned well stay in the dark."

Unwillingly, Catrin finally agreed to his demand. "All right. I'm sure Papa hasn't any interest in your latest escapade, anyway. I should think he's already heard enough to last him a lifetime. I never told him about the stream of mysterious visitors you entertain when he's away. I've never even asked *you* about them. Ness, are you involved with criminals? Is that the reason for such secrecy?"

"Thank you for your overwhelming faith in me."

"I don't want to accuse you, but, after all, you've never bothered to explain yourself. Cloaked figures slipping into the garden in the middle of the night, furtive comings and goings at all hours of the day—you have to admit its highly suspicious. Are you in trouble?"

His hard face softened as he detected a plaintive note in her voice. "Dear Catrin, you haven't changed. You stood up for me, suspecting that? Why didn't you ask me sooner? I never meant to cause you worry."

"To know you're drinking like a fish worries me the most. You know drink killed Father."

"Father! Father! What's he got to do with it?" Ness exploded, jumping to his feet. "Is that all I'm going to hear from you? Well, I'll show you how much like Father I intend to become. All those people who visit me—Comyn, Easter, David Stewart, too—and countless others are at this very moment plotting high treason."

Catrin's sharp intake of breath was audible in the quiet room as, with sinking heart, even before he confessed the truth, she guessed his secret. Those remarks of his—"a man without a dream" and wanting to be "just like Father"—told her all she needed to know.

"We're working on behalf of the King Across the Water. Not like those spineless Jacobites who call their sons Charles and James and toast the King Across the Water like members of an exclusive club, planting white roses, spouting reams of empty promises . . . he's coming, Catrin! He's already under sail with a French fleet at the back of him! Even now he could be landing off the Scottish coast."

"Oh, Ness, no! Don't follow in Father's footsteps. It'll be your ruin too. It'll fail just like the last time. Please, listen to reason . . ."

Ness angrily flung off her restraining arm. "I'd expected a little more enthusiasm from you—after all, you are a Blair. Perhaps I've been ill advised to betray our friends. Have 'Papa dear's' Whig policies overcome your inborn loyalty to the Stuarts?"

Ness's growing lucidity continued to surprise Catrin. Had she not seen him stumble she would never have suspected him of being in the least intoxicated. "You know your secrets are safe with me. All my life I've listened to talk about restoring the Stuarts. How can you expect me to believe this scheme has any more hope than the rest?"

"This time it will work."

"Admittedly he's a Stuart, but King James is hardly the personality to inspire loyalty."

"It's not James this time, but Charles, the Prince of Wales, who comes to claim the throne for his father. He's a born leader of men. Handsome, charming . . . they say where he goes men flock to his side. Oh, Catrin, Catrin, we come from a long line of Stuart supporters who've suffered much for the cause. Will you desert me now that we've come this far?"

She shook her head, but her heart was heavy. "You know I won't. Even if you proposed hiding the Prince in my wardrobe, I'd help you. But it's so dangerous. This isn't something Papa can bail you out of. You know what a staunch Whig he is . . ."

"Dammit, Catrin, I don't want old Millbank to do another thing for me. I'm in this with friends . . . and, contrary to popular opinion, not all my friends are drunken sots. These are brave, dedicated men willing to sacrifice their all for a dream. Just as Father did. And you don't need to be so scornful of Jacobites—it's only because of David Stewart that you're out of the Fleet. He's a vital part of our organization. Comyn's gone to Wales to rouse Welsh support. The network of dedicated men spreads from Land's End to John o' Groats."

"Oh, Ness, you don't realize the danger. Stop now while there's time."

"I'd as leave stop breathing. Besides, I'm in far too deep to stop now, even if I wanted to. We have lands to reclaim, past injustices to right. It's the glorious adventure we were born for, the fulfillment of the dreams of past generations . . . but I can see I'm boring you." Ness stopped abruptly, aware that his enthusiasm fell upon deaf ears. "If the cross-examination is over, I have to change. I've an important meeting to attend." Without another word he marched to his dressing room and slammed the door.

Chapter 4

Two weeks had passed since Catrin's ordeal in the Fleet. Easter was feeling much stronger and baby Douglas was thriving under the expert and doting attentions of the household staff.

Tomorrow afternoon Humphrey Millbank was due back from Bristol, and before his arrival Catrin had to find other lodgings for her friend. Comyn had still not returned from Wales, and though Easter was ever optimistic, Catrin wondered uneasily if all was well. Had Comyn been discovered about his treasonable errand and arrested? Out of deference for her friend, however, she kept her worries to herself.

Ness, too, had grown edgy, for he knew Comyn should have reached London days ago. Since their heated discussion of his Jacobite sympathies on that sunny afternoon two weeks ago, Ness had not reopened the subject. Whenever he went to the Cocoa Tree coffeehouse, a notorious Jacobite gathering place, Catrin held her breath, praying her brother was not getting involved in even more dangerous intrigue.

"We can take Eacy to lodgings off the Strand. I know a place there that belongs to a friend," Ness suggested when Catrin revealed her concern for Easter's welfare.

"I suppose that will do temporarily. If only you'd let me confide her position to Papa, perhaps he would . . ."

"Good God! You'll have us all hanged!"

"I didn't mean tell him everything, just a few selected points. Easter looks quite presentable. There's no reason for him to suspect she's anything but a friend from Rome temporarily without lodging."

"No, it's far too dangerous. There are too many lives at stake. Humphrey Millbank's a coarse, unprincipled man, but he's no fool. He'd soon ferret out the truth and turn us in. He's loyal as they come to that fat German."

"Hush! For someone who keeps warning me to be cautious, you don't follow your own advice." Catrin went to the door to make sure none of the servants were listening. "At least, now I know where your loyalties lie, I can understand why you couldn't take up the law."

Ness grinned, running his hand through his wavy chestnut hair, loose and unpowdered at this early hour. "I could never have sworn a loyalty oath to the house of Hanover. Still, it's safer to have 'Papa dear' think I'm a wastrel without ambition than to confront him with the truth."

Catrin agreed. She was hesitant to reopen the touchy subject, which was never far from her mind, yet growing concern for her brother's health forced her hand. "Ness."

"Yes." He paused, his hand on the doorknob.

"I know you're not the drunken wastrel Papa supposes, but you do drink far too much. Coming in reeling drunk several nights a week can hardly be called sober."

"Have no fear, I can hold my tongue. Liquor doesn't loosen it."

"That's not what I meant." She faced him, finding his expression had turned guarded and surly. "Have you forgotten what killed our father?"

"A broken heart."

"Drink."

"I know that's what Mama always claimed—"

"She was his wife! Surely if anyone knew, it was she. In our family there's an inherited weakness for the bottle."

"Oh, so you assume I'm carrying on the old family tradition. Well, don't worry about me, Catrin, I can live my life without any help from you." Ness angrily wrenched open the door and marched outside.

Biting her lip in agitation, Catrin watched him go. Since she had discovered her brother's involvement with the Jacobite cause, Catrin did not know whether to be relieved or even more alarmed. True, it was a slight comfort to learn his mysterious companions were not from the underworld, or that his frequent engagements held more substance than endless carousing. On the other hand, the grave danger of plotting against the crown vastly outweighed these crumbs of comfort. Catrin was not without remorse at having grossly misjudged her brother, dismissing his life as one dissolute round when in truth he had been involved in gathering arms, men, and money to support the cause. Furthermore, the knowledge that Easter, Comyn, and even their handsome laird, David Stewart, were Ness's fellow conspirators merely added to her unease. There was a vast difference between fashionable Jacobites who habitually raised their glasses to the King Across the Water and desperate men and women plotting to overthrow the government.

Catrin was also concerned for David Stewart's safety; though anxious not to reveal her interest in the dark-haired exile, she did not question Ness about his fellow conspirator. So far her emotion had been somewhat wasted on the dashing Mr. Stewart. Well aware now of both her identity and her whereabouts, he had made no effort to get in touch with her. And Catrin's disappointment was severe. She consoled herself with the idea that he had no time for dalliance, or that her close relationship to Ness made him wary of pursuit; it was too hard to admit that he might have no further romantic interest in her.

During their stepfather's absence Catrin had promised Ness she would join him at a masquerade ball in Ranelagh Gardens as the guest of Booth Merriam, a rich young man-about-town whom Ness had met at Oxford. Had he been at home Catrin knew her stepfather would have forbidden the outing. Ever since its opening she had longed to visit the famous pleasure garden, and that longing made her recklessly indifferent to Humphrey Millbank's wishes. She intended to have a final heady taste of freedom, for September and her marriage to Bryce Cavendish loomed uncomfortably close.

The thought made Catrin shudder with dread. When her stepfather proudly submitted a wedding invitation for her approval, the engraved words had made everything seem so terribly final that she might as well have been reading an invitation to her funeral. Once she was married she could no longer be happy and carefree—Bryce would expect her to begin nurturing his heir. Foolishly, as she pictured the gold engraved card, she substituted the name David Stewart for Bryce Cavendish. Pleasant warmth suffused her face and her heart began to flutter. She knew that had she been marrying the handsome Laird of Garth, she would have been counting the days until September.

* * *

Ranelagh Gardens had opened three years before, the new pleasure gardens rapidly supplanting popular Vauxhall as a haunt of the upper classes. On this golden summer evening, with barely a whisper of wind to disturb the leafy trees lining the broad gravel walks, the Merriam family celebrated Booth's twenty-fifth birthday with a supper and masquerade ball, to be followed by a firework display. Though most of the Merriams' wealthy friends had already retired to the country for the summer, they had returned to London in droves to attend Booth's lavish birthday party.

Hazy gold washed the evening sky as harlequins and columbines, pirates and gypsies arrived in carriages and sedan chairs, on horseback, or glided up the Thames. Many guests wore black masks to conceal their identity, while others seemed only too anxious to be seen as they strolled unmasked amid the garden's gaudy flower beds and sparkling fountains.

The Merriam family was a fashionably disreputable group, definitely not the companions Humphrey Millbank would have considered suitable for his stepdaughter. As Catrin looked about eagerly at the exotic company, that knowledge made her feel deliciously wicked. She was tired of being watched over like a baby in a nursery. And though her rebellion against restriction was mild, it was a rebellion nonetheless.

Brightly painted lanterns decorated with Oriental motifs swung overhead in the tree branches, awaiting dusk to turn the gardens into fairyland. In front of the famous pavilion their host greeted them, dressed as a mandarin in aqua brocade with a black velvet pork-pie hat and a preposterously long pigtail hanging down his back. Catrin noticed that the hand he politely extended to Ness bore grotesque silver talons affixed over the nails. Tucking his hands inside his wide embroidered sleeves, Booth Merriam bowed to her in true Oriental fashion. Beyond an appreciative smile when Ness introduced them, the popular Booth ignored Catrin, turning his attention to the fashionable ladies and gentlemen of the court who were his honored guests.

Being overlooked did not offend her; Catrin preferred to remain an anonymous bystander at this noble gathering of richly jeweled, gossiping ladies in their sumptuous gowns. She wished Easter had come with her, instead of declining her invitation because she feared the party would be too tiring.

Ness had gone in search of refreshments, and on a wooden bench beneath the trees Catrin awaited his return. Tonight she felt unlike herself, in a daintily sprigged cream silk gown with a pink overskirt and black laced stomacher. A chip straw hat tied beneath her chin with pink satin ribbons added a demure note. The ribbon-decorated crook she carried identified her as a shepherdess, though the romantic attire was more suited to a china figurine than a tender of sheep. The costume was on loan from one of Ness's actress friends. Many of the other women balanced gigantic jeweled creations on top of their heads making even walking through the gardens a hazardous ordeal. At least her simple costume, though cut decidedly low, was no detriment to enjoyment.

Ness finally arrived bearing two glasses of champagne and a plate of flaky mushroom pasties. He was wearing a three-cornered black hat over a knotted red kerchief. A black patch obscured his left eye and a brace of pistols gleamed at his belt. In his worn leather jerkin, full sleeved white shirt, loose black breeches, and bucket-topped boots, Ness made an attractive pirate.

Tables stood on the grass beneath the trees. A picnic supper instead of more formal dining inside the stuffy supper boxes had been chosen tonight. A string orchestra played on a raised dais and brightly dressed musicians mingled with the guests. Eating, drinking, dancing, and gambling were to be the entertainments of the evening. And the chatting, laughing guests seemed bent on drinking as much as they were able in the shortest possible time. Gentlemen were already at the card tables, abandoning their ladies to partake of the excitement of whist and piquet.

Ness escorted Catrin the length of the pleasure garden, pointing out the various marvels, including the spectacular galleried rotunda whose roof could be opened in dry weather to form an open-air concert hall. They strolled beside the ornamental lakes dotted with water lilies, past beds of fragrant stocks and carnations, past rose gardens and herb borders until Catrin's feet began to ache.

The long summer day gradually faded in a spectacular crimson blaze. The Oriental lanterns were lit and the heavy-leaved trees came alive with twinkling lights, casting mysterious shadows over the masked partygoers. The lighting of the lanterns signaled the beginning of the buffet supper.

Dozens of servants in green Merriam livery waited behind the white-clothed tables to serve their guests. The supper tables themselves were a minor work of art, loaded with delicacies and artistically decorated with fruit and flowers. Catrin saw dishes completely foreign to her, for, though he kept a good table, her stepfather's taste did not run to exotic food. Smoked salmon, caviar, and delicately flavored French cheeses shared the board with cold platters of sliced jellied brawn, tongue, and roast beef. Deep rose china dishes of hot chicken breasts afloat in malaga sauce stayed warm over lighted candles. Great mounds of exotic fruits, each topped by a gilded pineapple, served as table decorations. Next to platters of thinly sliced brown bread surrounded by green earthenware pots of butter were flower-decked wicker baskets heaped high with crisp glazed brioches. At each end of the table scooped-out melons filled with syrupy mixed fruits swam in a sea of sugar-frosted purple and green grapes. Delectable custards, assorted fruit pies, and silver platters of crisp dainty biscuits provided the dessert course. A four-tiered cake covered with rum icing and artistically decorated with lifelike marzipan fruits stood in the center of each table, flanked by small crystal dishes of pastel-colored ices, beginning to melt in the warm evening air.

Ness had already drunk too much champagne, and he lurched slightly as he handed Catrin a filled plate. Anxiously she tugged at his sleeve, leading him toward a secluded bench beneath the trees. Her heart sank as she noticed he was balancing two more glasses of champagne on his gold-rimmed plate.

The food was delicious. So excited had she been by the colorful spectacle, Catrin had not realized how hungry she was. When they had finished the first course Ness brought her a dish of strawberry ice and a handful of fragile *langues de chat* to accompany it. He also brought Catrin a bunch of frosted green grapes and a pomegranate before excusing himself on the pretext of talking to an old acquaintance he had met at the supper table.

Catrin finished her fruit, feeling conspicuous sitting there by herself. She handed her empty plate to a passing servant, and anxiously sought Ness's tall figure in the crowd. Though there were several pirates among the guests, none was her brother.

"What a pleasant surprise! Mistress Catrin Blair, is it not?"

Catrin glanced up as she heard her name spoken. Her stomach lurched in excitement as she saw David Stewart, dressed as a magnificent highland chieftain in tight-fitting tartan trews and riding boots, standing beside the bench. His gold-buttoned coat of royal blue velvet matched the blue bonnet crowning his dark hair; an eagle feather stuck in it proudly proclaimed his rank.

"Mr. Stewart! This is indeed a surprise," she mumbled, her breath tangling in her throat.

Without asking her permission, David Stewart seated himself beside her. Not too close, yet close enough to start a curious tingling sensation in her veins. Shyly she glanced at him, magnificent in his ancestral costume. At his throat was a froth of lace, snow white against his tanned skin; his cuffs likewise ended in billows of lace that emphasized his lean brown hands. A gold ring, the coat of arms surrounded by dark red stones, caught her eye. Uncomfortably Catrin fixed her gaze on the ring, growing even more embarrassed as the minutes crawled silently by. He must think she was a complete loon! A man's company had never kept her tongue-tied before; in fact gentlemen generally remarked on her interesting conversation. But those gentlemen had never generated such a disturbing surge of excitement.

"Do forgive me, Mr. Stewart," Catrin managed at last, after repeatedly clearing her throat, for her voice came out as little more than a croak. "I seem to be rather at a loss for words."

"Overcome by my magnificent appearance, no doubt."

"Perhaps . . . yes, that must be the reason."

"This is the ancestral dress of the Stewart laird of Garth."

"I thought Scotsmen wore kilts."

"A laird rides, so he must wear the trews. But I'm no great chief—laird of Garth's an unimportant title."

"And currently held by another man."

He glanced sharply at her, but the tension in his face gradually softened as he agreed. "That it is."

"My father forfeited his lands, my mother's family too."

"There's a long line of treachery in many a family history."

His dark face had turned so somber, Catrin decided not to pursue the subject. David Stewart must harbor bitter memories of old feuds best left buried. "Did you recently arrive from Italy?" she asked, deliberately changing the subject.

"Yes. But how did you know? Surely there's not that much of the Italian about me?"

"I usually recognize my own kind. As Comyn and Easter have only recently come to England, and you are their laird, I thought you must have lived near them."

"Comyn's family were tacksmen under my father and grandfather," Stewart explained. "In case you don't know what a tacksman is, he rents land from the laird and then in turn rents it to others. Easter's a Carmichael; the Carmichaels were long-time tenants of Comyn's family. The Stewarts and the Carmichaels have suffered much for their beliefs. And now, Mistress Blair, no more talk about the past. Can I bring you another glass of champagne?"

"Please. The evening's warm and I'm very thirsty."

Catrin sat back and tried to control her shallow breathing as she watched David Stewart walking proudly across the narrow stretch of grass to the buffet table. This was not the first time she had noticed this deep, inborn pride among the Scots. And though he had been born in Rome, at heart David Stewart was probably as Scottish as any man born in the homeland.

When he returned with the champagne their fingers brushed casually as he handed her the glass. Catrin fought the exciting shudder that crept along her arm.

"I'm sorry I was rude to you at the Fleet," she apologized at last.

He grinned. "Stung by jealousy, perhaps?"

"Jealousy?" Catrin could feel herself blushing. "Your private affairs are your own business. I just thought that Easter's safety came before . . . anyway, seeing that you did not fail us, I suppose I should forgive you your weakness."

"You are very generous, Miss Blair."

The mockery in his voice annoyed her. "I'm trying to be," she retorted stiffly.

"You find it difficult?"

"Very."

Catrin's mouth tightened as she remembered the woman in the shadows, that nameless creature who merely awaited her departure before flinging herself into David Stewart's eager arms. "I trust your mistress made your delay well worthwhile."

"My mistress would have done so, yes," he agreed, laughter in his green eyes. "Unfortunately, my midnight visitor was no more attractive than a middle-aged envoy from the king of France."

"An envoy!" Catrin gasped, taken back by his unexpected explanation. "Not a woman?"

"Not a woman. Disappointing, but it can't be helped. Kings' envoys are definitely not to be put off, Miss Blair, I'm sure you understand."

Embarrassment at her mistake made Catrin's cheeks almost

crimson, and though he smiled in amusement she could hardly feel at ease. "Oh, Mr. Stewart, it's my turn to apologize. How could I have been so stupid? You must admit mine was a natural assumption. At that time I didn't know about your involvement . . ." She stopped and glanced quickly behind her, making sure they were not being overheard.

"Have no fear, we're not being spied upon. Ness told me he'd confided in you. He also told me you aren't one of us."

"But I'm not a Whig," Catrin defended quickly, "I've no political leanings, Mr. Stewart."

"Then it's up to me to persuade you otherwise. And please, don't keep calling me Mr. Stewart. You make me feel as if I'm in my dotage," he chided gently. "We've been introduced, so surely you can call me David."

"Then you must call me Catrin."

"It will be my pleasure."

They sat beneath the trees in the fading dusk while he told her about his life before he came to England. David Stewart had seen service in several foreign armies, including fighting for the French at Fontenoy. Compared with his stirring adventures Catrin found the recounting of her own life dull. After a second glass of champagne, she felt more relaxed and their conversation flowed freely. She was no longer tongue-tied by his presence, and she no longer cared that the other guests were strangers, or that she had not seen her brother in over an hour. Catrin was aware only of the man at her side, lost in an unreal world of gentle summer breezes, tinkling music, and romantic lanterns winking like giant fireflies in the night.

Much later, when David Stewart casually suggested they stroll along the lantern-lit paths, she knew it was the invitation she most wanted. The landscaped gardens lay in shadow, beds of pale flowers gleaming ghostly as they passed. From the nearby trees a nightingale sang, pure and sweet, and they paused to listen to its song.

"Do you miss Rome?" he asked her.

"Not anymore. And you?"

"I already miss the warm climate, and they tell me there's worse to come up north. My blood may be pure Scots, but it's been somewhat diluted by the Italian sun."

They laughed and walked on. It seemed most natural when David Stewart slipped his warm, lean hand in hers. Catrin tried to suppress a shudder at his touch, hoping he was not aware of her reaction; her instinct told her she was out of her depth.

As they walked through the park she had seen women openly ogling him and she knew it was not his unusual costume, or even his handsome face, which held their attention. David Stewart had an indefinable air that women couldn't ignore. His lazy smile, his swiftly appraising glance, revealed he was no novice in matters of the heart. And the knowledge that she was helpless as a lamb among wolves was both exciting and frightening to Catrin.

They approached the pavilion, from which issued the sweet strains of violins playing for the gavotte and the minuet.

"Would you like to go inside to dance?" he asked, guiding her between high walls of shrubbery fragrant with honeysuckle, the perfume so strong it made Catrin dizzy. "Perhaps your brother will be there."

"I doubt Ness can still stand, but yes, I'd like to dance."

They entered the building, ablaze with candles dripping and guttering in their holders, the hot wax falling on the bare shoulders and wigs of those dancing below. Catrin paused to drink in the spectacle of brightly garbed dancers moving like mechanical dolls to the rigidly elegant measures of the minuet, her eyes alight with excitement. Unconsciously she gripped David's strong arm beneath his blue velvet coat. Only when he squeezed her hand against his body in reply did Catrin become aware of her action. Extracting her hand, she allowed him to lead her onto the floor to join the line forming for the minuet.

Because her stepfather considered dancing a waste of time, Catrin had never been to any of the London balls. Her only dancing experience, outside of lessons, had come from the Cavendishes' musical evenings, when the musicians sometimes played for dancing after their recital was over. The one ball she had attended had been in Rome, when she was twelve, a party at which the young Stuart princes, Charles and Henry, had been guests. Though Catrin had been far too young for Prince Charles to notice her, she remembered him clearly: a tall, fair youth, of almost girlish beauty, full-lipped, with large dark eyes inherited from his mother, Clementina Sobieska. Charles had been the darling of the court, a lively dancer, already exhibiting the promise of the enigmatic young man who had sailed to a foreign land to recapture his father's throne.

Glancing sideways at David, Catrin smiled at his serious countenance as he concentrated on the unfamiliar steps of this particular measure. She allowed herself a delicious shudder of pleasure as she decided she would not exchange him for the dashing Stuart prince if she was given the choice.

After three more dances, he suggested they leave the stuffy room and enjoy the cool of the evening. "It will soon be time for the fireworks."

Though Catrin was reluctant to leave the dancing, the heat from the candles and hundreds of packed bodies inside the vast room made the atmosphere stifling. On the dance floor David Stewart's Continental upbringing was more readily apparent, as were also the envious glances she had been receiving from the other women, eager to make the acquaintance of her handsome beau. Outside at least she would have him to herself.

As they walked into the balmy darkness, Catrin smiled with pleasure. This entire evening was so wonderful, she wished it would last forever. Warning bells jangled in her head, but she was far too happy to heed the danger of David Stewart's company. Soon she must marry Bryce Cavendish and resign herself to becoming a sedate matron. Tonight might be her last chance to be carefree and gay. Recklessly she dismissed all nagging misgivings about the wisdom of her actions, heedlessly following where David Stewart led. She could think of no other with whom she would prefer to spend her final night of freedom.

They crossed the lawns, halting at the shrubbery-fringed perimeter, from where they would have an uninterrupted view of the firework display. Here they leaned against a broad tree trunk, and Catrin did not object when David slid his arm around her shoulders, drawing her close against the welcome warmth of his body, for the river breeze blew chill.

"You're the loveliest woman here, Catrin Blair," he flattered huskily, his breath hot against her cheek.

"Thank you," she replied, making no effort to move away from the warmth of his body, which thrilled and made her uneasy at the same time. Catrin was highly conscious of his hot mouth hovering about her hairline. Then, as she had known he would, David brushed her cheek in a gentle kiss.

"Why did we not meet in Rome?"

"I was schooled at a convent. I doubt you frequented such places," Catrin explained mischievously, vastly enjoying the gentle movement of his lips against her skin, though it set her legs trembling.

"Correct. Convents were not favorite haunts of mine."

"Perhaps they should have been."

"Would you have welcomed me there?"

"Life became quite boring. I think you would have been a pleasant diversion."

He chuckled as he lightly traced his hot fingers over her cheekbones, gently turning her face toward his. "Tonight is stolen from my destiny. It has no beginning, no end. Oh, Catrin Blair, I've no place in my life for you, but God, God . . ."

As she stared up at him in the dim light of the lanterns her eyes misted. How darkly mysterious his face appeared, overshadowed by the swaying branches of the sycamore. His heavy brows, his prominent nose, his firm exciting mouth painted a far different picture than she remembered. David's eyes were black as night. Was it her imagination, or was there a strange intensity in his face she had never seen before? Whatever the cause of his changing expression, her legs began to shake until she had to exert her utmost control to conceal it from him. Catrin was alarmed to discover how much she yearned to feel his mouth on hers . . .

Their lips met and a hot wave of excitement sped through her veins until she thought she would melt. Though Catrin had been mentally prepared for his kiss, her own reaction to it filled her with awe. Totally disarmed, she gazed up into David's unfathomably dark face, far too close now, his warm breath fanning her brow. She could still taste the sweetness of his passionate mouth on her lips. Any thought of danger, her own natural caution, was swept away in a heady wave of longing for this man's lovemaking. She knew, and yet she did not know, the source of this painful delight which made her long to nestle in his arms, pressed hard against his protective body. Catrin gasped at the realization of what she actually craved.

David's mouth curved as he correctly interpreted her reaction. "Sweetheart, no, don't pull away from me. Don't be afraid," he whispered reassuringly, his voice smooth, soft, ensnaring her ever deeper in the net of her own downfall.

She did not say they should go, did not urge him to take her back to the lighted buffet table where she knew she should seek out Ness and ask him to take her home. She mentally acquiesced, his for the taking. When David whispered huskily that he loved her, she never questioned his words, but basked in them instead. Of their own accord her hands slid about his neck where she marveled at the touch of his skin, smooth and hot beneath her fingertips. She slid her fingers up into his crisp dark hair, taking off his proud blue bonnet and dropping it on the grass. Her action amused him; she felt his mouth curve against her exploring fingers. Catrin rejoiced in the power she was exerting over him, never once considering herself irretrievably lost as her will merged with his.

"I've never loved a man before," she confessed softly.

"You love me?"

"Yes, oh, yes, you make me feel so intoxicated. At first I thought it was the champagne . . . now I know it's not."

He drew her closer. They slid from the gnarled tree to the mossy ground, stretching full length on the grass. And Catrin yielded against his hard body.

"Oh, Catrin, I love you too. It's insane . . . I hardly know you . . . I didn't intend this . . . you must understand . . . oh, sweetheart."

His mouth engulfed hers in a blaze of heat, rocking her body with pleasure until she almost swooned. When he pressed even harder against her, she began to long for something she did not understand, aching to cleave to him, to be his for all time. Suddenly, the unbidden memory of her stepfather's angry admonition as he reminded her of her noble groom awaiting an unspotted maid made her gasp in shock.

"What is it?"

"Oh, David . . . I . . . I'm betrothed to another," she admitted in a horrified whisper.

"Give no more thought to him," he whispered back, his hands gently reassuring as he stroked her face. "We'll steal tonight from the future. Though this blissful gift isn't mine, I'll treasure it nonetheless," he whispered ardently, his voice husky, his breathing shallow.

Innocently she pressed even closer to him, delighted by his kisses even as she tried to fight the mounting heaviness in her limbs. Burying her face against the warm sweetness of his neck where the crisp lace flounce scratched her skin, she confided, "I want tonight to last forever."

"So do I. And it will, sweetheart, if only in our hearts."

An unexpected explosion echoed in the background as a shower of golden sparks lit the dark sky. Exclamations of pleasure and sporadic applause from the guests greeted the beginning of the firework display. Behind David's dark head Catrin could see the bursting gold stars, which added to the unreality of the present. Since the first time she saw him she had dreamed about David Stewart, imagining love to be all romantic kissing and exchanged vows. But the insistence of his body, the tingling response in her own blood kindled her slumbering passion. Love, romance, passion, in his arms they all became the same thing. His will was hers, his desire hers also.

"I swear I love you, Catrin, 'tis not something I say easily to every wench I meet," he whispered, his voice uneven as he gently stroked her face.

She smiled up at him, confident, no longer afraid of the depth of their emotion. It was as if she watched herself in a dream, as if this were not really Catrin Blair lying on the grass beside this handsome stranger. She knew his name; she knew he was involved in a plot to place a Stuart king on England's throne; but beyond that, handsome David Stewart was an unknown quantity. And that mystery merely heightened his attraction. Willing him to lean down to her, Catrin touched his face where the smooth olive skin burned hot beneath her fingertips.

"You needn't explain yourself to me. Perhaps from the beginning I knew it would come to this. It's all right. I'll not blame you."

He crushed her body against his own, pressing her soft yielding form into the mossy ground, his steel-hard muscle cutting into her. "I long to love you, Catrin, but you must promise to love me back."

In reply she took his face in her hands and drew his intoxicating mouth to her own, drowning in the sweetness of his kiss. She reveled in a growing passion she could not explain but experienced joyfully. His mouth was hard now, the soft heat gone. The pressure of his body had become thrilling yet menacing as he imprisoned her beneath him. Above the shadow of his head she saw bursts of red and blue stars, and the smell of gunpowder vied with that of the cloying honeysuckle.

"I can't promise you anything but my heart," he whispered as he deftly unlaced her bodice.

Flame seared Catrin as she became aware of the touch of his long slender fingers. She gasped as he gently molded her breasts, increasing the pressure as she thrust upward, eager for his touch. The pleasure was connected to every part of her body, growing into a quivering network of passion. "Your heart is all I ask."

"All?" he questioned against her ear, his hands rousing her to trembling heat. "Surely not all."

Catrin giggled, her excitement building at the meaning behind his words. "Not all. Please, David, be gentle. I'm afraid . . ."

"Be not afraid of me. Trust me. I'll try not to hurt you."

For all his assurances she knew panic as he slid his hands beneath her silken skirts, his hot caress traveling to her thighs and beyond. David slowly kissed her into submission so that she no longer clamped her thighs closed against his searching hand. The building sensation she experienced when she allowed him access to that secret place overwhelmed her as a mutual bolt of fire shot between them.

For some time Catrin had been aware of the building pressure against her thighs as his swollen manhood bruised her flesh. The unexpected intimacy of this alarming discovery made her draw back. When she drew away from that demanding heat, he did not chide her for her modesty. He placed her hand against the bursting pressure inside his clothing, gently kissing her mouth and urging her to caress him. Though mentally Catrin shrank from the discovery, her passionate nature had boldly asserted itself. Sexual passion was an experience her mind rejected yet her body craved. How often she had sighed over literary love scenes, which had prepared her not at all for this physical intimacy. The eager throbbing heat clamoring against her hand promised pleasure as well as pain.

David kissed her passionately, his mouth moving to her breast where he caught her nipples between hard lips, igniting such fire that she no longer analyzed the act. With a gasp of surprise she curved her fingers about his blazing flesh, unaware until now that he had unfastened his clothing. The knowledge that he longed for her intimate caresses, that she could make him shudder with pleasure, turned her bolder. Now she marveled at the strong hard heat of his swollen flesh, darkly engorged with blood; she even wished for daylight so she could admire him more fully. Her gasps of pleasure, her exclamations of wonder and delight only fired him to greater heights. He groaned beneath her caresses as she slid her left hand inside his fine lawn shirt, tangling her fingers in his curly black hair. She fingered his dark nipples, which were hard as her own, surprised to find those two parts of his body curiously connected, the one seeming to inflame the other, for the swollen surfeit in her hand leaped anew at the contact.

Time stood still. Neither of them considered the presence of hundreds of fellow guests watching the firework display. They pulsed to a clock of their own devising, fraught with heat, tenderness, and love.

David rolled Catrin onto her back and gently spread her legs, kissing her, soothing her, until she gradually relaxed, sufficiently aroused to allay her muscle-tautening fear as he pressed heated flesh to heated flesh. Then he thrust hard, until the final barrier was breached and Catrin cried out in surprise and pain. He did not allow her to linger on the threshold of pain, but carried her further, sweeping her to the sweet oblivion of mutual passion as he moved rhythmically inside her, caressing her with his hands, his mouth, his body. Catrin soared ecstatically, her emotions welded by heat and love to a molten climax.

Spent, David held her in his arms, comforting her as she slowly came back from that dark world of passion where she was an unseasoned traveler. Catrin wept against his shoulder, her tears marking the blue velvet coat. Around them colored stars were bursting against the black sky as the grand finale of the firework display took place.

"Oh, David, love, I never dreamed I could feel like that," she whispered in awe, pressing her lips against his hot neck. "I don't think I'm able to walk back . . . not yet."

He smiled in understanding and kissed her gently, his lips trailing softly down her cheek. "We've all the time in the world," he assured, drawing her close against the warmth of his body.

Catrin lay in limbo, wanting to weep for the depth of her emotion. Never before had she understood the deep involvement of all her senses, the complete surrender called making love. On this man she had chosen to bestow the gift that was hers to give only once in a lifetime. That treasure, which by rights belonged to Bryce Cavendish, she had bestowed upon David Stewart out of love and passion. She did not regret the sacrifice.

The wind stirred her soft hair against the back of his hand and, torn by emotion, David bent to kiss her mouth, his lips lingering on hers. "Say you're not sorry, Catrin," he whispered at last when she failed to respond to him.

"Not sorry because we made love, sorry only because you're not the man I'm to marry."

He drew away from her, the softness leaving his face. "There you're most fortunate. I'm a poor marriage prospect. An attainted Jacobite without a home to call his own . . . you're far better off without me."

"But I love you," she whispered tearfully.

Their mouths joined in a desperate kiss. David had not intended to hurt her, and though her sincere vow made his senses soar, he felt guilty because he had destroyed her security. He prayed that this one passionate act would not destroy her future.

When it was time to go he helped her smooth her dress, which was a mass of wrinkles, and retrieved her straw hat from the ground. Jauntily he placed his own velvet bonnet at a rakish angle, anxious to regain some of his bravado. The effort was in vain. He longed to promise her lifelong fidelity and care, yet in all honesty he could promise nothing, for his life was no longer his own.

They walked toward the buffet tables, where guests were gathering for refreshments after the firework display. David detached his arm from about her waist, not anxious to advertise their intimacy.

At their approach Ness lurched forward, a slurred greeting on his lips. "Catrin, love, where the devil have you been? We should have left an hour ago."

"Watching the fireworks," she replied innocently, aware her voice was still husky with the aftermath of passion.

"She was with me," David supplied quickly as he reached out to support the swaying man. "Come on, Ness, you look as if you need your bed. And a strong arm to lead you there."

Laughing, his spirits buoyed by champagne, Ness linked arms with them, his legs buckling as they headed toward the gates of the pleasure garden. As they went Catrin felt her elation rapidly evaporating. In place of the heated pleasure of passion there was only cold emptiness, a lonely wave that engulfed her until she wanted to weep. The wind from the river blew increasingly chill and she fancied she felt rain against her cheek. When he caught her eye, David Stewart smiled at her, but she thought his expression strained. Was he already regretting his impassioned words? She doubted he regretted their lovemaking.

Sanity returned in a flood long before they reached the wrought-iron gates where the rows of waiting sedan chairs and coaches stretched far into the night. Tomorrow David Stewart would be gone from her life, and she might never see him again. In all likelihood the precious memories of what they had shared tonight were all she would ever have of him. She had not only given him her virginity but also the deepest devotion of her heart. Catrin prayed that in the months to come, while he followed the fortunes of his Stuart prince, he would not cast her gift aside.

"Good night, old chap. Thanks for looking after my sister,"

Ness mumbled as he leaned against the first hackney they reached, for his legs had grown alarmingly weak. "A hellcart's best for me . . . river might sober me up too fast, eh!" And he chuckled foolishly, leaning on the tall wooden wheel, grasping the spokes as he shook with merriment. "Come on, Catrin, David hasn't all night. He's to be away first thing in the morning."

So her worst fears were true! Catrin's heart sank as, at Ness's insistence, she climbed up the steps and ducked to enter the hackney. David's hand was warmly supportive on her elbow, but the reminder of his electrifying touch was more than she could bear. There was no time, no privacy to say what she longed to say to him. They had not even discussed their limited future. As he had said, tonight was stolen from their destinies, a beautiful memory to treasure. Perhaps, when she was old and gray and surrounded by grandchildren, she would recall how, beneath the flickering lanterns, her ecstasy mirrored by exploding fireworks, a Jacobite fugitive had made passionate love to her on a fragrant summer evening in Ranelagh pleasure gardens.

"Good night, Catrin . . . Ness."

David's voice was deep with emotion as he squeezed her hand.

"Good night. And thank you for . . . everything," she whispered, afraid to say more in Ness's presence.

Then David stepped back, signaling to the driver to begin their journey. The hackney lurched forward, the horses' hooves crunching on the gravel walk. Through a blur of tears Catrin watched David Stewart move beneath the shadowed sycamores, turn down the avenue to the right, and walk out of her life into the dark summer night.

Chapter 5

The hackney entered the square, which was virtually deserted at this early hour. Metallic gray tinged the eastern sky and birds had begun to twitter in the plane trees as Catrin alighted from the conveyance. With the exception of a flickering flame in the basement kitchen where a servant had already lit the fire, the Millbank house was in darkness.

"Here you are, my man, and it's far more than you deserve. My backside'll be bruised for a week," Ness said crossly as he handed the hackney driver a handful of coins.

Catrin shivered in the predawn chill as she waited for her brother to join her. "Hush, must you speak so loud? You'll wake the neighbors," she snapped unfairly as he stumbled up the steps.

"Bitchy tonight, ain't we? Parties don't seem to agree with you, me dear. Not going to knock, you know, have me own key."

Triumphantly Ness produced a key which, with great difficulty, he fitted into the lock. The key turned and the door groaned with damp as Ness thrust it open.

Thankfully Catrin stepped inside the darkened hallway, where a single candle burned on the walnut sidetable beside the silver plate used for letters and calling cards. It was odd that a candle had been left burning all night, but she quickly dismissed the thought, longing for the privacy of her room. There was so much she had to consider, not the least of which was her deep involvement with David Stewart. She needed time alone to put

61

her jangled emotions in order, to learn how to cope with her newfound love . . .

"A fine how-do-you-do! What's the meaning of this?"

Catrin's blood froze at the bellowed question. To her horror she saw their stepfather emerge from the shadowed doorway of the front parlor wearing a voluminous nightgown, his tasseled nightcap askew on his shaven head.

"Papa, you weren't due back till tomorrow!" Catrin gasped accusingly as she fought for control. Desperately she searched for a plausible explanation of her conduct, though she knew there was none that would satisfy.

"Came home early, and damned lucky I did. What's the meaning of this? And you, you drunken wastrel, what have you to say for yourself?" he shouted, rounding on Ness, who was weaving in the open doorway, shocked at the sight of their angry stepfather. "Shut the door! Do you want everyone to hear our business?" Millbank bellowed. "As if tongues haven't started wagging already at the sight of you two, got up like a dog's dinner. Where've you been dressed like that?"

Taking a deep breath, Catrin stepped forward, prepared to tell the truth, for Ness was making no move to explain.

"We've been to the Merriams' masquerade party, Papa."

"Merriams? Who are they?"

"Booth Merriam—Ness's friend from Oxford."

"Oxford! You mean that young puppy who led you into more scrapes than even you could devise?"

Catrin's choice of the truth proved ill advised; she had forgotten their stepfather had already made Booth Merriam's acquaintance.

"Papa," she began again, but he stepped forward and cut her short, seizing her arm angrily.

"Traipsing through the streets, a daughter of mine! Showing off your bosom for all the world like one of your brother's actresses. And what are you done up as, my lad? A pirate, eh! Well, that's a bloody good choice, anyway."

"Catrin's done no wrong. She only agreed to attend the party at my insistence. If anybody's to blame, I am."

Catrin flashed Ness a smile of gratitude, almost happy that he had finally found his tongue and come to her defense. He stood beside her and slipped his arm about her waist.

"Oh, undoubtedly you're to blame. I never had any doubts on the matter. You're at the back of everything that turns sour in this household . . ."

"That's not fair, Papa..."

"You shut your mouth, miss. I'm speaking to your brother."

"Sir, if we have any differences to discuss, let us do so in private."

"Nay, what I've got to say can be heard by the entire household... including your explanation."

"Explanation? Papa, I've explained already! We were at a party and lost track of the time..."

"I told thee to be quiet!"

Catrin stepped back, surprised by her stepfather's cold rage, the full force of which was usually reserved for her brother.

"Now, my fine fellow, explain, if you can, what that fancy woman's doing in my guest room?"

Brother and sister gasped in unison. They had forgotten Easter.

"Oh, so you do know she's there. Well, that's a change. I expected you both to pretend you'd never set eyes on her before." Humphrey Millbank pulled out a straight-backed chair and thankfully dropped down on it, breathing painfully hard. His face had grown purple and his bulbous eyes were starting out of his head. He continued in a rasping voice, "And furthermore, me young cockscomb, I assume that puling scrap of humanity the wretch has with her belongs to you. Now, don't deny it, damn you—that woman's bairn's your bastard! It's plain as the nose on me face."

"You're wrong, sir. The lady's our friend; the child—"

"Wrong, you say! Enough lies. You, Catrin, let's have the truth."

"It's as Ness says, Papa. The lady's Easter Stewart, a friend from Rome. It was she whom we visited in Chiswick."

"If she lives in Chiswick, what's she doing here?"

"The landlord evicted her and I couldn't turn her out on the street."

"Now I've heard it all! To think you'd defend him in his lies—and immoral lies at that. At least I thought that just this once, you'd give me the truth."

"It is the truth! Ness had nothing to do with fathering Easter's child. She's married to Comyn Stewart."

Wearily Humphrey Millbank levered himself from the chair. "That does it! You—pack your bags and get out. I've tried to be a father to you, Ness Blair, tried damned hard at times, but this is the final straw. I've had enough!"

The maidservants, awakened by the uproar, were crowded

over the banister, their faces a white blur in the gloom. When he saw them Humphrey Millbank bellowed like a wounded bull and the women bolted with squeals of fright.

"Listen, Papa, you have it all wrong. I'm not lying for Ness. Easter Stewart . . ."

"Never mind, Catrin, you're just wasting your breath. 'Papa dear' prefers to believe the very worst about me. It'll be a relief to be out from under your foot, Mr. Millbank. Damned if I know why I've stayed this long."

"I do, lad. Cash. Filthy money. That's what's kept you here. Well, now you'll 'ave to find your own wherewithal to pay for your gambling and your brandy and your poxy trollops, because you won't get another penny out of me!"

"Oh, please, Papa, don't put Ness out of the house. When we've all calmed down he can prove he's telling the truth. If you'll just ask Easter—"

"I've asked her already, for all the good it did. It's only to be expected that she'd lie, or get backhanded by Prince Charming here. She seems a decent enough sort—that is, until she took up with 'im. Probably told her this was his house. Must've been a surprise when I came home early. Go on, what're you waiting for? You found that ridiculous getup good enough for traipsing through the streets last night; it'll do for leaving this morning. I'll give thee two hours to be gone. And take your woman and her brat with you."

Catrin clung to her stepfather's arm, pleading with him to relent in his harsh judgment. Ness shook his head at her, not wanting her to be distressed over his misfortune.

"As for you, miss, you've got summat coming to you too, so you'd best save your sympathy for yourself. It's off to Isobel's with you. And not for a couple of weeks this time. You'll stay till the day before your wedding—that's if there is a wedding. I wouldn't be surprised when word of this gets out if young Cavendish calls the whole thing off. You're going to Lancashire before tongues start wagging. Mebbe we can lie, say you've been there all along . . ."

"I won't go! You can't make me go to Aunt Isobel's!"

"Oh, can't I? We'll soon see about that."

Catrin clung to her brother's arm. Ness could not be turned out; he had nowhere to go. "What will you do? Oh, Ness, reason with him."

Ness laughed sarcastically. "Reason? He doesn't know the meaning of the word. Don't worry about me, Catrin, I've plenty of friends . . . and they'll take care of Easter too."

"Let me talk to Easter, explain to her. She'll be so afraid."

Humphrey Millbank barred the way. "You're talking to no one. Now get up to your room. I'll deal with you later."

Defiantly Catrin stood her ground. "I won't leave until you've given us a chance to explain."

"Right, miss, you've made your choice."

Three menservants materialized from the stair and Millbank ordered them to take Miss Catrin to her room forcibly. She flung a final agonized appeal to her brother to save her, but Ness stood there blinking in surprise, still trying to grasp the rapid passage of events.

Apologizing for their orders, and trying not to hurt her, the menservants swiftly bore her upstairs to her bedchamber. Some time later Catrin heard tapping at her door. "Who's there?"

"Ness. Can you hear me?"

"Oh, Ness, are you leaving now?" she cried tearfully, knowing she could not even kiss her brother goodbye. "Can you get a key? The door's locked."

"No, Millbank has them all. I told you he was no fool. Now, listen, Catrin, I've only a few minutes."

Wiping her tears and sniffling, Catrin knelt behind the door, pressing her ear to the keyhole. "Goodbye, Ness. Let me know where you're staying. And please, take care of yourself . . ."

"Stop worrying about me. Listen carefully—I want you to go along with Millbank's plans. Go quietly to Liverpool . . ."

"I certainly will not! Go I may, but it won't be without a fight."

"I commend your spirit, but we need you there for our purposes. Can't you let him think he's won, just this once?"

"No. I won't back down. I can't . . ."

"You must."

Catrin silently considered her brother's suggestion. Defiance was what she had anticipated using as a weapon against the hated edict; to acquiesce, as Ness suggested, was more than she could bear. Her stepfather and hated Aunt Isobel would consider themselves victors.

"Catrin, are you still listening?"

"Yes, I'm listening."

"I want you to go to Liverpool and wait until someone gets in touch with you. No one will suspect a young woman visiting her aunt. We badly need someone to carry money and documents. Our man was intercepted and barely managed to get away with his life—now he's known, we can no longer use him. Please, Catrin, it will help me and countless others if you'll agree. It's not dangerous. I wouldn't ask you to do anything dangerous, you know that. Just take the packages with you and wait until someone asks you for them. We can say they're gifts for dear Aunt Isobel. Will you do that for me?" he broke off as footsteps sounded on the stair. "Catrin, will you?"

"Oh, all right," she agreed reluctantly, her heart pitching at the idea of becoming involved in a treasonable plot.

"Goodbye, love, I'll get word to you as soon as possible..."

The sound of her stepfather's rumbling voice in the background alerted Catrin to his approach. "Goodbye, Ness. Take heat. And look after yourself. Remember, I love you..."

No answer came from beyond the door, and in disappointment Catrin concluded her brother had already left by the back stairs.

She had agreed to carry important papers, money too, and she shivered in apprehension at the reminder. Today she had finally taken sides. David would be proud of her—David! Her heart twisted as she repeated his name, and tears filled her eyes. How she longed for him. If only she could go away with him instead of having to stay with despised Aunt Isobel. Come September she would merely exchange one prison for another. Though she had never felt affection for Bryce Cavendish, now that she was in love with David, the enforced sentence of an arranged marriage was even harder to bear. David Stewart was her lover, they had exchanged vows of passion and love; yet she knew not where he was. More painful even than not knowing where he was—she did not know if he was still hers! And Catrin buried her face in her hands and wept.

Heavy throat-clearing on the other side of the door eventually roused her from her storm of self-pity. How long she had crouched here weeping Catrin did not know. Her legs were stiff and cold as, like an old woman, she struggled to stand, supporting herself against the door.

"Who is it?" she asked thickly, hoping her visitor was Ness.

"Don't cry so hard, lass. Going to our Isobel's isn't the end of the world."

Catrin's mouth tightened as she recognized her stepfather's penitent voice. "You can say that because you aren't going. I needn't go if only you'd listen to me. Why won't you believe..."

"I don't intend to discuss the unfortunate matter any further. Ness is gone and good riddance to 'im. You're to leave for Lancashire this afternoon. There's not an hour to lose if we're to say you've been at our Isobel's all along. The maids will be coming to pack your bags and I want you civil, do you hear? No shouting and raging. The poor lasses are only doing their job."

His unexpected concern for the maids touched her. "Don't worry, Papa, I don't intend to treat them badly. In fact, I intend to behave quite well."

She could have laughed aloud for the obvious pleasure her statement caused. He sighed with relief, and she pictured the satisfied beam suffusing his seamed face. The irony of the situation made her smile. His good humor was brought about because she intended to further the Jacobite cause! It was amusing to think that this loyal King George's man, this staunch Whig, was unwittingly aiding the enemy.

"There's a good lass! You're to have a new cloak for the journey. I had to hurry Miss Pence and it cost me plenty, but you're worth it. Now, cheer up, it can't be that bad staying at our Isobel's."

"No, Papa."

When Catrin refused to respond further to his attempts at conversation, Humphrey Millbank stumped away angrily.

Rain pelted against the carriage windows as Catrin traveled on the final stage of her journey to Lancashire. They had left the King's Head in Chester at dawn that morning in the midst of a thunderstorm. Her journey to Liverpool had been every bit as tedious as she had anticipated. To add further to the unpleasantness of traveling in wet weather to a destination she loathed, Catrin had been placed under the chaperonage of Mr. and Mrs. Fisher, who had been conveniently departing for Nantwich in Cheshire that same day. The elderly couple had graciously allowed her to continue on to Liverpool in their carriage rather than make her endure the rigors of travel by common mail coach.

Milly, Catrin's maid, had ridden with the coachman for much of the journey, giving up her seat inside the coach to Dorcas Fisher's maid, who was as large as her mistress. Now Milly lounged disrespectfully on the opposite seat, intending to enjoy the luxury of dry leather upholstery for the short time left to her.

"How long before we get there, milady?" Milly finally asked, as she sat up to peer outside at the sodden gray landscape.

"Two hours from the last posthouse. But with this rain we might find outselves axle-deep in a mudhole long before then."

Milly pulled a face as she settled herself more comfortably, holding onto the edge of the seat as the coach lurched around a corner. "Don't they never 'ave no sun in this place?"

"Rarely," Catrin remarked grimly as she nervously pleated the folds of her blue merino traveling cloak. Rarely sun, or laughter, or pleasure . . . Milly would find out the worst soon enough. "Cheer up. You'll probably have the servants' hall to yourself. Aunt Isobel's far too miserly to employ more than a couple of servants."

Milly grunted in disgust and they both gazed wanly at the watery landscape as the coach rapidly covered the last few miles to Edgehill. The passing fields, bordered by tall trees bent beneath the onslaught of the summer storm, looked desolate. Water filled deep ruts in the road ahead and the carriage lurched frequently as the Fishers' coachman skillfully avoided the obstacles.

At least Catrin was thankful to be free of Dorcas Fisher's constant scrutiny. She had virtually hugged herself with glee when nosy Mrs. Fisher discovered the supposed "gifts" for Aunt Isobel in her tapestry valise and praised her for her thoughtfulness. Had she opened the packages and found damning documents, and Jacobite gold with which to purchase an army's supplies, she would have fainted away. The weight of the larger bundle had elicited some comment until Catrin revealed that inside the wooden box was a bronze likeness of King George. She hoped Dorcas Fisher would not discuss her generosity with her stepfather or she would have to elaborate on her lie. The need to lie at all distressed Catrin greatly, lying not being a vice that came naturally to her.

It was late afternoon before they reached Edgehill. The bustling port of Liverpool, grown rich from trade with the Indies and with Ireland, boasted wide new streets and grand civic buildings. Shunning the city itself, Aunt Isobel lived in the more respectable environs to the south, denying Catrin even the colorful entertainment of life in a large port.

During her previous half-dozen visits to Cedars of Lebanon, the prim, respectable household maintained by the widow of the Reverend Oliver Stiles, late pastor of nearby St. Winifred's church, their daily routine had not varied. After the first couple of visits Catrin gave up expecting any change. Awaiting her was a monotonous existence of spartan light, heat, and meals, punctuated by church services, daily good works for the poor, and sedate walks during which Aunt Isobel would lecture her unmercifully on her many failings.

"Coo, is that it?" breathed Milly fearfully as she peered through the rain-spattered window at the forbidding three-storied brick house set amid dark cedars. "It looks haunted to me!"

"I assure you, any self-respecting ghost would soon find more joyful accommodations than Aunt Isobel's."

The coach clattered up the short drive and stopped before the red-brick villa's front door, which was reached by three curved steps. The coachman swung down from the box and shouted for assistance. A startled boy in a leather apron appeared at the side door. When he saw the coach with its steaming team, he darted back indoors, calling to someone named David to help with the bags.

His use of that particular name was a painful coincidence. At the poignant reminder Catrin shuddered and swallowed the lump that rose to her throat. Even the chance mention of his name made her heart race. Catrin's efforts to put all thought of David Stewart from her mind had been unsuccessful. Yet reliving the past would only bring on the melancholia she had fought since that blissful night in Ranelagh Gardens. Tears pricked her eyes when she recalled his exquisite kisses, the memory creating a heavy languor that spread rapidly through her body. Such deep emotion was difficult to conceal from others, though she knew her lover must remain a secret.

"My dear Catrin, welcome."

Forcing a wan smile, Catrin alighted from the coach. She took Aunt Isobel's small mittened hand in her own, finding her aunt's greeting decidedly chilly.

Dressed in a dull maroon gown of Indian cotton with a plain starched apron and a prim cap to match, Isobel Stiles appeared grim and unbending. A plain, mousy-haired woman of forty-five, whose tight-lipped mouth and colorless face proclaimed her deep piety, she eyed her fashionably dressed niece with disapproval. With all that bright hair and striking face and figure, Humphrey's girl could easily have been mistaken for an actress. No wonder he was having difficulties with the flighty baggage! Look at that full red mouth pouting in open invitation to a man's lusts.

"This visit is at such short notice. I trust all's well with your dear papa?"

"Quite well, thank you. Papa merely wished me to meditate in the tranquil surroundings of Cedars of Lebanon during the weeks before my wedding," Catrin lied outrageously, not sure if her aunt knew the actual reason for her banishment. The swift tightening of Isobel's colorless face told Catrin the worst had already been relayed to her. How much more severe would be her punishment had either Aunt Isobel or Papa guessed the extent of her wantonness at the Merriams' masquerade ball!

"Really, Catrin, we can hardly explain away your visit so innocently. Humphrey has prevailed upon me to do my best to guide you . . . be careful with those trunks, boy."

Catrin sighed with relief as her aunt's attention was diverted.

"What an extraordinary amount of baggage!" Aunt Isobel exclaimed, viewing the growing mound of bags and boxes with disapproval. "You'll have no need of all this clothing. We lead a very quiet life here."

A very quiet life had been putting it mildly! Catrin thought bitterly as she recalled her aunt's words. Life here was so quiet it was like being entombed. For three weeks she had stoically endured this miserable household, until now she was nearing desperation. Walking on the village green with pious Cousin Ruth in tow was the most daring outing she had been allowed. Milly had been sent home; an extra mouth to feed was considered an unwelcome burden. To Catrin's disappointment, not even Cousin Adam was here to brighten the days, he having recently moved to the Lake District to become an assistant rector. Unfortunately, Ruth was here as a constant reminder of all that was expected of a proper young woman.

Intercepting Catrin's mutinous look, Ruth asked, "Have you finished your sewing?" knowing full well Catrin was only halfway through her sampler.

"No. I intend to make it last me till autumn."

Ruth smiled smugly and patted her own neatly stitched work with dainty white hands. "This afternoon we're to sort clothing for the destitute."

"How exciting," Catrin commented sourly as she stabbed the square of linen with green silk. "Is that before our bible class, or afterward?"

"You're wicked to speak sarcastically about our good works."

Catrin glanced out of the window at the bare garden. No gaudy summer flowers graced the pristine lawn or edged the low brick wall; likewise the furnishings within this prim house were devoid of color. Each room was curtained in serviceable plush velvet in a dark shade of green; the mahogany furniture was plainly functional. On the bare polished floors were scattered homemade rag rugs of indeterminate colors. In the two small adjoining bedchambers used by Catrin and her cousin, white and dark brown were the prevailing colors. A narrow bed—Catrin was convinced the mattress had been chosen for its lumpiness—a chair, a small dressing table, and a wardrobe were the only furnishings.

Sometimes, after they were settled for the night Ruth tapped messages to her on the wall, or whispered at the keyhole when she knew her mother was occupied downstairs. Even this mild display of disobedience surprised Catrin, for in Aunt Isobel's presence Ruth was the picture of decorum, pale eyes downcast, white hands demurely folded in her lap.

A mousy, unappealing child, Ruth had become a mousy, unappealing young woman. Her rather colorless light hair was secured in a severe bun at the nape of her neck; every chance tendril that escaped its fastening was quickly thrust out of sight beneath her lawn cap. Ruth's plain gown was of paler stuff than her mother's, but of identical design. The only bright piece of clothing she owned was a cloak of Lincoln green wool given to her by Uncle Humphrey on her sixteenth birthday. Ruth was envious of Catrin's pretty clothes, her ribboned accessories and luxuriant chestnut curls, an envy exhibited in spiteful comments and tale-bearing.

Because Aunt Isobel was always eager to listen to Ruth's reports, Catrin suspected she had thrown them together for that very purpose. She must be delighted. Smarmy Ruth was an accomplished spy.

A warm breeze entered the room, stirring Catrin's hair against her brow. The soft caress tugged at her memory, rekindling the intense pleasure of David's touch, the feel of his mouth against her skin—quickly Catrin forced away the memory. Ruth was watching her intently, apparently eager to catch her in ungodly thoughts.

"Why don't we sit on the lawn to sew?"

"Mama says I'll get sunburned." Ruth continued to stitch, the subject dismissed.

"Are you always going to do what Mama says?"

Ruth's head came up, her light eyes wide. "You are wicked! Of course I do what Mama says. She knows what's best for me."

Catrin's lip curled, but she did not contradict Ruth's words. One look at the portrait over the bureau depicting stern Reverend Stiles, with his thin nose and turned-down mouth, convinced her that Ruth was merely a product of her upbringing. It was foolish to expect spirit from the offspring of so colorless a couple.

She had often wondered how her stepfather and his sister could be such complete opposites. Humphrey Millbank was forthright, even crude in his speech and behavior, whereas Isobel's every word and mannerism were a study of gentility, or at least Isobel's interpretation of gentility. Brother and sister had one trait in common, however, a trait Catrin had been amazed to discover in her straitlaced aunt. They both worshiped the quality. Aunt Isobel's frequent references to "Dear Lady Margaret and Lord Walter" purposely conveyed that the lord and lady of the manor were her very good friends, when in fact their relationship was only one of polite acquaintance. Catrin's discovery of her aunt's obsession with being accepted by her betters had provided her lone hope for salvation.

The day before, an invitation had arrived by messenger, not from Lord Walter of Bickerstaffe Manor, but from his neighbor at nearby Thorpington Hall. They had all been invited to a late summer gala ball to be held in the Hall's sumptuous grounds. Aunt Isobel's immediate reaction had been an emphatic no. Yet Catrin was convinced her aunt was beginning to yield after she had cleverly pointed out how advantageous it would be for Ruth to attend such a gathering. Their quiet life at Cedars of Lebanon kept Ruth from the local social functions where it was traditional to show off daughters as future marriage prospects.

Though Ruth insisted she had no wish to attend the ball, Catrin knew she was lying. When they were alone her cousin plied her with endless questions about balls and parties and the nobility in general, anxious to know what would be expected of her if she did attend the ball.

"Refreshments, girls." Sounding unusually cheerful this noon, Aunt Isobel breezed into the parlor carrying a tray of fish pasties and two glasses of milk. In this austere establishment the food was likewise uninspired. Stolid oatmeal porridge,

accompanied by an occasional kipper or fried egg, dry toast—
"very good for the complexion"—and milk, formed a typical
breakfast. A bowl of thin soup, or a small, tasteless pasty,
accompanied by unbuttered slices of coarse bread, and another
glass of milk, was their staple lunch. Dinner varied a little, but
never achieved acceptable culinary heights.

"Have you decided if we can go to the ball?" Catrin asked
after they had said grace. She selected a cold cod pasty and
found it tasted as dreary as it looked.

"It's unseemly of you to keep asking me, Catrin," Aunt
Isobel reprimanded her. "By the way, I discovered you've not
finished sorting the hymnals I brought home last week. They're
urgently needed for dispatch to missions in heathen lands. It's
very wicked of you to shirk your duty. Instead of accompanying
us to church, you will stay behind to complete your task, as a
punishment."

The edict was not unwelcome. At least sorting hymnals
allowed her time alone and Catrin would probably be finished
in plenty of time to walk in the garden.

"And lest you think you'll soon be finished," added Aunt
Isobel, evidently reading her mind, "you will then transcribe
certain hymns for playing on the harpsichord. Humphrey tells
me you have some musical talent. It will be a pleasant surprise
to see you exhibit some talent while you are here for something
besides constant complaints and wails of discontent."

Behind her mother's back Ruth stuck out her tongue and
Catrin longed to retaliate. She was, however, a little old for
such childish behavior.

When Isobel and Ruth had left for church, Catrin flung wide
the windows to admit the breeze. The casement groaned as if
unused to being opened. With a deep sigh of pleasure she leaned
far out into the sunshine, mentally picturing heavy-leaved green
trees and riotous borders of scented summer flowers. When
Catrin first arrived at Cedars of Lebanon she had longed to
rebel, but today she did not defy her aunt by going outside. It
was as if the restrained atmosphere inside the staid household
had already invaded her personality. A few months longer and
she would be so submissive no one would recognize her!

Determined to liven her mood, Catrin went to the harpsichord and played a lilting song, something she remembered
from that exquisite night at Ranelagh Gardens. If only David
knew where she was. Liverpool was not far from Scotland,

and Ness could give him directions to Edgehill . . .

She sighed and stopped playing. David would not visit her here—he had not chosen to visit her in London and he had known her whereabouts there also. A tear trickled down her nose. To how many others had David Stewart promised his heart? She slowly replayed the haunting tune, painfully recalling how it had felt to be held in his arms, to taste his passionate kisses . . .

"An exquisite piece, Catrin, my love."

She spun around, startled to discover she was no longer alone. Fleetingly she wondered if the man were David, or perhaps Ness, but the masculine figure who came through the doorway was neither.

"Bryce! I wasn't expecting you," she gasped as he marched toward her, the barrier between them growing with every step. This broad-chested, ruddy-complexioned army officer dressed in brown brocade coat and breeches, his sturdy legs in mirror-bright kid riding boots, was her future husband! Forcing herself to repeat that statement sent successive chills down Catrin's spine. Her husband! This man was going to father her children, would make demands on her body she was reluctant to grant . . .

"Thought I'd surprise you, my love."

Even the affectionate touch of this floridly handsome young man in his curled yellow wig repulsed her. His watery blue eyes searched her face as Bryce pressed her hand to his full lips. "Beautiful as ever. How long has it been since I've seen you?" When he received no welcoming response, Bryce cleared his throat uncomfortably and switched topics.

"From what I hear the old woman's something of a dragon. And being a fearless soldier, I came to rescue you from her clutches. Gad, not even a stable—you are leading a spartan existence. Cheer up, me dear, I vow to lift your spirits the only way I know how."

Catrin was quickly enfolded in his arms, and the looming closeness of his face, the smell of his perfume, stifled her. When Bryce tried to kiss her mouth she quickly turned her head so that his eager kiss fell on her cheek.

"Please, Bryce, my aunt's a model of propriety. We'd both receive the lecture of our lives if she saw us kissing," Catrin protested, sidestepping his loose embrace. "Now, pray tell me what you're doing in Lancashire?"

"Just passing through on the way to my Yorkshire estate. Thought I'd best look things over before the shooting season.

I'll hate leaving you alone so soon after we're wed, my love, but I always go up north for the sport and I doubt you'd find it entertaining. Of course, if you've a mind, you're more than welcome to join me."

Aghast, Catrin could only stare at him. They might already be married the way he was including her in his plans. But of course, they would be married not long after grouse-shooting started!

Desperate for a diversion, Catrin rang for the housekeeper and ordered glasses of Madeira and cake. While they awaited their refreshments she listened to Bryce's exciting account of his latest military adventures. He spoke affectionately of "Billy," King George's second son, who, as duke of Cumberland, commanded Bryce's regiment. Sometime back Catrin had been introduced to Bryce's commander at the Cavendishes' Mayfair home. To her disappointment the celebrated royal was rude, and unflatteringly corpulent; his coarse manner she concluded to be his heritage from the parade field. In a way, though presently he was much slimmer and better looking, Bryce reminded her of Cumberland. Give him a few more years in the field, more feminine conquests, more comradely drinking parties and, as he neared thirty, she imagined Bryce could be taken for Cumberland's brother. The idea was thoroughly distasteful to her.

The housekeeper brought their refreshments and pointedly left the door open, as Catrin assumed she had been instructed to do by her mistress should Miss Catrin entertain any gentleman.

Catrin tried to make conversation, without much success. This man had become an obstacle to her happiness almost overnight. She kept comparing him with David and finding him lacking in all respects. It was unthinkable that she should lie with Bryce, allowing him the intimacies she had eagerly bestowed on another.

"Shall we take a stroll in the garden?" Bryce suggested at length, putting down his empty plate and glass before he joined her at the window. "Gad, looks bare as a parade field. Perhaps there's a country lane nearby, somewhere frequented by lovers, what?"

"No, I'm sure there isn't. Why don't we stay here? We can talk undisturbed. Aunt Isobel and Cousin Ruth are at church. They won't be back for hours."

"That so? 'Pon my word, they've uncommon good sense,

those two," drawled Bryce, slipping his hand over her neck. "So white, so soft. Demme, but you're a ravishing creature, me dear. Any man would be proud to name you wife."

Catrin thanked him for his compliment, smiling as she moved away. Wife was not what Bryce had in mind today, she was sure; sweetheart, mistress, perhaps, both roles she had no intention of playing.

"Would you like more wine?"

"No. Wine lacks appeal in your presence. For intoxication your beauty surpasses even the stoutest potion."

Lazily he stroked the back of his hand down her soft cheek, his large blue eyes glistening in the sunlight as he drew her close.

Catrin stared up at Bryce's thick blond eyebrows, at the two V-shaped nicks on his cheek, mementos of Fontenoy, and she felt trapped. Though she longed to thrust him away from her, long years of conditioning prevailed. He was her affianced husband; he must be allowed certain mild privileges. She gazed at his ruffled lace shirt straining at the neckband, his muscular neck too thick for the delicate garment. "No, Bryce," she protested shrilly, pushing him away, suddenly brought back to earth by the unwelcome invasion of his wet mouth. Angrily he seized her and welded his mouth to hers.

The kiss delivered, Bryce finally released her. "Stop it, demme, no struggling. You'll be my wife in a few weeks." He angrily straightened his coat, annoyed by her resistance.

Indignantly Catrin smoothed her hair and her crushed skirts. "I think you'd better leave. Aunt Isobel might return early."

"You said she'd not be back for hours," Bryce reminded her, and he deliberately crossed to the door and closed it with his booted foot. "That was a careless slip on your part . . . or maybe it was intentional?"

Catrin backed away, but her anger mounted when she realized he was determined to try to seduce her. She thrust him away angrily when he again tried to embrace her.

"You're being a little too much of a tease, my love. A little sport whets the appetite—too much angers," Bryce snarled, his temper getting the better of him. "In a month you'll be my wife."

"Then perhaps I'll welcome your lovemaking. Not before."

Bryce's full lip curled in derision. "Come now, don't pretend all virginal innocence with me. The reason behind your swift banishment up north is all over London."

The blood drained from her face. Catrin stared at him, white as a sheet. "What do you mean, 'reason'?"

"Everyone knows you kicked over the traces. You attended the Merriams' scandalous ball while Papa was away. Anxious to keep me to my word, old Millbank bundled you up and sent you off to Lancashire like a naughty little baggage. True?"

She swallowed, clutching the edge of the bureau for support. "My father did send me north as a punishment for disobeying him, yes."

Chuckling, Bryce moved toward her, his gaze locked on hers. "As coldly prudish as you've been acting, I even wonder if you deliberately went to Ranelagh Gardens hoping to make me call off the match." Catrin gasped, surprised he knew her reluctance to marry him. Bryce smiled cruelly as he seized her slender wrists. "Caught you, eh! So you did want to be rid of me! Well, me dear, it would take far more than Booth Merriam's party to scare me off. I need you, dammit, Catrin Blair, in more ways than one. Too bad poor Humphrey didn't know that, or you needn't have endured this unnatural torment at the hands of your pious aunt, whatever her name is."

"Isobel."

"Isobel. Well, I still want you, Catrin, because you're one of the most luscious pieces of eligible skirt in England, but primarily, my love, because your dear Papa has a sizable fortune of the greatest interest to me. I'm not the luckiest man at the tables, and at the moment I'm going through a patch of financial embarrassment. With the Millbank fortune backing me, my creditors will be only too happy to extend my accounts. Now, no more maidenly protests. I've attended Merriam's parties myself and I know you must have been up to something for your papa to have packed you off like this."

Catrin thrust his hands away. "Stop it! Papa was afraid you'd learn I'd been to Ranelagh Gardens unchaperoned and would consider me soiled. He believes you to be a gentleman, a foolish assumption, I realize."

Bryce seized her arm and swung her about. "Enough, damn you! Do you think I've ridden this far for nothing?"

Relentlessly he bent her back across the bureau, his breath hot on her neck and cheek, his wet mouth searching her flesh. When Bryce encountered her mouth, tightly compressed against his lips, he swore beneath his breath. Cruelly he forced his kisses on her, brutally demonstrating his mastery over her. His fingers gouged her soft flesh until bruises appeared. Though Catrin struggled, Bryce pressed her back against the mahogany bureau. Imprisoning her there, his thighs steel hard, his arousal clamoring against her, he devoured her neck, his sweating face scarlet with lust.

Shouting for help, Catrin ineffectually pummeled his back. Bryce's strength and his dogged insistence on forcing his love-making upon her changed what had been merely anger and disgust into a panicking wave of fear.

"Damn you, why are you fighting?" He grabbed the back of her neck, positioning her face for his kiss. "Enough! Are you to fight like this when we're wed?"

"How dare you, sir? Get out of my house at once!"

Startled, Bryce spun about, his bulbous eyes wide, his face flushed. An indignant Aunt Isobel stood in the center of the parlor, ramrod straight, her lips tightly compressed against the outrage that threatened to take place under her own roof.

"Get out, I say. Begone this minute or I'll have you thrown out."

Straightening his coat, then his stock and wig, Bryce blustered, "Demme, have you any idea who I am, madam?"

"Your identity is known to me, sir. I repeat, get out of my house. This young lady is under my guardianship until her marriage. The fact you are the intended bridegroom means nothing. When you are wed in the eyes of God you will have access to her and not before. You've violated the hospitality of our home. If you don't leave at once your reputation as a gentleman will be severely damaged."

Both Catrin and Bryce stared at the small stiff figure in the middle of the room who stood her ground, stern as any soldier. Catrin felt an alien surge of pride in her aunt for daring to defy the Hon. Captain Cavendish.

"You'll regret speaking to me so. Demme, if you won't. I'm virtually Lord Cavendish. I could buy and sell this hovel ten times over any day of the week. Demme, madam, this lady is my betrothed!"

"Please refrain from cursing under this roof."

His blue eyes popping, Bryce swung about, speechless at being addressed like a small boy with his nurse. Snarling in rage, he seized his riding crop from a nearby chair.

"You've no right to forbid me access to my betrothed!"

Calming somewhat, Aunt Isobel considered his words. "Perhaps you are right, sir. If you will conduct yourself in a gentlemanly manner, you may stay to visit Catrin—in my presence, of course, as I'm sure her father would wish."

"We're adults, we've no need of chaperones..." Bryce began, swinging about, frustration written all over his angry face. Fists clenched, Cavendish glanced from one to the other, unsure how to proceed. Damn this jumped-up poor relation with her prim manners for arriving home at the wrong time! Catrin would have come around, given time, he was convinced of it.

"I've no wish to share a room with you, madam, so I shall leave. But you'll hear from me. I'll not stand to be insulted like this."

"Nor would you have been insulted had you behaved as the gentleman you profess to be," Catrin announced coldly, stepping protectively toward her aunt. "Please leave. I've no further wish to speak to you."

Aunt Isobel nodded immediate approval of her niece's careful speech.

Fuming, Bryce rounded on Catrin. "Dammit, madam, you've not heard the last of this. You'll be mine before the year's out. We'll be wed soon, dearest, and then you'll pay well for today's insult." Turning to Aunt Isobel, he bowed stiffly. "I remain your servant, madam. May we never have the displeasure of meeting again." With that Bryce stormed from the room. A few minutes later he could be heard clattering down the driveway and onto the highway.

"Poor Catrin. And it's all my fault! Oh, I'll never forgive myself for leaving you alone. That foolish Collins should have known better than to admit a man while I'm away. I suppose his being a gentleman, and considering he is your betrothed, she did not think it improper... can you forgive me, my dear?"

"You could not have known Bryce would call. I was never so glad to see you. Thank you for rescuing me, Aunt Isobel. I've no idea why Bryce suddenly acted in such an ungentlemanly fashion. He's never treated me before with disrespect."

Isobel stepped back, the sympathy fading from her face. "And why, pray tell, do you think he's changed in his attitude toward you? Reputation, that's what it is, young woman. Likely your wild behavior's attracted much unfavorable publicity. You've only yourself to blame. But I promise you, as long as you're under my roof it shall never happen again. You'll not be left alone for an instant."

Having reached this final comforting resolution, Aunt Isobel turned and marched from the room, leaving a speechless Catrin staring after her.

Chapter 6

The Lancashire farmland dozed peacefully under sunny August skies. Catrin leaned against a wooden gate to survey the ripening corn, realizing that for the first time since she had left London she felt happy. That morning Aunt Isobel had released her from prison, sending her into the village to meet the mail coach. For weeks Isobel had been anxiously awaiting news from her son, Adam, who had gone to a small Lake District parish as assistant rector.

The cornfields shimmered like bronze silk, the heavy ears of grain rustling in the breeze. Crimson poppies blazed among the corn; bright blue cornflowers and chamomile edged the fields. Tall sycamores, faintly tinged with yellow, lined the road and blackberries sheltered under the twining bindweed lacing the hawthorn hedge. Above the cornfields a kestrel hung suspended and Catrin watched as the bird dropped like a stone and disappeared from view.

Catrin picked up her wicker basket of brown eggs and honey, gifts to Isobel from a local farmer's wife. Reluctantly she retraced her steps down the winding lane leading to Cedars of Lebanon. She began to hum as she reviewed the startling announcement her aunt had made at breakfast: both girls were to be allowed to attend the ball at Thorpington Hall! With less than two days to prepare for the grand event, Catrin had almost given up hope.

Ever since her arrival at Edgehill her life had been in limbo. To her surprise she received no letters from London. She had not thought her father's anger so great that he would not even write to her. Neither had she heard from Ness, which would not have been remarkable—for her brother was ever reluctant to put pen to paper—had she not been expecting instructions for the disposal of the money and papers he had entrusted to her.

Fortunately her valise had a lock, or by now its contents would have been revealed to all. Though Ruth heatedly denied it, on several occasions Catrin had caught her trying to pick the lock with her brooch pin. She was beginning to wonder what she should do with the packages.

Almost as soon as she crossed the threshold of Cedars of Lebanon, her happy mood was destroyed. Aunt Isobel saw Adam's letter and snatched it from the basket. Exclaiming in annoyance at how long Adam had taken to write, Isobel hastened to the sunny window. Agitated, she tore open the sealed envelope, her brow knitting as she quickly scanned the page. "The ungrateful wretch! After all I've done for him . . . oh, how dare he!" she cried shrilly, clutching her throat.

Catrin and Ruth both stopped what they were doing to stare, astonished by the fierce emotion radiating from this normally placid woman.

"What is it, Mama? Has Adam not been given his post?" ventured Ruth hesitatingly.

"That treacherous . . ." At a loss for words, Isobel leaned against the windowsill, her face gray. "Not only has he resigned his post, he's . . . he's . . . oh, his father will turn in his grave!"

The letter fluttered to the floor. Ruth, alarmed by her mother's reaction, made no move to retrieve it. Catrin picked up the letter, wondering what the shocking news could be. Holding the paper to the light, she labored over Adam's hurried writing, skipping the obligatory polite greetings to "Dear Mama" and his regrets about resigning his post as assistant rector at Penhallow Parish Church. Then her eyes widened as he read further.

You will understand, dear Mama, that my conscience will not allow me to swear allegiance to a man whom I do not accept as our rightful king. Fear not, I will not forsake my calling. However, it is as a non-jurant minister I will be joining Prince Charles's army. I remain your obedient son, Adam.

Aghast, Catrin met her aunt's shocked gaze. For the first time she saw pain in Isobel's small, colorless eyes, yet even as she identified the emotion it was swiftly replaced by rage. "That's right, Catrin, your obedient Cousin Adam's joined the rebels. Well, good riddance to him. He's no longer a son of mine."

Ruth's jaw dropped at the angry pronouncement and her face whitened. "Are we still to go to the ball?" she blurted unthinkingly.

"You wretch, you're as ungrateful as your brother! Is a frivolous ball all you can think about when our livelihood's being threatened by that wicked—" Isobel brought the palm of her hand sharply across Ruth's face, leaving a scarlet mark on the puddingy flesh. Rounding on Catrin, she cried, "As for you, miss, where are your manners, that you read another's private correspondence?"

The letter was snatched from Catrin's fingers and flung into the fire, where it smoldered in the grate, the paper resting on a log before it slid to its demise in a mound of gray ash.

Straightening her shoulders and rubbing her hands in a businesslike manner, Isobel smoothed her already neat hair before picking up the basket of eggs to take to Mrs. Collins.

"I'll thank you never to mention his name again in this house."

"Yes, Mama," Ruth parroted obediently.

"Catrin?"

Fixed with a malevolent stare, Catrin swallowed, understanding it would be wiser to agree as Ruth had done, yet knowing her conscience would not allow such spinelessness. "When you've recovered from your shock, perhaps you'll feel differently," she began hesitantly. "Adam will still be a minister, which was what you wanted . . ."

"I want him to be respectable! We'll not be able to hold up our heads again. Never, not in a thousand years, will I change my mind! Adam's disobeyed God's plans as surely as his namesake all those years ago . . ."

"And is he also to be cast out of the garden of Eden?"

"There's no need for sarcasm, miss. Had I not already given my word to Lord Mainwaring that you girls would attend the ball, you would both stay home for your insolence."

For the rest of the day Aunt Isobel raged tight-lipped about the house, ordering scrubbing, polishing, and sweeping, turning cupboards out, throwing contents of drawers to the floor in a frenetic attempt to purge herself of her emotions. Catrin pitied her aunt for her inability to accept Adam as he was, or to even accept her own anger over his decision.

Not until the morning of the ball were Ruth and Catrin finally allowed to pause in their untiring round of housekeeping. Already clean, Cedars of Lebanon virtually squeaked as they walked through its rooms. The windows, usually besmirched with Liverpool grime, gleamed bright as mirrors, while the reflection of the barren furnishings on the waxed floors shone clearer than ever.

"What am I to wear to the ball, Mama?" Ruth ventured, pulling off her cap to examine her limp hair in the parlor mirror.

"Your Sunday-best gown should be most acceptable."

Though she did not like Ruth, the younger girl's woebegone expression at the thought of wearing her starched linen gown to so splendid an occasion touched Catrin's heart.

"I've a blue gown that is almost too small for me. Would you let me alter it to fit Ruth?"

On the verge of saying no, Aunt Isobel relented. "We'll look at it. It must be modest, mind you. No shockingly low necklines."

"I assure you it's most decorous."

Though the dress was too large in the bodice, the sapphire satin brought color to Ruth's eyes and made her thin hair appealingly blond. With the addition of a headdress of pink rosebuds and lover's knots in sapphire ribbon, Ruth became almost pretty. Tears of delight shone in her eyes as she admired herself in the mirror, never having imagined she could look so lovely.

It was on the tip of Isobel's tongue to refuse the loaned gown, yet even she had to admit that plain, mousy Ruth blossomed in this stylish gown with its soft lace flounces and fichu neckline. Perhaps in that elegant dress their neighbors would reconsider Ruth as a desirable marriage prospect. Now that Adam had thrown away his chances for the future, she must look elsewhere for security in her old age—though no doubt Humphrey could provide for her if necessary.

"What a kind heart you have, Catrin dear."

The sugary compliment took her so much by surprise; Catrin stared open-mouthed before she gathered her wits sufficiently to say, "I want Ruth to look her best." Arranging Ruth's hair over her shoulders, she twisted it to form ringlets. "Can I have permission to use curl papers on Ruth's hair? She'd look very attractive with curls."

Lips pursed, Isobel surveyed her plain daughter. Catrin was right, Ruth would be more attractive if her fine straight hair had even the slightest curl. Lord Mainwaring had two sons close to Ruth's age . . . dare she hope?

"You're such a sweet girl to think of your cousin. Yes, you may curl Ruth's hair if it makes you happy." Raising her voice above Ruth's excited squeaks, Isobel asked, "And you, my dear, what gown do you intend to wear to the ball?"

Catrin swallowed. She had been hoping to avoid that question. Her intention had been to reveal herself at the last moment when it was far too late to change her dress. She had a lovely magenta silk gown she had never worn, made for her last Christmas by a French dressmaker. The beautiful hooped gown had a skirt of ruched magenta silk worn over a petticoat of silver. Deep silver lace flounces trimmed the elbow-length sleeves. Unfortunately her stepfather had forbidden her to wear the creation, deeming the rich color and low neckline too immodest for an unmarried girl.

"My gown was a recent present from Papa. I've not yet had an occasion to wear it. I thought this important ball would be the perfect place."

Isobel nodded as she lifted handfuls of Ruth's hair, looping it to the side as she pictured a cascade of smooth ringlets. Her spirits lifted anew as she mentally created the scene of Lord Mainwaring being astounded by her daughter's beauty and insisting they draw up an immediate marriage contract with his son—the oldest boy, of course, because he would inherit. There would be no need to beg charity then! When he returned Adam would be amazed to find them well housed, beloved by their tenants . . .

"A gift from Humphrey," Isobel said absently, barely glancing at her niece. "Yes, the gown sounds most suitable. Ruth, you must be very careful not to shake your curls loose once they're arranged. Your hair's so fine, it's nearly unmanageable."

Catrin smiled at Ruth's reflection in the mirror. Everything was going to be all right.

Later that night while she prepared for the ball, Catrin was surprised by a knock on her bedroom door. She had been struggling without much success to dress her hair in a becoming formal style. When she opened the door she found a young woman on the threshold.

"I came from his lordship to help you prepare for the ball, miss," said the woman, curtsying to her.

The hallway was so dark Catrin could not see her face clearly. "Oh, come in, do. I'm almost ready. My aunt sent my maid home last month or I'd not still be trying to dress. Can you arrange hair?"

"Yes, miss, I've many talents," the woman remarked confidently as she stepped into the room.

Considering her comment strangely boastful for a maid, Catrin sat before the mirror, moving the lone candle until it shed as much light as possible on her hair.

Picking up the silver-handled brush, the woman swiftly brushed Catrin's shining curls, complimenting her on their silky texture. Soon the unmanageable cascade of chestnut ringlets was anchored at the back of her head by magenta satin ribbons and silver roses firmly secured with bone hairpins.

"Oh, it's lovely! You're so much better at dressing my hair than Milly," Catrin gasped in genuine delight. The woman chuckled as she reached for the hand mirror, intending to show Catrin the back view of her head reflected in the dingy dresser mirror. Catrin's gaze fell on the maid's perfectly white manicured hands. They were devoid of rings, but they might just as easily have been dripping with diamonds. Those hands belonged to no maid. Turning in her chair, she peered intently into the shadowed face half obscured by a frilled mobcap.

"Who are you?"

"A maid sent by Lord Mainwaring."

"That's not true. You may have come from his lordship, but you're no maid."

The woman chuckled. "My goodness, how quick you are. Well, I see we've no further need to delay. You've some items in your possession that I've come to retrieve."

"Items?"

"Please, spare me the mock surprise. A rider awaits outside. The gold, wench."

The woman's attitude swiftly turned haughty as she straightened her shoulders, her stature seeming to grow six inches. Catrin wondered if she was the Jacobite sympathizer she was expecting or merely a dangerous imposter.

"I don't understand. What money?"

"You're carrying our money. I've no interest in the documents—a man will ask you for those this evening, so bring them with you. Even I don't know who he is yet. Just hand over our gold."

"Is he to contact me at Thorpington Hall?"

"Aye, at Thorpington Hall. You surely don't think you little nobodies were invited because of your charming personalities, do you? There's generally a purpose to Henry's madness. Now the gold—I swear, why he thought you could be valuable to us escapes me."

Catrin bristled at the woman's scornful attitude. The stranger appeared to know enough details to be genuine, and as Catrin had no further way of testing her, she knew she must trust her.

Impatiently the woman thrust the heavy box of gold inside a valise similar to Catrin's own, after carefully examining the lock to make sure it had not been tampered with.

"Are you a friend of my brother's?"

"Brother? Who is he—then perhaps I can tell you," the woman snapped, her hand on the door.

"Ness Blair."

"Oh, so Ness is your brother. I'd never have guessed. Had I seen you together I probably would have thought him your lover—he's every other woman's lover, my dear." And, chuckling unpleasantly, the woman disappeared into the gloom.

Catrin had barely recovered from her unsettling visitor when Ruth rushed in, fussily adjusting her hair and patting her skirts in place. She twitched nervously at her lace fichu, trying to pull it higher to cover her meager chest. Ruth gasped when she saw Catrin's low-cut gown and her ample breasts swelling high above the lace-edged neckline. She stared, mesmerized by the unexpected display of flesh.

"Like it?" Catrin asked at last, made uncomfortable by Ruth's stare.

"It's wicked . . . but I think it's lovely," Ruth whispered with a nervous giggle. "Oh, I wish I looked like you. But then, Mama would never let me wear a gown like that."

"Nor will she me. I intend to cover it with my cloak. I won't reveal the daring neckline till we arrive at Thorpington Hall. I assure you, only you and your mama will be scandalized. Gowns like this are commonplace in London."

Enviously Ruth fingered Catrin's amethyst pendant. "Oh, how lovely. I haven't any jewelry. Mama says owning jewelry is a wicked luxury."

More than likely they could not afford jewels, Catrin thought. "Would you like me to lend you something?" she offered kindly. "I've a plain pearl and gold necklet I'm sure your mother wouldn't object to."

Ruth eagerly accepted the offering, her hands trembling with excitement as she clasped it about her neck. "Thank you, Catrin," she replied dutifully. Though she appreciated Catrin's generosity, she was rather disappointed at being offered such a paltry piece. Her cousin's splendid amethyst necklace, its diamond-shaped stone nestling in the creamy curve between her breasts, far outshone this schoolgirlish pendant. So taken was Ruth with Catrin's necklace, she fingered it again lovingly, almost wishing she could steal it.

Aunt Isobel's voice drifted upstairs, admonishing the girls for their tardiness. Hastily they pulled on their cloaks before snuffing out Catrin's candle; Ruth's they carried downstairs to light their way. Outside, they hastened to the waiting carriage sent from Thorpington Hall.

After some time they approached the double gates of Thorpington Hall, set between tall gray stone pillars. The drive wound through wooded parkland, where mysterious paths branched off between low hanging branches of fir, cedar, oak, and ash. Lights from the vast house glimmered through the trees long before the coach rounded the final bend and drew up before the square stone house. Thorpington Hall's brightly lit windows fashioned a shimmering halo from the mist. Ivy crept across the stonework and darkly festooned the mullioned windows. The old building, a combination of timber and stone, had been added onto over the centuries to greater and lesser degrees, according to the waxing and waning of the Mainwaring fortunes. Its former moat had become a smooth grassy slope from which a flight of stone steps led to a shallow terrace bordered by flickering lanterns. The Hall's great iron-studded oak door was flung wide to welcome the guests.

Lanterns swung from the branches of the stately trees in preparation for the outdoor festivities, but a change in the weather, ever to be expected during the Lancashire summer, had driven the entertainment indoors. Catrin was glad. To have attended a ball in these lovely wooded grounds would have been too painful a reminder of David and that magic night at Ranelagh Gardens.

"I wanted to dance beneath the stars," Ruth complained,

her bottom lip projecting in a pout. "It's not raining now. Why can't we?"

"Because Lord Mainwaring doesn't wish it," Isobel explained, patting her own severely arranged locks, upon which perched a small lace-trimmed cap with a single navy ribbon streamer. Though her panniered skirts were lavishly tucked, they too were navy, peeking modestly from beneath her navy wool cloak. Isobel wore her best mourning dress; even a fichu of white lace and a nosegay of crushed artificial roses had done little to lessen its somber, funereal air.

Catrin's heart thudded with excitement as they left the coach and mounted the steps. Liveried footmen in powdered wigs stood at the door, while curtsying maids in starched lace-trimmed caps waited inside to divest them of their cloaks.

Aunt Isobel turned about smugly to survey her charges and her jaw dropped as she saw Catrin's gown.

"Catrin, how dare . . ." was as far as she got.

"Dear lady, welcome to Thorpington Hall. We should have invited you here long before now, an oversight on my behalf."

Catrin joined her aunt in curtsying to the elegant, bewigged man who stepped forward and swiftly took her hand, pressing it to his lips. This must be their host, Lord Mainwaring. The middle-aged nobleman was splendidly attired in oyster brocade, a diamond pin nestled in the froth of lace at his throat. When their eyes met she saw appreciation twinkling there.

"And you, my dear, where have you been all these months? Your wicked aunt has kept you hidden from us all. For shame, dear lady, you've deprived us of a great beauty."

"My niece Catrin is betrothed, my lord."

With mock sorrow, Lord Mainwaring bowed politely and released her hand. He turned his attention to Ruth, who made a flustered curtsy, blushing at being singled out for attention by his lordship.

"And this lovely creature?"

"My daughter Ruth, who is *not* betrothed," Isobel added pointedly, wishing Ruth would not giggle in that foolish, high-pitched manner. "She's very young, my lord, barely out of the nursery."

Now it was Ruth's turn to look daggers at her mother, and her smile subsided into an unbecoming scowl.

"Charming, charming," mumbled his lordship, his gaze coming to rest on Catrin's daring décolletage. "May I get you some refreshments, my dear Miss . . . Blair, is it not?"

"Yes, it is. And I'd love some refreshments."

Ignoring Aunt Isobel's shrill protests, Lord Mainwaring swept Catrin with him into the milling crowd of guests. They were soon lost from sight in a swirl of jeweled brocades and ribboned lace flounces, the atmosphere athrob with laughter and tinkling music. The heavy-beamed, paneled oak hall had been decorated with colorful banks of summer flowers, their perfume heady in the warm atmosphere. Splendidly attired strangers crowded around them, eager to be introduced to the delightful newcomer; the men ogled Catrin while their womenfolk viewed her with a mixture of envy and spite. To be plunged into such exotic surroundings after the cheerless frugality of Cedars of Lebanon was almost more than Catrin could endure. She felt giddy with excitement.

The surging emotion turned her increasingly reckless. What matter if Aunt Isobel made her pay dearly for tonight? This strange, building mood was similar to the abandon she had known the night of the masquerade ball.

"Sparkling wine for a sparkling lady," complimented Lord Mainwaring, bowing as he offered her a tall crystal goblet in which bubbles were bursting. "You're a ravishing creature, my dear, simply ravishing."

Catrin backed away, wary of Lord Mainwaring's intentions. In his younger days Lord Mainwaring must have been handsome, but a life of pleasure had taken its toll. Now deep furrows creased his face and his gray eyes were couched in heavy folds of flesh.

"Well, our plain little miss has blossomed remarkably well," commented a sharp, spiteful voice.

Catrin turned in surprise to behold her erstwhile maid wearing shimmering violet satin, her powdered red hair piled high on her head and secured by a cascade of flowers and gleaming precious stones.

"You've met? But of course, how foolish of me. You mustn't be so catty, my love. Tonight our little Miss Blair puts most ladies to shame," remarked Lord Mainwaring. "Miss Catrin Blair, let me present you to my very good friend, Lady Susannah Fox, widow of my late lamented neighbor."

Catrin curtsied, immediately on guard. The lovely, pearly skinned face, surrounded by a frosted red halo, reflected pure malevolence. Though still beautiful, Susannah Fox was past the flush of youth and she viewed Catrin with pure spite that only a fading beauty can muster for a younger rival.

"Yes, we've met, my lord. I'm still very much in your debt, Lady Fox. My maid never arranged my hair so attractively." Catrin did not understand the flash of temper in those glittering green eyes.

Lord Mainwaring chuckled as Susannah Fox haughtily swept away.

"What did I say?" Catrin ventured at last, aware of the chill of the other woman's displeasure.

"One can not always understand Susannah's moods, yet perchance your reference to her waiting on you was not well received. Playing maid is vastly beneath her dignity, yet the only ruse I could devise to put her in a certain place at a certain time."

He winked, his hand burning through Catrin's magenta silk bodice as he pressed his palm against the hollow of her back.

Catrin was unsure how much to reveal. It was said Lord Mainwaring was a dedicated Jacobite, not merely a titled buffoon who pledged eagerly with his mouth but grew faint-hearted when called upon for action. Could she trust him? Outwardly he was a typical gentleman of his day, always ready with flowery compliments, splendidly dressed to the point of foppishness, seeming to have no interest beyond pleasure, yet when he was caught off guard, an uncharacteristic alertness gleamed in his eyes.

"I did as I was bidden," Catrin confided hoarsely, leaning close so he could hear her whispered words. The intimate action was much to his liking, for Lord Mainwaring insolently brushed his full lips across her soft cheek, the caress so slight she wondered if she had imagined it.

"I trust you always do as you are bidden, sweetest. And if that's the case, then you will go far."

Catrin did not want to create a scene by misinterpreting Lord Mainwaring's statement, nor did she wish to encourage his ardor. "My obedience relates merely to certain matters," she retorted firmly, stepping away from him.

Far from making him angry, her rebuke make him chuckle good-humoredly.

"Fiery too. I like that. There are many men in this room far younger than I, but few who are as experienced—still, we have the rest of the evening for that decision. First you must drink, and eat, and dance."

Catrin breathed a sigh of relief as Lord Mainwaring guided

her to a loaded supper table, where he ordered a fair-haired young man in rose silk brocade to fill a plate for Miss Blair and take care of her until his return. Catrin watched her host stride purposefully toward a side door where another man was waiting. The stranger had his back to her and Catrin saw only that he was dark-haired and heavily cloaked. Perhaps this was the courier to whom she must give the papers.

The foppish young man at her side introduced himself as Darcy Mainwaring, his lordship's younger son. Catrin had to strain to catch his lisping speech above the clamor of the noisy guests.

When their light supper was finished, Darcy Mainwaring led her onto the floor to dance the minuet. People stared at them, remarking what a handsome couple they made. As Catrin danced past, she noticed her aunt glaring hostilely at her. Ruth, who appeared to have been crying, looked mutinously in her direction, refusing to return her smile.

After five dances Catrin begged leave to go outside. The noisy hall was stifling; the atmosphere reeked of candle wax, stale perfume, and sweat. As she walked onto the terrace a cool breeze swept refreshingly across her hot face and shoulders; sighing in pleasure, Catrin lifted her curls to allow the air to fan her neck.

As they stood outside in the darkness, distinctive feminine laughter, and the flash of a violet gown slipping around the corner, revealed that Susannah Fox was entertaining an admirer. Darcy raised his voice in an effort to mask Susannah's words, noticeably relieved when that lady swished past them through the open French windows leading to the Hall. As she passed Catrin noticed that Susannah's ribboned hair ornament was disarranged and her mouth and chin were reddened. Was that why Lord Mainwaring had excused himself? Had a flirtation with Susannah, not a meeting with a fellow conspirator, been the reason for his hasty departure?

"Is she your father's mistress?" Catrin asked curiously.

Mainwaring colored and nervously cleared his throat. "Yes, I think so, but I don't know. Papa doesn't confide in me. Would you like some wine?"

Catrin agreed that she would.

Mainwaring excused himself, reappearing a few minutes later, flustered and stuttering. "P-papa . . . says you're expecting someone . . . m-my cousin several times removed . . . says you have a letter for him . . . have you?"

His injured expression touched her. "Well, Darcy, in a way, what he says is true, I do carry a letter from a mutual friend. But I don't actually know your cousin," Catrin explained, hoping she had soothed his ruffled pride.

"Oh, good. I thought maybe you were in love with him too. All the women fall head over heels for him. It's sickening. He was here all day yesterday and now he's back again. I'd hoped he'd gone for good. Susannah thinks he's so delightful, I'll warrant he'll be in her bed before the night's out—if he's not been there already."

Catrin wisely made no comment on this confidence, smiling politely as Mainwaring led her back inside the lighted ballroom. The gleam of violet against the scarlet velvet curtains immediately alerted her to Susannah's presence.

"Miss Blair, Mr. Parnell's come for his letter," Susannah hissed, catching Catrin's arm, her long fingernails digging into her flesh. "Give it to me."

Catrin pulled free. "I can give it to Mr. Parnell myself."

Susannah hissed in anger, her expression swiftly changing as a dark shadow spilled across the terrace. She simpered to the approaching man, "Here's our little messenger, Mr. Parnell."

Catrin looked up at the man who stood framed in the open French window and her heart stood still. Emotion turned her legs to jelly and her throat ached with the pressure of building tears. It was David!

Shock crossed his dark face, and almost imperceptibly he shook his head in warning. "You have a letter for me, Miss . . . ?"

"Her name's unimportant. Well, wench, give it to him," snapped Susannah.

With shaking hands Catrin reached beneath her flounced overskirt where the packet of papers rested in a linen pouch. Sanity was returning in hot, uncomfortable waves as she remembered Susannah had been kissing someone on the terrace. Perhaps the man had been David, not Lord Mainwaring.

"Here's your letter, Mr. . . . Parnell."

Silently he accepted the folded papers and slipped them inside his laced red velvet coat. "Thank you. You are a very appealing messenger."

Finally gathering her wits, Catrin smiled politely as David made a stiff bow over her hand.

Impatient to be rid of the young beauty, Susannah slipped

her hand possessively beneath his elbow, urging him outside. "Come, there's something I must tell you," she whispered as she led him onto the terrace.

Catrin was stunned. David had acted as if they were strangers, giving her no recognition beyond that faint inclination, the tiny frown forbidding her to greet him as friend. He must not want Susannah to know they were acquainted.

Darcy Mainwaring cleared his throat, growing highly uncomfortable as she continued to ignore him. "You lied to me," he complained accusingly as he finally grasped Catrin's arm and steered her back to the supper table. "You do know him. I could tell."

"I didn't lie intentionally. When I met him he . . . he . . . called himself by another name. I'd no idea he was your cousin."

"Nor did I know he is my cousin. Papa's always introducing me to people whom I never see again. I'm beginning to think he's involved in some kind of plot."

Catrin swallowed, aware that Mainwaring was staring intently at her, awaiting her comment on his shattering revelation. "A plot? Isn't that rather melodramatic? Perhaps your father has a lot of casual acquaintances. Many people have friends of whom they're not especially proud."

She changed the subject, and the young man handed her a plate of crystallized fruits and dainty iced cake fingers before blushingly excusing himself. Catrin had no intention of waiting for his return. Across the room she could see Aunt Isobel frantically signaling to her to rejoin the family, but she pretended not to notice. Instead she walked onto the terrace, down the steps, and into the shadowed flower garden.

Waves of shock over seeing David coursed through her body. How often she had dreamed about their meeting, couching those dreams in sweet words and smiles of love, fantasies that had no place in reality. Had he been indifferent because Susannah Fox was the current recipient of his protestations of love? Angry tears pricked Catrin's eyes and she walked even faster, past a romantic couple entwined on a wrought-iron bench, past statues and perfumed flower gardens drenched with rain . . .

"Catrin. Catrin, stop."

It was David! He must have followed her outside. Panic seized her and Catrin's first inclination was to run. For a few moments too long she hesitated, until she could hear his brisk steps crunching behind her on the gravel. Swallowing, Catrin turned to meet him, desperately blinking back tears.

"Oh, Catrin, sweetheart," David breathed huskily, holding out his arms to her.

She hesitated, injured pride and fear of discovery holding her back. They stood in the shadow of the walled garden, and though music and laughter from the ballroom penetrated there, they were alone. The magnetic pull of his presence suddenly became too strong to resist; capitulating, she fell into his strong embrace, hiding her pain in the warm comfort of his arms.

"Not in a thousand years did I expect to find you here."

"Didn't Ness tell you I was at my aunt's in Liverpool?"

"I haven't seen Ness since that night at Ranelagh Gardens."

David held her slightly away from him to look at her lovely face, finding her features little more than a blur. Light shed by the lanterns swinging from the nearby trees cast wavering shadows over the lawns, but here everywhere lay in darkness.

"I'd no idea you were to be the person to get in touch with. What are you doing at Thorpington Hall?" Catrin asked as she buried her face in the warm hollow of his neck.

"I might ask you the same thing—but who cares *why* we're here, only that we are. Oh, sweetheart, I never dreamed I'd be able to hold you in my arms tonight. You've been constantly in my thoughts. How have you been?"

"Well," she whispered, deciding not to reveal she had been banished for her attendance at the masquerade.

David cradled her face in his hands, tilting it upward to receive his passionate kiss. The touch of his mouth on hers made Catrin shudder and she ached to blend her body with his, finding she had little willpower to fight the attraction. Just then a familiar burst of shrill laughter came from the garden to shatter her peace of mind. When she pictured Susannah Fox in his arms, the painful reminder turned her pleasure to gall.

"What is it?" asked David in surprise. He had braced himself against a low wall, preparing to take her weight against him, when Catrin pulled away.

"Are you involved with that woman . . . Susannah Fox?"

"Involved?" he repeated, playing for time, unsure what to admit.

"Don't play me for a fool! You know what I mean. Were you her lover? Are you still?"

"To hell with Susannah Fox. Tonight's been given to us, let's not waste it discussing—"

"So you are her lover."

Her words came out flat and dead. Catrin stifled a sob which rose achingly in her throat. "I should have known. According to Darcy Mainwaring she's not the only local woman who's set her sights on you."

"Mainwaring! That milksop should've been a girl. I thought you'd have more sense than to listen to him!"

"In this instance he's probably right."

"Can I help it if women are attracted to me? I've never professed to be celibate."

"Do you love her?"

"No."

"Have you ever?"

"No."

Catrin digested his indignant reply. Strangely she found little comfort in it. "Has she the right to expect your faithfulness?"

He chuckled, the derisive sound chilling. "No woman has that."

Catrin added, silently, "Not even me." "So the vows we exchanged meant nothing to you."

"Are you calling me a liar?"

"Only if you speak lies."

"Everything I told you was the truth. Nothing's changed. A thousand Susannahs won't change my feelings for you. Has our love degenerated into mutual accusation? What happened to the grand passion we shared?"

Catrin hung her head, tears splashing to her silk bodice. "I'm so jealous of all the Susannahs in your life."

"You needn't be."

"David, I must know—do you love me still?"

He did not reply. Catrin became aware of his fingers biting painfully into her arm. Then he swore beneath his breath.

"What's happened between us?" he demanded at last through clenched teeth. "Surely you weren't expecting me to fling my arms around you? If that's the reason behind this outburst, I'm sorry, but I won't jeopardize lives to salve your pride. I always thought you understood—I was wrong. Maybe it's just as well. You'd never have been happy with me. Go back to your betrothed—at least he can give you something I never can."

Choked by tears, her voice sounded as if it came from a great distance as she asked brokenly, "What's that?"

"Security—something you won't have with me."

David released her abruptly and stepped back. Even though

his touch had been angry, the loss of his warmth made her feel
coldly bereft.

"David, please, don't let's quarrel."

"Quarreling wasn't my idea. In fact, I was foolish enough
to think I might persuade you to come to Edinburgh with me . . ."

"Edinburgh! You're going there?"

"Aye, in the morning, or tonight, if I've a mind to leave
. . . and before you ask, I travel alone. The likes of Susannah
Fox don't relish sleeping beside the road. Now, go back to
your aunt like a good little girl. It's where you belong."

Without another word, David turned and walked away, his
footsteps crunching on the gravel.

"David—oh, please, stop . . ." Tears choked her voice. Catrin stood trembling, the gay mockery of the ball echoing around
her. She felt empty, as if her heart lay trampled in the wet
grass. What had gone wrong? Why had their meeting not fulfilled the delight of her dreams? But she already had the answer.
Jealous accusations had spoiled what might have been the most
wonderful night of her life.

When Catrin finally returned to the brightly lit hall she found
the gaiety of the ball tarnished. She forced herself to smile as
she accepted the flattering compliments of the men who flocked
around her, begging for the privilege of the next dance. None
of these well-dressed men who eagerly paid court to her made
much impression, she was too intent on watching David, now
surrounded by a bevy of giggling females. Susannah Fox kept
a sharp eye on the other women as she held tight to his arm,
revealing by intimate gestures that she alone had claim to him.

Lord Mainwaring had not returned to the hall. Young Darcy
Mainwaring, however, was still very much in evidence as he
repeatedly caught Catrin's eye, indicating by his smug smile
that he considered her his very special property. His older
brother, a spotty-faced youth with sandy hair, partnered her in
a gavotte, changing Darcy's smile to scowls of displeasure.

Brother Martin was more loutish and even less appealing
than his sibling. Catrin bravely endured his heavy hands and
wine-tainted breath, wishing she had never come to Thorpington Hall's grand ball. The excitement and the laughter had
become a bitter sham, as false as their titled host's indolent
disregard for anything other than luxury and amorous conquest.
An almost palpable undercurrent of danger swirled menacingly
beneath the glitter. Never again could she comfort herself with

the fact she was merely a casual observer. By acting as courier she had become a Jacobite conspirator whose punishment on disclosure could be death.

This startling fact continued to plague her during the following dance, a noisy country round. To her discomfort Catrin saw that David and Susannah were among the dancers. Though she tried not to watch them, she could not overcome the torment of seeing his slender, olive-skinned hand resting possessively in the hollow of Susannah's violet satin waist, nor overlook the attentive smile he gave his partner.

To Catrin's horror, when the dancers changed partners, David stood before her. It was no coincidence that he took this place and she knew he had contrived to partner her. The smile on her face was forced. She stiffened as his warm hand slid into hers and she felt the weight of his arm about her waist.

"My dear Miss Blair, how very clumsy of me. Pray forgive me," he apologized after stepping on the hem of her gown for the third time.

"Stop it," Catrin hissed, wondering what game he played. David Stewart was far too skilled a dancer to make those mistakes.

"I've no idea what you're talking about," he dismissed smoothly, nodding and smiling to the others as they skipped past the line of dancers who stood hands joined to form an arch. Under the long arch they skipped; instead of slowing down as they reached the end, they picked up speed. While the other dancers chose partners and moved into formation, David propelled Catrin from the hall.

"What are you doing? We're out of step," she protested, annoyed yet strangely excited by the grim expression on his handsome face.

Through the doorway they went and down the dark chill corridor beyond. When she tried to pull away from him, David gripped her arms, pushing her into a shadowed alcove at the foot of the twisting stair.

"Ever since we quarreled I've been smarting with anger. I won't let you do this to me. Tonight may be the only time I'll ever see you. And, by God, I'm going to taste your lips if it's the last thing I do."

Shocked by his angry statement she stared up at him, finding his face darkly mysterious in the gloom. David grasped her, forcing her soft body against his. When she threatened to falter, his arms moved supportively around her back. His kiss burned her mouth. For the few minutes they were locked in that embrace, time stood still. Catrin wasted no more thought on Susannah or her own injured feelings, aware of little beyond the thrilling contact with her lover's hot, hard, arousing body. Drinking in the accustomed scent of his skin and hair, she allowed herself to be engulfed by waves of pleasure.

"Now ask me if I love you!"

His angry demand dampened a little of her delight. "Please, no more quarreling. I know you love me. And I love you—nothing can change that."

David crushed her to him, his seeking mouth hot against her face and neck. A few minutes more and she would be beyond redemption. This place was too public to allow him to make love to her.

Breathless, she finally wrenched her mouth from his. "We mustn't love here. Can we meet later?"

"Trust me, I'll find a way. Of course, you could always come to Edinburgh with me and meet the Prince," he whispered, trying to lighten the mood. He sweated, his ardor hard to bring under control. Catrin was right, they could not carry their lovemaking to its natural conclusion here. But later . . .

"You're insane. How can I do that?"

Footsteps in the corridor startled them and they leaped apart. Though they no longer touched, it was as if unseen fetters still bound them. Catrin could hear David's labored breathing as he gently touched her face before turning away.

"You're the only woman I'd ever ask to travel with me," he whispered in parting. Then he was gone.

Catrin leaned against the wall, trying to quiet her pounding heart. She knew she must return to the ballroom before she was missed.

Picking up her skirts, she hastened toward the noisy, lighted hall. Belatedly Catrin wondered if her face revealed the pressure of his mouth, betraying what had recently taken place. Her lips burned and the surrounding skin was hot to the touch. Resolutely she thrust away the unpleasant reminder of Susannah Fox, knowing that if she continued to torment herself with suspicion, she would lose him. Tonight David Stewart was hers. Perhaps that was as much reassurance as she could ever hope for. Sense told her Susannah Fox was not the first woman with a claim to him and she would probably not be the last. Since that magical night in Ranelagh Gardens Catrin had honestly assessed David Stewart's skillful lovemaking, understanding his was a talent not refined by disuse.

"I saw you," squeaked Ruth. She caught Catrin's elbow and spun her about as she came inside the hall.

Too late Catrin's hand flew to hide her aching mouth. The footsteps that had disturbed them must have belonged to Ruth.

"I don't know what you're talking about."

"Oh, yes, you do."

Ruth drew her cousin to the corner behind a tapestry screen.

"I saw that man kiss you. You even put your arms around him! It was shameful!"

Catrin gave her cousin a push, annoyed by her smug, self-satisfied smirk. "You're wasting your time. No one's interested in your tales. A dozen women are probably being kissed at this moment."

"My mother'll be most interested. In fact, when I tell her, she'll probably scold you in front of the other guests."

"You spiteful little cat! You'd tell her just to see me humiliated."

"Not if you give me your pendant."

"I can't! It's far too valuable."

"Then I'll have to tell her. She'll be scandalized to think you're—"

"Wait. I have to think," Catrin cried, seizing Ruth's arm before she darted away. "If I give you my pendant, what will I say when my papa notices it's missing?"

"Tell him you lost it," Ruth suggested, covetously fingering the gleaming stone, warm from Catrin's skin. "So wanton were you both, you made me blush."

A group of local matrons were heading their way, smiling in greeting. Forced to make a swift decision, Catrin whispered, "I'll let you know later."

"You've not long. If you don't give me the pendant by eleven, I'll tell Mama."

"Come, my dears, there's going to be a masque. We don't want you to miss the fun."

With angelic smiles on their faces, Ruth and Catrin turned to greet the ladies. Ruth could not resist giving Catrin a spiteful pinch as they moved into the crowd.

Across the room Catrin caught David's eye, and he smiled warmly before turning aside, wary of betraying their intimacy to the others. Ruth caught her eye also, clearly reminding her of the dire consequences if she chose not to fulfill their bargain.

The evening's theatrical entertainment was already under

way. To a gay orchestral accompaniment, six male dancers
dressed in animal skins tried to elude capture by a young blond
woman wearing a garland of flowers. To the guests' delight
the lovely nymph finally subdued the wild creatures with kisses
and caresses, until the ferocious beasts lay submissive at her
feet.

Catrin assumed the masque portrayed some incident from
mythology, yet so engrossed was she with the dilemma of how
best to outwit Ruth, she paid scant attention to the action. Even
faced with the imminent danger of discovery, she could not
keep her mind solely on her cousin's threat of blackmail. Sweet
memories rekindled by David's mouth made her heart race. If
only she could go with him to Edinburgh. Beyond doubt she
knew she loved him. No other man could ever make her feel
as he did, no other could ever possess her so completely. At
that moment David was hers. She might never have any better
guarantee than that, but then, love did not come with guar-
antees . . .

Taking a deep breath, Catrin walked deliberately toward
Ruth. It was already twenty minutes to eleven—not long in
which to make a decision.

"Ruth, come into the corridor. There's something I must
confide . . . I can't keep it secret any longer."

Though at first she was suspicious, Ruth finally accompanied her cousin into the darkened corridor where they stood
shivering in the draught from the open door.

"What secret?"

"If you promise not to tell your mama, I'll tell you about
our secret rendezvous."

"Oh, I swear not to tell." Eagerly Ruth gripped Catrin's
arm. "Tell me, do."

In the darkness Catrin smiled. Ruth must think she was a
total fool.

"I'm going to meet him in the gardens at midnight."

"Catrin!" Ruth gasped, scandalized. "Oh, take care—you
mustn't go. What will Mama say?"

"She won't know unless you tell her."

"I promise I won't. Your secret's safe with me. Who
is that man? The ladies all think he's charming and handsome.
Why did he pick you?"

"I don't know . . . oh, Ruth, I'm so lucky! I'll tell you everything tomorrow. Now, please don't tell Aunt Isobel, will you?
Even though I can't give you this pendant because Papa spent

such a lot of money on it, I've lots of other lovely things. I'll let you choose what you want."

Ruth's mouth tightened. "You're not going to give me the pendant?"

"No, I can't. You do understand, don't you?" Catrin gripped Ruth's clammy hand and squeezed it reassuringly. "Now, please, promise not to tell."

"No, of course I won't tell, I promise. At twelve you say, in the gardens?"

"That's right. Oh, I'm so excited. He's very handsome and has such a terrible reputation with the ladies, I can hardly wait. I'm really afraid, but I'll never let him know."

After a whispered goodbye, Catrin hastened away, taking pains to mask her laughter. How long would it take Ruth to run to her mother to reveal all the scandalous details?

Catrin scanned the dancers, looking in vain for David. Aunt Isobel was standing by the empty hearth talking to Lady Margaret. Her back was to the door and Catrin breathed a sigh of relief. How tragic if she had been spotted and made to join her aunt now, when she must find David to tell him her decision.

To Catrin's dismay, David was nowhere to be found. She left the hall and hurried to the cloakroom, where she took her cloak from the maid. Each time she contemplated the decisive step she was about to take, she shook with excitement.

"Can you tell me where Mr. Parnell is?" she finally asked the footman at the door, not anxious to alert others to her interest, yet knowing time was running out.

"In the stables, I believe, madam."

The stables! Unease churned through her stomach. Surely David wasn't going to leave without saying goodbye. No! Why must she always think the worst of him? With thumping heart, Catrin pulled her hood over her head and sped toward the stables.

A group of men stood talking, their voices low and agitated. She hung back in the shadows, not wanting to be seen. Presently the group dispersed and she moved even deeper into the shadows when Lord Mainwaring, cloaked and spurred, passed within a foot of where she hid. Two other men leaped into their saddles and galloped out of the yard leaving a lone cloaked figure talking to a groom.

"David?"

He turned, his face serious. Catrin's heart pitched uneasily, for she had expected to be greeted with pleasure. Quickly David waved away the groom before saying in an undertone, "My God, what are you doing here? Get back to the hall."

"I have to talk to you."

"There are things you mustn't know for your own safety."

"I heard nothing."

He began to relax then, and he smiled as he held out his hand to her. "I'm sorry, sweetheart, perhaps I'm being unduly cautious. It's just that you were someone I never intended to involve in all this."

"You didn't involve me, I involved myself. Besides, I thought you'd be pleased that I'd finally taken sides."

"Pleased . . . and worried." He kissed her, his mouth gentle, the pressure of his lips lingering on hers. "Now go back indoors. A man will be arriving any minute and he has no wish to be identified."

In shock Catrin saw full saddlebags on the ground beside his black stallion. "Are you leaving already?"

He pulled her out of the pool of lantern glow just in case someone watched. "I'm sorry, Catrin, but I must leave within the hour. It can't be helped—a sudden change of plans."

His news came as a shock, and Catrin battled the disturbing thought that perhaps David had intended to leave without saying goodbye. She had no actual reason for thinking that, yet David Stewart came and went so mysteriously, one could never be certain of anything.

"Then I must hasten also—I'm coming with you."

The sudden joy in his face brought tears to her eyes. Gone were her doubts. David's protestations of love had been true, after all.

"Oh, my darling! When did you decide that?"

"Thirty minutes ago, so you'd best take advantage of me before I change my mind. Be warned, I've nothing but the clothes on my back. All my baggage is at Aunt Isobel's."

He hugged her to him, showering her face with kisses. "That's of no consequence. When I've fulfilled my plans, you'll have everything your heart desires. Now go. I hear him coming now."

Hoofbeats thumped over the ground and Catrin found herself thrust deep into the shadows. Reluctant to leave, she blew David a kiss, waiting until the snorting of a labored horse drew close before she sped away.

Catrin virtually hugged herself with delight as she contemplated the next glorious hours galloping beside him through the summer night. So romantically appealing was the vision, she gave no thought to how they would eat, or sleep, or even survive in the wilds of Scotland, her thoughts centered only on her lover.

Inside the lighted hall Catrin caught Ruth's eye and signaled to her, smiling as if in conspiracy over their mutual secret. Ruth waited until she was sure Catrin was out of earshot before she hastened to her mother's side. Isobel still stood before the hearth, holding forth on her views about distributing charity to the worthy poor, a subject vastly boring to Lady Margaret, who viewed the surprise appearance of mousy Ruth as a heaven-sent deliverance.

"My dear, how pretty you look this evening. Walter also remarked on your appearance," Lady Margaret complimented, holding out a beringed white hand to Ruth.

"Thank you, your ladyship." Ruth curtsied, surprised and pleased. She was so delighted she almost forgot to deliver her startling news. "Oh, Mama, can you spare a moment?" she blurted, remembering her true mission. "There's something very important I have to tell you." Relieved by the interruption, Lady Margaret nodded and hastened away.

"What is it?" Isobel snapped, annoyed at having Ruth terminate her longest conversation to date with her ladyship. "Why haven't you shown yourself more? Both the Mainwaring boys have noticed you. If only you'd—"

"Mama, listen, this is very important. It concerns Catrin."

Isobel was immediately on guard. "Catrin? What about Catrin? Where is that young miss? I haven't seen her in some time. This is the last time you girls talk me into bringing you to an event of this nature. I've been thoroughly humiliated by Catrin's forwardness—as for you, miss, timorous as a church mouse for the most part, or sulking like a baby—when we get home I'll have plenty to say to both of you."

Ruth was dancing about in agitation as the hands of the great clock crept closer to twelve.

"Catrin has a rendezvous with a man!"

Isobel's mouth tightened to a grim line. "Are you sure?"

"Positive, Mama. She told me so herself."

"That wicked creature! But she knows no one here . . . does she?"

"It didn't take her long to make an acquaintance. He's the dark man all the ladies were flocking around."

"Never mind *who* he is." Gripping Ruth's arm, Isobel propelled her aside out of the noise. "Now, tell me everything you know."

"She's to meet him in the gardens at twelve."

"We'll see about that! That evil-minded wretch! After Humphrey entrusted her moral welfare to me, as well. To think, a betrothed girl, pledged to become another's wife in less than a month . . . the shame of it! Twelve, you say?" Isobel glanced at the clock. There were ten minutes left. Ten minutes in which to save a wayward soul from eternal damnation.

Dragging Ruth with her, Isobel marched purposefully toward their host, who had just stepped inside the hall, a glass of wine in his hand.

"My lord, I've just discovered some very alarming news."

"News, madam?" mumbled Lord Mainwaring, paying scant attention to Isobel's cross face as his gaze roamed over the dancers.

"My niece has formed a scandalous alliance with one of your guests."

"Eh!" he mumbled, his attention caught as he turned back to the two agitated females. "Your niece? An alliance? What do you mean, madam?"

"I mean, my lord, that one of your iniquitous guests has made a secret tryst with my young niece. Catrin will be dishonored if we don't intercede. If we're too late, I'm holding you personally responsible."

Bathed in indignation as she was, Isobel forgot herself sufficiently to glare at the nobleman, who retreated a defensive pace.

Lord Mainwaring finally grasped the source of this woman's agitation. So that was where Catrin was! The little fraud! Giving him the impression butter wouldn't melt in her mouth and all the while she was making a secret assignation with some blade. Who the devil was he? Quickly he glanced to where his young sons stood stuffing themselves at the refreshment table. Well, thank heaven, it wasn't either of them. And that was as well. He'd have flayed their hides if one of them had stolen that wench from under his nose.

"Madam, I'm shocked to hear it. We'll order an immediate search party."

"What an admirable idea, my lord," Isobel gushed, remembering her manners before it was too late. Prepared to do battle with their host, she had hardly expected such immediate understanding from a man she had already labeled a libertine. Maybe her judgment had been a trifle hasty.

"If your dear niece should come to any harm on my estate I'd feel eternal remorse," said Lord Mainwaring, while he simmered inwardly. By God, he'd make sure the lovers were disclosed before it was too late. He had no intention of letting Catrin slip through his grasp.

Ruth was panting with excitement, anxious to see her cousin exposed about her evil doing. "I knew you'd want to be told at once, Mama. I felt it my duty to save poor Catrin from disgrace."

"And rightly so, rightly so," agreed Lord Mainwaring, eyeing the dowdy little mouse with distaste. A terrible, simpering, spineless creature. He had no idea how she could be related to the other one. His breathing quickened as he contemplated losing beautiful Catrin to some nameless opportunist who had cleverly stolen a march on him while he was engaged in secret negotiations.

Catrin huddled in her cloak in the shadows, shivering with excitement as she waited for the clock over the stable to finish its sonorous chime. Twelve o'clock. Two horses stood in the yard, saddle bags readied for a journey. Her hands began to shake and her knees went weak as she watched a dark cloaked figure emerge from the stalls. David glanced about in concern when he did not see her. Catrin hesitated, enjoying her new-found power to cause him distress.

"Here I am," she whispered as she emerged from the darkness.

David grasped her in a crushing embrace, kissing her brow in relief before he set her aside. "Come, you little witch, are you trying to give me apoplexy? We're late. I'm already supposed to be on the road."

"Listen."

"To what?"

"All the noise coming from the gardens."

"Drunken guests, I suppose."

"No, it's a search party looking for me."

A look of alarm crossed his face. "Then we've not a minute to lose."

"They won't be here for a while. I told Ruth I was meeting my lover in the gardens. I knew she'd be bursting to tell Aunt Isobel. The gardens lie in the opposite direction, so we can leave without fear of being seen."

He chuckled as he cinched the girth on her horse. "You're

wilier than I thought. While they're beating the bushes for you we'll be on the road to Edinburgh."

"Exactly. Oh, you've bought yourself a scheming baggage, David Stewart, so you'd best be warned."

He gripped her waist and lifted her to the saddle.

"Bought? I don't recall paying a penny for you. I understood you came as a glorious gift."

Catrin's heart was full as she leaned from the saddle and kissed his warm cheek, shuddering at the contact. "I love you very much," she whispered, her voice shaking.

"Not any more than I love you. Now come, let's begin our adventure."

They walked the horses across the stable yard. As they skirted the trees of the surrounding parkland, lights bobbed in the dark and shadows scurried back and forth through the formal rose garden; searchers called to each other in harsh whispers, dismayed that their efforts were proving fruitless. Catrin could hear Aunt Isobel's shrill angry tones rising above the rest, and Ruth's distinctive whine could be heard in the background. She shuddered. Tonight she would leave behind the hated restriction of her aunt's joyless household. Resolutely Catrin turned her horse's head toward the dark road stretching far into the night. A new chapter of her life had begun. It was she and David Stewart against the world. She found those odds most appealing.

Chapter 7

The summer night smelled sweet. A salt-laden breeze coming off the tidal River Mersey blew cool in their faces. As they headed north, David said little, anxious to put distance between themselves and Thorpington Hall. Not until he considered them safe from pursuit did he slacken the pace. Valiantly Catrin clung to the saddle, her limbs aching from the unaccustomed exertion.

When David finally drew rein, dawn was already brightening the eastern sky. They had traversed the flat Lancashire plain without mishap. For the past several miles the flat terrain had gradually given way to hillier country and Catrin, ignorant of geography, wondered if they were nearing the border of Scotland. When she voiced her question, however, David laughed heartily.

"Scotland! You ninny, we've half of England to ride over yet. Come, you must be tired. We'll rest at that farm. Friends of the cause live there."

By the time they rode into the farmyard, scattering a litter of barking puppies, Catrin could barely keep her eyes open. The obliging farmer had been expecting only one guest, and he eyed the woman with suspicion.

"This is my wife," David assured smoothly, handing the man a couple of extra coins for his pains.

Heavy-eyed, Catrin barely noticed the poverty of the small room to which she was led. The bed smelled clean and the floor was swept; beyond that she had no concern.

When David returned to their room Catrin was asleep. He covered her with a blanket to keep off the morning chill before going back downstairs to discuss the following day's route with the farmer. This man and a dozen others along the way had been earmarked by Lord Mainwaring as loyal Jacobites, willing to shelter a courier to further the cause.

Bees droned in the honeysuckle that climbed the stone wall outside the open window. Catrin stirred, wondering at the insistent sound. As she gradually awoke she could identify other sounds and smells drifting through the open window. Cattle lowed in the distance, while the shrill yaps of playing puppies came from the farmyard below; she was also aware of a pervading odor of cow dung, which gradually overpowered even the sweet fragrance of honeysuckle.

Catrin stretched, wondering where she was. Suddenly she sat upright, recalling that this was the first day of her journey to Edinburgh! A thrill shot through her. She glanced around the room to assure herself David was not there. She experienced a flutter of unease as she wondered if he had left without her, before angrily dismissing the thought. David would not bring her this far to desert her in a stranger's house.

Footsteps on the bare floorboards outside the door alerted her to sómeone's approach. Her heart leaped when the door opened and David strode inside the room, yet his tense expression, his very movements, suggested either haste or danger.

"Thank God you're awake. We've got to get back on the road. Sanders spotted a party of riders heading this way. They could be innocent travelers, but I can't take the chance."

Then he was gone. Catrin blinked, coming even wider awake, wondering at first if she had dreamed his abrupt message. She stretched beneath the warm covers, almost drifting back to sleep when she heard his agitated voice below the window.

"Hurry, sweetheart, we haven't much time." The jingle of harness as he saddled their mounts snapped her into action.

Catrin leaped from the bed. There was a chunk of bread and cheese on the crude nightstand and she grabbed the food in one hand, her cloak in the other. As she slipped on her shoes, she was already heading out the door.

David was waiting impatiently in the yard, the horses saddled for the journey. The dour farmer hovered in the background, anxious to see the back of his dangerous guest. They urged the horses forward, heading for high ground, continually picking up speed until they had left the poor farm far behind.

Similar hasty departures, after only a few hours' sleep, became the pattern of their days. Catrin was surprised when David revealed his suspicions that they were being pursued by a party from Thorpington Hall.

"Why? Surely they can't hope to catch us in open country. It's like looking for a needle in a haystack," she complained loudly after yet another swift departure.

"I asked myself the same question until I realized Mainwaring must be behind the pursuit."

"Why would he try to capture us?"

David smiled as he reined in on a small knoll where he could survey the road leading uphill. "Mainwaring's the only one who knows my route—he gave me the map. Yet if he was trying his utmost he could have overtaken us days ago. He's trusting me to keep moving, knowing I won't be taken. I suspect that when we reach the lakes, he'll give up. He must be making a good showing to appease your papa."

Catrin was shocked by his suggestion. She had considered Lord Mainwaring a friend. "Why would he bother? Papa means nothing to him."

David shrugged as he turned back onto the road. "Pity the man, sweetheart. He loyally supports the cause, therefore he must not catch me. But I suspect he secretly yearns after you. Besides, your rich papa may have offered him good recompense for diligent effort. The cause always needs gold."

It took several more days to convince them that their pursuers had finally given up the chase.

Now they were riding through the wildly beautiful Lake District, where the hillsides' grassy slopes were a tangle of pink spotted foxgloves, saxifrage, and parsley fern. Beside the path berries grew profusely in tangled thickets of vegetation. Here the air was so pure and fresh Catrin's lungs tingled when she took a deep breath, finding it a far cry from London's hazy skies and Liverpool's murk.

Yet though their surroundings were beautiful, tears of disappointment and frustration gathered in her eyes. Always pressing north, sparing few hours for sleep, David was on edge, making him short-tempered and silent. Far from the glorious romantic adventure she had envisioned, their journey had been little but hard riding and deprivation.

To add to her disillusion, David had paid scant attention to her, let alone made passionate love. With each bumping hoofbeat angry disappointment welled stronger, until she began to glare hostilely at his broad back as he moved slowly before her up the narrow track. The ground was high and far to their left glittered the lakes David had spoken about. He did not even suggest a short detour from the route to admire the spectacular beauty spots; they merely passed forward, eating unpalatable scraps donated by grudging farmers, sleeping under the eaves of impoverished cottages if they were fortunate, or in a hay barn if they were not.

They crested a sharp rise. Seething with pent-up emotion, Catrin pulled her mount up short and blocked his path.

"David, we must talk. This has gone on long enough," she snapped, frustration making her reckless. The anger that momentarily clouded his face normally would have warned her not to proceed, but so incensed was she over her dying dreams, she did not heed the warning signs.

"What has gone on long enough? I assure you there are many miles to go before we reach our destination."

"And are they all to be like this?"

"The country's much the same—"

"That's not what I meant!" she shouted, her gray eyes flashing in temper. "Are we always to act like . . . like . . . polite acquaintances?"

"I fancied we were something more than that—I hardly share a bed with polite acquaintances," he countered evenly, his eyes slitted against the bright sunlight. "Come, let's dismount. Perhaps you've been spending too many hours in the saddle."

Catrin got down, but his suggestion merely increased her anger. "It's not me who's at fault, it's you!"

"What do you want from me? I'm about a mission to deliver a package of important papers with as much haste as possible. You knew that before you decided to accompany me."

"I thought our journey would be loving, that we'd renew the affection we shared in Ranelagh Gardens. 'Tis the only reason I came with you. I had no need of an escorted tour through northern England. Can it be you're no longer in love with me?"

His face set, David turned away without answering. He walked a few feet down the narrow track, stopping at an outcropping where he leaned against the gray rock. Catrin had followed him, but she kept her distance, refusing to join him when he held out a comforting arm.

"Constantly being on the run hardly sets the stage for passionate lovemaking," he defended, his voice tight. "Besides, you're always tired, or asleep, or—"

"Or what?" Something about his argument did not ring true. Uneasily Catrin approached, still keeping out of reach, her heart twisting as she anticipated learning something she would rather not know.

He turned toward her as she stumbled over the rough ground, his face taut. Dark shadows, from lack of rest, accentuated his large eyes, and the tension in his face made his cheekbones more prominent and set his mouth in an unyielding line.

"Catrin, though not in the manner in which you suggest. I have deceived you."

His statement was like a physical blow. His tight voice was a stranger's, the words blown about the fells and echoing through the boulder-strewn valleys of this barren countryside. "Deceived," she croaked, clutching the cold hard rock for support. "How have you deceived me?"

"You came with me assuming I was bound for Edinburgh."

"And you are not?"

"Yes, that's where I'm bound—eventually."

"Then wherein lies the deceit? Do you no longer love me? Is that what you're trying to say?"

Tension lessened in his face and he smiled at her, his eyes softening. "Little fool, on that score you've no worries. I love you no less than I did before."

"Then why?" she whispered tearfully, feeling uncomfortable about asking him why he had not made love to her.

"Catrin, would you have come with me had I told you grave danger lay ahead, danger that has little bearing on the cause?"

She swallowed, made uneasy by the sudden intensity in his voice. "Had you told me we were going on a crusade to the Holy Land, I'd have come, provided you still loved me."

Her answer made him sigh with relief, yet still he was not completely at ease. "These past days I've wrestled with my conscience, afraid of losing you, yet knowing I must divulge the truth. The nearer we get to the Scottish border, the more pressing becomes my decision. After you've heard me out, if you wish, you can turn back at Carlisle. I'll provide you with money to take a stage home."

"No. I want to stay with you . . . if you still want me."

Tears trickled down her soft pink cheeks, revealing to David the hurt he had caused.

"I'm sorry, Catrin, for deceiving you. I never intended anything but truth between us, yet I was afraid if you knew my actual destination, or the danger involved in this venture, you'd never agree to come."

"Can you not be honest with me now? I've come too far to turn back."

David took her hand, his clasp warmly reassuring as he led her to a natural seat shaped in the mass of rock. From here they could look into the valley, its scraggy grassland scattered with rocks and gorse thickets golden with blossom.

"Because one is never sure of one's friends, not even Lord Mainwaring was entrusted with the truth. He assumes I'm to arrive in Edinburgh on a prescribed date. Instead I'm to give these papers to a contact in Carlisle. I carry promises of support from a hundred loyal Englishmen, listing their assets and the number of men they can raise for the cause. This document alone could destroy them if it fell into the wrong hands. And all the time you were carrying it in your valise, unaware of its power."

"It was as well I didn't know. I'd have been even more worried."

"Though things fortunately went well, discovering you carried such damning evidence caused me grave concern." David glanced at her, seeing tears gathering in her soft eyes. He continued his explanation. "After I've delivered the papers I'm bound for the highlands."

"Is Edinburgh there?"

"No, we must travel much further north, into Appin country. Catrin, love, I'll be arriving in Edinburgh only *after* I've reclaimed my inheritance. Do you remember my telling you I was rightful laird of Garth?"

She nodded, also remembering the bitterness that had twisted his face when he spoke about old treacheries. "You intend to regain your land? But how? You've no army. You can't wrest a castle from its owner singlehanded."

Ignoring her practical reminders, David gazed into the mist-wreathed distance. Somewhere beyond this range of hills, beyond the lawless borderland, lay his inheritance. Like the royal prince, he too had land he was born to rule, wrested from him by treachery. He might die before he could lend his strong arm in support of Prince Charles, but he could not live with himself if he did not try to right the wrong of three decades past.

"My uncle treacherously betrayed my father, condemning

him to death. Always covetous, Gordon Stewart wanted Garth for his own. My father's old retainers have given me detailed maps and information, everything I need to find my way to Garth. Though I was born abroad, there's a strong love of Scotland in my blood. As long as I can remember I've known my rights to that corner of Appin. It's true, I've no army. My only hope lies in the tenants' love for my father and their hatred of his brother. I deceived you into believing it was devotion to the cause that took me to Scotland."

"And aren't you dedicated to that end?"

"Yes, but only after I've regained my own land. It's an ambition that's burned inside me all my days, the single-mindedness of revenge being far stronger than loyalty to a cause. Someday I knew I'd stand before Garth Castle and challenge Gordon Stewart for possession of the land. It's a dangerous ambition. And I've no guarantee of success."

For a long time Catrin silently considered his words. His revelation had come as a shock. She had to admit she had pictured them arriving in Edinburgh and joining the young prince's court, attending parties and balls, enjoying all the gaiety preceding a triumphal Stuart march into England. At her side would be her laughing, passionate lover, his foremost dedication being to make her happy. So died the dream. This new David, though no less handsome, had quickly cast aside the suave manners of a courtier, dispensing with the flattering compliments, the playful lovemaking, revealing instead a steel-hard ambition of long standing that could shatter forever their dreams of happiness.

"Why have you turned cold toward me?" she blurted suddenly, realizing he had still not explained the problem that lay closest to her heart.

"Oh, sweetheart, not cold—I could have taken you a dozen times. But I wanted only truth between us. Had I taken further advantage of your trust, my conscience would have been sorely tried. I had to let you make your own choice. You knew only that I was a Jacobite. Reclaiming Garth has little bearing on the Stuart claim to the throne. I seek vengeance for my father's death—and I've been waiting thirty years to claim it. If I succeed you'll be lady of a castle, there'll be money from my estates—"

"And if you lose?"

"I can promise you nothing, not even food in your belly or a roof over your head. Now, considering those odds, is your decision still the same?"

Catrin took both his hands in hers and without hesitation put her lips to his ear to whisper, "As long as you're with me I'll brave anything, anywhere."

"Oh, my darling."

David crushed her against him, holding her close, not speaking as he cherished the longed-for feel of her soft body in his arms. Then suddenly, he set her aside, his abruptness startling her.

"What is it?"

"You've got thirty miles before we reach Carlisle. I'll not touch you until then. You must be sure—I owe you that much."

Aghast she stared at him, at the determined set of his jaw, the steely determination in his eye as he turned from her and walked back to the horses.

"Damn you," she cried suddenly, rage building inside her. "Didn't I just tell you I was sure? I've a mind to stay here and let you go to your own suicide."

David swung into the saddle, trailing the reins of her mount loosely behind him. "You must make your own choice, Catrin Blair. I won't let it be said I persuaded you against your will."

"And when I've made my choice, why aren't you man enough to accept it?"

"If you aren't serious about staying here, you'd best mount up. I can't waste much more time." He flung the reins at her, walked his horse to the crest of the track, and dropped over the other side.

Fists clenched in anger, Catrin watched him go. Her horse stood cropping the grass at her feet, the reins trailing in the dirt. With an exclamation of exasperation, she finally grasped the reins and yanked up the animal's head. Using the rocks as a mounting block, she scrambled clumsily into the saddle, afraid she would fall as the horse shifted. Smacking her heels against the animal's flanks, she labored up the trail and dropped over the skyline, urging her mount to a reckless pace as they went downhill. David cantered a few hundred hards ahead, not actually waiting for her, yet by his slower pace she knew he was stalling to allow her to catch up.

As she rode up he said, "So you decided to come after all?"

"Yes, I did, but only because I don't know my way about this wilderness."

"I thought you missed me too much to stay."

"What's to miss?" she snapped, forcing her horse to a gallop as she left the path to ride around him, pulling ahead on the downhill grade.

David smarted in anger as he watched her go, her hair streaming in an unruly banner behind her. It was increasingly hard to keep to his resolve; every nerve in his body screamed for her. He considered pursuing Catrin and dragging her from the saddle, taking her out here with the rough grass for a pillow and the birds circling overhead. But he did not. Mouth set, he kicked his horse's flanks and galloped after her. There were many hard miles to go before they reached Carlisle.

Before sundown they had left behind rugged Shap Fells, lodging the night in Shap village. The following night was spent in a barn outside Penrith, and though Catrin sorely tempted him, to her annoyance she found David had no intention of breaking his word. She moved as far as possible from the tantalizing warmth of his body, burrowing deep in the straw as she shed tears of angry frustration over his stubbornness. It would serve him right if, when they reached Carlisle, she accepted his offer of a stage and left him to his fate. It would serve him right—but she knew she would not do it. Even without the looming threat of Aunt Isobel's vindictive chastisement and the horrid prospect of marriage to Bryce Cavendish, she would never leave David.

It was raining hard when they entered Carlisle. This was not the sun and showers they had encountered in the Lake District, but a driving gray pall. Catrin's cloak could no longer repel the incessant beating rain and she became soaked to the skin as they rode back and forth in search of a lodging house near the castle where David would deliver the papers.

"Go inside the inn out of the rain. We'll stay there. I'll go back and try again," David shouted to Catrin through the downpour, pointing to a half-timbered hostelry with the sign of the crown and anchor swinging over the door.

So thoroughly out of sorts did she feel by now, Catrin had a mind to argue with his decision. But the rain was so coldly penetrating and her ruined ballgown was uncomfortably plastered to her body. "What am I to use for money?" she snapped, trying to pull down her hood.

"Here, this should suffice."

David pitched her a small leather bag and Catrin surprised herself by catching it.

Wasting no more time, he wheeled his horse about and was soon lost in the press of cattle and farm carts thronging the main street as he retraced his journey in search of Mr. Jodrell's elusive rooming house.

Catrin rode inside the inn's yard and shouted for an ostler. A wild-haired, hare-lipped lad answered her summons. At first she thought him to be the local idiot, but, as he appeared to know how to care for her mount, she finally relinquished her horse to him. Struggling with her saddlebags, too wary of thieves to leave them with the horse, Catrin staggered inside the inn.

Welcome warmth and the tempting aroma of roast beef assailed her senses as she dropped the heavy saddlebags on the wooden floor.

"Are ye seeking a room?"

Catrin had few smiles to spare for the mobcapped female who poked her head around the doorjamb. "Aye, I am," she repeated, unconsciously using the local vernacular. "Have ye any?"

"If ye've gold to pay."

"Then warm one up and bring me water for bathing."

Catrin opened her drawstring purse and showed the woman the gold coins before carefully refastening the bag. Only after David's arrival did she intend to part with any money. They likely would not cheat him. A woman alone was always fair game.

The maid told her to wait on the settle in the draughty hallway while she went upstairs to prepare a room. After what seemed like hours she reappeared.

"At the head of the stair. Are ye alone, Mrs.?"

"No, my husband will join me shortly. Kindly direct him to our room."

A boy materialized from the kitchen to carry her saddlebags, preceding her up the stair. The room was by no means grand, but its dark oak paneling glowed with polishing and a welcome fire burned in the grate. The large bed was heaped with soft, clean covers and on the bedside table stood a bowl and jug for washing. After her recent spartan lodgings, the Crown and Anchor's guest room was like a palace.

"Have them send me water to bathe—a bathful if it's available," she told the lad after he had dumped the saddlebags beside the bed. "And bring whatever food's fresh and hot . . . I can pay," she added as he looked questioningly at her bedraggled dress.

The boy backed out and closed the door.

The bath arrived and a maid began to fill it with hot water. The girl had to make so many trips up the winding stair carrying pitchers of water, Catrin was convinced the bath would be stone cold before she was allowed to enjoy it. When she had finally gone Catrin peeled off her sodden skirts, bodice, chemise, and petticoat. Until now she had not realized how hopelessly ruined her clothes were. She stared in dismay at the stained, tattered skirt that had once been so fine, its silver embroidery tarnished and torn, the fine silk damaged beyond repair.

The bathwater was still hot. Holding her breath, she finally lowered her body into the water. The girl had brought a bar of fresh soap, and though it was harsh and unscented, at least it would cleanse her. The only other time Catrin had felt this filthy and unkempt had been after that loathsome night in the Fleet.

She soaked in the bath before the blazing hearth, sighing with contentment. After soaping and rinsing her long hair, she spread it across her shoulders to dry before the fire.

David was taking a long time about his business. Fear flickered in her stomach when she considered how long he had been gone; she even wondered if he had been arrested, before quickly dismissing the thought. David Stewart would not let them take him now. He had come this far fueled by hatred for his uncle; he would not allow the delivery of a packet of papers to defeat him before he had taken his revenge.

Presently the maid returned bearing a tray containing a platter of roast beef, boiled turnips in a cheese sauce, and a flagon of ale. While she luxuriated in the bath, Catrin nibbled shreds from the succulent roast, savoring its flavor, finding it marvelously different from their usual fare of coarse bread and cheese.

A sudden icy touch on her warm shoulder made Catrin start in alarm. She must have dozed before the fire.

"David!"

When she turned about she found him standing behind her, the orange firelight flickering across his dark face. In the shadowy light his eyes gleamed black with highlights of bronze and red and his grim expression made her shudder in anticipation.

The hand he placed on her warm pink shoulder was wet with rain, yet the strength of his grasp pierced her flesh with heat. His sodden cloak clung across his broad shoulders; rain darkened his red velvet coat and his white doeskin britches were plastered uncomfortably to his body.

"Are you trying to seduce me?" he asked huskily.

Catrin smiled, excited by his tone, her feelings of anger and disappointment gone. "Are you that old and feeble I have need to plot? Tonight's the time of reckoning, or have you forgotten?"

"No, I've not forgotten."

"I haven't changed my mind, though I've been tempted, you've treated me so surly of late."

His grip tightened before he abruptly released her to fling his wet cloak over the foot of the bed, and crossed to the hearth to warm himself. "I'm sorry, sweet. I apologize for my surliness. Now the papers are safely delivered, I'm free to go about my own business. Your decision to accompany me to Appin's probably not the wisest choice you've ever made . . . but I love you all the more for it."

The huskiness in his voice brought a lump to her throat. Catrin pulled herself up, her skin gleaming with water as she slowly emerged from the bath, the firelight gilding her body. His gasp of wonder was loud in the quiet room as he gazed for the first time on her beauty unclothed. Beneath the saturated doeskin David's passion swelled visibly, his reaction giving her a surge of pride.

When he held out the large towel Catrin wrapped herself in it, quickly rolling along its length until she landed soft and inviting in his arms.

"You schemer, you knew once I saw you like this I couldn't resist," he whispered, nuzzling her damp pink ear.

Catrin smiled, yet she had not purposely planned a seduction; in fact she was rather annoyed with herself for having missed several opportunities. David was her first romantic experience, and her feminine wiles were not as finely honed as they might have been.

"Is the bath still warm?" he asked as he turned back to the fire.

"If you hurry."

He took off his coat and waistcoat while Catrin huddled in the towel, openly admiring his broad-shouldered, well-muscled torso as he took off his sodden lawn shirt. Golden flesh stretched smooth across his straight, square shoulders and a dark triangle of rain-wet ringlets furred his chest. Her pulse quickened as David unfastened the band of his breeches, slowly peeling down the slick wet doeskin from his flat belly, easing the skin over his firm, unblemished buttocks. Though she had often imagined how he would look unclothed she had never seen him naked. Catrin's burning gaze followed the painfully slow movement of the saturated leather until his swelling manhood was finally revealed, full, heavy, and firmly fleshed, more magnificent than she had imagined. Uneasily she wondered if he would consider her bold for staring at him unclothed before she realized her pleasure in his body would more likely delight him.

"You're beautiful," she whispered, going to him and resting her head against his hard, cold shoulder.

"Not nearly as beautiful as you," he whispered, kissing her brow before he stepped into the bath. "Now, slave, you can wash my back," he ordered sternly when she offered him the soap.

Laughing in pleasure over her new role, Catrin lathered his muscular back, thrilling as his smooth skin warmed beneath her hands. As she rinsed off the lather he leaned back to kiss her soft white underarm. Catrin had tucked the top of the towel firmly above her breasts to form a narrow tunic. Eyes closed, David rested his head against those soft twin pillows as she vigorously soaped his chest.

Filling the pitcher from the bath, Catrin rinsed the soap from his chest. Then, making David stand, she tipped another pitcher of water down his back. He grinned as she stroked his shoulders, marveling at the hard flesh, golden as if cast from precious metal. Moving downward, her fingers tangled in the matted hair on his belly as, suddenly shy, she hesitated, her hand poised within inches of that arousing dark pillar of flesh.

"What, are you still a little convent mouse?" he whispered huskily while he tantalized her bare shoulder with his hot mouth. "You have leave to scrub me all over, wench."

Eyes downcast, for she could not hold his gaze while performing such intimacies, Catrin carefully lathered his throbbing flesh. The soapsuds slid over his smooth skin, her fingers gently stroking the fiery tautness of his growing erection. She marveled at the strength of him, how he leaped alive beneath her touch. Diligently she rinsed away the foamy white, shuddering as his gleaming tawny flesh emerged. Tentatively she fondled him, vastly enjoying the deliciously arousing sensation as her fingers slid along his slick flesh.

David finally stayed her hand, his breathing ragged.

"Aren't you enjoying it?"

"Far too much," he whispered, resting his head against hers.

At first Catrin thought David intended to kiss her until she felt his strong white teeth tugging loose her towel, sending it slithering to the floor. She squealed in surprise and excitement as he came out of the bath, streaming water like some magnificent sea god, broad-shouldered, narrow-hipped, darkly handsome, and fully aroused.

After a perfunctory dab with the towel, he lunged for her and brought her crashing onto the heaped bedding, sinking in a sea of feathers. His mouth burned over hers; his hard body covered her own. Catrin's hands fastened in his hair as she clung desperately to him, devouring his mouth as if she would unite their very souls in this deep, passionate kiss.

"I love you like no other. You're mine for ever," he vowed huskily, covering her neck and shoulders with kisses. Growing aware of the room's chill, he dragged covers over them, rolling their bodies in a downy cocoon. When he kissed her hungrily, and touched her breasts, she reciprocated with increasing ardor.

"Oh, David, never stop loving me," Catrin begged, trembling with emotion.

When David teased her erect pink nipples with his hot mouth, she cried aloud in pleasure. The fiery passage of his hands went down her smooth back, molding her softly rounded buttocks, her silky thighs, as he thoroughly explored every inch of her beautiful body. This privilege had been denied to him before and he intended to indulge himself to the utmost. Eagerly David urged Catrin to caress him, longing to feel her passionate response to his desire. A feeling of intense longing rocked him as she slid her hand over his taut belly, tormenting until she finally captured that magnificent treasure.

Their breathing became increasingly labored as he moved his hand high between her thighs, exploring the silken chestnut portals he longed to breach. Catrin responded to his intimate touch, squirming in delight at his firm but gentle manipulation. When David placed the velvet tip of his manhood against her burning flesh she moaned softly. The burning brand moved rhythmically against the core of her passion, inflaming her all the more when it nudged gently, insistently for admittance, making her quiver to contain him.

Catrin grasped David's slender hips and thrust her hips toward him, desperate to have his steel-hard strength inside her. Exerting all the control he could muster David only partially invaded the fiery depth of her body, until Catrin, growing ever more impatient, drove him to the hilt inside her.

"Oh, love me now, don't make me wait any longer," she pleaded in a torment of desire she had not known herself capable of feeling. A throbbing sensuality had seized her from his first caress and she was sure if it were not soon assuaged, she could no longer endure it.

David quickened his movements, sweeping Catrin toward a wild and consuming ecstasy, then suddenly, he plunged again and again, no longer showing mercy. He drove her deep into that bottomless darkness where light and sound rushed past her. She cried out, struggling to endure the pleasure of their mutual needs.

So deep was their shared emotion, Catrin wept softly while David held her, panting, cherishing her spent body against his own.

"Now do you doubt I love you, ninny?" David whispered much later, his mouth soft against her brow.

"Never again . . . not as long as you make such magnificent love to me."

Her throaty answer made him grin and he hugged her close, looking above her tousled chestnut curls at the leaping fire. Pray God she would never regret the decision she had made today. Even he knew his chances for success were slim. And he had never intended to bring a woman with him . . .

"You're looking grim again and I won't allow it. There's only one grim expression you can wear," she chastised, seeing the stern set of his features, which, moments before, had been softly relaxed in the aftermath of passion.

"And what is that?"

"The one you wear when you're contemplating taking me . . . oh, I know that special look, it's something I dream about when we're apart . . ."

But he was no longer listening. Instead David wrapped her hand about the furnace of his rousing flesh while he buried his mouth in her soft neck, devouring her with kisses. His worries about reclaiming Garth Castle he would reserve for the morrow. Today—and tonight—he would take his fill of this beguiling woman, making passionate love to her until she begged for mercy.

Chapter 8

The long summer day was already fading into dusk when Catrin first saw Garth Castle black against the twilight sky. Built on the banks of a brooding highland loch and ringed by dark mountains, the tall narrow fortress looked like something from legend.

Catrin shivered as she gazed at the majestic sight. The sun had all but disappeared from view, imparting a strange unearthly light to the green Appin peninsula. Bands of silver, lemon, and mauve girded the loch where the still water was disturbed only by the passage of a small boat, the rhythmic splash of its oars breaking the silence.

"Quick, get behind those trees," David ordered, grabbing her reins and urging her to shelter.

"There's no one about for miles."

"The boatman might see the horses. Who knows whether he's friend or foe. If Gordon Stewart knew I stood before his castle, he'd send a party to kill me."

David's grim pronouncement reminded Catrin of the danger lurking beside this placid loch and she grew tense with fear as the scene took on a sinister appearance.

"What do we do now?"

"When the light's dimmer we'll ride back to that cluster of cottages beyond the trees. With luck I can find out how the land lies from the crofters there." David smiled at Catrin and squeezed her hand in reassurance.

Catrin smiled back, though her heart remained bleak. She

could not shake a terrible feeling of foreboding that had descended with the dusk, a feeling so strong she experienced a wave of panic. Was David to die here on these shores in a vain attempt to repossess his land? Was that the basis for her sudden premonition of doom? Making a great effort, she shrugged off her fright and spurred her horse after David's as he skirted the woodland on the narrow track leading to Garth village.

At the first cottage they reached a rushlight was glinting in the unshuttered window opening.

David dismounted and knocked on the weathered door, praying his reception would be good. Despite his bloodline, despite his lifelong determination to one day set foot in Scotland, that longing nurtured by others' nostalgic dreams of home, David was a stranger in this land bordering Loch Linnhe. The discovery had come as a shock. So long had he fostered visions of this day, his imaginings had left the realm of reality until he almost expected to recognize both the land and its people as if he had lived there all his life.

An old woman in a white cap poked her head warily around the door to inspect the stranger, swift to notice the fine clothes that stamped him as gentry, despite his disheveled appearance.

"My wife and I seek lodgings for the night. Do you know if anyone hereabouts takes in travelers?"

The woman promptly disappeared inside the cottage where she could be heard consulting with someone else. Presently she reappeared. "Ye're welcome to say here," she announced. "Ye can take the animals to yon barn."

After he had seen to the horses, Catrin followed David inside the whitewashed cottage; the doorway was so low, they had to duck to enter the one-roomed dwelling. This cottage was reasonably clean, the beaten-earth floor swept. Unlike many dwellings they had shared since they left Carlisle, here the farm animals were housed elsewhere, a discovery that vastly relieved Catrin, who had no wish to endure another night inhaling the acrid stench of a cow byre. A peat fire glowed in a central hearth, sending a column of blue smoke weaving toward a smokehole in the thatched roof. A cast-iron girdle of oatcakes projected above the flames, tended by a young woman with straggling black hair. When she saw the strangers, the woman scrambled to her feet and bobbed her head in shy greeting before returning to her task.

"We've broth, oatmeal drammach, and oatcakes to offer ye to sup. And my man's got brose and a drop of good strong whisky if ye've a mind to join him."

David thanked the woman, saying any food would be most welcome, for they hadn't supped since leaving Oban. The interior of the cottage was blackened by the open fire, and though several rushlights glimmered in holders about the room it seemed to be in a perpetual twilight. Soon Catrin's eyes began to burn from the smoke and she sneezed as it tickled her nose.

"Your wife is'na ailing?"

"No, it's just the smoke," David explained. "She's very tired. We've traveled from Carlisle since Thursday."

"Have ye now?"

Still eyeing the strangers dubiously, the old woman went to the hearth and filled a wooden plate with fresh oatcakes. When she returned with the offering, accompanied by a pitcher of honey, she asked him, "D'ye speak the Gaelic?"

"A little. My father was an Appin man. But my wife doesn't understand it."

"I'm the only one hereabouts who has the English," the old woman informed him proudly. "I traveled to Edinburgh when I was young in the days of laird Somerled, which was a long, long time ago."

They ate crisp oatcakes washed down with warm milk drunk from wooden bickers, and spooned up thick oatmeal from a porringer with horn spoons.

David questioned the woman further, finally asking, "You were fond of the old laird, then?"

She pursed her mouth and drew her brows together in annoyance. "Fond? The old laird was beloved by all his people— not like the one who's laird now. We could all starve and he'd be put out only because we couldna tend the crops." And the woman turned aside, muttering beneath her breath.

David smiled as he recognized the unflattering Gaelic epithet frequently used by his father's retainers.

"When are you going to tell her who you are?" Catrin whispered after the woman crossed the smoky room to attend to her family's needs.

"All in good time. First I must see how far their loyalty goes." Catrin felt weary, and her eyes were so heavy they began to close. She nodded against David's shoulder.

Presently the woman's bearded husband approached through the blue haze of peat smoke, holding out a horn quaich, the Highlander's communal whisky drinking cup. David accepted the quaich and took a long swallow of the fiery liquid; Catrin turned down the offer, hoping the man would not be offended.

The crofter smiled and pointed to a box bed, indicating Catrin should retire there to sleep. She was grateful for his suggestion. It was the only bed she could see, yet so tired was she, if the crofter had chosen to give up his own bed she was not going to argue with him. The last thing she could remember was putting her head on a scratchy pillow stuffed, she realized later, with heather and bracken, the distinctive aroma filling her nostrils as she slipped into oblivion.

David hoped his Gaelic would be fluent enough to converse with the crofter. This family remembered his father with affection and he could think of no better household in which to learn the feelings of the villagers, on whom he must rely for assistance in retaking what was rightfully his. After much passing of the quaich, he began to draw the old man out, encouraging his stories of old loyalties and fierce battles. The crofter made no secret of his dislike of Gordon Stewart.

"Why do you follow him if he's hated so?"

The crofter's white eyebrows raised in surprise. "He's the laird. We owe him our loyalty."

"But you said he was not your rightful laird."

"Nay, but good laird Somerled be dead these many summers. No other has a better right than Gordon Stewart. We Garth Stewarts are sworn to follow our laird. Though the chief of clan Stewart is but a little lad, the Appin men are loyal to him. It's that simple, lad, we follow as our fathers did and their fathers before them. Being a Sassenach, you wouldna understand a clansman's loyalty to his own laird."

David considered his next statement before asking, "What if laird Somerled had had a son?"

The old man leaned forward, his eyes brightening before he realized the stranger was merely supposing. "Aye, but he didna. It's been thirty years or more since he's been gone."

"But if he had? Would you follow him instead of Gordon Stewart . . . would the other clansmen support him, considering his prior claim?"

The quaich passed around again.

"Aye, we would. The English attainder means nothing to us—laird Somerled's heirs are the rightful lairds of Garth. What do you know, lad, that ye're not telling?" asked the old crofter suspiciously. His wife and his scraggle-haired daughter had also drawn closer, after glancing warily toward the door lest they were being overheard.

"First tell me if Gordon Stewart's tacksmen would support another's claim to the land."

"Do ye know of such a lad?" demanded the old crofter, not answering David's question. "Is that it? Did laird Somerled leave a bairn across the water? I know his pretty lady escaped . . ."

"Laird Somerled's son stands on Scottish soil at this moment."

The old crofter's head came up, his blue eyes steely. "You're sure of that, lad—and of his right? You wouldn't mislead old Tam, now, would ye?"

"He has the sacred birth medal passed from generation to generation, laird Somerled's ring and his bonnet and clan crest—aye, his claim's just enough."

An awestruck hush had descended on the small room. Presently the crofter asked, "And is this lad man enough to risk a fight to rule us?"

"Certainly."

"First I'd have to see proof . . . see him. None of the tacksmen would choose to follow Gordon, so hated is he, had they a rightful heir to support. They listen to me—I'm the village spokesman. I'll call them to a meeting. When can ye present the lad?"

"Hold the meeting tomorrow and he'll be there . . . but only after he's convinced of the clansmen's loyalty."

"Tomorrow! Och, that's too short notice. We need more time."

"There's not more time. If Gordon Stewart gets wind of the meeting, he'll snuff out everyone who takes part in it. You know that."

The old crofter looked keenly at his guest, peering through the murk in an effort to see him clearer. "Aye, lad, I know that, but how did ye?"

David smiled and said no more.

Later, when he lay sleepless beside Catrin in the dark box bed, he prayed fervently for the success of his venture, offering thanks that he had been guided to this cottage.

True to his word, the next day Tam roused a number of interested tacksmen and their tenants to a meeting in a barn behind the cottage of the village's old bard, Blind Micah, who in his youth had composed many verses in praise of brave laird Somerled.

While the Garth tacksmen and their tenants met, David rode

through the wooded land beyond the loch, wary of being spotted on this bright summer day. Garth Castle was much smaller than he had imagined. All these years while he was being regaled with stories of his birthright, he had envisioned a grand edifice of stone, looming mighty from the waters of the great loch. Eyes slitted against the silver glare off the water, he gazed at Garth, foursquare, surrounded on the three sides by water— four during seasons of flood. This green peninsula of Appin, sliding gently into Loch Linnhe, stirred his blood, awakening some inborn memory of the generations of Stewarts who had bled to keep this land.

On an islet in the loch stood Castle Stalker, home of the hereditary chief of the Stewarts of Appin. From here he could not actually see the water-bound fortress he had ridden past this morning. Gentle men, the Appin Stewarts were loyal to the Stuart cause. When—he refused to say if, even to himself—he recaptured Garth Castle, David was sworn to raise an army in support of his prince. The Appin Stewarts would come out for him. Their clan chief being a minor, his tutor, Charles Stewart of Ardshiel, had signed his name in support of the cause long before Prince Charles had left French shores. David had no doubt his own tenants would likewise rally behind him and follow Ardshiel.

David arrived at the meeting place at the appointed time. He had told Tam he would present laird Somerled's heir after first securing his assurance of the clansmen's good intent. The creak of the barn door told him someone had been watching his arrival.

"Well, where's the lad?" demanded Tam, as he stepped into the sunshine, his expression angry. "Ye said he'd come with ye. We'll not be deceived."

"All in good time. First I need the assurance of the tacksmen. Chances can't be taken with so dangerous a guest. What if one of Gordon's spies were watching?"

Tam's face softened. "Aye, you're right, but ye can rest assured not one of Gordon Stewart's men is here. The few friends he has left are holed up inside the castle." And chuckling at his own remark, Tam opened the creaking barn door to admit their guest.

David glanced around the stone barn with interest, finding a dozen fierce, bearded men in assorted worn tartans squatting on the earth floor. Several men reached for their dirks when they saw the stranger, but Tam swiftly assured them they need have no fear, that this was the lad who was to present their rightful laird. If the clansmen wondered why he wore so heavy a cloak on this fine summer's day, drawn close about his body, no one commented. David waited in the shadows while Tam spoke with Blind Micah.

"We're all loyal to laird Somerled's son. The MacColls, the Carmichaels and the MacLeays are represented here also. Bring him forth, stranger, so we can kneel in homage to him," intoned Micah in his quavering old voice. A stir went round the assembly as men craned forward eagerly, looking intently at David.

"First, here's the birth medal for you to examine."

Reverently Tam took the hereditary gold talisman David proffered and gave it to Micah. The blind man felt the raised surface, nodding his white head in agreement that the metal was genuine. The ancient gold ring with the blood-red stones followed. This too was approved.

"If you're convinced of his rightful claim to Garth as heir of Somerled Stewart, I give you David Lachlan Stewart."

A gasp of surprise echoed through the barn as David pulled open his dark cloak to reveal his blue velvet coat with the silver buttons, snug-fitting tartan trews, and black kid riding boots. A silver-hilted dirk gleamed in his belt, a silver-handled pistol beside it. From his pocket he took a blue bonnet clasped with his father's oakleaf crest and placed it on his head.

"You!"

Aghast, Tam creaked to his knees. One by one the others came forward to pay homage to their new laird. Tears flowed from many an old eye as sentiment for dead laird Somerled was stirred by the appearance of his son. Some stared into David's face, remarking that now they looked close, they could see he had the look of laird Somerled about the eyes and mouth, while others shook their heads, not wholly convinced by this dark stranger who spoke Gaelic with a foreign accent.

Catrin was washing David's shirts in the burn behind Tam's cottage when he returned from the meeting. To her surprise David now wore the chieftain's dress he had worn to the masquerade. He must have changed after he left this morning. Even more surprising than finding him attired in tartan was the sight of the grizzled, reverent clansmen who accompanied him. Old Tam walked at the head of the small procession leading

David's horse. After assisting him to dismount, the old crofter dropped to his knee as his laird walked inside his cottage, the other men following suit.

By the time Catrin had overcome her surprise and gathered her washing, the men were already inside the cottage. Heads lifted at her entrance; the tacksmen had not known their new laird was not traveling alone.

"The laird's pretty wife," introduced Tam, nodding in her direction.

After a quick greeting, even David returned to the discussion in Gaelic, which left her feeling shut out. Catrin sighed philosophically; what had she expected? She must be grateful that David had won the clansmen's acceptance, his first step on the road to victory. The crofter's wife motioned to her to leave the men to their plotting and gave her a bowl of hot broth for her noon meal.

With great speed the plans for overcoming Gordon Stewart were made. Everyone concerned recognized the need for stealth and haste. A chance word betrayed to the wrong ears could bring swift vengeance to shatter their hopes.

For some time rumors of Prince Charles's landing in the Hebrides had reached Garth, spread by messengers from other clans anxious to know who would "come out," and in what force, before committing themselves. Only yesterday they had received word from Charles Stewart of Ardshiel, tutor to the Stewart clan's minor chief, asking for clansmen to rally to his banner. Tam had tacked the summons on the door of the Blind Micah's barn, though few villagers could read. Ardshiel intended to join the Prince's growing army at Lochaber.

After pondering this latest news and receiving no command to prepare to march from Gordon Stewart, Garth's fighting men voted to replace their hated laird with Somerled's son while they awaited further developments.

Prince Charles could not have landed at a more advantageous time and they intended to make use of the situation. As they argued back and forth, that day, well fortified from the passing of the quaich, Carmichaels, MacColls, Stewarts, and MacLeays who represented families from the hills surrounding Garth evolved a plan, using Ardshiel's call to arms as an excuse to arm themselves and march on Gordon Stewart's stronghold.

Daft Dougal, the blacksmith's son, was known to bear tales to the unpopular laird, so when the plans were set, he was deliberately taken into their confidence. Dougal's eyes popped and he could hardly wait to deliver the startling news that Garth's ablebodied men were prepared to follow the Stewart clan into battle, and on the morrow would go to the castle to learn if their laird was for Ardshiel or against him.

The next morning, when David kissed Catrin goodbye, he insisted she stay safe in Tam's cottage until his return. Then he mounted his horse and rode to the village meeting place in Blind Micah's barn. Though it was August, the dawn was gray and chill. The cloudy sky threatened rain.

"Aye, come in, lad," called Tam as he rapped on the door.

Inside the murky barn were assembled forty armed men carrying studded leather targes, dirks, highland broadswords, and Lochaber axes. To a man they knelt before David to swear allegiance. The sight of those bowed heads, the sound of the mass Gaelic oath of fealty, brought tears to his eyes as an unexpected surge of pride and love for these, his people, swept over him. These simple clansmen had accepted him almost without question and were now ready to lay down their lives, if need be, to restore what was rightfully his. In a small way he supposed his feelings duplicated the emotion felt by the young Stuart prince when he stood on the shoreline at Glenfinnan and raised his standard before the assembled clans who had rallied in support of his cause. As David looked at his kneeling tenants, the strangeness of this rainy, mountainous land, of the Gaelic tongue, disappeared as it merged with all those splendid dreams of Scotland he had dreamt beneath Italy's sunny skies. He had come home at last.

"Thank you for your loyalty. May God bless our right," he declared in a tight voice, his words followed by a gruff chorus of amens from the clansmen.

Tam spread out a length of green wool tartan. He quickly showed David how to pleat it over his belt to form the kilt and the plaid, then, by lying down and rolling himself in the length of fabric, how to dress in the all-purpose garment. With the removal of the belt, the woolen plaid became a blanket for sleeping. David donned knitted hose and deerskin shoes and a faded yellow shirt under a tartan jacket of a finer weave. The worn jacket was frayed about the wrists, for which Tam apologized.

Until the moment of truth inside Garth Castle, David was to pose as the son of Kenneth MacColl, a grizzled, gray-haired warrior who beamed with pride over the honor. Armed with his own sword, a primitive targe, and several daggers in his belt, David fell into step with the others as they emerged in the gray morning light.

The armed men walked through the village, singing a clan fighting song that stirred the slumbering love of battle that beat in every Scottish heart. The women and children crowded in doorways to watch them pass. Few women were aware of their men's actual mission. They were familiar with the Clan Stewart chief's message and believed the story that the clansmen, impatient to depart, went to rally their laird to the Prince's cause.

Along the shoreline the men marched, their step sprightly. Although David was overwhelmed by the men's support, he doubted the fighting ability of some of these soldiers, grizzled graybeards who had likely been out in the '15 and young, smooth-faced lads who had only lately left their mother's skirts. Still, beggars could not be choosers and his desperate gamble relied solely on surprise and his clansmen's skill. As he gazed at the stern forbidding walls of the castle, David wondered how many armed men watched their approach; he also wondered if any treachery had been breathed. Even now death could be trained upon them, their secret plans betrayed by someone loyal to Gordon Stewart.

Without incident they crossed the narrow causeway, passable on foot at low water, and reached the iron gates of Garth Castle. As if they were expected, those gates swung open and kilted clansmen within the castle walls greeted the invaders jovially. The men marched across the cobbled apron surrounding the castle and inside the outer defenses. The rising wind blew cold off the loch, holding the first sting of rain in its depth.

The gate to the inner courtyard was opened to them and, still without hindrance, the men marched up to the studded oak door leading inside the castle's great hall.

David could not recall a time when he had not dreamed of standing in Garth's courtyard, of touching the rough-hewn stone with his own hands. Yet at this moment all he could think about was their desperate plan and whether it would work.

They entered the castle hall, quickly assessing the number of armed men who stood about the room. The rumor they had heard this morning must be true—Gordon Stewart had sent a third of his small force to neighboring lairds, anxious to learn their sentiments before committing the men of Garth to the Prince's army. By his talebearing Daft Dougal had unwittingly done them an even greater favor.

Overhead the gray arched ceiling was low, formed of slabs of hewn rock, which jutted roughly from its surface. No adornment graced the hall's bare walls or softened the stone-flagged floor. Several chairs upholstered in red velvet, two camp chairs, and a long oak table comprised the hall's sparse furnishings.

On one of these velvet upholstered chairs, set atop a short flight of stone steps, which formed a dais, sat a spare, gray-haired man dressed in tartan coat and trews and wearing a blue bonnet to which were pinned a silver oakleaf crest and three feathers. Gordon Stewart had been expecting them.

"What brings you here this gloomy morning, Tam?" asked Stewart, stepping down from his throne. He fixed a smile on his thin mouth, quickly glancing toward the two dozen men stationed about the hall to reassure himself it was safe to approach the clansmen. "I see ye're all done out for fighting, lads."

"Aye, and fighting we aim to do," said Tam, bending the knee out of habit to his laird.

"Isn't it the laird's place to call out his men?"

"Then why have ye not? We've had Ardshiel's summons for two days."

"What's the hurry? Before we act we must see where our neighbor's sympathies lie. Charles Stewart is not our chief—he's only the lad's tutor. Let's not forget that." Eyes narrowing, Gordon Stewart asked suspiciously, "Think you to better yourselves by declaring for Ardshiel over me?"

"Nay, we were just wondering if ye were man enough to fight," declared an anonymous voice from the rear of the armed delegation.

Anger whitening his face, Gordon Stewart walked toward them, stopping short of mingling with the surly clansmen. He motioned for his armed retainers to move closer. At his bidding a dozen men came out from the gloomy corners of the room to await further orders.

"'Tis a serious charge to call your laird a coward," spat Gordon Stewart, drawing his sparse frame to its full height.

For the first time, David gazed full upon his uncle, experiencing all the loathing he had been conditioned to feel at the sight of his father's murderer. His hand quivered over his dirk and Kenneth MacColl laid a restraining hand on his arm. To his relief David saw Gordon Stewart bore no resemblance to his father's portrait, for Gordon had been only half-brother to Somerled. Gray-haired, sharp-featured, his eyes steely blue,

Gordon reminded him not at all of his father, a fact for which he was grateful. He had always wondered how he would be able to kill someone who resembled the painted likeness in his mother's treasured locket. A strangely unsettling thought struck him as he watched Gordon Stewart conversing with his men: murderer though he was, this gray-haired man was his only living blood relative on either side of the Channel, unless he counted these clansmen, bound by ancient kinship and loyalty to the Stewarts, though often bearing different names.

The muted strains of bagpipes echoed over the water, the sound growing louder by the minute. Gordon Stewart glanced quickly toward the open door, a scowl of displeasure on his sharp face as a piper entered the hall and stopped in the doorway. To his amazement, the man ignored his command to desist.

By prearranged signal, while most eyes were on the piper who continued to play, amazing the assembly by his disobedience, two MacColls, two Carmichaels, and assorted MacLeays and Stewarts moved behind Gordon Stewart's loyal followers.

Suddenly a bloodcurdling yell echoed through the vast stone hall; it was Callum Stewart, giving the battle cry. Gordon Stewart's startled men were seized from behind and those who resisted were immediately dispatched. Kenneth MacColl had stepped unnoticed behind Gordon Stewart and in that first wave of confusion grabbed him, locking his arm about his chest, a dagger poised at his throat.

Eyes wide with terror, Gordon screamed for help. Two men ran forward and were stabbed immediately. All the time the piper continued to play as swords clashed and daggers found their mark, the rousing music stirring men's blood and strengthening their resolve to avenge old injustices. A group of clansmen ran from the hall up the narrow stair to the guardroom, to dispatch what few soldiers Gordon Stewart held there in reserve.

"What's the meaning of this? I never said I'd not come out. You're insane! How dare you lay a hand on your laird—release me at once, and at least you'll be assured of death with dignity," Gordon Stewart growled at brawny Kenneth MacColl.

"The meaning, Gordon Stewart, is that you're no longer laird of Garth."

His blue eyes rolled upward to encounter David standing before him. Kenneth MacColl chuckled in amusement at his captive's shock as, vastly enjoying the coward's fear, the brawny Highlander raised his dagger another notch, drawing a trace of blood on Gordon's sagging ash-gray skin.

"Who are you to dare such treachery?"

Kenneth MacColl clapped a huge hand over Gordon's mouth, silencing him efficiently. "Now listen to the laddie," he commanded with satisfaction, "and ye'll find out."

"You're no stranger to treachery, for 'tis how you engineered my father's death. You betrayed him because you coveted this land. Other men were later pardoned and he might have been also, had you not produced forged testimony against him. I'm David, son of Somerled, here to reclaim my birthright."

As he spoke David drew his sword.

Eyes gleaming with the light of battle, Kenneth MacColl released his captive, eager for the swordplay to begin.

Hesitating, until he realized he could not avoid clashing swords with this shocking reminder from the past, Gordon Stewart struggled to draw the sword still hanging at his side. With a furious oath he leaped forward and engaged David in combat.

Men jumped back, clearing the way. While they fought a cheer rose from the kitchens when the servants were told their laird's cruel reign was over. The sound further enraged Gordon Stewart and he plunged forward, lunging furiously at David, slicing the bonnet from his head. Now David found his range and the swords clashed repeatedly as they parried and thrust, moving back and forth, intently watching each other. Violently cursing his existence, Gordon Stewart renewed his attack on his nephew, allowing emotion to overpower his skill. David kept tight control on his feelings, wary of unleashing the rage which bubbled inside him at the sight of his father's murderer. A cool head and a swift hand were needed to vanquish the enemy, and this morning he had both.

Gordon Stewart soon began to tire, and once he almost stumbled to his knees. Up again, he leaped about panting, more wary now of this opponent, who he realized was not an unschooled clansman in frayed jacket and worn plaid, but a welltrained swordsman who demanded his most expert handling.

The duelers moved back and forth until Gordon mounted the lower step, considering the added height an advantage. He already knew that if this duel was not soon over he would lose. Desperately he roared for aid from his retainers, who watched from the shadows, refusing to assist him. No longer restrained by the clansmen, they had simply decided to change sides.

"You cowards! You sons of dogs! Have ye no loyalty?" he bellowed, his face white with fury.

"Our loyalty's to Somerled's son," shouted one of his men, whose mouth streamed blood.

"Treacherous dogs! You knew my garrison was gone. You knew I had but a handful of men to protect me," screamed Gordon, losing control as he saw all his ill-gotten gains slipping away. The land he had schemed and murdered for was being stolen from him by this foreign-accented young puppy who might or might not have Somerled's cursed blood in his veins.

"Had ye a thousand men, they'd not support you against Somerled's lad, Gordon Stewart, their memories are too long for that. There are too many raped women, too many thieveries of cattle and land, too much cheating on rents—your tacksmen are even now meeting in the village and all have vowed allegiance to David Stewart."

This final appalling news made Gordon careless and he looked away, leaving himself open to the swift slice of David's sword. With a cry of pain he clutched his shoulder and fell to his knees, his sword flying from his hands.

"Finish him, lad, dinna let him live," cried a dozen voices as the bloodthirsty Highlanders crowded around for the kill.

David stood there, his sword poised above Gordon Stewart's scraggy neck, thoughts of the past and of the future coursing through his brain. This was the man who had robbed him of both land and father, stealing his birthright and widowing his mother. This man had laid waste to villages, rousing his tenants' hatred until they refused to support him against a stranger from across the sea. The rage bubbling in his breast gradually subsided as he finally saw Gordon Stewart for what he was—an old man, the burden of years apparent on his ashen face as he gazed fearfully at the victor, awaiting the coup de grâce. Why did he not press his advantage? Why did he not avenge his father's murder? David stared down at this pitiful old man, hated and despised, who had lost everything in this blood-spattered hall. And he could not kill him.

With a shuddering intake of breath, David stepped back and sheathed his sword. A disappointed chorus greeted his action, but the clansmen would not openly dispute their laird's decision.

"I haven't the stomach to kill an old man. Get up, Gordon

Stewart, and thank God I showed you more mercy than you ever showed my father. I curse you forever for causing his death, but I cannot cause yours. You're free to go in peace."

A gasp went up in the hall, and men looked askance at each other, wondering at the wisdom of their young laird's words.

"You have much compassion," Gordon Stewart ground out at last between clenched teeth as he grasped his bleeding wound.

"Your injuries shall be dressed and I'll give you a horse, a basket of provisions, and two body servants," David said coldly, averting his gaze as the bleeding man struggled to his feet.

"By God, you're a generous man, David Stewart."

David gritted his teeth at Gordon Stewart's sarcasm. "Go, before I forget whose son I am and take the vengeance that is rightfully mine."

Chapter 9

Catrin stood on the bank of the loch and gazed across the ruffled water to the distant, cloud-wreathed mountains of Mull and Morvern where wild goats roamed the misty crags. Closer at hand, drowsing in the dusk, lay the black outline of Castle Stalker, stronghold of the hereditary chiefs of the Stewarts of Appin.

This beautiful, mist-steeped land of rain, mountain, and bog, populated by a fiercely loyal and warlike people, was not as she had imagined the Scottish Highlands. Nor was life at brooding Garth Castle quite as she had expected. It was a primitive fortress raked by cold winds off the loch; the bare stone walls were unadorned, the floors uncovered, even the fireplaces failed to draw properly and so the rooms were always filled with smoke. Once the castle had been taken, Catrin had imagined an idyllic time shared with her devoted lover. And, while not expecting to be surrounded by luxury, she had at least assumed the existence of a few of life's softening pleasures. How different from her fantasies was the reality of life at Garth. But she would have cheerfully endured those harsh realities if David had given her more attention.

She sighed and began to walk along the loch. Tears filled her eyes and splashed inside the neck of her gown. At least she had been able to exchange her ragged finery for something which, if not as grand, was clean and in good repair. Dressed in this dark blue wool gown, a wool plaid draped about her shoulders to keep off the chill of the Scottish summer dusk, she looked a typical laird's wife. More self-pitying tears came and she angrily brushed them away. David had little time for her now he was laird of Garth. His hours were spent visiting his tenants, listening to the endless litany of injustices they had suffered under Gordon Stewart—wrongs he intended to right—and preparing his army for war.

Not that David no longer loved her; it was merely that reclaiming his birthright was the most important thing in his life. Catrin had begun to feel she was a poor second. And he still had not told his people that he and Catrin were not legally man and wife. When she had mentioned this to him he grew angry, saying he had enough on his hands without the whining of a discontented woman. So Catrin prudently held her tongue.

Two herons stood gracefully outlined at the edge of the water and birds twittered from the branches of a rowan heavy with scarlet berries. From an outcropping of rocks on the hillside sloping to the loch came the mews of wildcat kits. Apart from this, the lonely lochside lay silent. It was unthinkable that this remote and peaceful land might soon be filled with the sounds of war, or that these simple clansmen, who for the most part had never left their picturesque glens, could soon die. The silent permanence of mountain and lake suggested peace inviolate, yet Catrin knew such security was merely illusion. She was relieved that her premonition concerning this place had been unfounded—David's takeover of Garth could not have gone more smoothly—yet, as she reviewed her feelings, she was worried to find that sense of foreboding unchanged.

A rising breeze suddenly ruffled the water, sending lapping waves against the shoreline and startling the wading herons. Even the wildcat kits became strangely quiet, as if this majestic land were awaiting some great awakening—or could it be an impending tragedy?

"There you are!"

Catrin spun about to see David trotting down the rocky incline to the loch shore on a huge black stallion, newly acquired from Gordon Stewart's stable. She stood in a trance, unable to shake her melancholy mood; she was so slow to move that before she could collect herself he was already out of the saddle and striding toward her across the shingle. With a sigh, Catrin surrendered her fears to the comfort of his arms as David swept her from her feet.

"Oh, sweetheart, I've missed you so much," he whispered

tenderly, his lips lingering on her hair.

"David, please, hold me close, hold me."

"What is it?"

"I'm afraid."

"Why? The land is mine, everything went better than even I dreamed possible. Don't be afraid now we're on the threshold of glory."

"You sound like Ness."

"I'm a happy, optimistic man, not a reckless dreamer. Why are you sad?"

It seemed foolish to admit to unknown fears when she was safe in his arms, when her face rested against his and the exciting pulsing of his veins thundered in turn with her own. The temptation to cast aside her fears, not to own to this premonition of doom, was strong.

"Is it this place?" he demanded sharply, glancing about the deserted loch shore. "Surely to God you haven't the second sight, as my people call it."

So distressed did he look, his mouth tight, his eyes narrowed, that Catrin deliberately shrugged off her fears and sadness to set him at ease. She would be a fool to doom his venture from the start, for there was more of the superstitious Gael about David Stewart than he chose to admit.

"Perhaps it's just lonely beside the water. When I felt like this that first day, I thought you'd be hurt retaking Garth, but you see how wrong I was. Oh, David, just love me. I'm growing morbid because I've spent so many hours alone in this place listening to a language I don't understand."

He smiled and stroked her soft cheek. "Sweet, I apologize for leaving you to your own devices, but there was so much unfinished business. Tonight I intend to remedy that. I'll not even give audience to a courier if he thunders on the castle door."

They laughed and wrapped their arms about each other's waist as they strolled along the silvery shore, frequently stopping to kiss, each embrace growing longer and more passionate.

"I'd thought to make you my wife before we left Garth. Now we must wait. There's not a priest available to perform the ceremony at such short notice. Do you mind living in sin with me a little longer?" he asked huskily, drawing her down beside him on the purple heather-covered bank.

"A ceremony means no more than the vows we've already made to each other. Your people already believe us to be wed."

David smiled and he kissed her brow. "Aye, but my 'people' have a rather casual approach to marriage. Handfasting is still a common practice here. We stay together for a year and, at the end of that time, if there are no babes, and we both agree, each is free to go his or her own way. What think you of that?"

"It's sensible if both parties agree. It certainly makes more sense than childhood marriage contracts. Why have we need of formality, David Stewart? I thought your vow to love me forever was binding."

Her answer was a chuckle as he drew her close and showered her with kisses. The intoxication of his nearness was working its power on Catrin as she struggled to keep her senses, fighting against the softening heat that consumed her thighs and burned through her belly as he drew his fingers gently over her wool bodice, bringing her nipples erect.

"Oh, damn you, David Stewart," she hissed. "I'm a helpless fool when you start to work your magic."

"I was beginning to wonder if I'd lost my touch," he confessed huskily as he fondled the soft prominence of her breasts beneath the wool plaid. "You were sounding so serious. In fact, I've seen little of you lately when you weren't either serious or asleep."

Catrin lunged at him, cuffing him across the ear. The blow was light, but it stung and his angry reaction was to pin her beneath him in the heather, crushing her deep into its springy surface.

"Now I'll teach you a lesson, Catrin Blair, or Stewart, whichever you prefer. A good laird's wife doesn't strike her husband. She's subservient to him in every way."

Ignoring Catrin's indignant snort, he spread her hands wide, pinning her there while he bent to kiss her mouth. His tongue broke the resistance of her clenched lips, his teeth forcing against hers until he invaded the hot sweet moistness of her mouth. Still not releasing her hands, he traced a passage to her soft white neck and shoulders, exposed now the plaid was thrust aside. Moving lower, he pressed the moist warmth of his mouth over her breasts until she squirmed and moaned, desperate to take him in her arms. Punishing her in this delightful manner, with his knee David pushed up her skirts and pressed high between her thighs, gently rotating the pressure. They were both highly aware of the searing heat of his own increasing arousal.

Tears gathered in her eyes and spilled into her hair as Catrin's emotion increased to fever pitch. "Please, David, let me hold you close," she whispered brokenly.

"Say you love me forever, whether we are wed or nay."

"I swear it. You are my true husband now and forever."

He gazed down at her. How beautiful she looked, her face silvered by the light of the rising moon. She lay helpless beneath him in the heather like some lovely pagan captive. And a primitive part of him was highly aroused by the thought. Though David was many generations removed from his ancestors the Gaels, that same love of plunder, the wild, primitive arousal of taking captive flickered in him still. So must Appin men have brought women here in the mists of antiquity and mated with them in the heather beneath the moon.

The strange expression on David's face made Catrin tremble as she gazed up at him. The pale moon, risen in a dusky sky that never really grew black at this time of year, cast an unearthly glow over the loch and its shore. The summer night was sweet with the fragrance of heather, grasses, wild flowers, and herbs. She listened to the gentle lap of water and David's harsh breathing, aware she would never forget this magical night on the shore of the loch.

"David," she whispered, afraid, yet strangely excited by his face. "What is it?"

He had released her hands and she touched his cheek, surprised to find the flesh warm and alive. Grimly David caught the soft hand that caressed him and pressed his burning mouth against her palm.

"For as long as I live, Catrin, I'll love no other," he vowed intensely, his face somber. "Though we both took roundabout paths, we've found a home at last in each other's heart."

"Oh, sweetheart, I love you so much."

Their shadows mingled fiercely as they clung together, suddenly afraid this might be their final bliss. Mouths and hearts cried out in the intensity of their emotion as his tears mingled with hers. Though they had thought to make endless love beneath the moon, so desperate did they become, their flesh almost caught fire.

The gold talisman David now wore around his neck pressed against Catrin's breasts as he kissed her deeply. She wept and could not stop. How she ached to become one with him, never to have to kiss him goodbye. Her hands shook as she stroked his hot shoulders beneath his unbuttoned shirt, as he slid her hands over his firm buttocks in the tartan trews, molded lovingly to his muscular thighs. He was like a god and his passion, his love, had in some blasphemous way become her religion. Perhaps, at some later time, she would pay dearly for this passion, but Catrin did not intend to relinquish one moment of ecstasy. David Stewart was her life—his lovemaking her sustenance.

"Never stop loving me. Oh, David, David, I couldn't bear it. I ache for you . . . sweetheart . . ."

David never allowed her to finish her impassioned speech, silencing her words with his mouth. He fondled her full breasts, pleased by the tremors she took no pains to hide. Of her own accord Catrin sought the strength of his passion, her grip crushing as her fingers closed, viselike, about his swelling flesh. In this state of maximum arousal David felt no pain beyond that of denial. He finally allowed their naked flesh to touch, to caress in passionate overture. Tonight, however, he did not wait for her to clasp him and drive him to the haft within the heated passion of her body; so aroused was he, so painful his shudders of repressed desire, he blazed inside her as if she were truly his captive and he her conqueror, enacting an ancient rite beneath the moon.

Catrin cried out in intense pleasure. Her muscles flexed and held him fast, crushing, devouring that heated pleasure he sometimes withheld until the last, taking all of him for her immediate delight. Her hands went into his crisp black hair, fastening his mouth to hers. So demanding were his kisses, David bruised her lips, yet Catrin strained upward, seeking more, matching the unity of mouths and bodies. There was no directing him now, for he had cast aside the measured pace of lovemaking. Raw passion seized him and he bore her away from that time and place, spearing her into eternity on the consuming flame of generation. Here, on the silvery shores of Loch Linnhe beneath a cold three quarter moon, their hearts, their bodies, and their souls became one single molten being.

Memories of that beautiful, magical night, when the summer moon must have made them both insane, filled her mind as Catrin mounted her horse before gloomy Garth Castle on that chill September morning. David rode from rank to rank, assembling his men for the journey. Word had been received that support for the cause was growing daily, and that the Prince intended to take Edinburgh and establish a court within the city. Now, instead of heading for Lochaber, they intended to go to Edinburgh. Ardshiel and the main body of Appin Stewarts had left to join the Prince's army weeks ago; the clansmen of Garth were the final contingent from the banks of Loch Linnhe and Loch Creran to rally to the Jacobite cause.

Dressing in his tartan trews, blue velvet coat, and bonnet, a heavy wool plaid fastened at the shoulder by an ancient cairngorm and silver brooch, David looked every inch the Scottish laird. Catrin found it hard to remember that a few months before he had been a gentleman of Rome, fluent in Italian and well versed in the customs of that land. She, too, had been Roman many years ago, yet she had found adjusting to life in England far more difficult than David did to life among his clansmen. So diverse were their backgrounds, she had wondered uneasily if these Scots would still follow their laird's son once they recovered from their initial joy of deliverance from Gordon Stewart's tyranny. She had reckoned without David's natural ability to command men. Without question they followed him, not out of fear, but out of love and respect. He was a born leader, and his service in the French army had also made him conversant with warfare and soldiering. Though he was not familiar with the clansmen's weapons, David had swiftly mastered the art of fighting with leather targes and Highland dags and dirks. His diligence had earned the men's respect. To a man they were willing to lay down their lives for him.

David cantered to Catrin's side and for one final time turned to look at Garth, slumbering peacefully against the background of mountain and loch.

From the tallest tower his father's personal standard flapped in the brisk wind. The Appin flag, a yellow saltire on a blue field, fluttered below the scarlet pennant of Somerled Stewart, depicting an oak spray split by a dirk. The strange device had been inherited from their ancestor, Maxwell Stewart, a natural son of the Wolf of Badenoch, who three hundred years before had constructed his fortress on the shore of this gentle loch.

"Garth was built to last forever."

"And so it shall, sweetheart, passing to our sons and grandsons," Catrin promised, wishing her words were founded on conviction. That morning, as she prepared to leave her adopted land, she was apprehensive of the danger which lay ahead. But she would not stay behind. David had offered her that alternative, which she had flatly refused. Going against his better judgment, which told him a woman was safer at home, he had agreed to let her accompany their troops to Edinburgh.

"After all, what manner of man am I to break a promise? I did offer to take you to Edinburgh," he had joked as he kissed her passionately, his warm embrace comforting in the dark night.

She turned in the saddle to look at him, his countenance stern as he gazed on his inheritance, and morbidly wondered if this would be his last sight of Garth. A chill swept over her as she gazed upon the sheer beauty of her man. No other would ever affect her as he did. It seemed as if she had been in love with him since the first time their eyes met. Perhaps there was something to be said for love at first sight after all.

Birds chirped in the chill air. The clarity of color in this lonely land was dazzling to the eye; blue sky and silver-gray water surrounded by rusting bracken and purple, heather-clad slopes spreading as far as the eye could see. Even the birch trees were tinged with gold and the fronded rowans hung heavy with scarlet berries.

Slowly the procession wound its way along the loch shore. David and Catrin headed the column mounted on Gordon Stewart's best animals; a couple of baggage wagons and two spare mounts came from the same source. The blue-bonneted clansmen strode along in their kilts and plaids, singing to the accompaniment of a piper, who walked behind David's horse playing rousing battle tunes of ancient times.

A flicker of red from behind a stand of birches took Catrin's attention and she was convinced Gordon Stewart watched their departure. There was no reason to think so, for no one had seen the deposed laird since that rainy day when he left, accompanied by his two old servants. David should not have spared him! Would he try to repossess Garth while they were away? Gordon Stewart had no followers to do his bidding, yet there were rumors he courted the grace of the Campbells, the Appin Stewarts' hated enemy to the south.

Their slow journey south across Rannoch Moor, and afterward along the course of the Tay to Perth, took its toll on both humor and strength. Though David did not push his men, several of the older ones were forced to turn back, too feeble to continue. When he saw the unashamed tears in their eyes, when they pleaded to be allowed to go on, his heart twisted, but he stood firm in his decision. He would not kill men before they had even tasted battle.

They traveled through the Ochill Hills, crossing the rolling green lowlands without incident, avoiding the cities of Perth,

Stirling, and Falkirk lest they encounter government troops. Catrin would not have cared if they had taken a year to reach Edinburgh, for she delighted in David's company, in the excitement of shared nights in barns, cottages, and taverns wrapped in the warmth of his heavy plaid, fulfilling her dreams of love. The beauty of their nights made up for the discomforts of long days in the saddle riding through wind and rain, of poor food and clashing tempers.

From Falkirk to Edinburgh they heard news of a battle at a place called Prestonpans. And not merely a battle—the Jacobites had been victorious. Sir John Cope's government troops had been defeated in a matter of minutes, outwitted by the Prince's army, which had surprised them by taking a path through the bog and confronting the Redcoats at sunrise behind their own lines.

News of this victory spurred the flagging spirits of the Garth men, lightening their steps as they swung along the final stretch of road that would bring them within sight of Edinburgh's jumbled rooftops.

Edinburgh's main thoroughfare teemed with people. Narrow stone buildings, some of them nine stories in height, lined the street, their upper wooden galleries, conical turrets, and crow-stepped gables shutting out the light. At street level tradesmen's stalls displayed all manner of goods. This was market day, for makeshift booths had been set up in the lawn market below Castle Hill, overlooked by the massive, impregnable fortress, which had resisted the invading Jacobites. Known as the Royal Mile, this main street began at the castle and ended at the gates of Holyroodhouse.

The cobblestones were an odorous mire of filth and offal. Drovers were bringing slaughter animals to market and the narrow street rang with the grunts and squeals of pigs and the baaing of sheep. Dark wynds and closes led from the street, giving access to dwellings in the rear. Women water caddies, with yoked buckets, and piemen and haggis sellers forced their way through the crowds, their raucous cries adding to the racket.

David was hard pressed to keep his men together, for they stood gaping at the fascinating city sights while the city's inhabitants gaped at them. Since the Prince had entered the capital over a month ago, kilted highlanders in stained plaids, bonnets, and rough deerhide shoes had become a common sight. Yet there were those who still believed the horrible stories of Highlanders who killed children and roasted them over their camp-fires. So, though the wild kilted troops were tolerated, they were always viewed with suspicion.

After making inquiries about the whereabouts of the Prince's army, David learned they were camped outside the city in the village of Duddingston. Each night the Prince returned to his men after holding court in Holyroodhouse. Though some of the army was billeted in Edinburgh and the surrounding villages, the citizenry had not been forced against their will to accommodate the troops.

David found temporary lodgings for Catrin in a tiny fourth-story room in an old bastel house close by the Mercat Cross. She did not want to be separated from him, but he insisted she could not stay at the military camp at Duddingston. And though he did not intend to follow the Prince's example of spending all his nights with his men, he was bound to control his clansmen and keep their morale high. Fortunately, after two miserable days in her draughty, unpleasant lodgings, Catrin was miraculously delivered.

Soon after his arrival David went to Holyroodhouse, anxious to pledge allegiance to Prince Charles. Overjoyed by the sight of his old friend, Charles gave him a private audience, and they discussed the current campaign. Charles quickly revealed his disappointment at the slow enlistment, for he had hoped to have twice the men he now had. To make matters worse, after Prestonpans many Highlanders had taken their loot home and had not yet returned. Knowing that this delay gave the enemy time to regroup after their recent defeat, Charles chafed to be on the march. On the other hand, by staying in the capital he hoped to give the straggling troops time to rejoin his banner and encourage new recruits to enlist.

Their unsettling discussion at an end, Charles inquired about David's fortunes and was pleased by the outcome; he also insisted that David house his lady at a more genteel lodging, giving him an address where several other ladies of quality were staying. That afternoon David went to the address the Prince had given him and to his amazement met Easter and Comyn Stewart entering the residence.

When he returned to his own lodgings he found Catrin wrapped in her plaid, huddled over the grate, where she was trying to warm herself at the meager flame. Feeling sorry for her, David laughingly swept her in his arms.

"You poor, poor girl, what straits I've brought you to! Take heart, I've procured far more luxurious accommodations for us, complete with old friends."

"Old friends?" Catrin cried, hugging him close, excited by his news. "Oh, who?"

"Easter and Comyn Stewart. They tell me your brother's also in town."

Catrin's eyes shone with excitement and she could hardly wait to be installed in their new rooms. All this time she had received no word from either Easter or Ness and she was anxious to know how they were.

Within the half hour she was packed and on her way, virtually running along the congested street, eager to reach her new lodgings. She carried a small bundle of possessions, leaving the rest for David to bring with their horses later that afternoon.

Easter met her at the door and enfolded her in her arms, her eyes shining with tears of joy.

"Oh, Catrin darling. Praise be. When did you arrive in Edinburgh?"

"Two miserable days ago."

"But we heard you were in Liverpool with your aunt."

Catrin grinned. She released Easter and stepped back to examine her friend, pleased to find her looking far healthier than she had been at their last meeting. Easter's face was still thin, but there was a bloom on her cheeks and the dark hollows beneath her eyes had gone. From her shabby appearance, however, Catrin concluded money was still no more plentiful.

"Your news is out of date, Easter. Oh, there's so much to tell you, I don't know where to begin."

Inside the pleasant parlor of their rented apartment, Comyn greeted Catrin like an old friend. She was surprised to see how much older he appeared since he had been about the Prince's business. Over glasses of Madeira and slices of meat pasty followed by a dark fruit-filled bannock, the women excitedly exchanged news. When Catrin revealed she was living with David Stewart, Easter was unable to hide her surprise. Yet neither did she withhold her approval, for, despite her ragged appearance and unkempt hair, Catrin had never looked so radiant.

"I should have known you wouldn't be able to hold out against his famous charm," was all Easter said, catching her husband's eye and shaking her head when he would have said more.

Catrin leaned back in the brocade upholstered chair and looked around the comfortably furnished room with satisfaction. Though the lodgings were modest, the windows fitted well and the fire drew, the bed appeared clean and comfortable, and the tables and chairs managed to rest all four feet on the floor at the same time.

"David said Ness is in Edinburgh. Where is he? I haven't spoken to him since Papa threw him out of the house. Easter, I'm so sorry for what happened that day. With Ness's reputation, I suppose you can't blame Papa for thinking him at fault, yet he's so stubborn, he wouldn't let me explain. I expect he's disinherited me too, now that I've disappointed him. Aunt Isobel will have given him a lurid account of my sinful departure for parts unknown."

Comyn smiled, somewhat amused by Catrin's breathless account of her adventures. He still wore his light hair unpowdered and tied back with a ribbon. Though of fine cut, his clothing was shabby. Absently tucking the frayed edge of his cravat beneath his lapel, Comyn said, "Ness should be back soon—he'll certainly be surprised to find you here. I'm afraid we're rather crowded with just two rooms. You and the laird can use the other room; it's smaller than this, but it has a fireplace and a comfortable bed."

Catrin thanked Comyn for his generosity, explaining that David would probably spend much of his time at the Duddingston camp.

The baby awoke then, and Catrin scooped the squirming bundle out of his cradle beside the hearth, somewhat startled to find Douglas hardly bigger than he had been when she first saw him. Hiding her surprise, Catrin cuddled the infant close, whispering endearments to him. A fleeting smile crossed his pinched face before he began to whimper for his mother.

Easter nursed her baby, but even milk did not satisfy him for long and he continued to wail and fret. It was some time before Douglas was pacified sufficiently for them to be able to resume their conversation. In the meantime Comyn had left the house, ostensibly to meet with some of the Prince's officers at the nearby White Horse Inn, but Catrin suspected the baby's incessant wails had driven him out.

"Is Douglas sickly?" Catrin ventured, as Easter tirelessly rocked the protesting bundle.

"He's never been much of an eater. Being so tiny, the poor mite had a bad start in life. It's a miracle he's survived. We pray he'll grow stronger," was all she said.

Tears filled Easter's eyes when she spoke about her baby, and Catrin decided the subject would be better left alone. She began to question Easter about Holyroodhouse and the Prince's court, in an attempt to divert her friend's attention.

"The court's quite spectacular, I'm told. One constant round of grandly dressed guests. We're invited there tonight and will have to accept lest His Highness be offended. Mrs. Brodie, the landlady, kindly offered to watch the bairn for a few hours. Will you come with us, Catrin, you and . . . David?" Easter still found it difficult to call him anything besides "the laird."

"I'd love to, but I'm afraid His Highness would have me thrown out. He'd think a begger maid had come calling," Catrin protested, her hand flying to her tangled hair. "Sleeping in barns and out in the open didn't prepare me to meet royalty."

"Nonsense. Once Douglas is asleep, we'll work together to make you presentable. His Highness will understand your situation—they say he's a generous, uncritical man. My sister's bound to have a spare gown to fit you."

"Sister!" Catrin exclaimed in surprise, racking her brain to recall Easter's family. "Oh, yes, the carroty-haired pest who plagued us to death."

Easter laughed. "Brenda—though I guarantee she's no carroty-haired pest these days. She's twenty-three and a flame-haired beauty. We've got to brush the men away with a broom. She arrived unexpectedly on our doorstep, having traveled alone from Rome, eager to get in on the excitement. Comyn would like to see her married off, though Brenda's not likely to settle for one man when she can have a dozen."

Somehow this unexpected news about Brenda Carmichael's presence in Edinburgh made Catrin uneasy. The chubby, red-haired child she remembered would have been no threat, but the grown-up Brenda sounded quite ravishing. She was not anxious to have a rival under their own roof. Like most men, David was susceptible to feminine charm, and Brenda probably shared her sister's love and devotion to their young laird.

Dusk was settling over the Cannongate when a commotion at the street door announced the arrival of guests.

"That's likely Ness," Easter said, jumping to her feet. "I hope he's brought Brenda with him. Though she argues the point, I don't think it wise for her to roam the town alone."

Catrin was eager to greet her brother, yet she decided it would be a far greater surprise if she waited upstairs for him.

With Easter's help she had washed her hair and dried it before the hearth. In her plain blue gown, her narrow plaid about her shoulders, Catrin typified the demure laird's wife she someday aspired to be. As she waited beside the hearth for Ness to arrive, she forced herself to remain composed, smiling as she considered his surprise at finding her here.

The door opened and five people came inside the room. The draught from the door set the candle flames dancing, casting gigantic shadows across floors and ceiling.

"Oh, you've got a guest, Easter, you should have told me," cried Ness, his hale and hearty manner evidently the result of an afternoon's drinking.

"She's someone who'd like to meet you."

"Well, by Jove, introduce us. I'm always interested in lovely ladies."

Ness stepped toward her and Catrin lifted her head and smiled up at him. "Hello, brother," she said.

His total surprise, followed by a slowly dawning smile, was a response worth waiting for. Catrin leaped to her feet and Ness threw his arms about her, laughing in delight.

"By all that's holy, Catrin! How did you get here? I thought you still at Isobel's. Surely you didn't travel alone—demme, sis, you didn't, did you?" he demanded, pushing her slightly away from him as he treated her to a stern frown.

"No, silly, not alone. Though had I a mind to, I could've traveled the distance. Just because I'm a woman doesn't mean I'm helpless."

Ness grinned as he slid his arm about his sister's shoulders. "Let's drink to my lovely Catrin, the best surprise of the week— after Brenda, of course," Ness added with a wink.

From the group crowding the doorway, a woman's laughter tinkled out.

"You're a gallant courtier, Ness Blair, but a terrible liar. Wasn't it you whom I saw with both Jenny Menzies and Maggie Colquhoun swaggering down the Cannongate large as life? You didn't act as if you were giving me a single thought."

Ness grinned sheepishly as a cloaked figure stepped toward the hearth.

"You're a heartless wretch, Brenda Carmichael, revealing my darkest secrets to my sister and her not here a day."

Brenda laughed and tossed back her dark hood to reveal a mass of red-gold curls tumbling about her shoulders. Her long, fine-boned face bore little resemblance to the snub-nosed, freckled tomboy of Catrin's memory, though the milk-white, translucent skin stretched over high cheekbones gave a hint of freckles across the bridge of her nose. Gone was the wiry tomboyish body, replaced now by voluptuous curves, while Brenda's flaring nostrils and bold, green eyes gave her an intriguing worldly quality.

"So you're Ness's sister. I can see the resemblance. Did you also come to Edinburgh for the excitement?"

When their gaze met, Brenda Carmichael had a sweet smile on her full pink mouth, but her eyes were hard. Catrin swallowed, taken back by the hostility that passed between them. Brenda must also sense a rival.

"I came to Edinburgh with my—" Catrin paused, unsure how to explain David to them.

Ness leaned closer, his brows drawing together. "Your what?"

"Catrin came here with the laird," Easter explained shyly, as she poked the fire. "His takeover of Garth is complete and now we're free to go home. Isn't that wonderful?"

Brenda smiled tightly at her sister's words. "Our laird . . . David Stewart?"

Forcing a smile Catrin nodded. "Yes, we're traveling together."

Ness's indrawn breath, followed by a muttered oath, showed his displeasure over the news, but he did not pursue the subject. The three army officers were preparing to leave, though they would all meet later at the Prince's reception in Holyroodhouse.

Barely had the officers' clanging boots and spurs receded before Ness rounded on Catrin in anger. "What's this? You're traveling with David Stewart? Am I dreaming . . . that is what you said?"

"Yes, that's what I said." She looked him directly in the eye, not expecting such emotion.

Diplomatically, Brenda withdrew to the sideboard, where she poured herself a glass of Madeira while keeping a watchful eye on the couple before the hearth.

"How can that be?"

"I left Liverpool with him. He was my means of escape."

"Left with him? You mean you're living with him as his . . . his . . . woman?"

Her cheeks flushed, but Catrin did not look away. "We intend to be married."

"But are not yet?"

"No."

Ness seized her wrist. "By Christ, I don't believe this. Aren't you aware of his reputation? You little fool, how can you be taken in by him? How can you believe . . . where is he? We'll soon settle this."

"There's nothing to settle. Stay out of it! My life's my own."

"Oh, indeed, you never expressed that sentiment when we discussed my life, sister dear. My habits seemed ever open to public criticism . . ."

"Stop it! There's no need to make a scene," Catrin hissed, embarrassed to think the others were listening. "Let it go. We'll discuss the matter another time."

"Damn it, Catrin, I should call him out, defend my sister's honor. He's got women in every town, every country, always has had. I'd have thought you'd have more sense than to fall for a man like that."

"Sense had nothing to do with it," she hissed in reply as heavy footsteps sounded on the stair. "Promise not to embarrass me further. There's nothing you can do now; it's far too late. I've no wish to have you defend my honor. David and I are in love and intend to be married. Surely you prefer him to Bryce Cavendish as a brother-in-law."

"Touché—you know how much I despise that pompous Hanoverian ass. I suppose any Jacobite dog, regardless of his morals, would be preferable to him."

Bristling with anger Catrin countered, "Morals—on what authority do you preach morals to me, brother? You, who have barely a notion of the meaning of the word. I'll have no more of it. David's laird of Garth and a trusted officer of the Prince. You'd do well to remember that and accept what you cannot change with a good grace. I'm no longer your baby sister— I'm a woman with a life of my own to lead."

Her final statement, delivered in an angry undertone, co-incided with the opening of the door. Comyn and David came inside the room and Easter breathed an audible sigh of relief.

"David Stewart! What a wonderful surprise. Fancy being in the same room as the handsomest man in all Scotland," Brenda cried, racing across the room to embrace him.

"Brenda Carmichael! The last time I saw you was in Rome— you were riding in the duke's carriage. Did you grow bored with him?"

Brenda smiled, but David's reminiscence did not please her.

"Vincenzo was always boring ... it was only his money I found amusing."

David chuckled at her honest answer. "Ah, well, at least we have the truth. As I've little money to speak of, I trust I'm safe from your wiles."

"Some men don't need money to be interesting," Brenda said throatily, before she flounced away with a coquettish show of slim ankles encased in red silk stockings. She crossed to the sideboard to pour wine for the men.

"Catrin, sweet—and Ness! I haven't seen you since London. Are things moving fast enough for you these days?"

His expression surly, Ness nodded, briefly shaking David's hand. "Things fare well enough," he muttered, glancing at his sister, who gave him a warning look. "You surprised me by bringing Catrin to Edinburgh. She tells me you two are to wed. Is this so?"

"Yes. We intended to wed before leaving Garth, but circumstance forbade. I apologize for seeming to have abducted your lovely sister, though I promise she came with me of her own free will. We met purely by chance in Liverpool—there were no elaborate plans to deceive. And I do intend to make an honest woman of her, Ness, rest assured."

Though he did not accept David's explanation with a good grace, Ness said no more. When he finally picked up his cloak preparatory to leaving, Catrin was vastly relieved.

"Will you come to the palace tonight, Catrin? I'm sure my sister would be welcome," he said gruffly.

"Thank you, Ness. We'll see you there."

Ness nodded to David and Catrin; then, bidding the others goodnight, he slammed the door and thundered downstairs.

"Don't fret, sweet, he'll be all right once he gets over the shock," David soothed, taking Catrin's hand, his eyes soft. Fool that he was, he had not given much thought to her brother's reaction. He should have spoken to Ness privately first and prepared him for reality.

"I don't care what he thinks," Catrin declared bravely, staring ahead through burning tears. But she lied.

Chapter 10

Holyroodhouse stood at the eastern end of Edinburgh's four connecting streets known as the Royal Mile. The palace, set in a wooded park, was adjacent to the ruined abbey of the holy rood; to the east lay the village of Duddingston, where the bulk of the Jacobite army was camped.

Tonight the great palace was ablaze with light as Prince Charles Edward Louis Philippe Casimir Stuart held court as regent for his father, the newly acclaimed King James III. A constant stream of well-dressed men and women flocked to the grand levees and councils held at the palace. While many came to pledge themselves to the cause, others came out of curiosity, eager for a glimpse of the fabled "Bonnie Prince."

The walk to Holyroodhouse from the Cannongate was short. The small party set out in good spirits, cloaked against the elements, for the night was chill; before they reached the Abbey Strand it began to spit rain. David and Catrin led the way, with Comyn and Easter close behind them. Brenda, who was escorted by one of the Prince's lifeguards, lagged behind, laughing and making jests, causing passersby to stare at her.

Wherever she went Brenda greedily claimed attention, regarding it as her due and sulking if it was withheld. It had not taken Catrin long to realize this, or that Brenda ventured to few places unless accompanied by an attractive male. The discovery that Brenda had set her cap at David had come as an unpleasant shock. Catrin would have had to be blind not to notice Brenda's inviting glances, or the laughing innuendoes

that peppered her speech. In Rome they might merely have
been friends, but Catrin was convinced that Brenda intended
a far more intimate relationship.

It was raining heavily when they hurried across the palace
forecourt. Holyroodhouse was entered through an elegant fa-
cade linking two massive turreted towers, which gave access
to the quadrangle known as the inner court. Eager to make
himself available to the ordinary people of Edinburgh, Prince
Charles did not maintain strict security. The guards stationed
at the entrance allowed most guests to pass unchallenged. Even
rumors that an attempt was to be made on his life were ignored
by the Prince, who placed too high a value on his relationship
with his Highlanders to surround himself with bodyguards. The
proud clansmen would have been insulted had it been suggested
their Prince needed guarding from them.

The reception was held in the impressive, hundred-and-fifty-
foot-long white and gold picture gallery. The room's splendid
molded ceiling and wall panels formed a rich background for
the sumptuously dressed, bejeweled ladies and gentlemen who
chatted and laughed beneath vast crystal chandeliers burning
with many candles. The walls were lined with portraits of a
hundred and eleven Scottish kings and queens painted by the
Dutchman De Witt. Undaunted by the fact that many of his
subjects possessed no known likeness—some, for that matter,
may never even have existed—De Witt cleverly invented distinctive features to promote a sense of unbroken bloodline.

David told Catrin about the pictures as they slowly worked
their way through the press of people milling about the room.
The Prince himself had told him the story, amused by the idea
of Jacob De Witt producing Stuart ancestors to order for the
modest sum of one hundred and twenty pounds a year.

The hooped ballgown Catrin had borrowed from Brenda
was of moss-green silk worn open over an embroidered petticoat; the stomacher was trimmed with a ladder of violet bows.
A cluster of her shining chestnut ringlets was caught at the
back of her head by a posy of artificial flowers. By her previous
standards Catrin's dress was simple, yet she rejoiced in the
sheer luxury of being clean, scented, and attractively dressed.
She knew Brenda begrudged lending her the gown, and had
she not considered her own to be far more noticeable she probably would have refused to.

Brenda wore sapphire blue satin laced with silver, a glorious
creation that would not have been out of place at court in

London. Her hooped satin skirts shimmered as she moved and the bodice fit so close the fabric appeared to have been sculpted to her full breasts. The color was a perfect foil for Brenda's flaming hair, which she wore in a chignon topped by a scintillating tiara. The sparkling stones could have been paste, yet Catrin thought they were probably diamonds from a rich admirer. Vanity got the better of loyalty, and Brenda had not donated her jewelry to the cause as had many other Jacobite ladies. Anger and more than a little jealousy made Catrin envious of the tall redhead, for she still regretted having to part with her lovely amethyst necklace.

"Don't you think Brenda's the prettiest woman here?" Catrin said, a trifle peevishly, as she saw David's gaze straying in that direction.

"After you, yes," he agreed, wisely refusing to be drawn into a dispute. "I suspect Brenda intends to snare His Highness, but I'm afraid her hopes are in vain."

"Has he a mistress then?"

"None other than the cause. Though he's charmingly attentive and much admired by women, Charles has little use for them. They say that side of his nature has been somewhat underdeveloped. Many Edinburgh women are eager to tempt him, yet so far he's not even danced with them."

Catrin digested this surprising fact, recalling the lively young prince of her girlhood who had delighted in dancing before an enraptured court.

The crowd parted, presenting a glimpse of the Prince's blond wig before the heads moved again to block their vision. The Prince, however, had already spotted his old friend and his command rang out in a clear, cultured voice with an Italian accent.

"Make way for my dear friend, Stewart of Garth."

Like the Red Sea the crowd parted, all eyes on the stranger, curious and most envious of this newcomer who immediately had the Prince's ear.

David stepped forward and bowed before his prince—he did not kneel, like many who curried favor. "Your Highness, you are indeed holding a royal court. It took us ten minutes to get this far."

Charles laughed as he extended his hand before turning to look at the woman standing behind David. Catrin sank into a deep curtsy.

"So this is your lovely lady. You've chosen well," the Prince observed pleasantly, offering his hand for Catrin to kiss.

"It is most kind of you to invite us, Your Highness," she said.

Catrin kissed the Prince's long, smooth hand, trying not to stare at this legendary figure who inspired such fervent loyalty among the Scots. The tall, slender prince was dressed in a tartan shortcoat with waistcoat and breeches, and wore tall black boots; the blue ribbon of the Garter lay across his left shoulder, the star of that order gleaming against his red tartan coat. Charles wore his own reddish blond hair combed over the front of a blond wig. His pale face was long with a rather sharp chin. Although there was a pleasant smile on his full, almost girlish mouth, it was his large brown eyes that captured Catrin's attention; deep hued, burningly intense, this legacy from his Polish mother appeared startlingly out of place in his fair-complexioned face.

Now Catrin understood what the Edinburgh ladies sighed for—an approving glance from those smoldering eyes. There was no trace of lasciviousness in his expression as he raised her from the floor.

"I hear your father was Alisdair Blair, a loyal supporter of my father's cause. You, like I, am a child of exile come home at last."

Catrin smilingly agreed with his rather poetic statement. She was given no further time to contemplate the Prince's words when Brenda, with seeming innocence, deliberately nudged her aside. She gazed boldly at the Prince, and then she curtsied, the gems on her elaborate hair ornament reflecting the blazing candles as she billowed low to the ground, her sapphire satin skirts flowing over the toes of the Prince's black boots.

While he did not outwardly reprimand her, Brenda's actions had not gone unnoticed by the Prince. Charles's tone was cool when he addressed her after she had seized his hand to bestow a loyal kiss.

"Your name, madam?"

"Brenda Carmichael, Your Highness, younger daughter of John Carmichael of Garth . . . Comyn Stewart's sister-in-law," she added when the Prince failed to recognize her father's name.

"Comyn . . . yes, now I place you. Welcome, Miss Carmichael. You must have had a long and tiring journey from Rome." The Prince beckoned to Easter and Comyn to come forward.

Not realizing the Prince's attention had shifted elsewhere,

Brenda began to speak, a seductive smile on her face, her body positioned to display as much as possible of its charms for Charles's appreciation. An unlovely scowl crept over her face when she realized she was expected to step aside to make room for her sister and brother-in-law. It was not the Prince but one of his gentlemen who impatiently waved her away, and Brenda was displaced by the advancing couple. Fuming inwardly, she gave the man a venomous glare; unperturbed, he smiled blandly, used to protecting his royal master from predatory females.

Prince Charles spoke privately with Comyn about the probable support he could expect from the Welsh Jacobites. Satisfied with Comyn's report and growing weary of the crowd, Charles then called David to his side. They began a lively discussion in Italian, much to the displeasure of those Scots gentlemen who did not understand the language.

At the far end of the gallery the brightly garbed guests danced to the strains of violins, elegant minuets and gavottes having replaced the lively reels with which the Highlanders were familiar. Catrin for one was relieved by the musical selection, for she had not learned to dance a reel. Her first experience of the Scottish dance had been on the night before their departure when the Garth soldiers had danced for hours atop the leaded roof of the castle, their whisky-induced gaiety rivaling the pipes for volume.

"Well, you seem to have fared no better than I with our 'Bonnie Prince,'" remarked Brenda as she handed Catrin a crystal goblet of wine from a sidetable. "Think you he prefers lads?"

"You could hardly expect him to invite you to his bed in public," Catrin retorted sharply, surprising herself by her frankness.

Instead of taking offense, Brenda laughed. "How did you guess that's what I wanted? I shall have to watch you closer, Catrin Blair, you've a sharp eye."

"There's little I miss, Brenda. You would do well to remember that."

Brenda's cat-green eyes narrowed menacingly as if she were about to take issue with Catrin's statement. They sized each other up like dogs spoiling for a fight until David's arrival halted their undeclared hostilities.

No longer bound to amuse his prince, David was eager to be with Catrin. "Come, sweatheart, will you dance with me?" he asked, ignoring Brenda, who plucked at his sleeve, silently entreating him to partner her instead.

Eagerly Catrin accepted David's offer, relieved to be away from Brenda's disturbing presence. David's eyes were warm with love when he smiled at her, rekindling stirring memories of their intimacy.

Tonight he was formally dressed in buff brocade with an embroidered red velvet waistcoat worn over a fine lace-trimmed shirt. His muscular legs appeared to Catrin somewhat naked in white silk stockings and black buckled shoes, for she was more used to seeing him in riding boots. When he bowed to her in the opening measure of the dance the rich fabric strained across his powerful shoulders and she shuddered to recall that wonderful night in Carlisle when she had first watched him undress. Even this foppish court garb did not detract from the powerful aura of virility he exuded.

The Prince refused to join the dancers even when several ladies seized his hands and begged him to honor them with his presence. Repeating again that he would dance only when his mission was fulfilled, the young prince cleverly changed their disappointment to admiration.

As the evening sped by Brenda was partnered by a dozen different gallants, their attentions bringing about a swift recovery from the slight delivered her by His Highness. When at last it was David's turn to dance with her, Catrin fought to hide her jealousy as Brenda smiled up at him invitingly, allowing her hands to roam about his neck and shoulders. Next Brenda boldly slid her slender fingers into his crisp black hair, pretending to find a gray hair as she joked about his advancing age; David had reached his thirtieth birthday while still in Rome.

So preoccupied was she in controlling her indignation as she watched Brenda flirt outrageously with her lover, Catrin failed to notice the stir among the guests as the Prince strolled about the room, and so was startled to find him standing beside her. When she would have curtsied to him, he stayed her arm, insisting on informality.

"David tells me you're an accomplished painter like your mother. Arabella Blair's talent was famous. Do forgive me, Lady Catrin, for not remembering."

He addressed her as Lady Catrin, giving her the title customarily granted to the wife of a chief. She wondered if he thought she and David were married.

"I'm afraid you overestimate my talents, Your Highness, they're of a very modest nature."

"Nevertheless, if you're willing, I intend to put them to the test. My likeness has never been captured by a lovely lady . . . it's an experience I'm looking forward to."

"Oh, Your Highness, I'm honored, but I fear I couldn't do you justice."

"Nonsense. Attend me tomorrow morning at eleven after my council and we'll see how modest your talents are. And bring that reckless adventurer with you—David shall amuse me while you sketch."

"Oils are a more familiar medium to me, Your Highness," Catrin ventured, encountering warmth in his deep brown eyes as he sought to put her at ease.

"Sketching is much faster. We are soon to march into England, Lady Catrin."

With a bow, the Prince walked away leaving Catrin with her hands clasped in shock as she considered his royal command.

The dance was over and David came over to her. "Come now, don't tell me Charles has made fools of us all. Can this confusion mean anything else? He's asked you to bed him," he suggested wickedly as he observed her excitement. He slid his arm about Catrin's slim waist and pulled her close, pressing his lips against her flushed cheek. They stood before the long windows at the far end of the gallery, partly hidden from sight by the heavy gold velvet draperies. Catrin allowed him to embrace her, rejoicing in his strength and the quick surge of blood his nearness caused. Held close against the beating of his heart, tasting the heated fragrance of his skin, Brenda mattered not at all.

"Not that—he asked me to sketch him!"

"Really. Well, that doesn't surprise me ·in the least," he whispered, his mouth softly teasing against her brow. "I think I may have mentioned how talented you are."

"Oh, David, you are sure I can please him? You've no idea how well I draw."

"You do certain other things so expertly, I've no doubt you'll produce a masterpiece," he assured her huskily. "His Highness also asked us to honor him with our presence at tomorrow night's gathering. Lord knows, at this rate you may never want to leave Edinburgh."

* * *

Bathed in mild October sunshine, Edinburgh assumed a different personality. The dark stone buildings took on a mellow glow and the broad expanse of blue sky beyond Arthur's Seat softened the brooding mystery of the city's highest point. Built, like Rome, on seven hills, Edinburgh could best be viewed from the summit of this extinct volcano, which offered panoramic views over the Pentland Hills and the Firth of Forth. At the western end of the Royal Mile loomed the black bulk of Edinburgh Castle, brightly colored pennants flapping defiantly in the breeze.

The citizens of Edinburgh were taking advantage of the unexpected sunshine. The streets were thronged with goods-laden tradesmen and women with baskets of produce on their hips, their dirty barefoot children clinging to their skirts as they stumbled on the filthy cobbles.

That morning Catrin wore her blue wool gown with a plaid about her shoulders, declining to borrow Brenda's finery again for their audience with the Prince. David was dressed in a gray worsted coat and breeches over a black damask waistcoat; his highly polished black boots had scarlet tops. At the last minute he decided against wearing the brightly colored laird's tartan he had lately adopted. Modest and somber, they appeared the perfect provincial gentry come up to Edinburgh for the day.

Though Catrin doubted David had lost his fervor for the cause, she had noticed a marked change in him since their arrival in Edinburgh. The unquenchable enthusiasm he had displayed on their journey south had evaporated; even his face appeared older, with deepening lines about his mouth, as if he was possessed of increasingly gloomy thoughts.

"Do you not like Edinburgh?" Catrin asked, tucking her hand beneath his gray worsted sleeve. At the contact with his muscular arm, she felt that excited fluttering in her stomach, an emotional reaction she had supposed would disappear with time. It was as if their love was too good to be true, and her lover was an illusion that would evaporate with the morning sun.

"Edinburgh's well enough."

"You're different here, more moody," she ventured, his answer not exactly what she sought.

"There are so many things to be considered for my clansmen's welfare."

Again that somewhat morose expression, and she still had

not put her finger on its source. The tall gates of Holyrood Palace were visible over the heads of the jostling crowd; if she was to learn anything she must demand an answer before they entered the palace precincts.

"David Stewart, you're so closemouthed I could scream. Do you know something I should know? Are there things you're keeping from me?"

He looked at her then, full in the face. Lately she had noticed he rarely met her eyes, a trend she found unsettling. As always, when David's behavior toward her changed, the specter of Brenda Carmichael's flaming beauty crossed her mind. She hastily dismissed the jealous conclusion, knowing it was unfair to condemn him without cause. A man had to want to be stolen for the theft to be successful.

They were passing the garden wall of a white stone house set back from the street. The wrought-iron gate stood open, revealing a stone seat screened from the house by a wall of shrubbery and framed by a trellis of pink roses.

"All right, I suppose you'll keep at me until you have it. Come in here. They can only ask us to leave."

Uneasy, Catrin followed him to the bench and sat down. David did not sit beside her; he rested his boot on the edge of the seat and leaned forward, his arm on his knee.

"I know your intention was to come south with me—I want you to reconsider, to go back to Garth."

"No," she gasped, her heart lurching at his unexpected decision. "You said we'd travel together."

"Things have changed."

"How?"

"The Prince has not the army I expected, nor the weapons, nor perhaps even the support of the English Jacobites. Too few have come forward..."

"We're not out of Scotland yet. Let's at least wait until we cross the border to judge. Surely the English will come forward then."

"I pray to God you're right. The support promised from France has not been forthcoming, nor the money, nor the arms ...Catrin, sweet," David leaned toward her, his grave face inches from her own. "It might be far too dangerous for you. What if the march fails? The Prince's advisers are ever at each other's throats. No two agree on the course to take. Charles generally favors a different plan in private, though in public he strives to accommodate his counselors. In short, the glorious cause on which we were nurtured has a fatally large number of loopholes."

Catrin swallowed, shocked by his revelation. "The Prince brought no supplies with him? No men?"

"Some arms from France, but not enough to supply the Highlanders, let alone any English volunteers. Charles landed in the Hebrides with seven men. I'm afraid he's not yet learned to be suspicious of promises made to him by the King of France."

"Oh, please, sweetheart, don't send me back," Catrin whispered, her lip quivering. "I couldn't bear waiting at Garth not knowing how you fared. Though I know you love the land dearly, it's not my land. I'm a stranger there. My only comfort comes from being with you."

David swallowed as he reached for her hand. Feelings of love flooded through him as he gazed down at her, seeing tears glittering in her large gray eyes. Sense told him to send her home, but passion deafened him to wisdom.

"Easter's going back to Garth; you wouldn't be alone," he protested gruffly, trying to convince himself not to yield.

"And Brenda?"

He looked down at the clipped grass at their feet. "She is to continue with the army."

"Then so will I!"

The determination in Catrin's voice made his head snap up. "For Christ's sake, don't let thoughts that I might succumb to her charms turn you into a fool."

"My worry is that thoughts of her will turn *you* into a fool."

Her taunt stung him and he swung away from her in anger. "Comyn didn't allow Easter any choice."

"She has a sickly babe. Had I a child I'd probably make the same decision."

"His Highness frowns on women traveling with the troops."

"When he banishes Brenda Carmichael from the train, perhaps I too will reconsider," Catrin declared firmly. She stood up, smoothing her skirts, watching him out of the corner of her eye. Anger darkened his face. When he turned to face her, she tightened her mouth, prepared for battle.

"You stubborn wench," he growled, gripping her shoulder. "Had I an ounce of sense I'd listen to my brain instead of my blood."

Catrin gasped, suddenly understanding his statement. "Oh,

David, sweetheart," she whispered, her resolve softening as he gazed down at her. "You want me with you after all."

David pulled her against him, his hands in her chestnut hair. "I never stopped wanting you with me. Just this once I thought to do what was right, to use sense . . . oh, darling, I ache for you too much to wish you two hundred miles away."

Their eyes met, and she saw all the love there, that deep emotion she cherished above all else. "This is sense, David Stewart . . . the other's only denial."

He kissed her, and a tremor ran through him. Absently he wondered if the owners of this house were aware of their presence in their private garden, then the thought left his mind as she pressed close to him, warmly yielding.

"Not sense, sweetheart. Call it a decision from the heart instead of the head. I've made too many of those since I met you."

The sonorous voice of a clock striking the hour brought them back to the present and the same thought simultaneously flashed through their minds: Prince Charles awaited them at eleven. "We'll be late," Catrin squeaked as she seized his hand, hurrying him through the gate and into the street. They ran over the Abbey Strand as the last notes of the clock died away.

Even Holyroodhouse looked less forbidding in the thin autumn sunlight. The trees in the park beyond the palace were veiled in gold, the surrounding woodlands bright as an artist's palette; scarlet sycamores, copper beeches, and pale gold elms contrasted brilliantly with the blue sky.

Catrin found the scene pleasing, yet she would never like this imposing palace, which seemed to brood under the sadness of the past. Last night, before they left Holyrood, David had taken her to see the infamous spot where the murder of David Rizzio had occurred. It was one of the palace's foremost attractions. She had chilled as she stood on the narrow stair leading to the Mary Queen of Scots supper room down which the Queen's husband and his followers had dragged the ill-fated Rizzio after stabbing him fifty times.

That morning they were challenged by Charles's guard, more alert now the council was in session. David presented their pass, written in Charles's own hand, so they were allowed to enter and were quickly taken by a servant to the Prince's private rooms.

Prince Charles awaited them before the hearth. He was

wearing the buff coat and red velvet breeches he had worn on the day the standard was unfurled at Glenfinnan; it seemed a fitting costume for his portrait.

David bowed and Catrin curtsied to the Prince, who waved aside their polite formalities. Deep obeisance was more appropriate for the Muti Palace than here. In Scotland the possession of an acre overlooking some insignificant loch could entitle a man to become an officer, while ownership of barren mountain tops and misty valleys turned some men into virtual kings. Scotland was not Rome, nor these gallant Highlanders the trained army of the Prince's expectations. Charles felt both love and hate for this wild land of his ancestors as he daily tried to reconcile dreams with the truth.

"Lady Catrin, will you take refreshment before you begin?" asked Charles, offering her a glass of malaga.

The small gold and white drawing room was decorated with exquisite floral sprays painted on the molded ceiling, the brilliant shades echoed in the upholstery of the gilt-framed chairs against the wall. Pale autumn sunshine flooded through the red velvet curtained windows, washing the room with light and making it the best place to sit for a portrait. An ornate gilt chair upholstered in red velvet stood ready before the window.

David lounged on the window seat nursing a second glass of malaga while he watched Charles posing in suitable kingly fashion and Catrin, still highly nervous of her assignment, perching on a small stool to his right, sketch pad and charcoal at the ready. Charles was different today, he decided, studying the Prince's pale face. Twin sunbeams gilded a halo around his head of unpowdered reddish-gold hair. David concluded that the morning's council must have resulted either in decision or in further heated arguments to turn Charles so thoughtful.

"Have plans been made for the march yet, Highness? November's but a breath away. It seems unwise to save our journey for winter."

Charles's heavy eyelids fluttered, though he resisted the impulse to turn his head. "We've already waited too long. Today Ardshiel suggested you be invited to council. Your kinsman speaks highly of you. Will you attend me tomorrow?"

Surprised and flattered by his Prince's request, David agreed. "I'll be honored, Your Highness, especially if my presence helps light a fire under their laggard behinds."

Charles laughed. "It's a furnace we need rather than a fire. We'd have been wise to follow up our victory after Prestonpans instead of giving them time to regroup." Then, as if suddenly remembering Catrin's presence, Charles dropped the subject abruptly and spoke no more policy. The conversation changed abruptly to reminiscences of hunting expeditions and fishing parties, to athletic pursuits and Charles's brief experience with war as a youth at the siege of Gaeta.

When Catrin was satisfied with her sketch, she nervously proffered it for royal approval. Silently Charles studied the likeness, his mouth pursed as he turned it to the light, critically viewing the long face with its full mouth and large eyes, the captured expression revealing his mixed emotions. At last he looked up, noting Catrin's nervousness; she was afraid he did not approve her handiwork.

"You say you're not at home working with charcoal, Lady Catrin?"

"No, Your Highness. Oils are my forte. Neither are portraits my usual choice of subject."

"Catrin was painting beside the Thames when I met her."

"And was that masterpiece ever finished, or did he so distract you that you abandoned your efforts?"

A dimple showed on Catrin's smooth cheek as she glanced toward David on the windowseat. "As you've guessed, Your Highness, my attention wandered too much to complete the task."

Laughing, Charles rose to his feet, and he handed the portrait to David. "Here, Stewart of Garth, see what your lady has done."

The likeness was good. Catrin had captured the fleeting emotions crossing the twenty-four-year-old prince's face, combining them in one unfathomable expression, neither serious nor gay. Not as flattering as most miniatures, but far more like the man, this sketch from an untrained hand perfectly represented Charles Edward Stuart as he was today, bathed in October sunshine in the drawing room of Holyroodhouse.

"Do you think it good?"

David glanced up at the Prince, realizing that was a question a wise man avoided. Having never earned a reputation for diplomacy, he grinned infectiously as he said, "Good or otherwise, Highness, this is the Charles Edward Stuart I know."

The silence stretched uncomfortably long before Charles turned to Catrin and reached for her hand, turning over her grubby, charcoal-stained fingers to kiss.

"You, my dear, are an honest woman . . . a rare commodity.

I'm delighted with your work. I shall treasure this likeness as a reminder of my stay in Edinburgh."

Catrin let out a sigh, long suppressed, as she saw the Prince's smile of pleasure. "Your Highness is too kind," she said, her voice cracking with emotion. "Someday, given time, perhaps you'll allow me to paint a portrait that does justice to your . . . rank," she finished, fumbling for the right word.

"God grant you can paint me in St. James's, Lady Catrin," he said, bowing over her hand with a flourish. "I'll not rest until a Stuart sits again on England's throne."

Chapter 11

The stormy council meetings during those final days of October 1745 failed to produce results. Charles, eager for battle, was anxious to meet General Wade's army at Newcastle while his army was no larger than theirs. Lord George Murray, the strongest of his counselors and the most vocal, and who on occasion had made decisions without consulting the prince, opposed him. Murray's opinions were usually backed by the great Scottish chiefs, Locheil, Keppoch, Clanranald, Glencoe, Lochgarry, and Ardshiel. The Irishmen, O'Sullivan and Sheridan, who had sailed with Charles from France, contented themselves, however, with whispering their viewpoints in his ear. During it all, while the different factions squabbled to the point of threatening to withdraw their men and go home, Charles tried to remain neutral.

French help was not, as yet, forthcoming, being represented merely in the form of an envoy; neither had the mass uprising of English Jacobites taken place. Charles grew desperate for action, insisting there was no further reason to delay on the strength of waiting for recruits. Lord George Murray convinced many of those present of the wisdom of his plan not to attack Wade at Newcastle but to march into England through Cumberland and attack Carlisle.

As usual majority ruled and Charles, going against his better judgment for the second time—the first being the failure to follow up their advantage after Prestonpans—finally agreed to Murray's plan. The army would leave Edinburgh on November

1, bound for Carlisle. Lacking the necessary intelligence, Murray was unaware of Carlisle's small garrison and poor defenses, assuming that such an importantly placed bordertown would be heavily defended and by the taking of it they would vastly embellish their appeal.

When David bore home the council's final decision, the small household in the Cannongate was sent into a flurry of activity. It was decided Easter should leave at once for Garth. Comyn made arrangements for her to travel with a kinsman and his wife who were ailing and considered home to be the best cure for their affliction. On the day of departure Easter bid Comyn a tearful goodbye before he rode with David to Duddingston camp. Only Catrin remained to see her off.

As the coach pulled away, Catrin waved cheerily to her friend, who was swathed in a dark blanket, her pale face visible through the window of the dilapidated coach. Catrin felt guilty for not accompanying Easter. Her friend's dejection at being separated from family and friends was painfully apparent. Though the offer of transportation to Garth had also been made to Brenda, she too had declined to accept it.

When Catrin returned to her lodgings, she was surprised to find Ness awaiting her. Since their initial meeting he had been avoiding her, preferring to lodge with friends at the White Horse Inn rather than confront his sister with her lover. Hope surged in her breast as she wondered if her brother's unexpected visit meant he had decided to forgive her.

"Ness, how lovely to see you. I'd begun to think you'd abandoned us."

Ness's smile was tight as he endured his sister's kiss, holding himself somewhat aloof. "I came to pack my belongings. Where is everyone?"

Backing away from him, Catrin sadly accepted his unchanged attitude. "Easter's left for Garth. Comyn and David are with their men."

"And what do you propose to do?"

"I'm traveling with David."

"I anticipated as much. You're still me sister, Catrin, though I'm damned if I approve of the way you're living. Anyway, I've arranged some comfort for you on the journey."

"Comfort? In what way?"

"A carriage, my love, to keep you from the snow and sleet." Ness grinned and held out his hand. "That bastard appears to be treating you well, so far. For the moment I'll reserve judgment," he pronounced gruffly.

Tears filled Catrin's eyes as she clasped her brother's hand. "Oh, Ness, I'm so glad. David loves me true. He has my best interests at heart, you'll see."

"If he doesn't, he'll have me to deal with," he said harshly, his face dark. "Ogilvie and Kilmarnock both brought their wives and several others have hired carriages for their ladies. You can travel and lodge with them. David will have far too much on his mind to be bothered finding decent accommodation for you. Besides, those ladies are your own kind."

As Catrin traveled the bone-shaking road to Carlisle, she reviewed their conversation with mixed emotions, not convinced this comfort had been provided with a selfless motive. She rather suspected Ness of using the coach as a ruse to keep her and David apart. And so far it had worked. Still, she could not complain unduly, for beautiful Lady Ogilvie, Lady Kilmarnock, and the handful of other hapless females who followed the army, had virtually no contact with their men either. Rugged terrain, inclement weather, and the constant demands of keeping their undisciplined troops on the move kept the menfolk tired and gruff, allowing them little time to assuage their ladies' boredom.

When the Prince's army marched out of Edinburgh it was five thousand strong and no longer only Highland in composition, for several Lowland gentlemen had brought troops to swell the ranks. Lord Ogilvie's contribution, besides his breathtakingly lovely bride, had been a cavalry regiment six hundred strong; Kilmarnock brought mounted grenadiers; Lord Balmerino and Lord Pitsligo, a hundred and eighty mounted troops. These latest additions, combined with Elcho's horseguards and the hussars commanded by the Irishman Baggot, formed two respectable troops of cavalry. Impressed by show himself, Charles assumed others would be also, so Elcho's troops, resplendent in their blue uniforms, preceded the army into each new town.

Apart from the cavalry Charles had thirteen infantry regiments of poorly garbed and ill-trained Highlanders. Dirty, bearded, wearing stained kilts, plaids, and bonnets, many of the clansmen were also barefoot. However, what the Highlanders lacked in supplies they made up for in enthusiasm.

The advance guard of the Jacobite army reached Carlisle

on Martinmas Sunday. Unaware of its weak defenses, Charles wasted valuable time laying siege to the city. Not anxious to repeat his Edinburgh failure, this time he demanded the surrender of both castle and town. Despite their commander's efforts, Carlisle's militia were reluctant to fight. They soon fled their posts and the undefended castle fell to the Jacobites. On November 17, Charles, riding at the head of his army, entered the city and took up lodgings at Mr. Highmore's house in the High Street.

No balls were held at Carlisle; there were no cheering mobs, and worst of all, no recruits. Disappointed, Charles left the city on November 22, for Penrith.

The unusually good weather that had blessed the army in Scotland did not hold. During their siege of Carlisle, it snowed and the roads south were a mass of snow and ice; the tortuous roads over the fells were blanketed with white.

The Highlanders were not wholly at a disadvantage with the changing weather, boasting good-humoredly that their plaids were better when wet because the wool swelled to keep out the bitter wind. Even the difficult terrain at the gateway to Lancashire failed to daunt them, becoming instead a reminder of home.

During the grueling journey over Shap Fells the ladies were often forced to walk beside their carriages. When Catrin had ridden over these hills on her way to Scotland, the valleys had been green, the slopes gentle, giving no hint of the frigid torment to come. As she trudged beside Lady Ogilvie without speaking—they must save their energy for the climb—Catrin succumbed to tears of self-pity. Cold numbed her fingers and reddened her cheeks; she had ceased to feel her toes an hour ago.

Since they had left Edinburgh David had become a virtual stranger. With the exception of a night in Carlisle, they had spent only a few hours together. The coaches traveled in the rear of the army with the baggage wagons and were neglected by all. During the day David rode with his men, as did the other ladies' husbands; they had not seen the gallant Prince since Carlisle. Catrin was billeted with the other women and lack of privacy robbed husbands and wives of the few nights they might have shared. The frigid weather meant nightly shelter must be found for the men in the Lakeland villages, and this need dictated their pace. Often, when the officers finally found shelter for all their men, the night was half over. And not until they reached Manchester did the situation promise to improve.

The rough terrain soon proved too much for Catrin's old coach; two days into Lancashire the axle broke and the vehicle was abandoned. To Catrin's amazement it was Brenda who generously offered to share her coach with her. Not looking forward to the arrangements, but having little choice, Catrin was pleasantly surprised to discover Brenda could be an entertaining companion as mounting boredom drove them to call a temporary truce.

Kendal, Lancaster, Garstang, Preston, Wigan; the northern towns slipped by, each one as cheerless as the last. While they rattled through the dreary, winter-drab landscape Brenda chatted with Catrin about Rome, regaling her with amusing accounts of her romances. She frequently steered the conversation round to David. But Catrin, determined not to present her rival with valuable information about her beloved, would swiftly change the subject. Now she was grateful for David's infrequent appearances, for she was not anxious to give Brenda the chance to flirt with him. To his credit David paid little attention to Brenda; in any case he was usually too dirty, cold, and tired for gallantry.

Catrin could not overcome her distrust of this new and friendly Brenda, wondering if her guise of friendship was a ruse to worm herself closer to David. Not usually suspicious by nature, where Brenda was concerned Catrin suspected ulterior motives behind the most innocent action.

At Preston a new surge of hope was generated by the support of a local Catholic gentleman named Francis Townley, and two Welshmen who brought with them a handful of supporters. This county being traditionally Jacobite, Charles was expecting great things from Lancashire. Their reception at Manchester would be a crucial indicator of the support he could expect from the region. A sergeant enlisted in Preston went ahead of the army with his mistress and a drummer to raise recruits. When Charles entered Manchester one hundred and eighty volunteers awaited him. Aware of the importance of this Lancashire town, the Prince paid great attention to his dress, donning a clean light tartan plaid, a gray wig, and a blue velvet bonnet with a white cockade.

Lodgings were found for the Prince in a handsome house in Market Street. Jacobite sentiment ran high and billets for officers and their ladies were easy to come by. After the reading of the usual proclamation pronouncing Charles as Regent for his father, King James III, the Mancurians lit welcoming bonfires and set the church bells pealing in honor of the Prince's visit.

Outside the Bull's Head tavern the following day, Thomas Deacon, eldest son of the non-jurant bishop of Manchester, was in charge of enlisting recruits. Each man was given a shilling and a blue and white cockade, which Deacon himself fastened to their hats.

Catrin stood in the crowd watching the proceedings. Today she felt melancholy. Those celebratory fires and joyful bells on their arrival had been misleading; the thousands the Prince had been expecting to enlist failed to materialize. The smattering of Manchester recruits who had joined them were mostly rough fellows of low standing, bought more by ale and promises than by loyalty to the cause.

The night before David had dined with the Prince before attending a council of war. He was unusually morose when in the early hours of the morning he had returned to their lodgings. After they had discussed the disappointingly low number of recruits and David had conveyed the Prince's mounting disappointment, he lay down and fell asleep the minute his head touched the pillow. So weary had he been, he was still asleep when she left. As they had this Manchester billet to themselves, Catrin hoped the pattern would not be repeated tonight. Charles could not need David any more than she.

"Catrin, is it really you?"

She turned in surprise to see a tall man in clerical garb pushing his way toward her through the crowd. He seemed familiar, yet at first she could not place him. Then suddenly she recognized her cousin Adam.

"Adam! Oh, I never expected to see you here," she cried, embracing him.

"Nor I you." He held her at arm's length, the better to study her. "You look well, I must say. Are you staying with Mama?"

"No, although I was visiting her when your letter arrived to say you were joining the rebels."

Adam's brown eyes clouded and his expression turned grave. "How did she take it?"

"As you expected."

"I'd hoped . . . Mama always had such dreams for me . . ." Adam broke off, forcing himself away from the painful subject. "Then where are you staying, Catrin? Surely this calls for a celebration. You must dine with us at our lodgings—you have my word we're all respectable men of God sworn to follow the Prince."

Catrin considered explaining David to Adam, then decided against it. A minister, not given to worldly ways, might interpret their relationship as sinful.

"I'm staying with friends . . . oh, there's one of them now," she said as she noticed Brenda standing at the fringe of the crowd. For once Brenda looked quite demure. "My cousin Adam," she introduced as Brenda joined them, her curiosity aroused by the sight of the minister. "This is my friend Brenda Carmichael."

"I'd no idea Catrin had relatives in the clergy. Are you with us, Adam? Do you follow the Prince?"

"Yes, Mrs. Carmichael. A Manchester regiment is being formed, to be led by Captain Townsley. I intend to serve them in whatever capacity I may."

"You're a brave man of the cloth." Brenda allowed her silky lashes to obscure her bright knowledgeable gaze. "Shall I tell the others you'll be back shortly?" she asked Catrin, who flashed her a smile of gratitude for her thoughtfulness.

"Please do."

Taken off guard, at first Catrin had been grateful for Brenda's tact. It was only later, when Adam eagerly led her toward his lodgings, that she began to doubt Brenda's good intentions.

Brenda hurried along the filthy cobbled street, eager to reach her destination. She paused at the street door to assure herself Catrin was still occupied with her relative before darting up the narrow stair that led to the room where David slept.

To her surprise Brenda found the door unlocked. Quietly she let herself in, placing her wicker basket of provisions on the floor. The bed stood in front of the windows, dimly illuminated by the pale winter light. David's dark head hollowed the pillow, his face turned away from her. No stranger to seduction, the sight of her long-desired love object set Brenda's pulses pounding.

She threw off her shawl and hastily unfastened her bodice, mentally concocting the lie she would tell. Her plan was a gamble, but today she felt reckless. Subtle hints about her interest in him he had treated with indifference. In the beginning, when she expected to capture the Prince, she had not fought hard for David's attention. Once that futility had been abandoned, David Stewart became the sole object of her affection. If only stupid Catrin had returned to Garth with Easter, her task would have been far easier.

Brenda shot the bolt through the door. David stirred at the sound, flinging his arm above his head. He did not wake.

She stood beside the bed looking down at him, sighing with pleasure at the sight. When, as a precocious girl of twelve, she first set eyes on him, she had yearned to possess him. Then, of course, she had not the weapons with which to wage that war—there had been too many French and Italian women, ladies and commoners alike, ahead of her. Now only Catrin Blair stood between them.

Shivering, Brenda slid beneath the covers and snuggled against his warmth. The room was chilly and without her russet wool gown she was cold. The pleasure of touching his naked flesh excited her. Gently she stroked his face, tracing her finger down his hard nose, over his high cheekbones, finding his skin smooth and hot. David still did not wake, though his sensuous mouth curved in pleasurable dreams beneath her caresses.

Mildly rewarding though this activity was, making love to a sleeping man was not the fulfillment Brenda sought. She longed for David to reciprocate, to fondle and admire her breasts of which she was most proud, to join his body with hers in throbbing passion. There were a hundred men in the Prince's ranks who would give their all to be her lover, yet David Stewart was the only man she had ever truly wanted. Perhaps, Brenda considered with a smile as she traced her lips over his cheek, her longing for him was inflamed by his indifference.

Pressing her full breast against his shoulder, she slowly slid her hand over his chest, tracing a passage down through the matted dark hair on his belly until she found what she sought. The soft stirring of his heavy flesh under her caress thrilled her. She marveled at the perfection she held in her slender fingers, at the throbbing heat as blood coursed through his body to swell the tissues. Each passing second made her passion mount. No longer able to contain herself, she finally pressed her mouth passionately over his.

David's eyes opened. "Catrin," he murmured, blinking as he tried to accustom himself to his surroundings.

"Davie, come, are you faithful even in your sleep?" Brenda demanded in exasperation as she slid her hand down his sinewy thigh.

"Christ—Brenda! What are you doing here?"

"I know exactly what I'm doing, darling," she crooned, forcing down his protesting arm.

A coldness washed over him. "When I want a woman in my bed, I expect to do the inviting," David growled, his dark face set in a scowl.

Brenda stared at him in disbelief. "You surely can't mean that? Has that little Blair girl got you so tied to her apron strings you're refusing me?" As she spoke, Brenda thrust aside the bedcovers to expose her full, pale breasts enticingly tipped with pink.

David quickly averted his gaze. And his action angered her.

"Well, like a fool you can save yourself for your little beauty if you wish. But when I left her not thirty minutes ago, she was entering another man's lodgings. A man who cleverly hides his identity with a cleric's garb!"

"You're lying!"

"Am I? No doubt there are others who saw their tender reunion."

Grim-faced, David gripped her upper arm, his fingers biting into the milky flesh. "You lie!" he repeated menacingly.

A flicker of fear passed over Brenda as she looked at him, aroused by a passion not born of lust. Anger darkened his eyes and deepened the lines on his face. She struggled to free herself. "Well, love, defend her if you must. I'm only telling you what I saw."

"It can't be true!"

"Believe me, it's true. I watched her hug and kiss him like a long-lost brother. And she has but one of those and Ness travels with us, my dear, trusting Davie. Have sense, you foolish man, you're not the first to be shabbily treated!"

David thrust aside her entreating hands. "No." The word was ground out, his jaw tense. "Be it true or false, at the moment I've no stomach for you."

"No stomach!" Brenda repeated, her eyes flashing. "No stomach! Damn you, you arrogant bastard!"

"You would stay to hear the truth, Brenda," he mocked, turning to face her. "Do you think I've been deaf and blind these past weeks? Because of my affection for Catrin I chose not to understand. Had I needed a whore I'd only to walk into the street. Now go, before I forget I'm a . . ."

"Gentleman!" Brenda supplied in derision. She leaped from the bed, her mouth curled in a scorn. "You're no more a gentleman than that chair!"

David leaped out of bed with total disregard for his naked-ness and grasped her shoulders, shaking her as she struggled to pull down her gown. She gulped, no longer fascinated by the dark emotion in his face. The thought of his vengeance made her tremble.

"I love you," she blurted, surprising herself with the pitiable excuse. "For all these years I've loved you."

David bit back his angry words, hardly expecting that ar-gument. Tears coursed down Brenda's cheeks and for the first time he realized there was a vulnerable side to her. She was not just a flirtatious charmer who collected men as easily as most women did ribbons. During this unguarded moment Bren-da's defenses were down. It was a shock he had not been prepared for.

Swallowing his anger, David said evenly, "Brenda, there's no need to quarrel. It's no shame to have unrequited feelings. Now go, there's a good lass. We'll still be friends."

"Friends!" She tossed her head defiantly, her coppery hair whirling about her shoulders. "You'd make a woman a poor friend—'tis only as a lover they'd seek you. Well, Davie Stew-art, so you've turned me down, more fool you. There are men aplenty who are none so particular—Toby Lomax daily gets down on his knees to beg my favors. Someday you'll be sorry . . . it may be a lot sooner than you think!"

Head held high, Brenda marched to the door, stooping to retrieve her basket and shawl. It was hard to ignore his na-kedness. A picture of his lithe, muscular, broad-shouldered body, with the gold-tinged flesh molded like precious metal about his sinewy frame, was indelibly printed in her mind. His form was perfectly tapered from straight shoulders that were square and strong, and upon which she longed to lay her head in feminine submission. Kisses from that firm sensual mouth, caresses from his lean, strong-fingered hands, should have been hers. The intimate part of him she could not bear to contem-plate; it was too harsh a reminder of his rejection.

"Goodbye, Brenda," David growled in reminder as she hes-itated, her hand on the doorknob.

Angrily Brenda wrenched open the door and flounced into the cold dark hallway. Drafts whistled through chinks in the wall and she pulled her shawl tight, shivering with mingled cold and emotion. Damn him! Damn him! she muttered silently, her eyes glazed with angry tears. How dare he turn her away!

Fleet-footed, she negotiated the stair, though her vision was blurred. Coming to her senses before she reached the last tread, Brenda paused, leaning against the wall in an attempt to muster her flagging courage and self-respect. Finally she tossed back her hair and straightened her shoulders. Fool! Why should she consider herself defeated? A man did not always know what he wanted. It was up to her to show him.

The street door creaked as Brenda let herself out onto the cobbled street. Dusk was falling on this short winter day; the north wind bore the sting of sleet. She glanced wistfully toward the lighted tavern beyond the market hall. There the cream of the Prince's mounted troops would be gathered, ever eager to flirt with her, jealously vying for her favors. For the time being she must be content with superficial love affairs.

The smile she forced on her full mouth was empty as she turned toward the tavern. A slim figure in a bright plaid materialized from the gloom. They virtually collided.

"Catrin," Brenda gasped in surprise, "I thought you were to sup with your cousin."

How strange to find Brenda emerging from their lodging! There was a second habitation above, yet Catrin knew instinctively that was not where Brenda had been. The flush of anger on Brenda's cheeks she mistook for passion's aftermath, the gleam in her eyes for the shine of fulfillment.

"You were with David!" she accused, horrified.

Seizing the opportunity to wound her rival, Brenda smiled knowingly as she tossed her abundant hair from her face.

"He's awake now," was all she said as she hastened away.

Catrin tried to quieten her pounding heart. A strange sickness curled through her stomach and into her throat as she reviewed the implication behind Brenda's words. Knowing Brenda's nature, and given the woman's current infatuation with David, she could come to but one conclusion: Brenda had shared his bed. Voicing the horrid realization, even to herself, stole Catrin's breath. Not David, not her beautiful, handsome laird who had promised so much . . .

Sleet began to sting her face and she hurried indoors. Each rickety wooden step brought her closer to affirming that which she most dreaded.

When the door opened, David was standing shirtless beside the bed. Thinking Brenda had returned, he spun about, a snarl on his face. To his surprise it was Catrin who entered the room.

"Sweetheart, where've you been?" he asked, trying not to betray the terrible knowledge Brenda had divulged. Chances were it had been said out of pure spite, a lie to bend him to her will.

"Out," she said tonelessly, glancing about the room for evidence of his crime. Rumpled linen hung over the side of the bed. He was only half dressed and this past four in the afternoon—she need lie to herself no further.

"Not being a total idiot, I gathered that much," he retorted sharply.

She watched him light two candles and place them on the table. All this seemed unreal. Brenda had craftily waited her opportunity, biding her time until today. And she, like a fool, had innocently aided her in her treachery.

"I thought you'd have been dressed hours ago."

"The time got away from me."

"So I see."

"And what is that supposed to mean?"

Catrin clenched her hands and stepped away from the pool of yellow light. "I met Brenda coming out the door," she croaked, her mouth going dry.

"Ah, well, now I have an answer for your strange mood. And you, being a jealous little baggage, put two and two together and came up with twenty-four, correct?"

David slipped on his shirt as he moved toward her, the white fabric gleaming against his dark chest. Tears pricked Catrin's eyes as she gazed at his image through a wavering film. When he put out his hand to her, she did not take it.

"She was here with you, wasn't she?"

He nodded, his mouth grim.

"Oh, God!" Catrin buried her face in her hands.

"Not like that, damn you! She was here, yes, but we didn't make love—I swear."

When he touched her shoulder Catrin could not respond to his touch, her mind filled with horrid pictures of red-haired Brenda in his arms.

"You think I lie, don't you?"

She did not answer, her grief too wounding.

"How fragile is your trust. It's well to know now how little faith you have in me, my love. Perhaps my faith in you is likewise unfounded."

"Me! You've no just cause to question me. I've never even looked at another man since we met. You know that for the truth."

"Do I?"

"What did that wretch tell you?" Catrin's eyes blazed with anger. Her head snapped up, her mouth tight. She looked at his face, dark and grim in the candles' glow. "Come, tell me. I know she planted some lie in your mind."

"Perchance it's no lie," he said evenly, taking a candle and holding it aloft so that it illuminated her face. "Did you, or did you not, enter a lodginghouse with another man this afternoon?"

Catrin gasped, her eyes going round. So shocked, so guilty did she appear, David had his answer. Not waiting to hear more, he turned away, his mouth set in an unyielding line.

"Wait, oh, David, it's not what you think," she cried, going after him and seizing his arm. "I did enter a house with a man—my cousin Adam, the non-jurant minister about whom we've spoken. I met him this afternoon watching the recruiting. David, surely you didn't think I was with someone else," she gasped, appalled at the new light this shed on the incident. "Brenda knew he was my cousin—I introduced them. You believed her lies—oh, David, how could you? You bedded her out of jealousy."

His hand came out and gripped her neck. "Damn you, I've told you I didn't bed her. What must I do? Do you want to examine the sheets for telltale evidence?"

"Stop, oh, stop," she groaned, tears spilling from her eyes. "I understand why you did it—you thought I was with another . . . oh, David, to think you had so little faith in me."

His gaze was stony as he looked at her. "You still don't believe me, do you? Not even now."

Miserably she leaned against the table as he seized his boots and struggled to pull them on; then he snatched his coat from the peg beside the door.

"David, please don't go."

"I can find a warmer reception elsewhere, Mistress Blair."

The sound of the slammed door echoed through the room, followed soon after by a second thud as the outside door was slammed also.

She did not even go to the window to watch the way he went in the sleet-filled dusk. Catrin had already guessed his destination. And the terrible finality of that night filled her with pain. She threw herself across the bed and cried herself to sleep.

Chapter 12

Catrin stood waiting for the coach to be readied in the bitter December dawn. Today the Jacobite army was to leave Manchester, bound for Macclesfield; from there they would continue their march south toward London. This morning Catrin could hardly stand the sight of Brenda, let alone travel with her, so she had asked Jenny Oliphant, wife of one of the Prince's aides, if she might share her coach.

Across the gloomy inn yard she spotted David, swathed in a thick cloak. Too many Roman summers had thinned his blood and he acutely felt the winter's cold. Southbound though they were, at this time of year England offered little prospect of warm weather.

He strode over the cobbles, no welcoming smile on his face. "So you're determined to change traveling companions. Are you sure you can ride with Oliphant's woman?"

"Yes."

"Good. I'd hate to leave you stranded."

They peered at each other through the lightening murk, searching for a glimmer of forgiveness for the suspicion of the previous evening. None was forthcoming as both stubbornly clung to their pride.

"Will I see you tonight?" Catrin asked, weakening at the last moment.

"We'll likely join up in Macclesfield. The Prince leads one division, Lord George the other. The enemy's south of us in

Stafford. Now Cumberland's been made Captain General, he's hot for blood. It may be an exciting march." With that he turned and strode away without saying goodbye.

Tears stung Catrin's eyes at his indifference, then the reason for his hasty departure became apparent as Brenda tugged at her plaid.

"You needn't beg Jenny Oliphant's charity," she said, watching David's departing figure. "I've no hard feelings, Catrin. You're still welcome to share my coach."

"That's uncommonly charitable of you," Catrin retorted through clenched teeth as she twitched her plaid from Brenda's grasp. "I'm sorry I can't share the same sentiments." Haughtily, yet stepping with care, for her eyes were full of tears, Catrin crossed the inn yard to the black Oliphant coach. Jenny greeted her sleepily and assisted her into the vehicle before she huddled down in her cloak and went back to sleep.

When the coaches finally rattled out of the inn yard well behind the main body of troops, Catrin had mastered her emotions. She pondered her behavior seeking a solution to her dilemma. Why should she allow suspicion to keep them apart? David could have been telling the truth. She longed to believe he had; yet so many women deluded themselves about their men's fidelity, she was wary of blindly accepting his word. Could she be satisfied with sharing him? Could she live with the constant suspicion that he made love to other women? Miserably she admitted she could not. David had become too important to her for that. In the beginning, when she had little claim on his fidelity, she had tried to accept the fact she might be one of many. Now she could no longer live that way.

"What gloomy thoughts make you scowl so?" Jenny asked as she sat up to watch the dreary landscape.

Wanly, Catrin smiled at her companion. Black-haired Jenny was young, but she was no simpering innocent. Before marriage her husband had gained a sizable reputation for hell-raising and womanizing, vices he had purportedly put aside. Though her first inclination was to make a lame excuse for her ill humor, Catrin decided to tell Jenny the truth.

"Jealousy."

Jenny grinned, her pert nose wrinkling. "With a handsome man like yours, that's an affliction you'll suffer the rest of your days."

"It's an affliction I find hard to endure."

"Even considering the worst's happened—what can you do about it? Past is past."

"Nothing, I suppose."

"Exactly. But you can make sure it doesn't happen again, can't you?"

Catrin shook her head dolefully. "Probably not."

"Fie! What a milksop you've become. That's not the answer I'd have expected from you." Jenny leaned forward, her dark little face earnest as she clasped Catrin's hand. "Forgive me for mentioning the lady by name, but I'd needs be blind not to identify her. Brenda Carmichael thinks she can have any man she chooses. You're surely not going to prove her right?"

Jenny Oliphant's summation was one Catrin might have made had she not spent the night wallowing in self-pity. Whether David had made love to Brenda or not, she knew she would be a fool to relinquish her claim without a fight.

"You're right. David's mine and I intend to fight for him," Catrin pronounced, freshly determined to mend their rift.

Despite her determination, not at Macclesfield, nor later at Ashbourne, was Catrin given the chance to smooth over their differences. Circumstance intervened and she was able to spend only a few minutes alone with David.

Alarmed by the growing dissension within his council, Charles sought comfort from old friendships; he appointed David his special advisor, a position that necessitated his continuing presence at his Prince's side. What for David was a high honor became a wedge to drive them further apart. Frustration made Catrin angry and morose. To add to her injury, Brenda's current lover, Toby Lomax, was also a member of the Prince's inner council. While Prince Charles did not encourage Brenda's presence, he did not forbid Lomax to bring her to their headquarters, though naturally she was barred from council meetings. While Catrin smarted in the company of the other noble ladies in their comfortable, if somewhat crowded lodgings, she jealously pictured David spending half his days and nights in flirtatious Brenda's company.

When news of the Jacobite army's advance through northern England reached Derbyshire, a local regiment led by the Duke of Devonshire was hastily formed. Expecting the Prince to veer west into Wales, Cumberland was already waiting at nearby Lichfield, his ranks swelled by Hessian mercenaries. After conferring with his commander, the discouraged Devonshire returned to Derby and ordered his troops to Nottingham. The departure of the gallant "Blues" left the city of Derby open to Jacobite occupation.

On December 4, Elcho's lifeguards entered the city, several officers having gone on ahead to secure billets for nine thousand men. Earlier that day the mayor and the Corporation had fled, taking most of their valuables with them. The usual manifesto granting religious freedom and the maintenance of the constitution and proclaiming Charles as regent for his father, King James, was read by the town crier in Derby marketplace. Throughout the afternoon the remainder of the Jacobite army trickled in to a reception which, though not enthusiastic, was not openly hostile.

In Derby Charles stayed at Exeter House, at the invitation of the Cecil family, and it was there his commanders dined with him. The following morning the Prince attended a service in All Hallows Church.

When Catrin complained that the women were being excluded from the activities, David curtly informed her that a reception was to be held that evening in Full Street. With this morsel of encouragement she had to be content.

On that dark winter evening Catrin spent a long time before the mirror, grateful for Lady Ogilvie and Lady Kilmarnock's assistance with her elaborate coiffure. Long days on the road had depleted both their wardrobes and their supply of cosmetics, but so neglected had they felt since leaving Edinburgh they agreed they would have attended the reception in their nightgowns if necessary.

The assembly room in Full Street was jammed with guests as people came from miles around to see the Prince. The heat from so many bodies, the glare of the massed candles, and the smell of close-packed humanity, was overpowering. There was no room for dancing and many of the richly garbed ladies were most disappointed.

Catrin stood on tiptoe to see over the heads of the crowd, looking for the Prince and his gentlemen. Charles's flashing smile was artificial. Unaware of the false gaiety of the Prince's mood, the local gentry were most impressed by his charming manners. Catrin did not know what it could be, but she sensed that something was greatly amiss. As she looked from one to the other of Charles's advisers, conflict and dissension crackled in the air. David stood behind the Prince, dressed in his formal buff brocade coat and red velvet waistcoat. Tonight even he looked unlike himself, his heavy brows forming a straight line, his mouth set in a mutinous expression.

Swallowing her nervousness, Catrin advanced slowly toward him, her progress checked by the unexpected appearance of Brenda attired like a princess in her sapphire blue gown and diamond tiara. Brenda grasped David's arm and leaned toward him, her face level with his. To Catrin's immense relief he shook his head, his expression unchanged. Brenda shrugged and tried once again to interest him until he forcefully put her aside; then she flounced away, a grim smile on her red lips.

As she threaded her way through the assembly Catrin wondered uneasily if she would have any more success in speaking to him than had her rival. Since they left Manchester it seemed their quarrel had kept them apart.

"David."

He turned at the sound of her voice, the expression that crossed his face indefinable. He winced as he gripped her shoulder and turned her about, pushing her gently backward to a space beside the steamy windows.

"What is it?"

"Are we not even to speak to each other?"

"That choice is yours."

"You've known where I was every minute of the day and night, whereas I'm not at liberty to invade His Highness's privy councils."

They eyed each other grimly and a pang of fear shot through Catrin's heart. He appeared unrelenting in his ill humor.

"I didn't choose to lay myself open to more accusations. God knows, I've troubles enough," he growled, glancing about to make sure they were not being overheard.

"That's what I want to talk to you about. Can we . . . please?"

David swallowed as he looked into her lovely face, where tears were gathering in her gray eyes. Staying away from Catrin had been a torment; a thousand times he had been tempted to storm the ladies' lodgings and demand she come out to talk to him, but he had not. And neither had she encouraged him. Whenever they passed he had noticed her determined little chin move several notches higher. Fleetingly he had wondered if there were tears in her eyes, though his pride forbade closer investigation. Tonight he need wonder no longer, the tears were there and her hand trembled when he touched her fingers with his own.

"Come," he commanded gruffly, "let's find somewhere a little more private."

Woodenly Catrin followed him as he pushed a path through the finely dressed citizens, heading for the double doors where even now more late-arriving guests tried to push inside the packed room. A table was overturned, breaking the royal standard. A gasp went around the room as this awesome omen was swiftly relayed to the assembly.

"Oh, David, they say the standard's fallen, that it's smashed," Catrin cried, staying his arm as she caught snatches of the tale.

He gripped her shoulder and propelled her forward. "To hell with superstitious omens," he said dismissively. "We've far more important things to discuss. Keep moving."

Catrin did as she was bid, hastening down a dimly lit corridor, round a corner and inside a small anteroom austerely furnished in blue and gray. David pushed her backward until her legs encountered a stiff brocade couch, buckled, and abruptly left her sitting on the shiny surface.

"Now, what do you want with me?" he demanded, his face grim as he glanced toward the noisy reception room.

"Why won't you speak to me? We're like strangers. Don't you love me any more?"

"Why do you ask such a stupid question?"

"You know full well why I ask."

His mouth moved slightly as if he would grin before he thought better of it. "Were I a wise man I'd forswear all women. His Highness may have the right idea, after all. I'm not moved in with Brenda Carmichael, if that's what you're wondering."

"Perhaps I was too hasty the other night."

"I'll grant you that."

Catrin twisted her hands together in her skirts, despising the gown, which belonged to Brenda. "You must admit I had grounds for suspicion," she defended, trying to stay calm.

"Just because a man's in the same room with a woman can hardly be considered grounds. But I'll not keep you to your bargain. If you've done with me, let's have it now. Come, speak your piece!"

"David! Oh, you don't really care if I leave you, if I . . ."

"Of course I care!" he growled when tears choked her voice. "It's just that I've little strength left to battle with you into the bargain."

Fighting for control, she reached for the hand he had begun to extend to her, before changing his mind. "Who else must you argue with?"

"Nearly everyone. One of the only men who does not openly

oppose me is Charles himself."

They were interrupted by giggling women coming down the corridor and David swung her to her feet. "This is no place to say what I must say. Where's your cloak?"

"I'll have to get it."

Catrin protested as he took her arm and marched her rapidly through an adjoining unlit room. They finally emerged in a narrow corridor where numerous cloaks hung on pegs along the wall. Snatching the first thick, good-quality garment that came to hand, David tossed it about her shoulders.

"There. That should be warm enough."

"But David, it's not mine!" Catrin squeeked, hurrying to keep up with him as he strode toward the door.

"It is now," he retorted, glancing back. Just for an instant the grimness lifted from his dark face and she thrilled as that beloved smile flickered and was gone. "Come, we've much to discuss."

They plunged outside into the icy darkness, hugging close to the buildings to avoid the odorous kennel down which all manner of filth flowed. A sharp breeze blowing off the nearby River Derwent sliced between the buildings as they headed toward a lighted hostelry near St. Michael's church. The lane where the inn stood seemed quiet and David hoped that this establishment would be respectable enough for a lady.

A welcome fire was blazing in the oak-paneled common room of the old timbered inn. Tonight the room was half empty, for many patrons had flocked to see the Stuart prince and had not yet returned to quench their thirst.

David ordered bowls of pea soup with rye bread and flagons of mulled ale, the standard fare of the establishment. When the landlord had gone, David rested his head against the back of the tall oak settle where they sat beside the fire. His eyes were closed, his mouth hard.

Tentatively Catrin put out her hand to him. Without opening his eyes he grasped her fingers in his own, the affectionate gesture so warmly loving that tears again pricked her eyes.

"First tell me what troubles you so," she suggested, laying her head against his shoulder.

With a sigh David sat up and glanced about the room to make certain they could not be overheard.

"What think you of our reception here in Derby?"

"Not enthusiastic, but then not hostile either. No more or

less than I expected. And we are only a hundred and twenty-seven miles from London."

"Exactly. And are not the men's spirits high?"

"We could hear them shouting and singing in the streets. Yes, their enthusiasm's undiminished."

David rubbed his tired eyes before looking at her, tension apparent on his face. "Today we held a council meeting which included many lesser officers and commanders. Our course is set. And there's nothing anyone can do to change it."

"For London?"

Grimly he shook his head. "We retreat at dawn."

Catrin clapped her hand over her mouth. She had almost repeated the word aloud before she remembered where she was. Eyes wide, she stared at him, finally understanding the reason behind his black mood. Retreat! It was unbelievable. Granted, the government had more troops, yet the quality of the home guard and foreign mercenaries was doubtful. Ill equipped though many of the Highlanders were, they still marched with pride and enthusiasm, prepared to take the capital and restore the Stuarts to England's throne. How would these hot-blooded clansmen accept the ignominy of retreat?

"Oh, David, why?"

"The council considers a march on London suicidal. Cumberland and Wade are too close for comfort and they quake at the thought of the militia camped on Finchley Common. Christ, what support will anyone give us if we turn tail? The word—from unconfirmed sources I grant you—is that the London Jacobites are set to come out, the Welsh are forming, even the blessed French army is ready, their courage bolstered by our miraculous invasion."

"And the Prince?"

David smiled grimly. "Devastated, furious, despairing—there aren't enough words to describe his reaction. He generally follows his intuition, which, when he's allowed to exercise it, can be startlingly accurate. Unfortunately Lord George goes only by facts . . . and those quite simply are that the enemy outnumber us five to one. Therefore, all things considered, we're to slink back across the border, out tails between our legs."

"How will you tell your men?"

"That's the worst part of all. Even Lord George knows the news will fill the clansmen with despair, so he's planning a grand deception. We'll leave before dawn while the mist's thick, supposedly to fight Wade."

Just then the meal arrived and they fell silent, burdened by their secret knowledge. They ate in strained silence, leaving much on their plates.

Occasional bursts of laughter from the street, and the sound of Scots voices as clansmen wandered by, only deepened the lines about David's mouth. He dreaded telling his men the council's decision. The men of Garth had gallantly endured hardship without complaint; how could they now accept the shame of retreat? Proud, brave to a foolhardy degree, his men would accept anything but that.

And what of Charles? That morning his blazing anger had been readily displayed. Tonight, once the false smile was no longer necessary, the Prince's mood would sink to its lowest depths. Likely there would be no heroic figure striding beside the soldiers on their journey north, for David knew Charles well enough to guess that the immaturity he sometimes displayed would be encouraged by this bitter disappointment.

"Surely not all agreed with Lord George."

"A few voices of dissent, but too few to sway the vote. No, sweet, like it or not, our course is set. Derby's to be the turning point. The fools expect to be safe across the border, but Cumberland won't rest, his father can't allow it. You know as well as I that the fat German's probably quaking in his shoes. Oh, God, why are we the only ones to see it?" he demanded in anguished tones.

Wordlessly Catrin gripped his hand, stunned by his revelation. The hopes of a lifetime were crushed by this fateful decision. What chance now of David retaining his land if reprisals were sought? She shuddered to picture the wrath of the overbearing, porcine Cumberland—Bryce's commander! The realization gripped her heart. Was Bryce with the troops camped a few miles away, awaiting daylight to pounce on the dispirited Jacobite army?

"Are we to give battle then?"

"Not even that, though we'll issue powder to give that impression. Cumberland's not close enough, nor is he privy to our moves. But I'll grant you, once he learns we've turned tail, he'll soon be breathing down our necks. Come, let us walk. This place depresses me."

Swathed in her borrowed cloak, Catrin caught her breath as the cold night air swept over her. Across the street a party of kilted Highlanders saluted David, recognizing him from the march. He grimly acknowledged their greeting. And his heart twisted as he considered the pain of these simple men who had come so far, achieving much against great odds. If only they could be given the chance to prove themselves, to gamble on a bid for the capital instead of bearing the shame of retreat as they scrambled for the doubtful safety of the glens.

Catrin tucked her hand beneath his arm as they walked the dark, unfamiliar streets without speaking. Eventually, unable to stand his silence, she tugged at his arm. "After such devastating news our quarrel seems meaningless," she said, surprising herself with the honest statement.

David forced a smile. "You were convinced I'd bedded Brenda, yet there was nothing of truth to it. You've made your own hell these past few days, you suspicious baggage. As for your infidelity, I soon discovered the Reverend Adam Stiles to be a devoted man of the cloth dedicated to salvaging the recalcitrant souls of his ragged Manchester regiment."

"You surely didn't believe Brenda?"

"I didn't want to believe her. But there's a lot of jealousy in my heart also."

Now it was Catrin's turn to smile as she laid her head on his shoulder. "You were really jealous, weren't you?"

Shamefaced, David agreed. "Beside myself at the thought of you in another's arms."

They stopped to embrace, leaning against the bowfront of a small establishment on the corner.

"I'll never seek another's arms. You have my promise," she vowed, her breath fragrant against his face.

"Must I make the same vow?"

Catrin squeaked indignantly until she heard him chuckle. Without further speech, David pulled her close, his mouth hot against hers. They kissed and she gave herself up to the strength of his arms, basking in the warm comfort of his embrace. Yet though she found great pleasure in his nearness, Catrin could not prevent a chill seeping through her veins when she considered the future. Retreat. Pursuit. Defeat. Those three words seemed fated to mirror their destiny. Afraid, she grasped him tight, pulling his face to hers and showering him with kisses.

"Oh, David, love, you're in such danger."

"Nay, don't fret about me, Catrin. It's you I worry about. If, and when, we cross the border, I'm not going to listen to any more protests—you're going to Garth. And that's my final word. The slender security I believed we had is gone. Now it will be a fight to the death."

His bitter words numbed her heart. Catrin did not argue with him, merely clung to his strength and tried to pretend nothing had changed. Soon David slid his arms from about her and they began to walk again.

"Where are we going?" she asked hopefully, longing to hold him in her arms, to dispel his pain and make up for the dissension that had come between them.

He smiled, knowing by that small hopeful tone what was on her mind. He hated to disappoint her. "You to your lodgings, sweet. Unfortunately, I must attend His Highness. He's probably already storming about his room demanding my presence. There's much work left to be done and not much time in which to do it. Few will sleep tonight . . . only the men, poor ignorant fools, will go cheerful to their beds."

Long before dawn the Jacobite army mustered in the Derby streets, shivering in the winter cold, yet encouraged by the mistaken belief that today they would meet the enemy. All officers had been sworn to secrecy, for Lord George Murray feared the mood of these wild men if word of their actual destination leaked out. Laughing and trading jests, assuming that being issued with powder and shot meant that they were marching to battle, the men quickly formed ranks in the misty darkness. Yesterday their weapons had been fine honed and their provisions replaced in preparation for this glorious morning when they would sally forth to give battle. Excitement over the coming fight rippled back and forth through the ranks of bloodthirsty clansmen.

It was well after dawn when first one, then another, spotted some familiar landmark passed the day before. It was only then that their mood began to change. Puzzled, but doggedly trusting their officers, the Highlanders kept faith until none could mistake the direction of their march. They were heading north!

When David could no longer ignore their questions, or the disgruntled chat between his men, he raised his head, steeling himself against the inevitable pain he was about to inflict.

"Aye, lads, you've guessed it," he said grimly as he rode alongside them. "We're on the way home. Nay, don't ask me why, I've as much idea as you. Come on, step lively, we don't want Cumberland's bayonets stuck up our arses."

A chuckle as someone suggested thrusting several bayonets in that exact spot, to be readily found on their corpulent enemy, only temporarily lightened their mood. A general air of despair began to seep through the ranks, the mood so contagious that even David's own clansmen grew silent. Some shed tears for all the hopes ground beneath their heels on this alien English soil. And though the clansmen repeatedly looked for guidance from their Bonnie Prince, he was nowhere to be seen.

Three hours after the main body of the army had vacated Derby in the black winter night, when even the rearguard commanding the Swarkstone Bridge, six miles outside the city, had been recalled, Prince Charles Edward emerged from his lodgings. Usually one of the first out of bed, enthusiastically readying the men for the march, he now allowed his own defeat to rule his actions.

He swung into the saddle without speaking to his guard and galloped ahead, passing the sullen ranks without a glance or a word of encouragement, refusing to answer the baffled clansmen's questions. Today he was not Bonnie Prince Charlie, the darling son of the Scots; today he was Charles, the half-grown princeling whose bubble had burst in this insignificant English town.

While the dispirited Jacobite army marched rapidly toward the border, passing through towns turned alarmingly hostile, jeered at by the country people, bitterly nursing their wounded pride, events a hundred and sixty miles to the south were taking place which, had they but known, would have changed their tears to laughter.

December 6, 1745, known as Black Friday, saw London in panic. Only on this day, when the Highland army was already in retreat, did word reach London of the Jacobite occupation of Derby. The Bank of England, besieged by panic-stricken Londoners, only escaped bankruptcy by paying out in sixpences. Many citizens fled the city and establishments were hurriedly boarded up. The panic was further increased by the open proclamation of King James by London Jacobites. Their German sovereign, not being a man of overwhelming courage, had his valuables packed aboard a ship that lay at anchor on the Thames, awaiting his flight to Hanover. Likewise, the hastily assembled militia defiling Finchley Common would have crumbled at the first sight of the Highlanders' screaming charge.

Had they but known, London could have been theirs. Yet Charles Edward, riding through the bitter winter weather, knew nothing of the truth. He smarted bitterly over the decision of his council, his bitterness gradually turning to deep resentment.

Charles could not accept defeat. So therefore he would not admit it. Sullen, no longer the charming Stuart Prince, Charles had buckled beneath the weight of his council's decision to cross the border again. Instinctively he knew, had he been man enough to admit it, from that moment on his cause was lost.

Chapter 13

Allowing Catrin no say in the matter, David arranged her transport to Garth. He was anxious to put as many miles between her and the enemy as possible. Catrin traveled ahead of the army, enjoying the company of her cousin Adam as far as Carlisle. In this gloomy northern land the short winter days were as frigid as the fear that gripped her heart. The local population displayed their growing contempt for the bedraggled rabble who had marched this way in triumph three short months before.

Ness rode beside the coach for many miles, trying to encourage his sister, refusing to be daunted by their changing fortunes. He had no men of his own to command, so he had thrown in his lot with Roy Stewart, acting as his junior officer. Ness ignored the overwhelming dejection of the Highland troops. Ever optimistic, and daily fortified by warming spirits, he considered the retreat more as an adventure that gave them a breathing spell to regroup and try again.

Adam was left behind at Carlisle, where he was later to be joined by the Manchester regiment that would hold the city for the Prince. Ness continued into Scotland as Catrin's escort. A gentleman riding with his sister aroused little comment, and though he was staunchly Jacobite, Ness wisely avoided drawing attention to his allegiance, putting his sister's safety before his own pride.

On a bitter January day with the bite of sleet in the wind, Catrin finally came in sight of Garth Castle. Black-shadowed in its pool of iron-gray water, the stonghold was as forbidding as a prison. The lonely countryside lay sullen beneath lowering skies. Dead bracken, stiff with ice, crackled mournfully underfoot as she alighted from the coach to bid Ness goodbye. He had refused the hospitality of the castle, preferring instead to rejoin the army, which was less than a week's march behind them.

"Thank you for your concern," she whispered, clasping Ness close, trying not to cry. "Be careful, Ness, please. You always take such chances . . ."

"Enough sisterly advice. We'll be heading south come spring, you mark my words. Charlie's not through yet," he assured, kissing her cheek. "I'll accept your hospitality next time we come this way. Say hello to Easter for me, and give her this letter from Comyn. Now I must be off."

Tears blinded Catrin as she kissed him again and said goodbye. For a few minutes she stood buffeted by the icy wind as Ness mounted and wheeled his horse about, heading south. At the crossroads he paused to wave before he spurred his horse forward, disappearing from view behind the bare trees.

The burden of the collective sorrow of the Jacobite cause seemed to settle on her shoulders as Catrin got back into the coach and told the driver to continue. Despite her thick wool traveling rugs, she could not get warm.

The driver refused to go up to the gates, afraid of disaster on the castle's narrow causeway. Assuring his passenger he would wait for the baggage to be unloaded, the driver scrambled thankfully inside the coach, leaving Catrin to travel the last hundred yards to the castle gates on foot.

The icy wind off the loch took her breath away, slicing through her cloak and the bright wool plaid she had wrapped about her body. At the gates she was challenged in Gaelic by a sentry.

"I'm Lady Catrin. Send for Mistress Stewart . . . Easter."

Not sure whether the man understood, Catrin huddled against the stonework, trying to shelter from the searing wind. Breakers marred the surface of the loch and the surrounding gray hills were only distinguishable from the angry water by the undulating snow line, which crept out of the pine and alder thickets to thrust frigid fingers among the brown heather.

To her joy and relief, it was Easter herself who ran up to the gates to greet her, accompanied by several kilted clansmen. "Catrin, love, what brings you here? Oh, you're a sight for sore eyes," gasped Easter, ordering the gates to be opened. She clasped her friend in tearful welcome when Catrin finally stepped inside the shelter of the walls. "I never expected to see you—and by yourself too! What has happened?" Easter asked, not waiting for Catrin's reply as she turned to the servants to delegate tasks.

Men were directed to the waiting coach to fetch Catrin's luggage before the two women hastened inside the great hall to the warmth of the fire that climbed halfway up the cavernous chimney.

Easter fussily saw to Catrin's comfort, insisting she remove her wet shoes and offering her dry wool stockings and a clean brown wool gown, which she donned behind a screen in the alcove beside the hearth.

The castle chambers had been frigid in summer and Catrin shuddered to think what they would be like in the depths of winter. She rather wished she could stay in the hall beside the fire, yet she knew she would be expected to take the large chamber she had shared with David.

Catrin accepted a steaming bowl of mutton broth, fresh oatcakes dipped in heather honey, and bannocks dripping with butter, all washed down by a milk concoction laced with whisky. As the warmth of food and fire penetrated her numb body, a feeling of well-being washed over her. Surprising herself by the admission, Catrin decided Garth was not as alien as she had expected. She welcomed the familiarity of these rugged stone walls, for they belonged to her beloved; this land was his inheritance, the fulfillment of his dreams.

Comforting though her memories were, as she looked about the austere hall her longing for David, which she had tried to forget, was reawakened. If only they could resume that humdrum existence which she had rejected in her foolish excitement over the cause. What had then seemed undesirable had become most appealing.

"Now, oh, now won't you tell me your news! How much longer must I sit in torment?" Easter cried when Catrin's hunger was appeased.

Catrin smiled, and she sighed deeply. Though perhaps it had not been consciously done, she had been delaying the inevitable questions. By her excitement and joy Catrin guessed Easter had heard nothing of the changing fortunes of their army. They were isolated here from the main Appin Stewarts, who might also be unaware that their grand army had turned tail.

"I brought you a letter from Comyn. Ness gave it to me before he left."

"Oh, then Ness accompanied you. Why didn't you bring him indoors to sup with us, Catrin? The hospitality's scarce in these parts. Perhaps it's not too late. He can't be more than an hour away. I'll send someone after him."

"No, Easter . . . no."

Easter's face sobered. "He didn't want to stay under the laird's roof. I understand."

"Not even that, for I think he's finally accepted our relationship. He felt his duty was to rejoin the army."

"What of their progress? How far are they from London? And why did you change your mind and come home? I remember you vowing to walk down the Strand on David's arm."

Catrin found the reminder of the vow she had laughingly made before their departure from Edinburgh painful. She took Easter's hand and made her sit on the bog-oak bench beside the hearth.

"Listen to me, Easter, for what I have to say isn't encouraging. The Prince went as far south as Derby before his council persuaded him to retreat." Ignoring her friend's horrified gasp, Catrin gripped Easter's frail hand tighter. "My cousin Adam traveled with me to Carlisle and Ness came with me through Scotland. We heard that the army safely crossed the Esk at Longtown, though it was swollen with winter rain. That was on the Prince's birthday, just before Christmas. The men were in good spirits, glad to be back on Scottish soil. That's the only news I have. The last I heard was that the enemy were close, so maybe by now they've given battle. David wanted me safe at Garth until he knew what new turn our fortunes would take."

Tears shone in Easter's eyes as she opened Comyn's letter. While Catrin waited silently for her friend to read her husband's words, she mentally relived the grueling march north through the bitter December weather. At least now the Prince was not sulking, having rallied his good humor to cheer the men. David, too, had been in better spirits when he rode alongside her for the first few miles out of Carlisle. She did not see him again. A homebound clansman of the Grants of Glenmoriston had brought her David's greetings later and informed her of the army's successful crossing of the Esk. As they drew closer to home, the Prince would be even more hard pressed to keep his army together, for the clansmen would desert wholesale, anxious to attend to the welfare of their families.

"We'll rally and continue to fight for our cause," Easter announced with determination. "Comyn says we're far from defeat."

Catrin lowered her gaze, unwilling to argue with the optimistic statement. Easter must take what comfort she could.

A woman hastened down the narrow stair leading into the hall bearing a writhing bundle wrapped in her plaid. Smiling, Easter took her baby from the woman, whom she introduced to Catrin.

"This is Jean, Douglas's nursemaid. She's very good with him . . . Tam's daughter," Easter added in an undertone.

Catrin barely recognized the wild-haired woman from old Tam's croft with her hair brushed and braided, her face scrubbed clean of peat smoke.

"Yes, I remember. How nice to see you, Jean," murmured Catrin, recalling the girl spoke only Gaelic. To her surprise, however, Jean greeted her in halting English.

"Welcome . . . home . . . Lady Catrin." Then, blushing, she hid her face in her folded plaid, embarrassed by Catrin's pleasure.

When Jean had taken Douglas to the kitchens, Easter explained. "Poor Jean has a tragic tale of her own. Douglas is a blessing to soothe her mind. Several years ago Gordon Stewart abducted her and treated her cruelly. She never told her family, but she hid in the heather and gave birth to a baby. The child was deformed and she killed it, fearing it was cursed by the fairies. Since that day her mind's been unhinged. Tam took her back, not understanding the cause of her witlessness. Since Douglas has been here, she's made a miraculous improvement."

"Poor Jean. I'd no idea. Are you teaching her to speak English?"

"I'm trying. She's slow picking up the words. She must like you to practice in your presence. That's a great compliment, for she's a shy little thing. If anything should happen to me, be kind to her, Catrin."

"Happen to you? What's going to happen to you?"

"You never know," was all Easter said, gripping her friend's hand. "Now, no more talk of gloomy things. Our main task is to keep the village functioning in our men's absence. And that's no small task. Years of deprivation have made near imbeciles of some of the women. Their children are like wild creatures.

I've taken them in hand a little and am trying to teach them to behave like human beings. You can help me with that. And then we're always in need of help in the kitchens. With the men gone, many of our women have gone back to their homes to care for their families. I made those oatcakes and broth you ate."

Catrin was suitably impressed by Easter's newfound domesticity. Yet while her friend chatted on about mundane village matters, she felt a growing sense of unreality. It seemed as if they should have been performing some great feat to aid the cause instead of living as if it did not exist.

As the freezing weeks passed, Catrin soon learned to take great comfort from those ordinary matters which at first she had despised. She purposely immersed herself in the boring repetition of teaching women to cook, to scavenge for something nutritious, and to keep their children clean, while she thrust to the back of her mind her fear for David's safety.

As lady of the castle, village disputes were also brought to her to judge. A young boy with a club foot served as her interpreter in these matters. Lachie had traveled with the clan last summer, but had been forced to turn back to aid his grandfather, who had not lived to see his beloved Appin hills again. Now Lachie had attached himself to Catrin, serving her with fervent loyalty. He was a simple lad with an aptitude for languages, having picked up English from Tam's wife while he helped her about the croft during her husband's absence. Catrin was grateful for the lad's help.

February and March passed without let up in the winter weather. April dawned, and but for the calendar Catrin would not have been aware of spring's approach. In London the crocuses would have bloomed already; daffodils would be edging the lawns with gold and buds would be bursting in anticipation of spring. At Garth April brought little change. Perhaps now the snow did not lie as long, and the ice on the burn was easier to break, but Catrin must look in vain for primroses and apple blossom.

The wind whipped sleet in the faces of the Jacobite army as they stood on Culloden Moor awaiting the government attack. Icy rain lashed against bare skin and numbing cold increased the gnawing pain of empty bellies. For days the men had eaten little more than a few handfuls of oatmeal or cabbage leaves stolen from impoverished crofts. Their supply train was nonexistent, rations of biscuit being barely enough to keep them alive. Dog tired, some from foraging far afield for food, others from an abortive night march over boggy ground in preparation for a surprise attack on the enemy that never took place, the soldiers weaved where they stood, swords bending beneath their weight. Many had thrown away their targes on the night march and stood without protection. The Highland line stretched sparsely for over a thousand yards and frequent exhortations to "close ranks" effected little change; the Highlander needed a good thirty inches to wield his weapons.

David had dismounted to stand with his men, who despite their hunger and weariness were eager for the coming fight. Wrapping his sodden plaid tighter about his body, he walked among them, his boots squelching on the boggy ground.

Culloden Moor, a portion of the high plateau known as Drummossie Moor, was a poor site for clan warfare, giving the advantage to the enemy artillery. It had been argued that better ground could be found across the Nairn, high ground that would suit the wild Highland charge and put Cumberland's horsemen at a disadvantage. But Charles, for once taking the initiative, and swayed more by flattery from his Irishmen than by common sense, refused to retreat in hopes that this would become a second Prestonpans. Falkirk, their other minor victory gained in January, had not the glory of that first battle. And glumly, as he eyed the stinging gray curtain driven in the Lowland wind, David instinctively knew today's action would resemble neither.

Dead, brown heather and boggy depressions, crude drystone walls and a few isolated crofts dotted this broad expanse of land edging the Moray Firth. The moor was used to pasture sheep in the summer. Five hundred feet above sea level, this stretch of windswept moorland was bitter even on a June day, with nothing to break the force of the wind from the North Sea as it roared through the mouth of the Great Glen. The few sod houses on the brown moor belonged to tacksmen of Mackintosh of Moy Hall. To their north lay the boundary of the estate of President Forbes of Culloden; to their south three farms, whose drystone walls stretched up from the River Nairn to the heather-clad moor.

The Stewarts of Appin were in the front line of the army's right wing, commanded by Lord George Murray who stood with his own Atholl men. The Camerons were on the Stewarts' right. Lord John Drummond had command of the army's center and positioned the Frasers to the Appin men's left; next to them came contingents of Clan Chattan, the clan of the cat. The combatants ranged along that broad front were aware of the identities of only their immediate neighbors, whose ancient names read like a roll call of clan history.

Grouped on this desolate moorland in the driving sleet the Highlanders awaited the battle that was to decide the fate of their cause. At the front of each clan, and therefore closest to the enemy, stood its chief or his representative, followed by his immediate family, his piper, and his handpicked bodyguard, consisting of two men from each company under his command. These companies were led by their own chieftains, as were the different septs owing allegiance to the clan chief. After the chieftains came their sons, or sons of sons. The leading ranks of each company were comprised of well-armed landholding men; behind them came lesser ranking men, the hierarchy going down to the wild-bearded common man, those bare-chested, bare-legged humblies as scantily armed as they were clad, yet still maintaining familial fighting groups of fathers, sons, brothers, standing together in defense of their clan honor.

Against the drab winter landscape the kilted clans made bright splashes of red and faded green. Their blue bonnets bore the Stuarts' white cockade, a knot of five bows of silk or linen bearing an inscription, the favors fashioned in hundreds by seamstresses from Edinburgh to Manchester.

The Jacobite artillery, such as it was, fired the first shot over the scarlet-coated enemy, a ball that hit a soldier in the rear ranks. Their aim was never to grow truer and, after five minutes the Prince's guns, manned for the most part by unskilled clansmen, grew silent. Now the high moor shuddered as the government guns replied, belching smoke that rapidly engulfed the waiting clans. The bombardment continued to deadly effect. Screaming men went down and the clansmen moved in to close the gaps. For an hour they stood in the bitter wind and sleet awaiting orders to move while they were systematically slaughtered by Cumberland's artillery. And the orders never came.

In a confusion of sleet and smoke, surrounded by the blood-quickening music of the pipes and the agonized screams of the wounded, the clansmen waited until they could wait no longer. Suddenly the line broke. Clan Chattan charged, uttering blood-curdling battle cries. A third of some of the clan regiments already writhed on the ground. This was not their method of warfare; fighting hand-to-hand combat with dirk, targe, and broadsword was all the clansmen knew.

Once the Mackintoshes, the MacBeans, and MacGillivrays of Clan Chattan were away, the Atholl men, the Camerons and the Appin Stewarts, with Ardshiel at their head, followed. Right arms lifted high, broadswords gleaming through the smoke, they came on, defiantly screaming their battle cries. A deadly hail of grapeshot met their charge.

In the thick smoke and the sheer force of bodies racing across the sodden heather, David soon lost sight of Comyn, who had commanded men to his left, and of Ness, who had stood on his right. All he could see were wild men racing forward, shouting their rage and despair, running into the mouths of cannon and musket. The line moved obliquely toward the enemy's left, emerging from the rolling smoke like a pack of ravenous wolves, deprivation forgotten now they were on a death run.

Something happened and men were suddenly colliding on the moor, either meeting the running horde of Clan Chattan blinded by heavy smoke, or being mown down by the deadly rain of grape. Men stumbled and fell over fathers, sons, and brothers in the dreadful slaughter. Many threw away their muskets without firing them, running in for the kill with sword and ax. The wind temporarily blew the smoke aloft to reveal rows of enemy musketeers forming an impenetrable wall of red coats, white gaiters, and deadly fire. The clans went down in great heaps in their mad suicide charge. Yet many men kept going, hacking, slicing, clearing a path in the enemy lines, driven by fury and despair as the grape and musketry took its terrible toll.

At last the fury slackened. Those who were able fell back in twos and threes, finally in whole groups as Stewarts, Camerons, and the assorted tribes of Clan Chattan detached themselves from the slaughter, leaving behind their dead and dying on the blood-soaked heather.

David went down, unaware of the extent of his own wounds as he reached for old Tam, whose head had been half blown off by a musket ball. The old man smiled, gripping his hand, before his face dissolved in a torrent of blood. The shock of the charge, the screams of the dying clansmen surrounding him, had numbed David to his own pain. Gradually he became aware of the wetness of his plaid; more than the sodden rain, this warm sticky fluid was of his own making. Beneath the red plaid his jacket sleeve was saturated with blood. The searing pain in his collarbone made him wonder if the bone was shattered.

All about him lay the little chieftains of the septs of Appin wrapped in their blood-soaked plaids, dying in this hostile land, raked by bitter wind and choked by drifting clouds of smoke. David did not know if Ardshiel lived. He had seen some of Ardshiel's family go down, including his old uncle Duncan.

Men writhed about him in their death agony, their chests, their heads, their limbs, half shot away. David buried his face in the dead heather, tasting dirt in his mouth, lying still as riders thundered past. He was too wise to raise his head to see if they were friend or foe, yet he suspected they were Cumberland's cavalry, for their own cavalry was now largely unhorsed.

In less than an hour the last gasp of the clansmen's fury had been spent. Outnumbered two to one, tactically inferior, lacking firepower and cavalry, the clansmen fought a primitive battle against modern military might, a battle they were fated to lose before it began. Half starved, exhausted, and outmaneuvered, though they claimed few of Cumberland's men in comparison to their own fallen, the clansmen had successfully penetrated the enemy ranks, a miraculous feat not anticipated by Cumberland's officers.

The battle was over. The war was lost.

Prince Charles fled the field with his officers, deserting the clans who had fought and died for his cause. Unknown to those simple men, they had been fighting for their own existence in the country of their birth. And now their enemies were to make the survivors pay dearly for the deeds of the fallen.

When David awoke it was dark. A bitter wind swept across the moor and he tried to huddle closer into his wet plaid. The pain in his arm and shoulder robbed him of breath and he had to rest between movements. As his eyes adjusted to his surroundings he saw lights flickering in the blackness and over the cries of the wounded he heard voices of people searching the heaps of slain.

Beggars, comrades, wives, and daughters wandered over the field. The government troops had done their work well, clubbing and bayoneting the wounded, though many still writhed in agony, stubbornly refusing to die.

Slowly, painfully, David pulled himself from under the dead

limbs that had trapped him face down in the frozen heather. He still had his plaid, as did most of the slain about him, but he understood well enough what was taking place on the desolate battlefield. The rough voices belonging to those shadowy presences were Highland ones. These were not ghouls from Cumberland's ranks, they were beggars from the nearby hills and sod huts systematically stripping the dead and wounded.

He crawled over the frozen ground, trying to avoid the bodies, for more exertion was required to clear obstacles. When movement or voices came close, he stopped, playing dead. He headed for a low wall to his right that would afford shelter. Every motion brought fresh blood gushing warmly down his arm. With his teeth he worked through his cambric shirttail, struggling to rip a length of fabric to tie about his arm. Sweat broke on his brow and trickled down his cheeks as he moved his arm, or attempted to move it, having little control of the afflicted limb. The fire in his collarbone was almost more than he could bear. With his teeth and one good arm he looped the cambric strip about his sleeve, but try as he might he could not bring the ends together tight enough to stop the bleeding.

Exhausted, he lay thankfully in the shelter of the wall. Finding a dead man nearby he stole his tattered plaid to give himself a second covering to withstand the night cold.

Footsteps crunched over the frosty ground, alerting him to someone's approach. David's eyes opened, but he did not move. It was still dark, but the bitter freshening wind and the thinning sky told him morning was near. How he would defend himself from the looters he did not know. He was determined to do what he could to keep his scant coverings. A woman crouched nearby, rolling over a body near the wall and stripping the plaid from the bloodied corpse. Another woman, finding her victim not yet dead, and tired of fighting his feeble resistance, smashed a rock against the wounded man's brow.

A white hand, ghostly in a feeble lantern flame, reached to the body closest to him, rolled over the corpse, then moved on. Not all the women looted; some where searching for loved ones. The same hand reached to him, preparing to turn him over. He heard the woman gasp as his eyes closed against the light. The impression of a white face half obscured by a muddied red plaid danced between the black spots under his closed lids. So weary was he, so weak from hunger and loss of blood, David could not fully comprehend. He thought the woman spoke his name. He liked to think she had, but when she tugged at him, trying to push him upright, he rasped in protest, wanting to be left alone to rest.

"Davie, help me. For Christ's sake, don't fail me now."

The woman tugged again. Then she prodded him, and he could barely endure the agony as she made him stand. His ankle buckled under him and to his surprise in the light of her lantern he saw a red stream gush from a crusted cavern in his shin. Fog descended as he stumbled and fell. The woman cursed. She slapped him, trying to rouse him. And in his turn David cursed her back.

"Let me be, you bitch," he muttered through parched lips where blood tasted salty on his tongue.

She slapped him again and he feebly raised his hand to defend himself. Then he was falling through blissful warmth without pain . . .

"Get up, damn you, Davie, help me."

She would not let him enjoy his peace, this damnable woman. Through glazing eyes he tried to identify her, but her features blurred in the gray light of dawn, lost in the folds of her ancient plaid. Now she was taking him against her, panting with exertion, moving him over the frost-rimmed ground. Shrilly the woman cursed others around her, who replied in kind. Someone struck at her and his rescuer kicked at the other creature, delivering a resounding blow that sent her yelping to the heather. When next David fell, lying face down on the slick white heather, he determined this was to be the last thing he would do.

Pink-edged dawn peeped from beyond the mountains and Ness shivered where he lay, trying to draw what was left of his tattered coat closer about his body. His head was on fire. Tentatively he reached to his temple, wincing at the unexpected pain of the sticky contact. He had been hit, yet the bullet must only have grazed him. For an insane moment, as he struggled to his feet, stumbling over corpses stripped naked on the ground, he wondered if he was already dead. Could he be dead and unaware of it? A ghost among these others, populating a world that no longer existed?

Shuddering, he swiftly dismissed the macabre notion. He would give his all for the sweet taste of whisky. Or perhaps a jug of ale from the nearest tavern. More acutely than food he craved a "dram," as the Highlanders called it. Or maybe he would settle for a glass of claret from the hogsheads raided from Governor Forbes's cellars.

Ness sweated and shivered as he struggled to climb through a broken drystone wall. He fell back, appalled at what he had seen. High against the pinkish sky stretched the moor, littered with pyramids of slain from which writhed white limbs, jerking spasmodically. Men clawed the ground, inching painfully along, going nowhere. There were cries and groans, pleas for water. And he had none.

Crouching beside the wall, Ness guardedly surveyed the moor. Figures wrapped against the bitter cold were moving everywhere like corbie crows stripping the wounded. He cried out in rage, but his voice seemed buried in his chest. When he came to his senses he was eternally grateful for his weakness.

A sod hut stood nearby and he staggered and crawled to its shelter, only to find it already crammed with dead and wounded. There was room to shelter beneath a leanto where hay was stored, and Ness burrowed deep into the warm hay. He was drowsy, but for a long time he did not sleep, unable to block out the groans from inside the hut or his own pain and hunger.

A sudden searing agony in his side brought him plunging from the hay, directly into the redcoated arms of a government soldier who had been systematically bayoneting the haypile. Blood gurgled and bubbled through the rent in his tattered coat as Ness stood swaying, momentarily baffled by his predicament. He suddenly broke and ran. But they caught him, clubbing him to the ground. He lay there a long time until he was finally roused by the stench of smoke. There was a crackling sound, which was shortly followed by screams of agony and a stench more horrible than he had ever smelled before. The soldiers had fired the bothy where the wounded clansmen lay!

Ness struggled to his feet, swaying. Soldiers stood about the blazing dwelling, ready to shoot any who tried to escape. He ran and fell and got up and ran again. But to no avail. Watching him, considering it great sport, the redcoats even pinged bullets around his feet, making no attempt to hit him. And when he was too spent to give further sport, they descended on him, bayonets raised. Only a sharp voice issuing a command to desist halted the descending steel.

A young officer ordered the man to drag Ness to his feet, noting the fine cut of his coat, his good leather boots, the last gold button dangling from his waistcoat. This man might be a worthy prize. When they beat him down again with the butts of their muskets, Ness did not resist.

Much later, he saw the sun struggling through the clouds and realized he was in a wagon bouncing along a road littered with civilian corpses. From another man he learned they were bound for Inverness and the Tollbooth jail. Ness took heart at the news, thinking that perhaps now he would have his wounds dressed, especially since the officer had already singled him out as gentry.

His optimism was unfounded. When Ness was thrown into a stinking room already crowded with moaning wounded, the floor swimming with filth, he discovered his nightmare had only just begun.

In a stumbling daze of pain, David was taken from the field. He was slapped, cursed at, upbraided constantly by the woman. Plead though he might, she would not allow him to rest. Finally, when he could go no further, she kicked at him in her frustration. He ignored the blows, too spent to be roused. Blissfully he lay there, finding the icy ground soft as a feather bed. His tormentress had gone!

Not for long the bliss of resting. In what seemed like seconds she was back. Cursing him anew, slapping his face to bring him to life. Now the confounded woman was trying to undress him! He yelled with the last of his strength when she pulled free his coat, jerking the agony of his arm, his shoulder. Remorseful, she patted his cheek, gentle this time, and when she leaned over him he was aware of her tears splashing on his face.

Between them they managed to put on the coat, she pleased at the accomplishment, he only grateful the pain had stopped. This coat she struggled to button about him was warm, its buff facings splashed with brown. It was not his, but it did not matter. He was beyond caring. Again she was beating him from the ground, railing at him. There were other voices too. And many red coats.

"My man's hurt bad. Where are the company surgeons?"

English voices answered and he heard the clink of coins, followed by feminine laughter, before the agony began again. David pleaded with her to let him be. She would not heed his words.

When he was finally allowed to stop, he was saturated with mingled blood and sweat. Gingerly he brought the sleeve of his coat to his brow, unable to remember if either of his arms still worked. In surprise he saw the sleeve was red. The woman had dressed him in an English regimental coat!

"We've little to aid the lads," said a Lowland Scots voice.

But the man came anyway. He forced back the coat and David screamed aloud his pain. Whisky was put to his lips and he drank long and deep, thankful for the favor. Through a dull haze he saw a figure bending over him, reeking of onions, kippers, and strong tobacco. Then a red-hot pain possessed him and he screamed until his voice broke; he went on screaming soundlessly as he plunged into a pit of darkness.

When next he woke David found himself in a small stone chamber. The air was frigid and the steady drip of water never ceased. The place felt and looked like a tomb! Fear raced through him. He looked about and by the light coming through a broken place, where tangled grasses invaded the stonework, he saw shattered coffins tossed about. Gripping his heart, he became joyfully aware that his hand leaped under the beat. They had thrown him in this vault and left him for dead!

Tentatively he moved his legs. One ankle burned like a furnace. When he tried to lever himself to a sitting position, he collapsed, biting his lips in pain. Glancing down he saw a white bandage, reddened, but otherwise clean, swathing his chest inside the hated red jacket. After much struggling he finally got to his knees and from there, with the aid of an ancient stone coffin, to his feet. He felt light-headed and a rushing sound roared past his ears. Gritting his teeth, he waited for the tomb to right itself.

The voice of his tormentress said, "So, you're back from the dead, Davie. It's about time."

And he knew he was not free. Today, all over again, she would torture him, driving him beyond endurance, forcing him to her will.

"For Christ's sweet sake, you cursed bitch, leave me alone!"

"Aye, and had I let you alone you'd be meat for the crows, or spitted on one of Butcher Billy's bayonets. You'd best thank your maker I found you first."

The voice was familiar. At first he did not know who the woman could be. Rustling from the dim corner alerted him to another presence as a man's weak voice called out, "Water, Brenda . . . water."

Brenda! His head reeled as he tried to remember where and when he had known a woman called Brenda. She tended other wounded; he could hear two different voices. The only Brenda he had known was Brenda Carmichael!

"Surely to God it's not . . . not Brenda Carmichael!"

"You needn't sound surprised. I'm a hard lass to get rid of. And yes, it's me, you ungrateful bastard. The others came quietly. You were hell on earth to bring in."

"Where are we?"

"A cozy tomb in a nearby churchyard. You're safer here than up above, though I wish to God it had a fireplace."

David's mouth twisted in what he fancied was a grin and he lowered himself gingerly to the ground.

"What's happened?" he asked later when she left the others and came to his side. "Are we being hunted?"

"Hunted would be a pleasanter way to go. Massacred is more accurate," she spat bitterly, offering him a piece of stale bannock. "Is your ankle easier?"

David felt his ankle, finding it splinted, his boot cut away. "What injury is there?"

"A musket ball splintered a bone. You took another ball in the neck which broke your collarbone, and a half pound of grape in the shoulder. Oh, you've done yourself proud, Davie lad."

"Have you news of the Garth men, or Comyn, or Ness?"

"No. I didn't find them, but they're likely out there."

"Who are the others then?"

"Toby Lomax, one of Ardshiel's tacksmen from Ballachulish, and a MacGillivray. You're faring better than they. I didn't think about trying to pass them off as one of Howard's regiment. At least you've been doctored by one of their surgeons."

"Thank God for that. Is there anything we can do for them?"

"Nothing." Brenda shook her head and looked away. "Soon I'll go up top. A woman's bringing me bread. Now lie still, Davie, get back your strength, there's a good lad."

Delivering a maternal pat, Brenda scrambled forward, wormed her way up through a shattered corner of the old tomb, and disappeared.

Sometime later David roused himself to attend to the other wounded. One body was cold and the MacGillivray whispered that the lifeguard was gone. There was not enough light to distinguish features, but David assumed the dead lifeguard to be Toby Lomax. He found water in a skin and he held it to the men's parched lips. There was little else he could do for them except move a rock for a pillow and struggle to pull the coat from the dead man to give to the MacGillivray, whose teeth chattered.

Scrambling overhead, followed by powdery rock falls, announced Brenda's return. She brought a loaf and a chunk of cheese, which she divided.

"Eat hearty, you'll need your strength," she said, thrusting a sizable portion of food at him.

David devoured the food as Brenda scrambled away to check on her other charges.

When she returned a few minutes later, Brenda dabbed her eyes with her plaid. "Toby's dead," she said. "The MacGillivray too. Can you help me get the Stewart man through the hole?"

"I'll try."

"We must be off. They say the burial parties are coming tomorrow to clear the moor. All rebels are to be hunted down. We can't risk staying here. I've bribed a lad to carry us to Nairn."

David woke hours later. So numb were his limbs he felt as if he were already dead. Scratches came from the rock overhead. Brenda answered the summons, urgently consulting with someone in the dark.

A few minutes later she was at David's side, urging him to get up and help drag the Ballachulish man toward the entrance. Weakness assailed him when he stood, putting his weight on his good leg and tentatively trying the splinted ankle. He managed to balance by holding on to the rocks.

Between them they dragged the man across the vault floor. His left leg was mangled and the pain of movement was so intense the lad bit through his lips to keep from crying out. Wrapped in the dry plaid of the dead MacGillivray and wearing Toby's boot on his good foot, the Ballachulish man staggered upright. They pushed him through the hole while the carter's boy pulled from above. So terrible was the exertion, David wanted to vomit; he even turned aside to do so until Brenda slapped him.

"None of that, you ungrateful sod. Have you any idea how hard it is to get food? Keep it down."

Normally her shrewish command would have angered him. Yet in his weakness he had grown accustomed to Brenda's orders, so David swallowed, gritting his teeth as he struggled to do as he was bid.

Getting through the hole with only one good arm was almost

more than he could manage. The carter's lad grabbed his injured shoulder and David could not keep from crying out, though Brenda thumped him for his foolishness. Inching over the rim, clinging to the vegetation growing there, David prayed his way to the top; he could credit no other way of managing the feat. He lay beside the Ballachulish man, his stomach heaving, aware of sweat trickling inside his clothing. Brenda followed swiftly, marshaling her charges to their feet, stricter than any sergeant.

As David clung weakly to the cart they were to ride in, he discovered it was full of coffins. The irony of the situation made him chuckle and, eyes blazing, Brenda slapped him into silence. While David lay in a coffin atop the swaying cart, he vowed vengeance on his tormenter, eager for the return of his strength if only to teach that red-haired amazon the value of humility.

Rain blew in the wind as they clattered into Nairn, stopping before the cabinet shop of Angus Macleay. The lad slid from his perch and Brenda followed.

They had been stopped twice on the road by parties of redcoats who joked that if they'd a mind to wait, they'd soon fill their coffins for them. Brenda distributed kisses, promising even more while she eluded their reaching hands, telling them to seek her out in a well-known Nairn tavern where she danced nightly for King George's brave men.

The cabinetmaker opened the wide door and several men pulled the caskets from the cart. The two full coffins were placed near the back, convenient to the rear door.

Brenda laughingly passed through the workroom, flattering the old cabinetmaker, and kissing him by the sound of it; to the lad she gave the buttons from Toby Lomax's coat, swearing they were solid gold. A swift kick delivered to the side of the casket, which sent David's head spinning and his arm throbbing, he assumed to be the signal to leave his stifling bed. The lid was loose and he easily pushed it up. Inside the cabinet shop it was dark, but not as dark as the coffin had been.

David helped the Ballachulish man out of his coffin as best he could, wondering how a man with a mangled leg would survive in Nairn. The lad smiled and nodded his thanks, his compressed lips forbidding speech. David took him to a bench to rest, noting with sorrow that his white beardless face was covered in sweat and grim with pain as he laid his head against the scarred wall.

"Take heart, lad, we'll do the best we can for you." But as

he left the shivering youth, David had little hope for him.

"Well, you took your time. I was beginning to think you felt at home in your coffin," Brenda snapped when David tentatively emerged in the rain-spattered alley. "Where's the lad?"

David inclined his head toward the coffin shed.

"Good. The cabinetmaker says he'll care for him. We'll have to leave the lad behind, we haven't time to worry about him."

"What are we going to do here?"

"Get this cloak over you to begin with. We'll have to find something else for you to wear. The red coat's served its purpose."

"I never realized how scheming you were, Brenda Carmichael," David remarked later, as they crouched in the doorway of a shed in a deserted wynd. She grinned as she bustled him out of the red uniform coat and into a damp shirt, stock, and fustian coat she had stolen from washlines in a neighboring close.

"Aye, well, you might live to sing my praises yet, Davie Stewart, but not if we don't shake a leg. I've a pony spotted down the wynd. We might just be in time to liberate the poor creature from its tether."

When they rode out of Nairn, David was astride a skinny highland pony, a minister's flat black hat perched on his unruly hair. Brenda also had a mount, a jenny ass bearing baskets of provisions she had spied tethered outside a tavern.

"We'd better ride a while before we sup," she suggested, eyeing the metallic sky. "Likely there'll be a deserted bothy somewhere on the moor."

A tumbledown bothy was found in which to shelter from the cold rain. For the first time in weeks David was full after feasting on fresh bread and baps, fruit scones, pies, and black pudding, washed down with whisky. More awaited them for the morrow. After their initial feast, if they were careful, the food might last till they reached Appin.

"Now, my lad, we'll head to a place I heard of. A cove where we can sell the animals for a passage aboard ship."

"No."

Brenda's head snapped up, her tangled red hair making her appear fierce. "What do you mean, no? I didn't ask what you wanted to do, I told you."

"And I'm telling you, woman," David growled, gripping

her slender wrist, his fingers leaving bruises on the white freckled skin. "I'm taking no ship. I'm going to Garth. Catrin's in danger and I'm not sacrificing her to the redcoats. If what you tell me's true, she is in for her share of reprisals. We must get there ahead of the soldiers."

"Don't talk like a fool!"

"If you won't come with me, I'll go alone. You can take ship for wherever you wish, but you take it alone."

They glared at each other in the murky light, dodging the pattering leaks in the bothy roof.

"You ungrateful bastard!"

"I thank you for saving me—I'll always be in your debt. My need to go to Garth has nothing to do with ingratitude. Surely you understand that."

Brenda's face looked old and haggard in the gray light.

"Oh, aye, Davie Stewart, I understand it well enough." For a few minutes she silently contemplated the situation.

"Besides, you've bullied me long enough. A man can only stand so much," David said breaking the silence.

Brenda glanced at him and saw his grin. She swallowed, tears gleaming in her eyes. "And so can a woman," she said bitterly. "Have it your way—to Appin it is. At least my sister will be pleased to see me."

Before dawn they left the moor, and as they rode south rain soaked them to the skin. Skulking over rough terrain, fording overflowing burns, and sheltering from the worst downpours, they made few miles. As the hours passed David began to grow hot until he thought his head would burst. They were coming up a bracken-clad slope, the sturdy animals surefooted on the springy ground, when the world began to spin. David pitched from the saddle.

"Christ, you stubborn man, you're burning with fever," Brenda clucked as she leaned over him. "Why didn't you say something?"

Struggling with his weight, she dragged him toward the bracken-fronded entrance to a cave on the hillside down which clear water thundered. Curiously, though she feared for his health, Brenda's heart lightened. Once again she was in command.

Chapter 14

The grass grew lush and green as warm May sunshine brought the hills to life. Spells of cold and rain still beset them, but the long-awaited spring had finally arrived. The breeze was laden with the scent of flowers and the sweetness of grasses. And David still did not come.

Each morning Catrin scanned the nearby hills in hope of seeing horsemen approach. But the hills were bare. She fretted at their isolation and contemplated sending men further afield to see if they could learn anything about the army's progress.

It was on just such a fine spring morning, after her customary scan of the hillside, during which she found nothing more promising than circling birds, that Catrin went back to the castle. Easter had been ill lately and much of the load of running Garth had fallen to her. A heavy flux, which to Catrin's alarm Easter had confided had flowed on and off since her baby's birth, had temporarily laid her low. Weak, but stubbornly struggling to pull her weight, Easter moved about the castle like a wraith, thin and white-faced, her cheekbones jutting through her delicate skin.

"Lady Catrin, will you come outside with me?" Lachie asked urgently.

Catrin obliged, wondering at the lad's haste as he scurried ungainly on his misshapen foot.

"What is it, Lachie? I've much to do."

"A man, Lady Catrin, a man," was all he whispered. Then glancing about, he said louder, "Come, I want to show you the fine goldcrest nest in the juniper scrub yonder. We can gather branches for smoking the hams at the same time. Hurry, Lady Catrin."

Completely baffled by his talk of goldcrests, Catrin stared at Lachie without comprehending. Only when she noticed one of the older retainers walking ahead of them toward the outer gate did she understand. Lachie had been reluctant to divulge his actual message in the man's hearing. They had no evidence, but her people suspected the old man of treachery and were careful what they discussed in his presence. Her heart raced as she followed Lachie, surprised by his speed.

"The thrushes are also fine this year," Lachie continued when they reached the gate.

Grunting, the gray-haired man swung open the gates.

Catrin pulled her plaid over her head and followed Lachie across the narrow causeway. Today the water was low and they crossed the bar without wetting their feet. Earlier in the year melting snows and spring rains had swollen the loch and trips ashore had to be made by boat.

They hurried along the shoreline. Lachie took the lead, glancing about furtively at every noise. At last, satisfied they were not being spied upon, he stopped and waited for Catrin. "I found a wounded man in the woods. He asked me to bring my lady to him."

Catrin clapped her hand over her mouth. David! Surely it was not David. "Is he the laird?" she asked the lad, running now, eager to reach their destination.

Blankly Lachie looked at her. "I don't think so, my lady. The laird's dark. This man is bandaged about, but his beard is yellow."

Her heart sank at the disappointing news.

Birds called shrilly to each other as they entered the birch and alder thickets. A scrambling noise in the undergrowth made them spin about, but it was only a fox or a badger, for the path was deserted.

Lachie led Catrin to the spot where he found the man. No one was there. Puzzled, the lad lifted bramble arcs and beat at gorse thickets with an improvised club he had wrested from a sapling, searching for the stranger.

"Are ye here, sir? I've brought my lady," he called in Gaelic, then again in English.

They waited and Catrin became aware of a prickling sensation along her arms and legs as she tensed, listening for some response. Suddenly the bushes parted and a man stumbled out of the tangled thicket. He was clad in rags of assorted tartans, a crude crutch beneath his arm, his face almost invisible under a filthy bandage.

"Ye're a good lad," he croaked through parched, cracked lips. "You're from Garth then?"

"I'm Catrin, Lady of Garth. Can I help you?"

"You're a sight for sore eyes, Catrin of Garth. Don't you recognize me, Mistress Blair, or should I say Stewart?"

The man partially pulled aside his bandages and a thatch of dirty corn-colored hair spilled free.

"Comyn! Oh, God, what brings you here? And wounded too!" Catrin embraced him, stinking rags and all.

"Is David home?" he asked hopefully, though prepared for her disappointing reply.

"No, I haven't seen him. Have you no news of him? Or of Ness?"

Hot tears blinded Catrin and spilled down her cheeks when Comyn revealed he did not know what fate had befallen her loved ones after the big battle they had fought outside Inverness.

Between them Catrin and Lachie supported Comyn as far as the road, where they bade him wait in the shelter of the beeches while they fetched a cart.

Eager hands helped lift Comyn aboard the cart, while Catrin cautioned the men to be mindful of his wounds. He was weak from exertion, lack of food, and loss of blood. Catrin must curb her impatience and bide her time to question him further about the battle.

Fortunately, when they entered the castle, Easter was still asleep, and Catrin decided it might be wise if she learned the worst before waking her friend.

At her orders the serving women brought whisky, fresh bread, and broth, which Comyn gulped down. Catrin cut a chunk of roast mutton and he speared it on his dirk, tearing into the flesh like a savage.

Between mouthfuls of food and swigs of warming spirit, he briefly recounted his adventures after escaping from the bloody battlefield on the shores of the Moray Firth. Catrin covered her face while she listened to his account of the clans' wholesale slaughter, now being followed by savage reprisals carried out throughout the Highlands.

"Will they come here?" she asked, knowing his answer before she spoke.

"David's a known Jacobite. They'll come."

"Perhaps we're too poor to interest them. Besides, this glen's so narrow and isolated."

Wearily Comyn shook his head. "Were it merely the width of a bothy, they'll come, Catrin. You're fortunate you haven't been harmed already. The devils must be waiting for good weather." Comyn glanced toward the open door, where pale spring sunshine dappled the stone. "This is good Jacobite-hunting weather. Post lookouts. When the soldiers are sighted you must hide. But first, where's my wife and little lad? I've longed for them all these months!"

Catrin would not allow Comyn to see Easter until the servants had ministered to his wounds. With gritted teeth she helped the women wash and dress his suppurating head wound and gagged in revulsion at the maggots infesting the hole in his leg. Comyn assured her it was a natural, often beneficial process, and directed her to pour whisky over the place. His wounds dressed, they trimmed his beard and brought clothing to replace his rags. After their ministrations, despite his bandaged head and swollen leg, Comyn appeared presentable.

"Now, you can see her," Catrin pronounced with satisfaction. "You'd have scared poor Easter witless if she'd seen you as we found you. Stay here and eat more. We've sufficient. I'll go up and wake her."

Catrin hurried from the room up the narrow stair to the bedchambers. Through an arrow slit she glanced at the silver loch glinting in the sunshine. The pleasant green loch shore still had the ability to make her blood run cold. Had her feeling of foreboding been a forecast of horrors to come? Now, when she strained into the distance searching for moving specks on the hillsides, she would be looking for redcoats. Today was clear and she could see shapes moving through the patches of sun and shadow, but she could not tell if they were cattle or King George's soldiers.

She prayed they were cattle.

"Easter, wake up, darling, I've a wonderful surprise for you," Catrin whispered, laying her hand gently on Easter's pale brow. Easter's lids were so terribly transparant, her blue eyes seemed to shine through the skin. Her lids fluttered and opened.

"Oh, Catrin, a surprise! Whatever can it be?" Easter smiled at her and clasped her hand. "Help me up, you know I always enjoy surprises."

Catrin frowned as she noticed a patch of blood on the sheet

where Easter had lain. It was only a small amount, but it was an ominous sign. All the potions of St. John's wort, the teas of lady's mantle, which Aggie, the castle wisewoman, had poured down Easter, had failed to halt the periodic bleeding. Sense warned her Easter could not bleed forever.

"Nay, 'tis not much, Catrin," Easter assured, aware of her friend's concern. "I'm feeling much better for the rest. Help me change my skirts."

With her hair freshly braided and dressed in a clean gown, Easter descended the narrow stair, eager for the surprise Catrin promised. In the hall below she saw a bandaged man hunched over the fire, a flagon in his hand. Easter smiled, guessing their laird had come home at last. Catrin had been so patient.

At the sound of their footsteps the man turned, revealing his distinctive corn-colored beard. "Comyn!" Easter shrieked in delight, stumbling on the final step before racing over the flagged floor, her arms outstretched.

As Catrin watched them embrace a lump rose in her throat and she came close to tears. She ached at the reminder of David's arms about her, at the memory of his kiss. She would give anything to be welcoming him at this moment. Dark thoughts of death had filled her mind as the weeks passed without word. That David had died on Culloden Moor was a possibility she could not deny. David could be a prisoner, or he could be hiding in the heather with his prince.

Above Easter's neatly braided hair Comyn glanced sharply at Catrin, worry lines furrowing his brow. Easter's appearance gave him just cause for concern. Yet Catrin shook her head in warning, hoping to dissuade him from commenting on his wife's gaunt condition.

Easter sent for Jean to bring down the baby for his father's approval. Soon the hall was abuzz with voices as retainers came eagerly forth to question Comyn about the fate of their loved ones. Jean carried in the baby and Comyn laughingly bounced Douglas on his good knee, finding the boy still undersized though apparently in good health. Douglas surprised them all by laughing at his father, unafraid of this bearded stranger with the deep voice.

When the joyful greetings and the questions were done, Comy reluctantly broached the subject he knew would destroy Easter's happy mood. He intended to keep stories of the troop's atrocities to a minimum, while still trying to impress on them the danger of their position.

"I was telling Catrin it will be best if you post lookouts. The redcoats are harrying the glens and I'm afraid for your safety."

"We've no need to worry about our safety now you're home," Easter cried, squeezing her husband's hand.

Comyn smiled, touched by his wife's faith. He shook his head. "Oh, Eacy, I'm little protection against a troop of soldiers when whole, let alone half crippled. Listen to me," he persisted when she would have shushed him into silence. "Post sentries at the head of the glen. Mayhap, if they fire Ardshiel's property first, we'll be forewarned. Yet if they come from the closest fort it's likely Garth will bear the brunt first."

"What if we keep a signal fire? Some of the men have suggested that to me," Catrin interjected.

The idea was sound. Comyn nodded, pleased that at least Catrin was being practical. "That's wise. But you must plan even further ahead than that. Once the redcoats are sighted, you have to be prepared to run. And far enough for safety. Into the next glen will only delay the inevitable. There are caves on the mountainsides; your people will know them. Stock one with drinking water and food, leaving a lad to guard it if you're afraid of thieves. You can hide there—if you've time."

At his ominous words Catrin's heart began to thud dully. Did these avenging soldiers come in the night, showing no mercy to women and children? She suspected Comyn knew far more than he was telling, but for Easter's sake she kept her mouth shut. As frail as Easter had become lately, added fear could prove dangerous.

"I'll tell our people what to expect. And we'll provision a place in case we need it."

Catrin got up, leaving husband and wife alone.

She took her plaid and called to Lachie to join her. The lad always sat in the corner, his gaze fixed intently on her like a faithful puppy awaiting her command. "Come with me. We must warn everyone in the village of the danger."

The sun was low, the day coming to a close when Catrin paused to rest on a sun-warmed boulder. She thrust her straggling hair back from her brow. Though the day had not been hot, her haste and excitement of her mission as they went from tenant to tenant to deliver their warning, had made her sticky and very thirsty. Shyly Lachie offered her a bannock from his pouch and she gratefully accepted his gift. Slithering on the shingled loch shore, Lachie stooped to fill his water skin, which he brought back to his lady.

Catrin patted his arm affectionately. "You're like my own son, Lachie. What would I do without you?" He said nothing, but his beautiful smile was reward enough. "Come," she said, when she had drunk her fill, "it's wise to be indoors before sunset."

That afternoon, while they were making the rounds of Garth village, Catrin had ordered the servants to carry provisions to the large cave known locally as the Old Man's Nest. She had discovered the cave several weeks ago after pursuing a runaway lamb up the mountainside. Even if the redcoats had the stamina to climb the mountain she doubted they would discover the hiding place, hidden as it was by tangled brush and shrubs.

The loch glinted dull pewter as the sun went behind cloud and the wind picked up. Catrin shuddered, not just because of the dropping temperature. They were passing that place where boulders and trees came close to the water, where the wildcat kits had been born and she had stood on the day of their arrival in Garth.

"Is this place cursed, Lachie?" Catrin asked curiously as she caught up with him. Lachie did not appear to hear, for he spun about, a peculiar expression on his face while he sniffed the air, rather like a dog scenting danger.

Puzzled, Catrin followed his gaze as he scanned the distant shoreline, which had come back to life as the sun crept from behind a silver cloud, changing the hills from black to spring green. Through the shifting patches of sun and shade there suddenly appeared a man, followed by another and another. Foot soldiers!

"Look, lady," Lachie cried, pointing to the figures.

"Redcoats! Run! We must get inside the castle."

The boy's face blanched in fear as he turned and bolted. Shouts from the opposite shore told them they had been spotted. A musket was discharged harmlessly into the loch, warning them to stop; more men on horses appeared.

Catrin ran as fast as she could, leaving Lachie stumbling behind. Her heart hammered in her chest and her throat was dry. What that morning had been unthought of, this afternoon had come to pass. If Comyn had not managed to limp home to Garth, they would have had no warning at all. If they took the path around the loch shore it would take the soldiers hours to reach them. A second narrow track, cutting off many miles, led into the glen, but that secret route would not be known to King George's men. With luck the soldiers would wait for daylight to begin their march. The lookouts in the hills would fire the hastily constructed beacon to warn the glen's inhabitants of the enemy's approach. There was not time to warn the Garth villagers. They must hope that the warning beacon would give them enough time to flee to the hills.

Catrin's news of the redcoats' approach brought panic to the castle's inhabitants. Had they a garrison it would have been wiser to try to withstand attack from inside the walls, but the few old men and half-grown boys by whom Garth was manned could offer little resistance to a well-trained detachment of King George's men.

The silver plate, the candlesticks and chalice from the castle's small chapel, and what gold and silver coins they possessed were quickly lowered into the cavernous well in the courtyard. Catrin allowed those who wished to leave the castle to rescue their families. They took what food they could carry and skins of well water. The rest of the retainers armed themselves with kitchen knives while several of the old men carried rusted claymores they had used at Sherriffmuir.

Catrin's abiding worry was what to do about Comyn. In his condition it would be impossible for him to climb to the cave. She must find a hiding place inside the castle. Beneath the floor covering in the piper's gallery off the hall was a trapdoor, and she decided to hide Comyn there.

Two old women and their husbands agreed to stay behind to care for the fugitive and serve the government troops if they chose to use the castle as a billet. Catrin hated to leave David's land to the conquerors but she could think of no practical way to defend it. If they showed no resistance the redcoats might be less likely to destroy the village.

Wrapped in their thickest plaids, for the nights were still cold, Catrin and Easter prepared to leave the stronghold. The smell of woodsmoke blew in the wind from the troops' campfires across the loch. At the head of the glen the sky glowed red from the warning beacon.

Jean carried Douglas and Lachie brought his lady's blankets and pillows, anxious to make her comfortable in her temporary quarters. The trapdoor was secured, the floor covering drawn over it to cover the hiding place. They were on the verge of departure when a commotion outside brought them running to investigate.

To Catrin's horror black figures appeared out of the night and the air was filled with the sounds of tramping feet as the enemy crossed the causeway. As she watched, soldiers reached the unmanned outer gate, scaled it, then opened it wide to admit their comrades. Catrin debated whether to run inside the inner courtyard and slam the yett. Such a move might buy them a little time, but without enough men to defend their position, the soldiers would merely scale the walls. The added inconvenience might turn the redcoats hostile.

She puzzled over how the redcoats had reached the castle so fast. They should not have been here before daylight unless a traitor from the glen had shown them the secret way.

White-faced and clutching each other for support, the women stood their ground. Catrin need wonder no longer who had betrayed them, for at the head of the redcoat troops, astride a gray horse, rode Gordon Stewart, his thin mouth curled in a cruel smile.

"Greetings, ladies. I've brought some visitors with me—some friends this time. We'll thank you to produce the traitor, David Stewart."

"He's not here," Catrin spat, glaring defiantly at this man who had deliberately betrayed his own kind to the enemy. When David did not take his uncle's life she had known he was making a grave mistake.

"I'm Captain Fox, Lady Stewart. It will go well for you if you turn your husband over to us at once," said the white-wigged redcoat officer who detached himself from the troop and rode forward. "We've reason to believe he's here."

Catrin stepped forward, boldly looking the English officer in the eye. "You have leave to search the castle, Captain Fox. I assure you my husband is not here. I've not seen him since January."

"Oh, we intend to search, ma'am. It would have been wiser had you produced him of your own accord. My men might have been far gentler with your possessions," sneered the captain, signaling for the soldiers to enter the inner courtyard.

"We've few valuables. There's food if your men wish to sup, and there are spirits in the cellars. We do not deny you hospitality."

"It appears so—you seem about to take a journey."

Catrin swallowed, knowing she could not pretend they were not prepared for flight. "Many of my people have families in the village. News of your coming made them afraid and I was allowing them to go home."

Though the captain nodded, the smirk on his thin lips told her he did not believe her story.

"Then, as you apparently have nothing to hide, you'll kindly stay out of our way while we make our search."

Catrin gripped Easter's arms when she would have raced inside the hall. "No. You'll betray him," she whispered urgently, forcing Easter to stay beside her.

When the men began wantonly to slash the few pieces of upholstered furniture and slice down banners from the walls, Catrin angrily marched inside the hall to protest. She was physically restrained. Clattering through the kitchens, raiding the cellars, the King's soldiers scoured Garth from top to bottom. Screams from the kitchens told Catrin the men were about their age-old sport. But when she protested at the rape of her scullery women, the captain swore at her and told her to hold her tongue.

When the men returned empty-handed, Gordon Stewart was not satisfied. "He's here. A wounded man was seen in the vicinity. There's still one place left to look." Deliberately, Garth's former laird marched toward the piper's gallery and ordered the floor coverings dragged aside. The soldiers exclaimed in anger when the lantern light revealed an iron ring set in the stone slab.

Easter grew faint and had to sit on the floor. The baby screamed and Jean tried in vain to quiet him.

"If you don't shut up that bloody kid, I'll bash its brains out," snarled a nearby soldier, raising his musket in a threatening gesture.

Catrin snatched Douglas from Jean, who was weeping in fear, and rocked him, trying to quieten him. "Don't you dare lay a hand on this child! What kind of soldiers are you that you make war on women and children?"

"Soldiers of His Majesty King George, and don't you forget it, you bloody Jacobite whore," retorted the belligerent soldier.

Their captain grinned at the exchange, refusing to chastise his men. He was vastly interested in the contents of the hiding place in the floor beneath the piper's gallery.

"Your husband's in there, is he not?"

"No, he is not. I've told you the truth. I've not seen him for months."

"We shall see. Open it!"

The men heaved on the ring and the aperture yawned open. Lights were shone below and a bellow of triumph told them Comyn had been spotted. Three men jumped down and subdued him before hauling him to his feet and dragging him roughly through the opening. Comyn was flung to the flags, screaming in agony from the pain in his leg.

"That isn't him!" bellowed Gordon Stewart, beside himself with rage. He rounded on Catrin. "Where is he? I'll kill the bastard with my own hands!"

"You know as much as I about his whereabouts. It's unfortunate that David didn't kill you when he had the chance. He spared you because he thought you old and feeble. He never reckoned you were so evil you'd betray innocent people—"

"Enough," snarled the redcoat captain. "Who's the prisoner?"

No one spoke. When Comyn refused to identify himself they clubbed him senseless with their musket butts. His head wound had burst open under the barrage and blood and fluid gushed through the bandages to the stone floor. When Easter and Catrin tried to aid him they were flung aside.

"You lied to us," snarled the redcoat captain, rounding on Gordon Stewart. "Are you perhaps not as sympathetic as you pretend? Is it possible you're a Jacobite also?"

"No! I told you true," cried Gordon Stewart, fuming impotently as he racked his brains for another hiding place. "I've even more reason to hate this self-styled laird of Garth than you. He wrested my inheritance from me. True, I'm seeking personal vengeance as well as loyalty to the crown, but you can trust me. She knows where he is, I'll be bound."

All eyes turned to Catrin, who tried to control the tremors that shook her knees. Brusquely the captain ordered her seized.

"You can be made to reveal what you know."

"Torture me if you will, but you'll learn nothing. I've no secrets to disclose. I wish to God I did know where he was, then at least I'd know he was alive. Likely he's dead."

The captain rounded on Gordon Stewart, who was emphatically shaking his head.

"No. I have it on good authority that he escaped from the field. It's only a matter of time before he reaches Garth—that's if he's not here already."

After some deliberation the troops decided to sup off the confiscated food and drink. They tied Catrin's hands behind her back and looped the rope through the iron door ring. A soldier was ordered to guard her.

While the men gorged themselves, Lachie seized his opportunity. He crept toward Catrin, unnoticed by the feasting troops. In his hand he carried a cup of water, but up his sleeve was hidden a knife.

"Hey, you, get away from her!"

Lachie held up the cup, showing the guard what he did. The man shrugged and allowed him to raise the water to Catrin's lips. She drank deeply and thanked the lad.

Before Lachie had an opportunity to use his knife, the suspicious soldier seized him and flung him to the floor.

As the whisky kegs passed freely among them the soldiers began to sing. The captain kept an eye on his men, finding little in their behavior to criticize. Even when they seized the serving women, many of whom were well past their youth, he refused to interfere with his men's sport.

To Catrin's horror several soldiers advanced on her, knives drawn, preparing to release her from her bonds. Not for a moment did she suppose their action to be out of pity. She shuddered to think of the sport for which they had earmarked her.

Then, and only then, did the stern voice of the captain bark. "Don't touch that one. She's mine."

His pale eyes gleamed in the glow of the fire as he stood before her, the smell of claret strong on his breath. "You're too refined a prize for this scum," he uttered thickly as he drew his white hand across her bodice. At first gently fondling, he suddenly pinched her nipple, his thin mouth curling cruelly when she gasped. "Later, little Jacobite," he promised, before he seized her and covered her mouth with moist slack lips.

Catrin longed to scrub away the vile taste of his wet mouth. A noise of scuffling, followed by a woman's shrill screams, took her attention. In horror she beheld the scene unfolding before her. The soldiers were dragging Easter to a trestle table, which had been hastily cleared of food and dishes.

"No! Leave her alone!" Catrin screamed, straining desperately at her bonds. "She's too ill. Someone help her." She looked in vain toward the few shuffling old men cowering in the shadows of the gloomy hall. Even Lachie refused to aid Easter, merely watching her struggles before he looked away. His loyalty extended only to Lady Catrin.

"No, damn you—she's my wife!"

Heads turned as Comyn struggled to his feet, lurched, and fell forward. His jaw smashed against the flagstones and when he raised himself, his mouth streamed blood.

"Your wife? Then you'll be most interested in her welfare."

Captain Fox's sarcastic voice sliced through the general hubbub in the hall. He ordered his men to carry their prisoner to a place of honor before the hearth. Tears trickled down Catrin's cheeks as she observed their black humor. Comyn was to be given a perfect vantage point from which to watch his wife's defilement!

"Now, you filthy Jacobite dog, you can watch what happens to the wives of traitors." Captain Fox turned to his lieutenant, nodding his approval. The officer raised his hand as a signal for the fun to begin.

While they tied her to the table, Easter remained quiet, too weak and spent to scream. One by one the men came forward to take their turn. She found her voice now and her tormented shrieks rang through the stone-vaulted hall. Someone complained about the blood. And Catrin hung her head, agonized over the proceedings, yet helpless to stop them. Dazed, she slumped where she stood, unable to reach the floor. She hung by her wrists until the pain became so intense she must stand again to relieve the drag.

Now the slight form spreadeagled on the table was unnaturally still. Men laughed self-consciously and some even murmured their remorse as their efforts to slap their victim back to life failed. Blood stained the scrubbed table and dripped on the flags beneath.

In horror Catrin looked to where Comyn slumped, lashed to Gordon Stewart's state chair, his chin sunk in his beard. To his own credit, Catrin saw that Gordon Stewart had not taken part in the sport, keeping to himself on the far side of the hearth while he allowed King George's brave soldiers to enjoy their own special brand of pleasure.

When they unfastened his wrists and legs, giving him his freedom, Comyn swung at the nearest soldiers in impotent fury.

"Will you try to run, Jacobite dog, or do you fancy a little sport first? Why not try to take as many of us as you can," suggested a drunken sergeant, his bulldog face thrust close to the wounded man.

Bellowing his rage, Comyn swung at them, seizing first one, then the other, by the throat. He fell and struggled upright. And they, vastly enjoying the spectacle, helped prop him up as he ineffectually fought for vengeance. Surprised yelps revealed that his strength was not wholly depleted, yet Comyn soon tired and fell to the floor. All further effort to support him for another round failed.

Catrin had screamed at them, demanding they stop their cruel sport, but her thanks had been a fist that smashed her lips against her teeth, bringing the salty taste of blood to her mouth.

This latest outrage to his lady finally roused Lachie to action. He had already decided outward defiance was useless. With due cunning, he slipped through the shadows, unnoticed by the drunken soldiers, who were busy flinging the inert Comyn across a bench while others dragged Easter from the table. Lachie slipped behind Catrin and slit her bonds.

"Wait, my lady, not yet," he cautioned hoarsely.

She nodded assent as he crept toward the door, his intention being to steal one of the officer's horses for Catrin to ride. But Lachie was not to succeed in his plan. A soldier bellowed a warning as he noticed the lad at the door. A musket shot rang out. Catrin screamed as Lachie fell.

She stood there in torment, knowing if she ran to assist Lachie she would sacrifice her chance to escape. Jean came from the shadows, the baby cradled in her plaid, and she leaned over the boy, who writhed a few times and was still. Raising her tear-streaked face, Jean looked at Catrin and shook her head.

Catrin shouted for the soldiers to come to the wounded lad's aid. A man finally stepped forward and turned Lachie over with the toe of his boot. Stooping, he mercifully closed the staring eyes before returning to his comrades.

Now Captain Fox was ordering the area cleared. After glancing toward Catrin as if to reassure himself she still awaited his pleasure, he sent his men to tap a second hogshead of claret.

The hours dragged on. Many of the soldiers slumped before the hearth in a drunken stupor. Captain Fox played chess with an ivory set they found in a cupboard; Gordon Stewart was his opponent.

By now Catrin's tears were dry. She looked about the room through dazed eyes, wondering how much longer this torment would go on. The more men who fell asleep, the better her chances of escape. Yet she could not leave Douglas to the redcoats' mercy; she owed Easter that much. It would be difficult to take the baby unless Jean came with her. Jean was slumped in a corner holding the baby snug in her plaid. Concentrating, she tried to will Jean to look up. At last the girl raised her head and Catrin offered a fervent prayer of thanks. She motioned to the door, hoping Jean understood what she wanted her to do. Painfully slow, Jean finally moved to the doorway where she crouched against the oak jamb. No one appeared to notice. Catrin did not know if Jean was aware her wrists were free.

Another round of claret, a second quick check of his captive and Captain Fox made a clever move. A muttered curse from Gordon Stewart was followed by laughter, and the two men continued with their game.

The sentry guarding the door was slumped against the wall, his chin on his chest. Stealthily Catrin moved, keeping an eye on the couple before the hearth and the dozing guard as she sidled through the doorway. Impatiently she motioned for Jean to follow. She prayed the baby would not wake.

A thick mist had come down with the night and moisture beaded her hair and face as she crept outside into the darkness. Jean was close behind her. Mercifully the baby slept. Across the inner courtyard and under the raised yett they fled, their soft-soled shoes soundless on the cobbled surface. Catrin raced onto the causeway with Jean at her heels.

Stumbling through the darkness, the two women ran as fast as they could along the loch shore. The cold and the movement had roused the baby and he began to cry. Catrin was confident they were too far away for his cries to rouse the soldiers, muffled as they were by the sound of waves breaking on the loch.

A burned barn and an outlying croft still smoked in the mist, but Garth village itself appeared unharmed. To Catrin's amazement many of the dwellings were still occupied, their inhabitants choosing to spend the night in their own beds instead of the cold, inhospitable mountainside. All her frantic efforts to warn them of danger had been for nothing! Anger and frustration possessed her as she banged on doors, sounding the alarm as they passed.

"Flee to the hills, the redcoats are at the castle. They'll be here before daybreak," she cried as curious heads poked from doorways along the track. "Save yourselves while there's still time!"

She had reached the last cottage which set back from the road before she realized the villagers did not understand a word of her warning. And Jean's English was too limited to use her as translator. Temporarily defeated, Catrin slumped on a rock doorstep, too tired to continue. Jean's warm hand slid comfortingly inside hers and Catrin rested her head against Jean's shoulder and wept.

The baby's screams of hunger finally roused them and Jean left Catrin to go in search of either a wet nurse or milk to feed the infant.

Dawn was merely a pink tinge in the sky when the unmistakable tramp of feet blew toward them on the wind. Alerted by the ominous sound, Catrin grabbed Jean and ran with her to a stone barn behind a clump of trees. With pounding hearts, they opened the door. Catrin urged Jean to take Douglas and hide in the hayloft.

Assuring the girl she would return, Catrin ran back outside. A scream echoed in the quiet dawn and to the east the sky was streaked with orange flames, bathing the huddled stone dwellings in lurid light. Now perhaps the villagers would listen to her!

At this end of the settlement, people were running from their homes. Eyes wide with terror, they were fleeing to the mountains to join the wise who had hidden in the caves after the warning beacon was fired.

Catrin ran among the more reluctant ones urging them to flee, literally pushing them onto the road as proud housewives hesitated to leave their paltry treasures. Desperate to convey the need for haste, she raced back toward old Tam's croft, hoping his wife could help her speak to David's stubborn tenants, who scowled at her as if she were the enemy.

Old Tam's wife was sitting at her croft door, but the sight that met Catrin as she drew closer made her recoil in horror. The old woman's skirts were hiked up, her limbs arranged in an indecent pose. Catrin was almost relieved to find that she was already dead, and glad that Jean was not here to see her mother's outrage. Hastily she pulled down the garments to cover the body decently, wary of approaching rough voices. Too late, she darted into the shadows behind Tam's croft.

The soldiers had seen her! Yelling and brandishing their muskets, the men began to run. One of them carried a blazing torch that he was using to set the cottages' heather thatch alight. Hot flame, thick, acrid smoke, and showers of sparks filled the lightening sky. Catrin coughed, gagging on the smoke as she tried to smother the sounds in her plaid.

"After her!" the lust-crazed men were shouting, their voices mingling as one.

Catrin dodged behind a stand of rowans separating the houses from the burn. Across the narrow water campfires sputtered and she turned back, not anxious to land in the arms of a second party of redcoats. Dodging behind the crofts, plunging deep into the shadows, she worked her way back through the settlement toward the barn where she had left Jean and the baby.

To Catrin's horror, as she reached the stone barn flames exploded from the hayloft. Redcoated soldiers, brandishing torches, leaped about the building like ghouls, dragging out women and children, clubbing the young boys and old men who tried to resist on behalf of their women. There was nothing she could do to save Jean and Douglas. Thick black smoke already issued forth in a choking cloud. Screams echoed in the darkness, but she did not know if Jean cried for help, or whether the sounds came from the women who were being systematically raped in front of their children.

Catrin hid in the shadows of the buildings, awaiting her chance to escape. She had to get away before it was full light. They would have been wiser to stay inside the castle, for even Captain Fox's demands would have been preferable to this. The soldiers were no longer searching for David. Now they slaughtered wholesale for the joy of it, the garish firelight revealing the zeal with which they performed their task.

After successfully skirting the burning cottages, Catrin reached the crown of the road where it dipped toward the loch. First light brought a gray, rainy day. The drizzle was not enough to extinguish the fires lighting the skyline, though it caused thick black smoke to billow forth and made the burning thatch hiss and spit.

The sound of many approaching feet sent Catrin searching for shelter. At this point there was none. Around the bend, up from the loch road, came a troop of soldiers from the castle, Captain Fox riding at their head. Catrin bolted for open ground, running until she thought her heart would burst.

Whooping, crying "tally ho" as if they rode to hounds, the captain and his young lieutenant left the main body of troops, galloping across the heather in pursuit of their quarry.

Too weary to go on, her breath searing in her lungs, Catrin fell to the boggy ground and lay still, gasping for breath. Hoofbeats thundered in her ears and the high-spirited animals snorted and whickered as their riders drew rein. Bracing herself for the onslaught, Catrin lay there, too spent to resist.

"By Jove, if it isn't me little captive," said Captain Fox in surprise as he pulled aside the sooty plaid. "I thought I'd lost you, me dear. It's unfortunate you decided to run away. Things could have been far more civilized for you."

Unspeaking Catrin stared up at him. The thin morning light revealed the dissipation in his face, his pouched, bloodshot eyes, the sharp lines framing his thin mouth. Captain Fox's wig was perfectly curled, his uniform freshly pressed—he had not yet taken part in the village slaughter, having come from the castle after a few hours' welcome rest.

"Don't touch me!"

"Or you'll do what?" he sneered as he leaned over her. He hesitated, eyeing the muddy ground. "Lieutenant Henry, take the captive over there," he ordered. "That spot looks more comfortable for a morning's sport."

With the last of her will, Catrin fought against capture. Despite his slight build, the young lieutenant was too strong for her. When he yanked off her plaid, the better to examine her body, his captain barked at him.

"Leave her, damn you! If you take a serving it will be after me."

The lieutenant kicked Catrin, his face surly. When they reached the spot sheltered by three huge boulders that Captain Fox had indicated, Catrin was thrust down onto the wet bracken. Pitching a horse blanket to the lieutenant the captain instructed him to spread it over the ground.

Catrin was rolled onto the blanket and the captain stood over her, eagerly contemplating his prize.

"Will you fight, me dear?" he drawled, taking his hat from his head and carefully placing it on the edge of the blanket.

"With my last breath," Catrin spat, hating him with all her being.

"In that case, you'd better hold her, Henry. Damned if I want a threshing virago. Much too early in the morning for that."

The lieutenant seized Catrin's arms and pinioned them above her head before bringing his knee to her chest, driving it under her chin until Catrin thought she would choke. She closed her eyes, blood pounding hot in her face, then kicked and screamed as Captain Fox ripped her skirts, wadding them above her waist. He grabbed her thrashing legs, wedging them apart. His knee came into play, catching her high between the thighs, making her scream in pain. In the background she could hear the chuckles of the common soldiers, their comments ribald as if they watched a bawdy entertainment. While ripping open her bodice, Captain Fox reprimanded the lieutenant for pressing too hard on her chest and obscuring that which he eagerly sought. Thankfully the pressure was released. A moment later Catrin felt a stinging pain as the captain sank his teeth into her breast.

Clapping and cheers followed the action. This renewed enthusiasm, however, annoyed the captain, who snarled at the spectators to "bugger off."

Through a haze of tears Catrin saw the blur of his red uniform, his white whig slipping askew, his pale face with those light metallic eyes. His lips were brutal on her bruised, bitten mouth as he forced himself inside her, the invasion calculated to wound. Catrin cried out, hardly expecting such pain, for she was no untried virgin, yet neither had she ever been so sorely used. The pain seemed to penetrate her bowels and sear along her backbone. She closed her eyes, praying for strength to endure when she finally felt the slithering release as he left her body.

Cool air washed over her exposed limbs. But the respite did not last long. Rewarding him for his loyal assistance, Captain Fox allowed the young lieutenant to take her. This time the pain was not as severe, but Catrin had to fight back growing waves of nausea.

Twice more they used her and she prayed desperately they would not then invite the common men to take their turn. When their thirst was slaked, when they had dressed again and replaced their wigs, the two redcoat officers stood looking down at her. Sneering, Captain Fox took two silver coins from his pocket and dropped them on Catrin's belly.

"There, 'tis twice as much as you're worth, you Jacobite whore."

She lay in her shame, naked in the heather, the silver pieces icy on her skin, and longed to die out there on the loch shore.

"Cover yourself," spat Captain Fox, flinging her smoky plaid over her nakedness. The two men shook her from the horse blanket onto the wet bracken, pushing her, nudging her with light kicks until the blanket came free.

"Guard her. I'll fancy some more come evening," said the captain.

Mounting his horse, he gazed down at her and spat in comtempt before wheeling about and heading for the road.

The common soldiers, who had been cooking something over a smoldering fire, crowded around her now and Catrin pulled her plaid beneath her chin. With the lieutenant there they made no attempt to touch her, and after a few minutes someone crouched down beside her. Through pain glazed eyes she saw a red coat.

"Here," the lieutenant held out a piece of charred fowl speared on a twig. "Eat. You need your strength."

Sullen, and only because she knew he was right, did Catrin accept the offering. The meat was hot and she had to blow on it.

A soldier perched on the mossy boulders to stand guard over her, eating hunks of meat from his knife while he waited. Another soldier brought him a canteen. Catrin could smell the alcohol on his breath when he leaned over her to say, "Here's a gown and a cloak from the lieutenant. He says you can dress behind the boulders."

Catrin was surprised by the lieutenant's thoughtfulness. Yet she did not thank him, unable to forget his part in her assault. Then nausea washed over her again as she looked up and realized she was dressing for his pleasure. Grinning, the lieutenant jumped down from the boulders to roughly caress her buttocks.

"Tonight, when the captain's asleep, there are things I'll do to you that even he shies away from. You'll like it, I promise. You've such nice round—"

"Lieutenant Henry, sir, will you come?"

The lieutenant spun about, angered by the soldier's interruption. Cursing, he slapped Catrin for no other reason than she was there, and then he went away with the man.

Throbbing fear seized her as she contemplated his words. She had not only to contend with the lust of Captain Fox but with that of his lieutenant as well. And she had no assurance that when they tired of her they would not turn her over to the ranks. Furtively Catrin looked about for a way to escape. As if he read her thoughts, a soldier thrust the muzzle of his musket into her back.

"Be a good girl, now," he admonished, sliding his hand over her breast when his lieutenant was not looking.

Catrin struck the man, who cursed at her, but he stopped his fumbling.

Across the heather toward the houses she could see women

crouched weeping over their dead. Some of the plaid-covered mounds were too small to be adults. Her heart ached for the mothers whose dead children lay unburied in the heather. The vengeance of King George's troops knew no limits.

The village of Garth was ransacked and burned. All who had not fled to the mountains were eventually killed. Catrin alone was left. The soldiers prepared to move on. In the distance she could see smoke issuing from Garth Castle, curling like serpents from the arrowslits.

Along the loch shore they led her in the faltering noonday sun. Catrin had not seen the captain since early morning. From time to time she became conscious of the lieutenant's lecherous gaze. The gown she had been given was too short and displayed a large amount of white ankle. His eyes strayed to her ankles, to her full breasts straining at the black wool bodice, and he licked his lips in anticipation.

Hoofbeats came up from the rear of the party and Captain Fox rode into view. Smuts marred his pristine breeches and the cuffs of his coat. Across his cheek was a lurid scratch.

"You. Halt," he snarled at Catrin.

She had been staggering, thankful the men's pace was lethargic. Too much liquor the night before and too much bloodletting that morning had sapped their energy. Now she stopped. One by one the redcoats passed her. Some of the men made obscene catcalls; their lieutenant said nothing, just scowled at his captain when told they were to take the secret route shown them by Gordon Stewart. Captain Fox promised to join the men shortly to aid them in their mission to destroy the outlying crofts and tenant farms scattered over the nearby hillsides.

Catrin looked about, desperate to escape. They had reached the small boulder-strewn peninsula that jutted into the loch, that terrible place of foreboding. Were her fears to prove justified today?

Impatient to begin, Captain Fox slid from the saddle as the last soldier reached the bend. He seized her and welded his mouth to hers, reawakening the pain in her bitten lips.

"There's a nest for us close by. How convenient."

Catrin looked to where he pointed and saw the outcropping where the wildcat kits had been born. Below them stretched the beautiful loch, a chill wind ruffling the water. The surrounding green-hazed hillsides were dappled in patches of light as rain clouds scudded across the sun. Now at last Catrin had an answer for her unexplained fear of this picturesque spot.

"There are wildcats there," she protested, hoping to dissuade him.

"They'll not harm us."

The captain seized her arm and dragged her up the boulder-strewn incline. When she struggled to free herself he swung her about, slamming her against a birch sapling.

"Damn you, desist! I want you receptive and I'll damned well get it," he threatened before he again fastened his mouth over hers.

Catrin drew up her right knee, thinking to catch him in the genitals but, sensing her move, he ground his booted heel into the top of her left foot. His spur ripped her flesh and Catrin cried out in pain.

Smashing her to the ground, the captain pinioned her beneath him. His breathing grew ragged as he smothered her with hot wet kisses.

"When I'm finished with you, there'll be no resistance," he threatened, cursing as his sword became wedged in the mossy boulders. Swiftly he disentangled it and removed his pistols. His hat and wig followed. Then Captain Fox quickly unbuttoned his gold-laced uniform coat and his breeches.

What happened next seemed unreal. Catrin clenched her fists in the heather. His sword and pistols lay almost within reach. But not quite. The pistol would be her best weapon, for she did not know if she had strength enough to run him through with a blade.

"Now, you little bitch, you're not fighting. Demme if you're not," crowed the captain, drawing back, surprised by her aquiescence.

"I've abandoned the fight." And though her lips tore with the effort, Catrin smiled at him. "Even a Jacobite woman knows when a man's her master. Far better we couple with delight. You have already taken me in anger."

Astonished that she had finally spoken civilly to him, Captain Fox gasped, "Delight!"

"Jacobites have hot blood too. Surely, captain, women have praised you as a handsome man before," she flattered, hating every lying word.

His face was no longer pale; he sweated and a dawning flush suffused his high cheekbones. He grinned and shifted so that she might have an uninterrupted view of his throbbing flesh which, unleashed from its prison, quivered to claim her.

Conceit had made him drop his guard. Catrin reached for his manhood, shuddering in revulsion as her fingers encompassed his hot flesh. Her reaction he mistook for desire. Aroused by her touch, he rolled on his side and pulled her into his arms as he passionately devoured her neck. Would that she could slice it off with his own sword, she thought demonically, working her fingers to increase his delight, though she almost gagged. She smilingly urged him to lie back, to close his eyes while she pleased him further.

"I'm as English as you," she revealed before she began to flick his searing flesh with her tongue. The taste of him made her want to vomit.

"English," he murmured breathlessly, not expecting this woman to offer him such delight. "From where?"

"I lived in Bloomsbury with my stepfather."

"I don't believe it," he gasped, a smile curving his mouth.

"I was brought here against my will by my Scottish husband."

He nodded. Smiling his pleasure, he sank deeper into the heather, totally off guard as he concentrated on this unlooked-for stimulation.

The pistol lay buried in the heather a few feet away. Forcing herself to manipulate him with her tongue, Catrin strained, scrabbling through the prickly growth until her fingers closed over the pistol.

"You're a man to be proud of," she flattered, her tongue sliding off him, her mouth rank with the taste of his flesh.

"Then be about it, woman. Don't stop now." His eyelids fluttered open and she kept her hand behind her. Setting to with a will, she lulled him into false security again while the swelling flesh inside her mouth nearly gagged her. He groaned again with pleasure.

Catrin raised the pistol. Her arm already rested on his chest. He groaned and panted, unaware that she was pressing the muzzle against his red uniform where his heart lay. She pulled the trigger.

The shot echoed off the hillsides. His eyes opened, disbelief and pain there as he started forward. Wildly he clutched his chest, where a smoking hole appeared.

Catrin leaped back, terrified she had only wounded him, that his comrades would come to his aid. The captain opened his mouth and let out a hideous cry, which she silenced by wadding up her skirts and thrusting them between his lips to shut out the sound. They struggled briefly before he lay still.

Dazed, she stared at him, lying on his back as indecent as some of Garth's old men, whom the soldiers had laid bare, placing their privates in their hands. Hatred bubbled within her for the degradation she had endured to buy her freedom. She did not cover his pathetic limp flesh.

Staggering to her feet she began to vomit, ridding herself of the bitter gall of shame for having intimately caressed this creature in order to beat him at his own game.

Chapter 15

A light mist had come down with the dusk, making Catrin even more anxious to reach the cave before dark. Scratched and bleeding, her feet blistered and her knees cut from repeatedly falling on the rough track, she had doubted she would ever find her way.

From inside the cave an unexpected challenge rang out in Gaelic. Virtually sobbing with weakness, she leaned against a stunted pine. After coming this far she had not anticipated being denied refuge by others who had arrived before her.

"I'm Lady Catrin of Garth," she croaked through swollen lips, praying these people were from Garth.

A bearded, half-naked man emerged from the cave to investigate. At first he failed to recognize her. Catrin warily stepped closer until her bruised face became visible through the light mist. The Highlander relaxed, his smile registering his relief.

The man's arm was bound with filthy bloodstained bandages and Catrin assumed him to be a clansman returned from the war.

"Come," he said, beckoning to her. He spoke a few words of English. "Water," he said, holding out a goatskin.

The cold spring water soothed her parched throat. Catrin could barely swallow. It was agony touching the goatskin with her swollen lips, which still oozed blood from the healing cuts. Bruises marked her face, and her foot, where Captain Fox had gouged his spur, throbbed red and angry.

Helping hands drew her inside the cave where a small fire burned in an upturned kettle, taking the edge off the dank atmosphere. Several women and children and the lad who had been appointed to guard the food, his old mother, and the Highlander in ragged kilt and plaid, gathered curiously around her, exclaiming over her condition.

The women made her comfortable on a bed of bracken. They bathed and bandaged her wounds, then gave her hot broth, still somewhat in awe of this foreign woman who belonged to their laird.

When the women left her alone to sleep, Catrin lay in the eerie darkness, unable to forget the past twenty-four hours during which their peaceful existence had become unspeakable horror. In a few short hours life in the glen had changed forever. Those who had escaped the redcoats' slaughter must eke out a meager existence like savages in hillside caves. She had no doubt the redcoats would eventually return to harry, rape, and plunder until, tiring of their sport, they marched further afield or were called home to fight another of King George's wars.

The steady drip of water from an underground spring echoed through the cave. Catrin tossed feverishly on her bracken bed, weary, yet afraid to go to sleep, frightened by the nightmare images that invaded her mind. Worry about her future only heightened her discomfort. Though today these people had been kind, they spoke a different language. And they still considered her more "the Sassenach woman" than their laird's wife. She wondered how much loyalty David's tenants would show toward her during the terrible months ahead.

Each time she tried to sleep Catrin saw before her Captain Fox's horrified face, pain and shock reflected in his pale eyes. His dying cries tormented her and she covered her ears to shut out the sound. It wasn't true, she couldn't have killed a man! Easter, Comyn, Jean—they weren't dead. It had to be a terrible nightmare from which she soon would wake.

High above mist-wreathed Loch Linnhe the survivors huddled in their cave, bound by a common bond of fear and grief. Smoke from the peat fire drifted about them in a comforting cloud. The moisture still dripped. Deep in the shadows a woman wept. A suckling baby whimpered in frustration at finding the breast dry, soon adding his cries to the others'. And nothing changed.

* * *

A week passed. Gradually the horror of what had taken place receded; unfortunately some of the protective numbness shrouding the events went with it. Catrin had to accept that she had killed the redcoat captain, nor could she overlook the destruction of Garth. Mercifully the horror of her own violation merged with the collective pain. Some things she would not reveal to a living soul. At night, thankfully she was no longer tormented by the dead captain's face. Now, if she pictured him at all, she forced herself to recall his sneers and sweating lust, emotions that aroused disgust instead of pity.

Eventually only the lad who had guarded the supplies and his mother chose to remain in the cave. When the redcoats did not return the others went to join another group of villagers who had fled to the caves at the first sign of trouble and were hiding on the other side of the mountain.

Weeks passed and there was still no sign of the soldiers. The villagers would not return to Garth, considering it cursed. They came down the mountain long enough to bury their dead, which the redcoats had left for the crows, and to scavenge among the rubble, but before nightfall they always returned to the safety of the caves.

When Catrin surveyed the blackened remains of David's cherished inheritance from the windswept mountain track, she wept. His castle was little more than a burned-out shell, his people reduced to a handful of ragged fugitives.

One sunny afternoon, when Catrin was returning from a foray into the village to salvage what edibles she could find growing in the plots behind the ruined cottages, she was startled by a shadow falling over the track. Catrin froze as a figure came from behind an outcropping of rock directly above her. Blinded by the sun, she could not see how the man was dressed. Terrified that he might wear King George's uniform, she turned, preparing to run for cover.

Signaling to her frantically, the man ran swiftly down the track. He was a Highlander, the design of his red plaid similar to that of a family at the head of the glen who had also taken refuge in the caves.

The red-bearded giant drew abreast of her, smiling and pointing to where a second figure was emerging from behind the rocks.

"What is it?"

The man could not speak her language, though by gestures

he tried to dispel her fear. Pointing again up the hillside, he took her arm, urging Catrin to follow him. When they neared the boulders, two other kilted men wearing plaids of the same set came into the open. Touching their forelocks in respect, the brawny Highlanders insisted Catrin examine what they had hidden behind the rocks.

Despite their apparent friendliness, she was wary of these strangers; only because she supposed one of their number to be injured did she finally agree to follow. The incline was steep and she slid to her knees before regaining her balance. Catrin finally reached the sheltering rocks to find a woman kneeling beside a plaid-wrapped figure.

At her approach, the woman rose, straightening to her full height. Wildly disarrayed red hair tangled like a bramble thicket about her shoulders. Yet ragged though she was, there was a certain familiarity about this tall figure. Even the woman's graceful movements, devoid of the ungainliness of the raw-boned crofters' wives, reminded her of someone she could not place.

They met on the path and Catrin's stomach turned over as she looked into the woman's face.

"Brenda Carmichael!"

"I've brought your man home," said she, her voice harsh.

Stunned, Catrin looked from this bedraggled figure to the plaid-swathed form lying in the heather. Her man! By that Brenda could mean only one thing.

"David, oh, David!"

In her haste Catrin stumbled, picked herself up, and raced on. Dropping to her knees beside him, she pulled away the plaid. He was pale, heavy-bearded, his black hair long and tangled, but it was David!

At her touch he opened his eyes, smiling in disbelief as he recognized the lovely face leaning over him. He croaked, "Christ, what ails me? Am I delirious?" Reaching out, expecting to claw at thin air, he was surprised to encounter the softness of a woman's flesh. "Catrin? Is it really you?"

"Yes, sweetheart, it's me. Oh, thank God, thank God, you're safe."

She laid her face against his chest and wept. All the fight left her body, the life, the strength. She could hardly believe her most fervent prayers had finally been answered.

Her racking sobs moved him so deeply that David was at a loss for words. Gently he caressed her hair, murmuring endearments. So weak had he become since Culloden he had almost given up hope of ever reaching Garth. They had struggled south over miles of rough ground, frequently pursued by redcoats. Sometimes fever and pain from his wounds had laid him so low he despaired of seeing another dawn. But, God be praised, his strong constitution had seen him through—that, and the persistence of that damned Carmichael woman!

Yesterday, when they came upon the MacColl brothers cutting peat, he had shed unashamed tears of joy, for he knew he was home at last. Rory MacColl had carried him to shelter, tending him during the night, for his fever had returned. Then the brothers had brought him here. They had heard that his lady was living on the mountain and promised to bring her to him.

When at last Catrin had recovered her wits, she directed the MacColl brothers to carry David carefully up the last few treacherous feet to the cave.

Brenda walked behind them, scowling, leaving no one in any doubt that she had no wish to be there. Had she not thought the shock would have finished David, she had even contemplated telling him Catrin was dead, clearing the way for their escape to France. In fact, when she saw Garth's scorched ruins, she hoped her lie had become the truth.

"Be careful with him. How badly is he wounded, Brenda?"

"Nothing that won't heal," Brenda commented sourly. "You can be sure I didn't bring him home out of any love for you."

Catrin inwardly recoiled from the hostility in Brenda's voice, though she did not know why it had surprised her. There had never been any love lost between them.

After David was made comfortable on the bracken bed, Catrin inspected his wounds. She shuddered at the sight, tears filling her eyes when she considered his terrible suffering. Cheerfully David assured her he was on the mend after being doctored by a wisewoman on the far side of the loch. Since the woman's ministrations his fever had broken and the suppuration of his wounds had cleared. While she bathed and redressed his wounds with clean rags, David told her briefly of his adventures since Culloden, reinforcing Comyn's story of the appalling fate of their clansmen. He had no news of Ness.

As she knelt beside him, Catrin gazed sadly at her lover's gaunt face. His cheekbones were very prominent, his eyes larger, his olive skin sallow against the bush of beard. Then suddenly the David she had known smiled back at her, his green eyes tender, and her heart pitched with love. He touched his black beard.

"It would be my greatest pleasure to shave if there's a razor available."

She shook her head. "The men hereabouts never shave. Perhaps we might find one at the . . ." she stopped, wondering if he was aware of the extent of the damage to his estate.

"Castle," David supplied, his mouth twisting bitterly. "I've already seen the ruin, you needn't try to spare me. It's still standing, Catrin. We can always refurbish the interior. Likely Garth's withstood worse—they also told me Comyn and Easter are . . . dead."

Catrin nodded and glanced away, wondering if he had been told the manner of his friends' death. "Does Brenda know?" she asked, glancing toward the tall figure standing at the cave entrance.

David nodded. Taking her hand, he kissed her fingers. "Don't fret over her, Brenda's strong. She saved my life. And though I won't ask you to love her, Catrin, please try to endure her."

"I will," Catrin assured, quickly brushing the thick curling hair from his brow. She stooped to kiss his lips, feeling great joy as sweet memories of the past were rekindled. "Now try to sleep. Rest and regain your strength. We'll talk some more tomorrow."

She covered David with the heavy plaid. After giving him a draught of a foul-smelling brew prescribed by the wise-woman, she left him, reassured the mixture would help him sleep and relieve his pain.

Mindful of David's kind words about Brenda, Catrin plucked up courage to approach the stiff figure standing at the cave's entrance. Moonlight spilled through the shrubs, dappling the cave's stone surface and palely illuminating Brenda's face.

"Brenda."

When Brenda turned Catrin saw that her cheeks glistened with tears.

"I'm so sorry about Easter. There was nothing I could do to prevent it. I did try to save the baby . . . it . . . it was no use."

"The MacColls told me everything."

Catrin swallowed, knowing there was little she could do to soften the truth. "Thank you for saving David, for caring for him. The words were hard to voice because, though David had been wounded, Catrin could not wholly overcome her jealousy when she remembered that Brenda had been with him night and day. After she considered the hardships Brenda must have endured to bring a wounded man all these miles, she was ashamed of her own meanspiritedness.

"I didn't do any of it for you," Brenda spat, shaking free the soothing hand Catrin rested on her arm. "I saved David for me. He's mine now, more so than ever."

Hatred flashed between them. Brenda's lean face was sharp with venom as she glared at Catrin. Then she moved out of the cave beyond the sheltering shrubs. Catrin watched her go, terribly apprehensive of the weeks to come, when this triangle must be resolved one way or another.

Almost from the day he arrived in Garth, David's strength began to return. Only his ankle, the injury worsened by his grueling journey, gave him constant trouble. He limped outside one sunny June day, wary of intruders as he sat sunning himself in a sheltered crevice facing the sheep track leading up from the glen. On either side of the mountain his tenants knew he was home, yet they would not betray him. As laird they owed him their loyalty. He wondered if Charles Edward was as blessed with loyalty now fortune had turned her back on him.

"Well, Davie, I managed to bring you home in one piece," Brenda remarked cheerfully as she squatted beside him. She offered him a piece of potato bannock hot from the griddle. "Sorry there's no butter for it."

David grinned ruefully and blew on the steaming food. "I'm sorry there's not a lot of things."

"You can't stay here. You know that, don't you?"

"When I'm fit to undertake another journey we'll head for the coast."

"We could've already been in France if you'd listened to me."

"You know I had to come back for Catrin."

"I hope she was worth it," Brenda muttered sourly. She got up and left him, not choosing to discuss her rival.

As she ascended the mountain track, Catrin met Brenda coming down. In a woven basket she carried greens and berries she had picked in the village. "Don't stay below too long," she cautioned as Brenda passed without speaking. "I saw smoke beyond the trees. The redcoats may have returned."

"Good luck to them if they can find anything worth having," Brenda said carelessly, tossing back her curling mane and almost pushing Catrin out of the way.

"Brenda's determined not to be civil," Catrin grumbled later when she joined David in his sunny spot. Once the words were out, she was immediately sorry. His face darkened in anger.

"I've enough on my mind without you two always squabbling," he retorted sharply. "Last night I could hear you going at it like fishwives. I'm not some bounty to be fought over and divided up, and by Christ I expect you both to realize that someday soon."

Tears pricked Catrin's eyes as she left him and went inside the smoky cave. The quarrel Brenda had picked with her last night she thought had passed unheard, for David had appeared to be sleeping. Now she realized he had only been pretending, reluctant to become a pawn in their accelerating feud.

During the past weeks David would have been unable to love either of them, even had he chosen. His strength was returning—and with it some of the old fire, for lately his kisses had grown passionate. Brenda also was aware of the change in him. Before long she would begin acting the coquette, determined to arouse him. From experience Catrin knew Brenda had no intention of giving up easily.

When Brenda returned to the cave in the hazy dusk, she carried five brown eggs in her plaid. "These are for David," she announced, producing them with a flourish. She would not tell Catrin where she had found them.

Naturally David insisted on sharing the eggs. Brenda refused her portion, doubly annoyed when Catrin accepted one. While Catrin ate her egg her eyes pricked with tears of shame for her inability to refuse the delicacy.

"Did you hear any news of the soldiers?" David asked when he had finished his meal and thanked her for it.

"They're camped in the next glen. We'll have to be more cautious about showing ourselves."

David frowned. This was another worry. "Don't go outside the cave alone, Catrin. Take the lad with you if you must leave."

Catrin nodded, alerted by Brenda's curiously cold expression. There was a puzzling gleam in her eyes, a contemplative, calculating light that boded no good.

This evening, the lad, whose name was Roy, had shaved his laird with a razor he had found in a discarded redcoat mess kit. He also brought David a new coat he had found stuffed in an abandoned saddlebag beside the loch. Glad of the garment, for his own was little more than a rag, David was not pleased by the discovery. It meant a redcoat had ridden past their hiding place. Were the soldiers anticipating making a second sweep through the glen in search of fugitives?

While Roy trimmed and washed his laird's hair, Brenda took Catrin's arm, drawing her away to the mouth of the cave where the fading crimson sunset imparted a rosy glow.

"The redcoats are looking for David."

Catrin's eyes bulged with fear. She had hoped they had abandoned their search. "Do they know he's here?"

Brenda shrugged. "Perhaps, or maybe they're just gambling. Either way one of us must stay with him at all times. He can be entirely too reckless for my liking. Gordon Stewart still rides with them. His knowledge of Gaelic stands him in good stead. Damn that vulture—Davie should have slit his throat when he had the chance."

"Oh, then he told you about their duel?"

"There's little he hasn't told me. We lived close on the road," Brenda remarked with a suggestive chuckle.

Clenching her fists, Catrin refused to be drawn into a squabble. Sense told her there could have been little of a sexual nature between the travelers, weak as David had been, yet she could not prevent her jealousy being sparked by Brenda's remark. "So you keep telling me."

Her barb failing to draw blood, Brenda continued with her story. "They say the Campbells are aiding the government troops. Butcher Billy's friends are making a thumping success of their scorched earth policy. Don't you know one of Cumberland's officers?"

In the gloom Catrin could not see the expression on Brenda's face. "Yes. Why do you ask?"

"Just curious. David told me he's your betrothed."

"A childhood arrangement only. I barely know him. I don't even know if he's still alive. His regiment fought at Culloden. It's possible they're behind some of the destruction, but Cumberland's got many friends. The chance that Captain Cavendish is close at hand is very remote. Besides, I don't really care what happens to him. He means nothing to me."

"Mmm. Davie has your undivided loyalty. Suppose this man appears. You'd be far wiser to go with him than stay with a fugitive. After all, you're not a Highland lass who knows nothing but these mountains."

"And I suppose you are ... don't think of it, Brenda Carmichael. I love David and I wouldn't dream of deserting him if ten Bryce Cavendishes rode into Garth. You're not going to have him handed to you, so you'd best stop conniving and accept the facts. You saved his life, it's true, but that doesn't make him yours. If I were called upon to save him a hundred times over, you know I wouldn't hesitate."

Somehow, when she thought about their conversation later, Catrin felt uneasy. Brenda had chuckled and remarked on her heated declaration without displaying any anger. Her good humor in itself was puzzling.

Catrin moved deeper inside the cave and began to scrape the wooden porringers and blackened iron skillet. David rose and limped toward her.

"Leave it," he commanded, his face grim. In the red glow of the peat fire his expression was strained.

Uneasily Catrin wondered if he had heard her discussion with Brenda and intended to take her to task for it. Words of apology sprang to her lips, but were extinguished before she had a chance to speak them.

"I can't stand this torment another night," David breathed huskily as he seized her and kissed her deeply.

So taken aback was she that Catrin faltered, her knees buckling as with difficulty he bore her up. The heat of his kiss was a balm for all her wounds. Fire leaped in her at the contact, ignited by the pressure of his hard body against hers. Catrin forgot David was wounded, forgot that he had nearly died, forgot even about Brenda who might return at any time; she remembered only that David was in her arms and how much she loved him.

"Oh, David, darling, are you sure?" she whispered in answer to his unspoken question, the message transmitted by his eager flesh. Her voice quavered with excitement as he caressed her hair, her face.

"I'm sure, sweetheart. Don't give that a thought. If it hurts I'll let you know."

Catrin went with him to the bracken bed, partially secluded from the cave's central room by a two-foot-high crumbling rock partition. Catrin wondered if Brenda or Roy would come indoors to surprise them. Roy would diplomatically retreat to the shadows, ever obedient to his laird's wishes; Brenda was another proposition.

"Stop worrying about their coming back," David admonished, reading her mind. "Just love me, sweetheart. Surely I've waited long enough."

"Not any longer than I," Catrin whispered, her hands shaking as she caressed his face. His cheekbones and jawline were more prominent now, the change apparent beneath her searching touch. Yet his lips were no longer thin and taut with pain; they had grown full with passion. "Oh, sweetheart, I was afraid I'd never see you again. Many a night I wept for you. I love you so much."

In the gloom she could see moisture glittering in his eyes.

"My longing for you brought me back to Appin. I'd have died trying to reach Garth—sometimes I was convinced I would."

"That's in the past. We're together now and we'll never stay apart again. As long as we have each other we can be happy. The castle, the land . . . they don't matter to me, David. It's you I want."

The sweetness of his tender kiss brought tears to her eyes. Undoing his coat, Catrin carefully slid her hand inside his rough cambric shirt, rejoicing in the steady rhythmic beat of his heart. Encountering the edge of his bandage she touched him timidly as she recalled how easily his heart could have been stilled.

Softly David chided her for her caution. "Didn't I tell you not to give it a thought?"

The hot sweetness of his neck was a refuge from pain. Catrin buried her face against his flesh, burrowing deeper, lost in the well-remembered fragrance of his skin. For a few minutes she lay still, wrestling with disturbing thoughts while she enjoyed the soothing touch of his hands on her hair.

"I'm afraid of this," she confessed at last.

"So am I."

She raised her head, surprised by his admission. "Why?"

"So much has happened since we've been apart."

"I'm no different."

"I can see that," he whispered huskily as he eagerly cupped her breasts in his warm hands.

Unease washed over Catrin as she reviewed his statement; David must be afraid his wounds had sapped his virility. Her own sudden fear of lovemaking had a far different origin. In a weak moment she even debated confiding the source of her fear to him, then thought better of it. If she did not reveal her shameful secret, no one need know, least of all her lover. She was so afraid that when David's body slid inside hers she would picture the redcoats' lustful faces, remember the pain and shame she felt when they violated her. Desire for David still stirred in her veins, yet it was a flickering emotion which Catrin suspected could easily be quelled. Today's passion was merely a pale ghost of the searing, all possessing fire of yesterday. The brutal redcoats had stolen her joy of lovemaking. And she was no longer sure she could respond to her lover.

"Why are you crying?"

To her surprise, when Catrin put her hands to her cheeks they were wet. Her tears had dripped on his face as she leaned over him.

"You're right, David, such a lot has happened since we've been apart—things that are hard to forget."

"Come, sweetheart, don't be afraid. There's no need for haste. We can make love as slowly as you want. Despite what we pretend, neither one of us is quite what we used to be."

Catrin forced her mind to the present, trying to banish her memory of rape, of the horror of killing the redcoat captain. The man in her arms was her lover, the only reason for her being in Scotland. For him she had thrown away a life of ease to live among these primitive clansmen. As long as he was beside her she did not regret her sacrifice. Life without David was meaningless.

Beneath the stirring manipulation of his hands warmth gradually began to wash over her. David might have lost much, but not the ability to send life singing through her veins. Gentle and tender, his kisses brought her back to life; when their tongues met in the hot fragrance of awakening passion there was no demand for submission, no clashing battle of wills. Gently she caressed him in return, ever mindful of his wounds. To Catrin's delight, when he finally uncovered her full breasts, his breath catching in his throat at the longed-for pleasure, blessed heat curled through her belly to ignite her laggard passion.

They kissed and held, arousing each other slowly as if they had all the time in the world. Thoughts of the others who might invade their privacy did not change their pace. Even when Catrin, made somewhat uneasy by sounds beyond the partition, tried to hasten matters, David would not allow it.

The hot insistence of his manhood seared against her thighs until Catrin could no longer ignore it. Apprehension about touching him intimately made her hesitate. When she grasped

that steelhard flesh would she recall the horror of touching
Captain Fox? To her overwhelming relief, when she plucked
up courage to grasp the heated brand, to renew shudderingly
her memory of this pleasure giving force, she felt desire without
revulsion. She was overjoyed to discover that the men who
had used her cruelly had created no barrier to her feelings for
David. A sudden burst of heat set fire to her passion as her
body took over from her mind.

Aware of the change in her, David kissed her joyously,
unconsciously increasing the pressure of his hands on her bare
breasts. He caressed the silky globes with his thumbs before
taking her erect pink nipples in his mouth and teasing them
with his tongue, his teeth. He was thankful she had been slow
to rouse, for he had been afraid he would shame himself out
of weakness were he required to perform too soon. As her
hands seared over his flesh, he thought he would burst. A great
wave of relief sang through his body. The horrors they had
both witnessed were finally vanquished by the powerful need
they felt for each other.

Catrin writhed against him and David rolled her to her back
in the sweet dried bracken. Ravaging her mouth with kisses,
he rejoiced in the soft feel of her body beneath his, the pillowed
breasts, the curving thighs and hips. When he thrust her skirts
above her thighs, when he kissed the quivering heart of her
passion, Catrin moaned in torment. Her well-remembered reaction aroused him to even greater heights. Slowly he slid
between her thighs, caressing her body with his own.

"I love you, David, more than anything in the world."

"Oh, darling, I love you too, so much."

Her hands tangled in his hair as Catrin pulled his face to
hers, devouring his lips. His mouth was life itself, and she
trembled, beset with mounting waves of desire. The sweet
torment of his throbbing manhood, stroking hot between her
thighs, was more than she could stand. Reaching down, she
fondled him, making David gasp with surprise. The delight
soon became too great. The velvet tip of his organ was poised
at the entrance; then, tensing, Catrin fought against entry. He
grunted, thrusting hard, finally asserting his right. And with a
deep sigh she opened to him, spreading her legs wide as she
eagerly fought him, barely able to withstand the pleasure
sweeping through her.

Mouths and bodies joined, they moved rhythmically in the
bracken, speeding toward that tumultuous end. David's en-

dearments were smothered in the tangle of her hair as Catrin soared, seeking relief for the agony of desire. Yet still she clung to consciousness, afraid to let go, afraid to cross that threshold where she was no longer in control. Impatient, David thrust harder, filling her body until she thought she would burst. Such a heavy surfeit of pleasure washed over her, she thought she would be consumed by his blazing flesh.

Crying out, Catrin clutched at his back, writhing frantically beneath him as she came up off the bracken. And he held her there, balancing himself on his good leg, taking her weight on his good arm; he drove deep, filling her with the heat of passion long denied. A scream, followed by groans of deepest delight, escaped her lips. Aware they might not be alone, he covered her mouth with his own before the insistence of his blood robbed him of all conscious thought. David soared with her to that place known only to lovers. All the fire, the longing, the love, was finally assuaged by this blending of flesh. Bodies racked by emotion, together they reached the pinnacle and plunged deep into the soothing dark aftermath of passion.

Arms wrapped about each other, they finally lay still, bodies joined, cherishing the emotion they shared. Love held them fast against the pain of life. Having each other and the pulsing warmth of passion was enough; they needed nothing else. Supremely content, they dozed.

At the cave's entrance Brenda sat wrapped in her plaid, shielding her face from Roy and his mother, who pretended not to hear the ecstatic sounds from the rear of the cave. Obsequious peasants! Damn them both, she fumed, angry tears prickling her eyes. She treated Roy to a venomous glare as he passed her to go outside to relieve himself.

Damn David, Catrin too! She had not thought it would come to this so soon. Each sigh, each cry, drove the knifeblade deeper into her heart. David was hers! Hadn't she brought him back from the dead? To save his life she had schemed and lied, stolen—maybe even killed, she thought in surprise, recalling the men she had cracked over the head when they stood in the way of their flight. And for what? Bringing David to Garth had also meant reuniting him with her.

Gasps and sighs of satisfaction made Brenda clap her hands over her ears. Had they no shame? she thought silently. Then in spite of herself she gave a rueful grin. Shame would not have entered into it had she been the one lying with him. During all the hours they had spent together David had not made love to her once; not in Edinburgh, not on the march, and certainly not during their flight from Culloden. It had been torment to watch him regaining his strength, his color, his old assurance, all in preparation for mating with that bitch!

Brenda sat brooding long after the sounds died away. Doubtless they slept in each other's arms, sharing that heavy-limbed peace that came after lovemaking. If Catrin were gone David would be hers. A plan that had half formed in her mind earlier that day surfaced and would not be stilled. Her anger and pain over what had just taken place between those two forced Brenda to put the finishing touches to her scheme. Surprisingly, she felt no guilt for what she contemplated. Conscience played no part in it. Once she had recovered from the pain of jealousy, revenge became her driving force.

It was ironic to think that the success of her plan hinged on Catrin's abiding concern for her lover's safety. She had said she wouldn't hesitate to save him a hundred times o'er; well then, let's see what you're made of, Catrin Blair. Brenda shuddered when she considered the consequences if her plan backfired. If the wretch failed her, it would cost her the dearest thing in her life.

Chapter 16

Catrin woke to the unexpected pleasure of David's kiss. The touch of his hot mouth aroused her.

"Good morning, sweetheart," he whispered, his hand softly caressing her spine. "Did you sleep well?"

"Better than I've slept in months."

Her tremulous smile made him quiver with sudden anticipation, which was swiftly dashed by clattering pans and the bustling activity of the others.

Catrin had also heard the sounds and she shook her head, not wanting to make love in the presence of their fellow cave-dwellers.

"Thank you for all the pleasure you gave me last night," David whispered. "Mayhap you're right. We should wait for night."

She smiled and burrowed against him, freshly aware of his wounded shoulder when he winced under the pressure. Catrin moved away from him, afraid last night's exertion had reopened the wound. And she would not allow him to embrace her again.

Today it was especially gloomy inside the cave, with only the fire for light. The mountain was steeped in heavy mist, leaving them isolated from the outside world as if they floated above the clouds.

To her surprise Catrin discovered Brenda had been gone for several hours. She would not have expected her to venture into the village under such treacherous conditions, yet Brenda frequently surprised her. Long ago Catrin had learned never to try to anticipate Brenda Carmichael.

Catrin helped prepare the oatmeal and oatcakes. She took a plate to David, insisting he eat before she changed the dressings on his wounds. Several days ago one of the Garth villagers had found an unburned bedsheet in the castle wreckage. Rather than use the sheet as a covering, she had torn and rolled the cotton to use for bandages. Now David could have his dressings changed more frequently, an improvement she hoped would speed his healing.

Gritting his teeth, then taking copious swigs from a whisky bottle young Roy held to his lips, David managed to endure the ordeal of having his wounds dressed. The crusted fabric adhered to the healing surface, in some cases almost becoming part of the knitting flesh. Catrin wept for the need to hurt him when she pulled the old bandages loose. To her untrained eyes the wounds looked terrible, yet at least they were not suppurating. The salves the wisewoman had given him were gone. Catrin had not told David, but she intended to go to the opposite side of the loch in search of the wisewoman, for whom she hoped to purchase more medicines.

Toward noon the mist began to lift. Catrin went with Roy's mother, Mab, to pick herbs to make a wash for David's wounds. After about an hour of walking over the rough terrain and finding only a handful of plants, Mab was too tired to continue. Now that she knew what to look for, Catrin helped the old woman back to the cave before continuing her search alone.

As she wandered downhill along the sheep track the mist began to come down again and she debated whether to continue. David had urged her to come back if the mist returned, afraid she would miss her footing on the treacherous terrain. However, this time, instead of sealing off the mountain, the gray blanket stayed several feet above the ground, allowing her to pick her way easily along the track.

For how long she wandered Catrin did not know. Sounds were muffled in the mist. She was aware of the distant bleat of sheep as she finally turned uphill, her apron full of herbs. All the plants she had gathered looked the same and she hoped she had plucked the right ones.

Only three tracks led out of the glen, one going directly over the summit, one leading to a shepherd's bothy, the other winding close to their cave. To Catrin's alarm the mist was thickening rapidly, and visibility was reduced to a few feet.

She picked up her pace, afraid of being lost on this isolated mountain. Despite the fact she had traversed the mountains regularly since spring, their rapidly changing appearance made her unsure.

A steady crunching sound alerted her and Catrin stopped, straining into the mist. Perhaps the bleating sheep grazed just beyond her vision. Ahead of her appeared the blurred outline of a building. To her dismay she found she had taken the track leading to the shepherd's bothy. Dispirited, Catrin turned around and started downhill. Every few minutes the mist thinned, then grew dense again. Uneasily she wondered if it would eventually blanket the mountain and leave her stranded in the heather.

Dark shapes suddenly loomed out of a heavy pocket of gray vapor settled over the mountain a hundred yards below. To her horror she discovered the sounds she had heard were not made by grazing sheep but by scrambling men clad in red coats carrying muskets!

Too late, she spun about, retracing her steps. The mist stayed sparse, no longer providing sufficient cover. As Catrin sped toward the shepherd's bothy, hoping to hide there, a warning shout told her she had been spotted.

"After her, lads."

Scrambling, sobbing, her herbs dropping erratically as she fled, Catrin had almost reached the bothy when rough hands grabbed her from behind and spun her about.

"Now, my pretty, where are you going? Not so fast. It isn't nice to run away from us."

Catrin compressed her lips, averting her face when the red-faced soldier seized her and put his tobacco-tainted mouth over hers. Several men hooted and jeered as they joined them. They all shouldered muskets, some with bayonets fixed. One man prodded her lightly with his bayonet, indicating she was to turn around.

So far she had not spoken and the soldiers assumed she only understood Gaelic. Content with that assumption, Catrin failed to enlighten them as they prodded her and kept asking where she lived.

Sounds from further down the mountain distracted the soldier's attention as more of their comrades struggled up the rough track. Shouting encouragement to their fellows and brandishing their muskets in greeting, her captors temporarily relaxed their guard.

Not waiting to debate the wisdom of her action, Catrin bolted through the heather. About thirty feet to the left was a trail leading over the mountain. If only the mist would thicken, she still might give them the slip. The redcoats had been able to creep up on her because of that mist, yet now she might be able to turn its cover to her advantage.

Shouts and curses filled the air as the soldiers stumbled after her. To her alarm, when she glanced behind her, Catrin saw the first redcoat emerge from the rapidly thinning mist. He was soon joined by a dozen comrades as more soldiers labored up the mountain track. Catrin ran as fast as she was able, frequently stumbling as she turned her ankle on the uneven ground. Her flight was to no avail, for the margin between them narrowed by the minute. Not until she was seized and hurled to the ground did she finally concede defeat. Great sobs tore at her chest as she gulped for air.

The soldiers formed a circle about her, prodding her where she lay gasping on the ground. Catrin's heart thundered until she thought it would leap from her body. Fear for David's safety still possessed her, yet growing fear of these soldiers, of being made to suffer again like the women of Garth, was uppermost in her mind. As she lay there, fighting to get her breath, a sudden commotion erupted among the soldiers. Her guards briefly lost interest in her as they shouted to each other and raced back and forth through the mist-steeped heather.

"Damn the bitch, she's given us the slip!" growled their sergeant when his men returned empty-handed. "I'd a fancy for that one. Bloody amazon she was. Are you sure you can't find her? She can't've gone far."

"Mist's thick as soup down there. We're not breaking our bloody necks looking for a piece of skirt."

While they grumbled, Catrin began to inch away, awaiting an opportunity to escape. A few minutes longer and she would be free to stand, to run...

"Hey, you, not bloody likely!"

Catrin screamed as she was kicked sharply in the ribs. The others crowded around her, their mood suddenly turned ugly.

"We've still got this one."

"Reckon she'll be sport enough."

"What about the captain? He should be here in a few minutes—unless 'is bloody 'orse broke its neck."

The soldiers retired a few feet away to debate what to do.

Suddenly Catrin ran. At first they did not appear to notice. Hardly believing her good fortune, she picked up speed as hope flooded to her breast, bringing renewed strength with it. Shouts of alarm rang out and she knew they had seen her, yet their pursuit was halfhearted. Her hopes for escape were not wholly dashed until she neared the place where the two tracks met. There she caught her foot in a pothole and pitched forward, the jarring thud knocking the wind from her.

She picked herself up, surprised the soldiers had not tried to catch up with her. They held back about twenty feet below, lighting pipes as they lounged against the rocks waiting for her to make a move. High on the mountain the last of the mist had lifted and deep in the clouds glimmered the golden haze of sunlight. Catrin stared at them, her heart thumping, watching as they casually passed their pipes. They laughed, they smoked and they waited.

The soldiers acted as if they wanted her to escape. Like a cat tormenting a mouse they gave her hope, robbing her of it only at the last moment. She got to her knees, to her feet, still watching them intently, aware they were making no move to stop her. Her ankle throbbed and it felt weak as she stumbled over the uneven terrain while the soldiers laughed and shouted encouragement. Suddenly something struck her in the back, slid over her arms and locked about her chest; a rope, expertly thrown, descended to halt her flight. Catrin fell, giving vent to sobs of disappointment. A sharp tug on the rope and she began to move, yet when she tried to scramble to her feet the soldiers tugged even harder, deliberately keeping her off balance. Over scratching heather, soaked with mist, over rock and scrub they pulled her until at last she was effectively hauled in. The landing of the captive was hailed by a resounding cheer.

"Look, she's crying, poor thing. Come on, let's have a quick one to cheer her up," suggested someone. The man's words were met with coarse laughter.

She was hauled upright, then prodded with bayonet tips until she began to run to avoid the pain. Allowed to go a short distance before the rope went taut, she was again jerked off balance and hauled in to more cheers and laughter.

Dazed with pain and fear, Catrin lay there, wondering if she was going to faint as sounds grew loud before receding in nauseating waves. Blood trickled from a dozen bayonet cuts and the rope had burned her flesh in angry weals. She did not know how much longer she could endure this torment, or even how long the soldiers intended to play their game before getting down to their original objective.

"Come on, you lazy bitch, on your feet," bellowed her tormenters.

A jerk on the rope, which aggravated the rope burns, soon persuaded her to stand. It was hard to get up with her arms bound above the elbow and she crawled, then tottered, until she had regained her balance. As she stood a cheer resounded. The men urged her to run again.

A sudden icy command rang above the soldiers' jeers as an officer on a white horse rode forward to stop the exhibition.

"Stop this cruelty at once! There'll be no more of it. You'll kill the wretch."

"Yes, captain, sir—there's plenty more like 'er in these parts. We're killing 'em all, sooner or later. What difference does it make," Sergeant Dixon grumbled half to himself as he ordered his men to remove the rope.

The soldiers sliced away the ropes binding her arms, cleverly slitting her gown in the process. Deep slashes on her bodice revealed tantalizing glimpses of white breast; the sleeves of her gown, already ragged after her ordeal, merely fell away. At their captain's command the soldiers thrust her forward.

Trembling as she obeyed, Catrin wondered if she would be able to move another step, so bruised and shaken did she feel. She hated being at the mercy of another redcoat captain.

"You, girl, come here. Closer!"

Eager hands thrust her stumbling toward the captain's snorting white horse. The redcoat officer was barely visible through a veil of dirt and tears. How immense he looked sitting astride his blooded mount, impeccably dressed in white and red.

Leaning from the saddle, with his riding crop the captain lifted her tumbled hair from her face. At his sharp command Catrin looked up, tears streaking rivers down her dirty cheeks. Every inch of her body burned and ached and she swayed with weariness.

The captain exclaimed in surprise, his florid face paling. "Look at me," he snapped again as she almost fell.

"Most of 'em don't speak nothing but their native gibberish, captain, sir."

"I'm well aware of that, sergeant. However, this one, I believe, speaks English."

Something about his voice, his mannerisms, riveted Catrin's gaze on the captain's face. She blinked again, focusing her pain-dazed eyes with difficulty. He was young, his hair hidden beneath a curled white wig. The face beneath his dark three-cornered hat was vaguely familiar.

"Surely it can't be . . . Catrin!"

Her mouth dropped as in a wave of anguished disbelief, she whispered, "Bryce Cavendish!"

"Oh, God, if only I'd known."

He swung from the saddle and to his men's sheer amazement Captain Cavendish reached for the captive woman and took her weight against him. With his lace-trimmed kerchief he wiped away the dirt and tears from her face, before pulling her in his arms.

"Damn you, you savages! You're no better than these creatures skulking in their caves. I'll have every one of you punished for this!"

"She tried to run away, sir. We only did what any soldier would've done . . ."

"Then God help His Majesty's troops."

Bryce turned on them grimly, his crop poised as if he intended to strike the first man who stepped forward.

"She's one of the Jacobites. We have it on good authority."

"This lady is my betrothed!"

A collective gasp of horror echoed from the ranks.

"But how? She's wearing their garb. She ran from us . . ."

"Who wouldn't run from you, and with good reason. Come, my love, you can ride back with me. We're quartered in a shed further down the mountain."

"Oh, Captain Cavendish, thank you," Catrin gasped, tears of relief spilling down her face.

As if in a dream she found herself lifted on Cavendish's saddle. Even sitting astride the animal made her hips hurt. Crumpling, she allowed herself to rest against his chest, giving no thought beyond the present. Bryce had saved her from a terrible fate. She did not know from whence he came, or why, just that he was here and she need endure the soldiers' inhuman torment no longer.

When they reached the shed Catrin was lifted carefully from the saddle. The disgruntled troops had filed down the mountainside after their captain, muttering to themselves, wondering at the strange twist of fate that had delivered Captain Cavendish's betrothed to them. No one had explained to them how she came to be here, or why she wore the plaid, or why she crawled dirty and windblown about this godforsaken place. It was not the common soldier's right to know.

"There, my sweet, sit here while I bathe your wounds."

Bryce was stern as he ordered the men to bring food, drink, and medicines to repair the damage they had done.

Catrin accepted a reviving gulp of brandy that burned her throat. It was Bryce himself who bathed her ankle and bandaged it, then tended her visible cuts. He appeared shaken by her treatment at the hands of his men, repeatedly insisting the deeds were done without his knowledge.

She ate bread and meat, finding her strength somewhat revived after the nourishment. However, when she finally gathered her wits, Catrin was less overjoyed about meeting her betrothed on this Appin mountainside. Bryce would surely insist on taking her to the nearest town. Solicitous and polite though he was being, she was not wholly taken in by his manner, suspecting the old Bryce lurked beneath this newfound penitence. And Bryce in command could be extremely dangerous.

Clumsily brushing back her wet hair from her face, he offered Catrin more bread, cold meat, and pickles. While he made notes in a book taken from his pack, she continued to eat in silence.

"Now, perhaps you can explain to me what you're doing in this godforsaken mountain? I still can't believe it's really you."

She smiled at him, wondering how she should answer his question. "And I can't believe you're here. You're the very last person I expected to meet."

"After your ordeal it's understandable that you're pleased to see me, but you've still not explained yourself."

"I was in Scotland visiting friends when the hostilities broke out. You can probably guess the rest. Soldiers vary little in their treatment of the enemy."

He glanced away, discomfited by her bitter tone. Clearing his throat, Bryce said, "Surely you aren't here with your father's permission."

"No, not exactly." Her imagination went wildly to work, trying to find a plausible explanation without endangering either David or herself. "The last time we met, you . . ."

Bryce pulled a wry face. "Me apologies, Catrin dearest. Demme, you were so infuriating! And that dragon of an aunt."

"She's the reason I'm in Scotland."

"I don't understand."

"I ran away from Aunt Isobel. You surely can't blame me—she's so pious! I felt stifled."

A slow smile dawned on Bryce's face and his thick lips curled speculatively. "Ran away, by Jove. Did you now! And what exactly didn't suit about the old gel? No chance to have any fun, eh?"

Catrin swallowed nervously when he moved closer and began to stroke her hair. "Though I admit I ran away for more adventure I never bargained for quite this much adventure. Thank you again for rescuing me. If you hadn't come along I might have been dead before morning."

"We'll clean you up, take you into town. Good God, I can't believe you're in this condition. It's shameful! They'll be punished for it, you have my word."

"Before I go into town I must let my friends know where I am. They'll be worried about me," Catrin hastily interjected.

"We'll tell them together. They must be out of their minds with worry, demme if they mustn't."

"I'd prefer to go alone. The sight of a redcoat officer might frighten them. There's been so much horror lately."

"Where do these friends of yours live? I haven't seen a decent habitation for miles. Even the castle looks as if it's only a burned-out shell."

"Over the mountain. It's not far."

"We'll go together."

"No, please, let me talk to them first. Surely you aren't afraid I'll run away."

Bryce grinned as he took her hand. "Aye, deathly afraid, my love. That's why I intend to come with you. You're slippery as an eel, Catrin Blair, and I don't intend to let you slip out of me grasp again."

"Bryce, please."

His grip tightened and he pulled her close. "You're planning to run away. What sort of fool do you take me for?"

Catrin found herself lifted from her seat until she reclined in his arms. Her struggles were met with renewed force. "Please, Bryce, let me go!"

"No protests, demme! I'll admit, you could smell better, yet after all this time apart, I can overlook a few discomforts. Now, what manner of friends are they that they can't face an officer of the King? Not bloody Jacobites, surely? By God, that's it, isn't it? These friends of yours are Jacobites! That's the reason you're in Scotland. The Appin Stewarts are Jacobite sympathizers and this is their land!"

"You're wrong. MacColls and Carmichaels live here also."

"Who gives a damn what they call themselves," he snarled, his bulbous eyes bulging with anger. "In fact, you're so eager to be off, I'd stake my next month's pay this 'friend' is a man . . . demme, Catrin, your lover's a confounded Jacobite traitor!"

At this point the sergeant reentered the hut, pointedly clearing his throat when he saw his captive seated on his captain's lap.

"Yes, dammit, what is it?"

"Your betrothed this lady might well be, captain, sir, but our informant said she's been aiding the fugitive."

"How very interesting." Bryce grasped Catrin's chin, twisting her face about. His mouth narrowed and his eyes were hard. "Your lover's the Jacobite fugitive, David Stewart, isn't he?"

Eyes wide, she shook her head.

"Up in caves they be, sir, hiding like animals. Likely she can lead us to him right enough."

Bryce motioned for the man to leave. Putting Catrin away from him he sat contemplating her in silence, chin sunk on his chest. At last he said, "So, you've been lying all along. I'll tell you what I'm prepared to do, considering my past feelings for you. If you'll come into town, live with me as my wife, we'll forget this ever took place—"

"Bryce, I can't! I know we were betrothed—"

"Still are betrothed."

"You know I never felt affection for you."

His eyes hardened at her honest statement and he jumped to his feet. "Silence, damn you! I'll listen to no more. If you won't come to town with me, you can damn well take us to your lover. Oh, don't play games, I saw it in your face while Dixon was talking. You know where he is all right."

Silently she regarded him, wondering what he would do now. Casually Bryce withdrew his silver-handled pistols and weighed them in his hand.

"You won't kill me."

"Really? What makes you so sure?"

Sweat beaded her brow as she contemplated the man before her, wondering how much information he had about David's hideout. Whoever had betrayed David might also have betrayed his hiding place. She had to get away to warn him. But how? Bryce was no fool. No conceited, claret-sodden Captain Fox.

Suddenly Catrin found the muzzle of a pistol pressed beneath her breast. Nudging the soft flesh, Bryce smiled speculatively.

Finally, unable to keep his hands off her, he fondled her breast, slapping her face when she kicked him. Then he cocked the hammer on the pistol.

"Be still, or I'll blow your tits away. Damned shame to have to destroy such a deuced fine piece of work. Now, what do you know about the fugitive? And no more foolish lies."

"I've told you, I know nothing about a fugitive. Why won't you believe me?"

Bryce smiled scornfully, one eye on the door as a rumble of voices grew louder. "Demme, Catrin, do you take me for a complete fool—Christ, what ails the scum now," he snarled in exasperation as the babble of sound entered the shed. Wheeling about, he stormed through the door, his voice ringing out, cutting through the excited clamor. The men caught scuffling hastily defended themselves as he bellowed at them in rage.

Catrin's heart pounded. For a few precious moments she was alone. This might be her last chance for escape and she could not throw it away. Desperately her gaze darted about the primitive dwelling, fastening on the rickety rear door half obscured by a packing case. She leaped across the room, stumbling over a heap of harness discarded on the floor. The rotting wood yielded to her thrust and she found herself standing on the spongy ground behind the shed. To her amazement the sentry she had expected to find had gone, adding his contribution to the dispute taking place in the front of the building. Mist swirled twenty feet beyond obscuring the craggy hillside. If only she could reach the safety of that swirling blanket she would be free.

Bryce's voice rang out as he addressed his men. Not bothering to listen Catrin charged forward, stumbling on the uneven ground, almost flinging herself into the shielding mist. No rough hands reached out, no trampling feet thundered after her. She could hardly believe her prayers had been answered. She was free!

Faster she went, faster, tears of relief spilling down her cheeks. The terrain was rough and she stumbled, unsure in the mist. She must warn David. Yet which way to the cave? The terrain looked all alike and the short horse ride had further confused her. Twice Catrin chose routes that ended in heaps of boulders. She could already hear the redcoats' voices echoing out of the mist below her and she began to panic. She could wander about in circles till nightfall and never find the well-hidden cave. Sooner or later they must find her, there were so many of them. And she was sure Bryce would not be so kind now she had given him the slip. It would be easy to find the main track. Why not head for the large cave where the Garth villagers sheltered? She did not speak their language but she knew they would aid her, their loyalty to David assured her of that.

Voices growing nearer hastened her steps and she ran along the wider trail, picking up speed when the mist thinned. Up the mountain track Catrin went, her legs aching until she thought she could not take another step. Here the sun was shining, while in the glen below thick white mist settled over the land. Only a little further and she would be free.

Catrin paused, fighting for breath. Up above she could see the mouth of a cave. She pulled off her tattered kerchief, waving it to attract the attention of the sentry posted by the Highlanders. Then, to her horror, as she moved forward for the last leg of the journey, she felt a hand about her ankle, trapping her.

Shouts and tramping feet spilled from the swirling mist blanketing the hillside as the soldiers emerged. She was quickly surrounded.

"Here she be, captain. Caught nice as pie."

Catrin thought she could not draw breath. Now Bryce himself, red-faced and puffing, appeared at the wispy edge of the thinning blanket.

"That was very unwise of you," he shouted. "I suppose you still insist you know nothing about the fugitive's hiding place."

A laugh rippled among the troops as all eyes turned toward the gaping hole above the next ridge, partially covered by vegetation but clearly visible. Catrin stared at him, overcome with panic. She could not get away now. Behind her lay the redcoats, still emerging from the mist; before her stretched the sunlit mountaintop, offering little cover.

Bryce gripped her arm, his fingers cruel on the soft flesh. "Go on, dearest, keep moving," Bryce snarled, his eyes on the yawning cave entrance. He pressed the pistol barrel hard into her ribs. "Introduce us to your friends."

They moved forward, nearing the crest of the jagged mountain peak. Bryce's breathing was labored as he panted uphill, unused to such exertion. A cheer sounded as the sunlight revealed a descending path dropping far into the swirling mist carpeting the neighboring glen. But Bryce was wary of what might be lurking below, hidden from sight in this damnable mist. The Jacobites were welcome to this inhospitable place.

Next week, when he was relieved of his duty, he determined never again to venture north of Carlisle.

Three children scuttering through the bracken had already betrayed the villagers' presence. After one terrified glance at the party of redcoats cresting the mountain, they raced for cover.

The cave was one of many formed in the barren mountainside. Not as well hidden by brush and saplings as David's hiding place, this larger place housed more than a score of homeless Highlanders. At the soldiers' approach the adults protectively grabbed their children, making no defensive move, merely staring sullenly at the enemy. One by one their gaze swiveled from the redcoat captain to the woman walking before him. Though they must have seen the pistol held to her back, no one registered concern. The only emotion passing between Catrin and these displaced tenants of Garth was hatred. In anguish she realized they believed she had deliberately betrayed them.

A party of soldiers went inside the cave, muskets lowered as they nervously probed the smoky darkness. Taking the villagers prisoner, the others herded them together on a flat plateau, keeping their muskets trained on them. Children sobbed and women defensively clutched them in their skirts to hide them from the soldiers. Two wounded clansmen, several young lads, and some old men were separated from the others. Even the men offered no resistance, their will to fight temporarily broken by cruelty and deprivation.

The soldiers searched the cave and returned empty-handed. All they had found were a handful of dirks and swords, some whisky kegs, and a haunch of smoked meat.

Bryce rounded on Catrin. "What trick is this? Where is he?"

"I told you I know nothing of any fugitive. Ask them, maybe they can tell you what you want to know."

Bryce attempted to communicate with the villagers, who viewed him blankly without comprehension. His face reddened as he furiously repeated his question for the fourth time.

"You speak to them. Damn it, Catrin, tell them what I want."

Using the few words of Gaelic she knew, combining them with the Highlanders' names for their laird and Prince Charles, Catrin fashioned several garbled sentences, which received a predictable response. Even had she been able to make them understand her, she was secure in her belief the people were too loyal to betray either of their leaders.

Cursing, Bryce glared angrily at these smoke-blackened peasants who huddled before him in their tattered plaids, barefoot, straggle-haired, the men bearded like patriarchs out of the Bible. And his stomach churned. What manner of people were they? He had so little in common with them he might as well have been fighting aborigines.

"So, our bird's flown, has he? What do you think, Dixon? Is that possible?"

"Could be, Captain Cavendish. Our informant didn't guarantee we'd find him, just said this one could probably take us to him. And she brought us up here, for what good it's done."

"Aye, for what good it's done. Where are these marvelous friends of yours, Catrin sweet? Surely these filthy stinking savages aren't they?"

She shook her head. "You can see they're only simple villagers. They've nothing of value. Everything they had has already been stolen from them."

Bryce's thick lip curled in derision. "Demme if you won't have me weeping before long. They're vermin, no better, no worse. What do we do with vermin, Dixon?"

The sergeant's bullneck reddened and his face was suffused with a smile of joy. "Dispose of it, sir?"

To Catrin's shock the soldiers roughly jostled the villagers until they were backed against the mountain's rock wall. By their wandering hands and hungry expressions, she knew the men had been expecting far more from this adventure. Apparently Captain Cavendish did not condone rape, exhibiting a flash of compassion she had not given King George's officers credit for.

"You're not going to kill them!"

"Of course. What value are they to us? We want David Stewart and if they don't know where he is, or won't betray his hiding place, they must die. Likely he's sulking in the heather waiting for us to leave, but I'm damned if I'll waste any more time searching. Dusk will be falling soon. A man could break his neck on these confounded mountains."

The women were weeping and wailing, trying to protect their children. They had understood nothing the captain and his men had said, but they knew when the redcoats lined people up in this manner it was for only one purpose.

"Bryce, please, don't kill them. They've done no harm.

They're only peasants. They farm these scrubby acres. Their only crime is loyalty to the clans they were born into. Please, don't kill them!"

"Eloquent, me dear, very eloquent. However, your concern is misplaced." Turning away, Bryce ordered the sergeant to prepare to finish off the captives.

Catching at his arm when he strode away, Catrin held onto his sleeve, tearfully pleading to save the villagers' lives.

"No!" Angrily Bryce shook her detaining hand from his sleeve, his blue eyes hard. "You're like a stranger! Demme, if you're not, Catrin! What can this filthy rabble possibly mean to you? They're like something out of the dark ages."

"They're human beings who don't deserve to die!"

He stared at her tear-streaked face, at the misery in her eyes without comprehending. Behind him the sergeant barked a command and the soldiers leveled their muskets. A fresh outburst of wails and moans followed the action but still the shots were not fired. Bryce had not yet given the word.

"What do they deserve, then, traitors that they are? They kill me men every chance they get, their officers too. One good officer was found shot by the loch, several others have been knifed. That's not the work of innocent peasants. Explain that if you will."

"Bryce, they've much to take vengeance for. The soldiers destroyed the village, they killed, they raped, people were burned alive . . ."

"People? I'd hardly call them that! Muttering gibberish like a bunch of natives. For Christ's sake, Catrin, remember the society to which you belong, or I'll begin to think you've lost your mind."

"I'll come into town with you if you'll spare them."

"You'll come into town with me anyway."

Swallowing, she stared at him, finding his expression unyielding. The sun was warm on her face and its rays gilded the billowing mist layered below them. An eerie feeling that they stood above the world, that they held the power of life and death in their hands, passed over her.

"If you spare them, I promise you won't regret it. I can be so much nicer to you if I'm pleased."

Unmoved, Bryce regarded her coldly. He glanced toward the sergeant who awaited his command. He began to raise his hand, thought better of it, and let his arm drop. He stared at her. "Nice! Demme, Catrin, what in heaven's name is that supposed to mean?"

She caught his arm and she leaned against him. Forcing away her revulsion, she pressed her lips against his, pretending passion she did not feel.

"That's being nice, Bryce. Surely passion's preferable to merely capturing a reluctant woman? You're no border raider. You're an officer in King George's army, a gentleman..."

Suddenly he chuckled. Catrin blinked, hardly able to credit the sound. Bryce was laughing at her, the tension gone from his face.

"Christ, you seductress! Let the damned vermin live by all means. Your promises intrigue me, demme if they don't."

Catrin was seized and Bryce planted his lips firmly over hers, smothering her with hot lustful kisses. Many pairs of eyes watched, took in what was happening, and drew their own conclusions.

"Will you spare them?"

"Today, yes. You have my word."

And Catrin breathed a deep sigh of relief over her victory.

Brusquely he turned and called to the sergeant. And they stepped a few paces away. A baffled expression crossed the sergeant's face, yet he did not argue, merely turned to do his captain's bidding. The soldiers, disappointed at being robbed of their sport for the third time that day, shouldered their muskets, glowering first at the prisoners, then at their captain.

"Go!" Catrin urged, ushering the villagers toward the cave. "You're free. Go!"

Uncomprehending, they stared at her. Finally someone moved. No shots rang out. Hardly able to believe their good fortune, the villagers bolted as one body, racing for shelter. Their final glimpse of the Sassenach woman was to see her enfolded in the arms of the redcoat officer, apparently relishing his kisses. Considering she was bound to their laird, they found the scene strange and shameful. But the villagers of Garth put down the woman's disloyalty to the fact she was a Sassenach whose actions could never be fully understood.

Down the mountain the soldiers toiled, with Catrin in their midst. The sun was sliding lower in the sky when they reached the hut to retrieve their supplies and the captain's horse. Her heart ached as she pictured David worrying because she did not return, wondering if she had fallen in the mist. She prayed he would not venture forth in search of her. Whoever had betrayed them could still lead the soldiers to the cave, but tonight at least he was safe. One of the villagers was probably already slipping through the heather to warn their laird of his danger. By dawn David would be gone. Catrin prayed he was strong enough to endure the rigors of travel. When she realized Brenda finally had him to herself, pain twisted in her heart. She fought back tears as Bryce silently hefted her up on his horse and swung up behind her.

As they traveled downhill, the mist that had been lurking in the glen came back and began to swirl up the heights like a wispy disembodied soul, drifting at random about the forbidding black crags. Somewhere a bird called, the sound echoing eerily off the water. Tears slid from Catrin's eyes as she thought of David and faced the agony of losing him. Surely the villagers would understand she had saved their lives by sacrificing herself. Surely they would reveal her bravery to their laird. Yet she was not wholly convinced they would.

Half expecting Gordon Stewart to materialize as they neared the foot of the mountains, Catrin glanced toward the misty stands of alder and birch surrounding the loch, iron gray in the early evening. Something stirred in the rocks above the road. A red plaid and fluttering skirts betrayed the watcher as female. When they rounded the bend Catrin felt a surge of nausea as for an instant she gazed full on her betrayer. Brenda Carmichael watched from the shelter of the trees before the mist swallowed her from view. How could she, who professed to love him, have endangered David's life?

As they turned onto the road leading around the loch, Catrin took a last look at Garth. Bleak, lonely, and gray, the landscape matched her own emotions. She realized now that the basis for Brenda's betrayal had been her own declaration to give her life for David's. When Brenda somehow learned Bryce Cavendish was the officer in charge of these soldiers, the opportunity to rid herself of her rival must have been too tempting to resist, regardless of the possible danger to David. Giving her her due, Brenda probably considered Catrin would come to no permanent harm in the care of her betrothed. By deliberately arranging her capture, Brenda had gambled on the strength of Catrin's convictions. And with her usual luck, the gamble had paid off. As anticipated, Catrin had gone with Bryce Cavendish, sacrificing herself to give David time to escape.

Turning to look back at the misty trees, Catrin could distinguish little of the sodden gray countryside. Somewhere in that gray mist was the man she loved, whom she might never see again. Her heart ached when she realized she had never even bidden him goodbye!

Chapter 17

"Davie, wake up. You're sleeping like a dead man."

He roused himself, wondering why it was Brenda and not Catrin who woke him. At first, while he struggled to clear his foggy brain, David thought he was still hiding in the heather, that they had not yet reached Garth. Then the reality of where he was flooded back and he sighed with relief. "Where's Catrin?"

Brenda gritted her teeth. Damn him! She might have expected that to be his first question. Without answering, she took his good shoulder, helping him to sit, then stand on his injured leg, which was often stiff when he awoke.

"Come to the fire. There are people here from the village with news."

"News! Has something happened to her?"

David could see the knot of people huddled around the fire warming their hands at the blaze. Though it was dark, beyond the cave entrance the darkness appeared curiously gray. The mist had come down again.

"What news?" he demanded, singling out Angus MacColl to be the spokesman.

The red-bearded man hung his head, loath to tell his laird what had taken place. The small party of villagers glanced from one to the other, wondering how to tell him.

"The redcoats are back," said Angus MacColl. "They came to the cave today."

David's hand flew to his dirk. "How many?"

"Thirty, forty, and an officer."

"Where are they now?"

"They've gone back down the mountain."

"Stop shilly-shallying. If none of you has the courage, if none of you is man enough to tell him, I'll do it," Brenda snapped, her patience tried. "Catrin's gone with them!"

"Oh, God, they've captured her!"

"No—she went of her own free will, riding the captain's horse."

"I don't believe you."

"Ask them."

Angry, David rounded on the Highlanders, who hung their heads, still reluctant to hurt their laird. The men said nothing.

"Damn you, speak to me! Is she right?"

Angus MacColl rubbed his bearded face and finally nodded.

"I don't believe it. There must be some misunderstanding."

"She brought the soldiers to our hiding place. Then she . . . she went with them willingly enough," he said, choosing not to repeat what the others had told him about the Sassenach woman's behavior with the redcoat officer. He would not shame his laird with such information.

Brenda, however, did not share his scruples. "God, tell him the rest of it! You're mealy-mouthed as a parson, Angus MacColl. Not only did she go with the redcoat captain, she greeted him like a long-lost . . ."

"Brother?" David's eyes narrowed in anger. "You've told me that story before, Brenda. I remember another such relationship—was it in Manchester?"

The reminder infuriated her but Brenda brazened it out. "Very well, Davie, I was trying to be kind. Long-lost lover's more accurate."

David raised his hand to strike her, stung by her accusation. "You're always trying to blacken Catrin's character. If she went with the enemy captain there has to be some reason for it."

"Oh, there's a reason, all right. The captain's name is Bryce Cavendish!"

Her disclosure was a shock. David's jaw tensed and a muscle began to leap beneath the surface. "Bryce Cavendish! How can you know that?"

"Captain Cavendish is in command of this detachment of soldiers. I heard his name spoken around. In fact, I've known for a week but didn't choose to tell you. It's Cavendish she went with, you fool, not just *any* redcoat officer. He's her betrothed—or have you forgotten?"

"No, I've not forgotten. Nor have I forgotten how she felt about him. They barely knew each other. There's some other reason behind this. Maybe they hoped she'd lead them to me. Angus, ask if the soldiers took her captive? That must be why she led them to the hiding place. I know Catrin wouldn't deliberately risk your lives."

Angus MacColl briefly conferred with the others. Then, with a heavy heart, he repeated what he had learned. "They say she brought the soldiers to the cave. They did search for you there, so perhaps she was trying to draw them away from here. Matt says she wasn't bound. And she went with them of her own free will. There was no force to it."

"But what did she say? She must have said something."

Angus shook his head, for no one had understood anything the Sassenach woman had said, picking up only a couple of words from the gibberish she spoke. "She betrayed our people, yet for some reason, at the last minute, the soldiers spared them. Their captain changed his mind."

The news sparked hope in David's breast. Catrin must have bargained with Cavendish for his tenants' lives. And they, not understanding English, had misinterpreted her motive.

"Don't you see? By going with Cavendish she obviously bought their lives."

"Stop it, damn you, Davie," Brenda cried in anger. "She went with him because he's her betrothed. We spoke about Cavendish some nights back, about the wisdom of following victor instead of vanquished. Do you understand what I'm trying to tell you? Sometimes you're stubborn as that rock."

"I understand that you're trying to convince me Catrin's left me for Cavendish. But it's a lie! She has no love for him."

Angus MacColl glanced up, seeing anger and pain seaming his laird's face. He had little love for the Carmichael woman, yet he did not want to see his laird hurt. To give a man false hope was more than he could stomach. Far better for his laird to forget the Sassenach woman and take a good Highland lass to wife.

"Doubtless the lady still has a deep regard for you . . ." Angus began, carefully choosing his words. "Yet she gave no resistance. In fact, the lads told me she greeted him warmly, with . . . kisses and such." His voice trailed away as he met the open hostility in his laird's green eyes.

"Damn you, how can you lie like that!"

"He's telling you true, Davie, whether you believe it or not!"

David was silent for a long time while the men cleared their throats and stared into the peat fire. At last he straightened his shoulders, trying to shrug off the burden of pain this news had caused him. He still believed there was a good reason behind Catrin's behavior, despite overwhelming evidence to the contrary.

"She'll come back. She went with them because she had no choice."

"Believe what you want, but you can't stay to see if you're right. We must leave tonight. The men will guide you through the next glen—Davie, don't be a fool," Brenda cried in exasperation when he stubbornly shook his head. "It's you they're looking for! And they'll keep coming back till they catch you."

He knew she was right. For some time he sat there brooding, trying to accept the truth. In his heart he could not believe Catrin had willingly left him to go with the redcoat captain, yet the people who had seen the event assured him it was so. He had no time to wait to hear her version of the story. By now there was probably a price on his head and he was not positive someone would not try to collect it.

David stood, steadying himself on his bad ankle, wincing at the sharp pain that speared him whenever weight was put on the limb. "Very well. You're all good loyal men who've dealt honestly with me in the past. I don't know if there's some other explanation behind this, but at the moment I can't afford to wait to find out. I'll get my things together, and then I'll be ready."

His decision caused Brenda to heave a great sigh of relief. In fact, a few weak tears pricked her eyes as she realized he was going to be easy to manage. The first bolt of hostility he had delivered had made her uneasy. Fortunately, sense and self-preservation had come to her rescue.

In less than an hour, swathed in heavy plaids and carrying their meager possessions, David, Brenda, and the four MacColl brothers, guided by several Highlanders, picked their way carefully along the mountain track leading into the neighboring glen. They would be heading north through territory already put to the torch; their destination was the west coast, where Angus MacColl had heard French ships sometimes lay off shore to take away Jacobite fugitives.

It was dark, cold, and treacherous on the mountain track, yet Brenda's heart sang with joy because David was hers again. At the moment he was not receptive to her affection, but time would change that. Lord knows she had been waiting for him since she was twelve years old—she could wait a little longer.

The house where Bryce and the other officers were head-quartered belonged to one of Ardshiel's relatives. Everything of value had already been earmarked for carrying back to England.

Catrin found these living conditions most luxurious compared with what she had been used to lately. She was surprised Bryce did not insist they share quarters. Though this had been his original intention, to his annoyance he discovered he did not have the billet to himself. His fellow officers, being of similar rank and class, would never condone such open flouting of convention were he to live openly with his betrothed. He almost regretted having told them how he had miraculously rescued her from a band of savages. Had he pretended she was merely a captive woman he could have enjoyed her without censure.

"You can take this room. I believe it belonged to the lady of the house and I expect it's decorated to a woman's taste."

Catrin smiled stiffly, wary of this polite Bryce who had merely kissed her hand as etiquette demanded, introducing her to his fellow officers and apologizing for her appalling condition without revealing that his own men were responsible for it. A local woman who had acted as maid to the mistress of the house was summoned to attend her. Catrin bathed, and washed and brushed her hair. Her tattered clothing was replaced from the wardrobe of her absent hostess. Now she felt almost human again. The local woman was not impolite, yet neither was she friendly toward her. News of her supposed betrayal of the villagers must have already reached Crannock House. That she had ultimately saved their lives seemed to count for nothing among these Highlanders. Holding her head high, Catrin tried to hide her pain as she dismissed the maid and retired to bed.

After making sure the woman had gone and the house was quiet, Catrin slipped on a cloak and shoes, then quietly unfastened the door. She had no idea how far she would have to travel to reach her former hiding place, but she was determined to make the effort.

"No, mistress, you're not allowed out."

A detaining hand shot out of the darkness and she heard the clink of a musket. Bryce had set a guard to watch her door.

"Am I a prisoner here?" she demanded icily.

"Not a prisoner, mistress. Captain Cavendish asked me to guard you for your own safety. You never know what these Scotch savages might do."

Even the windows had been secured. When Catrin managed to wedge open a small pane, harsh voices from the garden below told her sentries watched her window. In frustration she threw herself on the bed and sobbed herself to sleep.

"Did you sleep well, my love?" Bryce inquired solicitously when she appeared downstairs the following morning.

"No, I did not. Why did you set guards to watch me?"

"I can't take a chance on losing you now," was all he said as he caressed her neck. Though his touch was gentle, his eyes betrayed the barely concealed fires of lust.

His fellow officers began to file into the dining room where they then enjoyed a formal meal, polite as any Bloomsbury diners. The genteel gathering was so strange, considering the utter devastation of the surrounding land, that Catrin wanted to pinch herself to make sure she wasn't dreaming.

When the others departed to be about the day's orders, Bryce hung back to talk to her. "Choose what you want to take with you. The folderols in the wardrobes upstairs should suit you admirably. Simple, perhaps, but of good quality. They say Ardshiel's family were men of wealth. Prepare for our journey home next week. I can't wait to take you to Hursthampton. We'll be happy, I promise."

Protests came to her lips and Catrin quickly swallowed them. They were still too close to the glen to risk crossing Bryce. There was nothing to stop him carrying out his sentence on the villagers today, for he had slyly promised merely to spare them yesterday. He had not been able to enjoy the sensual rewards he had anticipated, so his temper was probably frayed. Instead of crossing him, instead of telling him she would never marry him, Catrin merely smiled and held her tongue.

"By the bye, you've not heard the latest news, have you, me dear?" Bryce asked, pausing at the door, his hand elegantly positioned on the knob where he could admire his large sapphire ring.

"What news is that?" Catrin ventured, almost afraid to ask.

"I'm now Lord Cavendish. Me older brother, God rest his

soul, finally succumbed to the consumption. Gad, I thought he'd linger on forever, poor sod! Hursthampton rivals anything in the county. You'll be proud to be its mistress, Catrin. And I'll be proud to have you there." His speech at an end, Bryce carefully placed his hat on his head and walked away.

Lady Cavendish! Catrin had never actually considered herself in that position. To be honest, since she had fallen in love with David, she had barely thought of Bryce at all. It was a shock to speak that title and realize she could well become its owner. Granted, at some future time she might escape from Bryce, but the further they traveled from Garth the less hope she would have of finding David.

Catrin leaned on the window frame staring out at the flower-decked garden dappled with morning sunlight. If it hadn't been for the black-shadowed mountains rimming the horizon she could easily have been in England. So peaceful did it seem it was hard to accept that beyond these walls lay the utmost devastation.

Survival alone in this desolate land would be impossible. It was hard to accept, yet by now David was probably miles away. No one but he felt any concern for her. The Garth villagers would probably kill her if she returned, hating her as much as the redcoats now they believed she had intentionally betrayed them. A woman could not endure long, friendless and penniless in a hostile land. Yesterday, while she stood on that summit above the gold-washed clouds, she had made a choice. When Bryce rode south she must travel with him.

Brenda stooped to fill a skin with water at the crystal loch, ever wary of discovery. The hilltops hereabouts were ringed with sentries on the lookout for fugitives and more particularly for Charles Stuart himself. After fleeing Culloden in April, the Prince had skulked through the heather to the Hebrides and back. It was September now, and though there was a price of £30,000 on his head he was still at large.

"Is there anyone about?" David asked as she approached their shelter built of tree branches and bracken.

"Not that I saw. Here, the water's fresh."

David took the skin and swigged the cold liquid. There had been no whisky since yesterday and they had only water to drink, which had hardly the same beneficial properties. He felt unreasonably disturbed this morning, haunted by a painful dream.

Reading his thoughts, Brenda snapped, "You dreamed about her again last night, didn't you?"

Sharply he glanced up. "Do you seek to rule my dreams also?"

Brenda held her tongue as he pushed past her, his scowl dark. She watched him move low through the thickets of gorse to the adjoining shelter where the four MacColls lived. They had come here from Glenmoriston, where they had met the fugitive Prince hiding with seven desperate men, not loyal Jacobites but robbers who had sworn to shelter him.

In the late afternoon they gathered around the campfire to roast a hare David had snared that morning. They had whisky Angus MacColl had stolen from a redcoat supply train. Bold to the point of foolishness, Angus could not long be parted from his "dram," risking any danger to obtain the golden liquid.

Brenda watched David, noting how much he was drinking; yet the whisky failed to brighten his mood. How she wished she could have ruled his dreams. He often dreamed about *her*. It was not hard to detect, for on those mornings he woke tormented and drawn. He stayed morose throughout the day and if there was whisky he drank far more than usual.

By now she had grown used to his indifference. At her insistence they shared a separate hut, for she didn't relish the companionship of the MacColls. The arrangement, however, led the brothers to believe her relationship with their laird was of a far deeper nature than was really the case. David had never made love to her, and many a night Brenda wept over his refusal to even consider her as a woman. Generally he treated her as if she were the MacColls' sister.

"A ship's at anchor off the coast. I heard talk about it yesterday," confided one of the MacColls. "Charlie's in the vicinity and they're hoping to contact him."

"The vessel's the *L'Heureux*," David added, staring wistfully into the smoky fire. "They say she's anchored in Loch nan Uamh. I'll bring Charles to them. I know his hiding place."

Thinking it was whisky talking, Brenda laughed. "Really, Davie, and is he your bosom friend then, these days?" He flashed her such a look of hatred, it silenced her sharp tongue.

"I'll have him told before nightfall."

The MacColls, who never doubted their laird's words, eagerly offered to accompany him. This territory was as strange to them as it was to David, but months of hard living had made them all reckless.

"You stay here," David ordered Brenda when she got up to follow them. "For once I'll have a few hours to myself."

Smarting at his angry words, she crouched before the fire, seething with plans to bring him to her bed. Around her neck hung a charm given her by a wisewoman on Benbecula, where they had awaited a rescue ship on a tip that proved unfounded. Deliberately she rubbed the stone and prayed. But it was not to the God of her childhood, in whose laws she had been well versed by the sisters; it was to a darker, more primitive deity who well understood the blazing fires of unrequited passion.

The small ragged party paused to rest, throwing themselves full length in the rusting heather. David's ankle throbbed and his collarbone burned, yet there was still too much whisky in his veins to make him see sense. Charles was up here on this mountain. They had spoken only two days ago, and if the ship was here to take the Prince to France, he was going to be the one to give him the news. The cave where Charles had formerly hidden was deserted; the redcoat patrols must have driven him onto higher ground. They must find him before dark. Redcoat sentries posted at the head of every glen would be on the lookout for fires, so if they were unlucky enough to be stranded up here, they would spend a chilly night.

"Come on, lads, on your feet. We've only a few hours of daylight."

Cheerfully the MacColls sprang from the heather, ever obedient to their laird. He might have been the Prince himself, so loyal were they to him. In their eyes, though there was still a certain magic attached to Prince Charlie, they admired David Stewart far more than the ragged stranger they had met last week and to whom they had bent the knee. David Stewart had never made them go hungry, nor had they ever had to face danger alone. Neither had he risked their lives unnecessarily—whatever risks they took were usually at their own behest.

They climbed ever higher, leaving behind the bracken already tipped with brown, rusting a tidemark around the mountainside. Soon the red stags would roar in the corries and skeins of geese would fly south over the snow-capped hills. A movement caught David's attention. The figure was dressed in dark garments, but he could tell immediately it was not a wild creature.

"Highness," David called softly, his voice urgent. There was no answer. Again he called, this time in Italian, using the familiar name Carluccio, which the Prince was called by his father. There was silence. They waited.

Very slowly the shadow moved, growing, finally emerging as a man, shortly followed by two more. Confidence mounted as David moved forward, hand outstretched to greet the Prince. Remembering his place, at the final moment he bent the knee before this ragged trio. Since his wandering Charles had become especially aware of his princely rank. Perhaps it was because rank was one of the only things Charles Edward had left.

Gone was the finely dressed charmer of Edinburgh and Manchester, replaced by a gaunt, ragged figure with a flowing red beard. Lousy, covered with sores from deprivation and infected midge bites, Charles made an unlikely prince. In his ragged black kilt, with a dirty shirt, brogues in holes tied to his feet with thongs, and a Highlander's soiled plaid looped about his shoulders, he was indistinguishable from a hundred other desperate fugitives who slept in the heather.

"Highness," said David, grasping the dirty hand extended to him for his kiss. "The boat's here. Your efforts to reach them have borne fruit. It's anchored off the loch."

"Thank you, Stewart of Garth, you've been one of my most loyal supporters. Tomorrow at dawn we'll set out. If the men knew the land better we could travel by night, as is our usual way, but I don't relish falling to my death. I've been too hard to kill for too long."

David smiled, looking up at Charles and noting the princely quality he still possessed despite his temporary degradation. "We'll join you, Highness. It's long past time to quit these shores. The winter will soon be upon us and I doubt we can withstand it in the open, poorly equipped as we are."

Charles nodded and offered him a skin of brandy. The spirits imparted an incongruous warmth and cheer to the ragged little band of men. During his travels about the Highlands and islands of Scotland, Charles had set a pattern of drinking that was to haunt him for the rest of his days, worsening with age and bitterness.

David accepted the brandy and took a hearty swallow. It was French, and excellent, not the usual fiery comfort of the poor Highlander, the whisky to which they had all become addicted.

"Thank you, Highness."

"Will you join us? We have enough game for all."

"No, thank you, we must go down before dark."

"God protect you, Stewart of Garth. We'll meet on the morrow."

To David's surprise, the red-bearded prince clasped him against his chest, kissing his cheeks in the Continental manner. Then they parted. Charles, thrusting his straggling blond hair from his eyes, waved until David and the MacColl brothers were out of sight.

It was dark when they reached the camp where Brenda was waiting.

"Did you find him?" she asked in surprise.

"Aye, the laird always does what he sets out to do, woman," reprimanded Angus MacColl, not liking Brenda's domineering manner. "It's not for you to question him. We found Charlie and he greeted us right royally."

David smiled, well aware of Brenda's seething resentment of Angus MacColl. "At dawn they'll make their move. We must be ready to join them. We'll be aboard that ship."

Brenda nodded, her eyes prickling with tears. Damn her weakness, she thought, turning away and going back into the shelter. She had been terrified he would not return. Some instinct told her that today was a turning point in his life. She had put her unease down to that confounded dream of his "beloved Catrin"; but perhaps it had been merely a foretaste of things to come. By this time tomorrow they could be headed for France. Thank God for that!

"You'd never recognize the Prince. He's even lousier than the MacColls," David laughed as he came inside the shelter. "When he lands in Rome they'll swear he's an impostor."

"You'd best get some sleep if we're to be away at dawn."

"Not yet." He thrust away her arm when she would have led him to his bracken bed. "Look, woman, I'm not an invalid. I climbed yon mountain and back again. I don't need help to lie on my bed."

David sat in the doorway drinking and watching the firefly flames of the enemy's campfires ringing the nearby hilltops. They were surrounded by redcoats. Each day he expected to be his last. Though he had never thought he would feel this way, he would be glad to leave Scotland. This was the place where all his dreams had died. In that respect he had much in common with his prince, yet Charles's bitterness had not the added anguish of lost love to deepen the pain.

Oh, God, Catrin! He gritted his teeth, rocked by emotion. For days he had tried not to even think about her. Last night his dream had been so vivid, he had wept silently when he woke to find it was only a dream. The experience had shattered the wall he had carefully erected about his heart. It was over, the love, the sweetness, the bond. Today he had given much thought to the past and realized he had never really relinquished his hope of having her back. Tonight, with the prospect of taking ship for France around the corner, he must finally accept the truth. The love and passion he still felt for her he would lock deep in his heart where it would lie untouched by any other woman. Whomever he met, wherever he went, he would never stop loving Catrin Blair.

"Davie, lad, come, lie down. The night's half gone."

Brenda laid her hand gently on his shoulder, her hair falling against his face. The soft feminine voice, which these days she rarely used, stirred within him a pagan fire. For all the time he had traveled with the Carmichael woman, he had not taken her. He always knew that, given the slightest encouragement, she could have been his, yet he had not made the effort. Instead of desire Brenda fired his anger with her constant reminders of Catrin's desertion. And when his anger was spent, bitterness began to grow until he found himself consumed by it. Over the weeks and months he had become a changed man. David gave Brenda much credit for helping him achieve that feat. Now, tonight, when he was at the lowest ebb of his emotions, she came to him, soothing, cozening, the way a woman ought to be. Copious amounts of whisky had removed his self-imposed restraint, warming his blood, which today had throbbed with memories of Catrin.

"You never give up, do you, woman?" he snarled, not calling her Brenda, reverting now to the MacColl brothers' speech. "For as long as I live you'll taunt me. And you mistakenly call that love."

Brenda gasped, alarmed by his angry tirade. "I've loved you for years. Only you were too foolish to see it."

"No, I was too discerning to accept it," he corrected bitterly. "You've striven to crush any finer feelings I had, ever quick to point out how Catrin deceived me. And do you know, Brenda Carmichael, though I can't prove it, I doubt your hands were clean in the matter. I fancy that somehow you arranged her defection."

"Davie, please, no more anger. Didn't I save your life? Haven't I cared for you faithfully since then? You've no cause to revile me."

He silently reviewed her words. Perhaps she was right. He had no actual cause for hatred. The whisky he had drunk constantly since his return was gone. In disgust he flung the empty skin aside. She had moved closer; the tantalizing softness of her hair was all about him. Brenda stroked his face, his hair, his beard.

"Love me tonight. I'll take away your pain. Maybe even your dreams of her. You can't ever have her again, Davie— but you can have me . . . as often as you want."

For a few minutes longer he resisted until the warmth flooded him from head to toe, insistent, all-consuming. With a growl more of rage than passion, he seized her and dragged her into his arms. Brenda's mouth was on fire as she covered his face with kisses, responding eagerly to his touch.

David shocked himself by the surge of feeling her nearness caused. How good it was to have a woman in his arms, to feel the soft pliancy of female flesh, the different fragrance, the pleasure of a woman's touch on his body. A gasp of longing for something he could not have lodged in his throat, coming out as a strangled sob when he allowed his hands the freedom of her luxurious curves.

Though Brenda rejoiced over her victory, later, when David drove her hard into the dried bracken bed, when the magnificent heat of his body cleft her in two and she writhed with sheerest delight, the name on his lips chilled her. In the depths of passion he had called her Catrin!

Chapter 18

On a pleasant September morning, Catrin stood at the window of her stepfather's Bloomsbury townhouse looking down on the street below. Milkmaids clad in blue-striped dresses, white aprons, and mobcaps carried their wares in pails hanging from wooden yokes resting on their shoulders. The cries of lavender girls and flower sellers mingled with the milkmaids' calls, their stridency increasing as they tried to make themselves heard above the rattle of wheels and the clop of hooves from coaches crossing the square. A familiar coach waited several doors away as Dr. Little paid morning calls on his titled patients.

Birds twittered in the plane trees. The sun was milder now, the air soft. Gone was the summer heat that had turned London's narrow streets into an airless prison. The garden was splashed with clumps of purple Michaelmas daisies and late roses filled the air with fragrance. Yet Catrin did not appreciate her surroundings. Too often her mind wandered to a rugged land of mist and mountain, of windswept lochs and red-berried rowans. It was a place she would never see again. But more than the place, her heart ached for the man she had left there. She prayed David had escaped the redcoats and her sacrifice had not been in vain.

Last week, to her joy and subsequent horror, Catrin had finally learned of her brother's fate. After Culloden Ness had been taken to a fetid Inverness jail. From there he was put aboard a vessel bound for London, where he had been imprisoned ever since. She had pleaded with Bryce to arrange his release, knowing it was well within his power as a personal friend of Cumberland. Bryce had finally agreed on the understanding that the date for Ness's release would fall after their wedding. The clemency was to be withdrawn at his discretion—in actual fact if Catrin failed to go through with their marriage.

She shuddered to think how Ness had fared during these nightmare months. Stories of the Jacobite prisoners' deprivation, which she had heard from several sources, filled her with horror. Bryce, telling her it was exaggerated nonsense, forbade her access to the informants. Despite his assurance, Catrin took no comfort from Bryce's words. He had forgotten she had been a witness to Butcher Cumberland's rout of the Highlands, which was currently being hailed as a victorious military campaign.

Daily Jacobite prisoners were brought to trial as a never-ending program of vengeance was carried out. It sickened her to see the shabby, illiterate men and women who last year had known nothing but their barren mountains being carted through the London streets before jeering mobs who pelted them with stones and filth. And all because they had supported a dream! Many of them barely understood the cause they championed, knowing only that their chief had called them out. Centuries of clan loyalty provided their answer. Now they were dying by the hundreds in terrible prisons, or were being shipped to the Indies as slaves to sweat out their lives on plantations . . .

"Miss Catrin, come quick! Your father's fallen and I can't lift him!"

Catrin spun about at Jessie's anguished cry, her heart racing. Running from the drawing room she found her stepfather slumped on the carpet, his face purple, his breathing shallow.

"Send someone to call the doctor, Jessie."

"Call him, miss?"

"Yes, his carriage is at number twenty-four. He's visiting the Carringtons."

Catrin bent over Humphrey Millbank and loosened his stock. Her heart fluttered as she tried to find his pulse and could not discern a beat. Finally, after much effort, she felt a feeble flutter beneath the mountain of flesh. While she held his wrist his pulse strengthened.

"Catrin," he whispered, his voice sounding strangled.

"Yes, Papa, I'm here," she answered obediently, soothing his brow with her cool hand. His skin felt clammy and now, instead of red, his face was gray.

"Ah, I was afraid I'd only dreamed you'd come home." When Humphrey Millbank smiled, Catrin's heart sank, for she saw it was with only one side of his mouth.

A few minutes later the elderly doctor arrived, puffing with exertion, for he was on the portly side himself. Alarmed by his patient's color, he creaked to his knees to examine Humphrey Millbank. Dr. Little then ordered the menservants to carry their master to his room.

"My dear Miss Blair, how can I tell you," Dr. Little began later over a refreshing glass of Madeira. "Such a tragedy, considering you've only recently returned home." Here he cleared his throat, coloring slightly, for the story behind Catrin's disappearance was the topic of much speculation around London drawing rooms.

"Perhaps if you would just tell me what's wrong with him?" Catrin suggested dryly.

"Yes, quite." Doctor Little looked slightly annoyed at being thus addressed. "Your stepfather's suffered an apoplexy. I thought at first it was his heart that failed him, but now I suspect a stroke . . . yes, a stroke's far more likely."

"When I saw his mouth lift on only one side, I suspected that. Is he going to be all right?"

"All right," repeated Dr. Little. "No one's all right when they have a stroke, me dear—apoplexy's a most serious condition. I would say, though I hate to dash your plans, that in view of your stepfather's health you should postpone your wedding indefinitely."

At that moment Catrin could have embraced the bumbling old quack. No news could have been dearer to her heart. In her excitement she temporarily forgot that Ness's freedom hinged on her following through with her obligations.

Even had she not been bound to Bryce to save her brother, Catrin's joy would have been shortlived. Humphrey Millbank was in danger of suffering a second crippling attack when she casually mentioned her conversation with the doctor.

"Never! I won't hear of it. Bloody nonsense . . . don't shush me, lass, I'll have my say! Haven't you been returned to me from the dead? Haven't we been blessed with a miracle because young Cavendish—Lord Cavendish—isn't going to write you off with a faretheewell? No. You'll be married with as much haste as possible. September it is . . . albeit a year late . . . but September, anyroad!"

* * *

September it was. And the grand edifice of St. George's in Hanover Square was the sight of the social event of the month. Scandalous speculation over the bride's recent conduct during her year of exile "up north" caused the pews to be filled to overflowing, bringing far more than the expected two hundred guests.

Catrin wore a gown of flounced white satin with magnificent silver trimmings, following a color scheme currently fashionable among brides. Bryce had personally favored an elopement, which had become a very modish arrangement, yet to please her father, whose lifelong dream this union had been, Catrin agreed to a proper ceremony. She carried a bouquet of orange blossom and white roses tied with silver ribbons, framed by a ruff of ruched silver lace to match the Brussels confection trimming her flounced skirts. Her silky chestnut hair was drawn high on her head, padded with false hair and adorned with loops of silver ribbon, lace, and sprays of fragrant white roses; two long ringlets trimmed with orange blossom fell over her left shoulder.

The roses had been Bryce's suggestion. When Catrin saw her groom's somewhat sarcastic smile as he viewed her elaborate headdress, pain speared her heart. In the numbness surrounding these unwanted nuptials she had not connected any hidden meaning to these white roses.

Now his thoughts were clear. His seemingly innocent suggestion had been in mockery of the Jacobite cause, for the white rose was its most treasured symbol. The chill that gripped her heart as she viewed her blandly handsome husband-to-be in his impeccable dress uniform was a forerunner of an emotion that would deepen as the weeks passed.

The minister was late. According to tradition Bryce should not have seen his bride before their wedding, yet it was he who adjusted her headdress and remarked upon the beauty of the roses.

"By the bye, dearest, I have a little news. That brother of yours is to be released today. Now, don't let me hear you say a Cavendish is not a man of his word."

The strains of the great organ reverberated through the building, and, nodding to her, Bryce walked away with his groomsmen.

Catrin's hands sweated as she wrung them together. Her bridesmaids, two of Bryce's fair-haired cousins, fussed over her gown, and her matron of honor, the daughter of one of her stepfather's closest friends, adjusted her flounced skirts. While she listened to the strains of organ music announcing the beginning of the bridal procession, Catrin tried to comfort herself with the news Bryce had just given her. Ness would be free today! Though perhaps Bryce had meant to cheer her spirits, she knew otherwise.

Catrin went through the wedding ceremony like a sleepwalker. Odd disjointed thoughts flitted through her mind as she knelt before the altar. Could Bryce have legally forced her to uphold her marriage contract? Her stepfather loved her in his way, yet there had been little hope of leniency from that quarter, for this marriage was the delight of his heart. By enduring Bryce as her husband she had saved her brother's life. Not only had she wed him, to ensure Ness's release Catrin remembered she had even promised to display affection for him. How could she fulfill that promise? Once Ness was safely aboard a vessel bound for the Continent, broken promises would be of little concern. It had been a vast disappointment when she learned she would not see her brother, for the conditions of his release were that he leave London immediately and never again set foot on English soil.

". . . take this woman to be your lawful wedded wife?"

Catrin's heart stood still as she realized she was paying little attention to the ceremony. No one seemed unduly concerned, so at least she must have correctly mouthed her own responses. She cast a sideways glance at her groom and gave him a tight, brittle smile. Bryce's answering expression told her she was not deluding him in the least.

Amid joyful pealing of bells, cheers from the crowd, and showers of rose petals, Catrin emerged from St. George's in the mellow September sunshine on the arm of her handsome groom. Officers of Bryce's regiment formed a canopy of crossed swords under which they walked.

A carriage drawn by milk-white horses and bedecked with satin bows, silver streamers, and roses waited before the church. Bryce handed Catrin inside the carriage before turning to smile and wave goodbye to his friends.

"You'd best try to look happy, my dear, you're married to me now for better or worse."

For better or worse, the rhythm of the carriage wheels repeated the phrase as they rumbled along the Kentish lanes. The peaceful, sun-washed countryside slipped past the window as they headed north under tall trees already tinged with gold. Beside the road the spreading hop fields were heavy with fruit while brambles laden with purple blackberries smothered the hedgerows. Dusty ox-eye daisies nodded in the wind of their passage and the bare stubblefields were bordered with creamy meadowsweet.

Bryce put out his hand to her and Catrin forced a smile.

"You're as lovely as any woman I've even seen . . . lovelier," he complimented, his blue eyes softening with emotion.

She regarded him coldly, her heart unmoved. "Thank you."

"You needn't be so formal with me. Demme, Catrin, we're man and wife!" he reminded a trifle huffily.

"Give me time to get used to this, Bryce."

He took his hand from hers and said no more. Slumped in the corner he watched the passing countryside, a scowl on his heavy face.

Nervously Catrin smoothed her pink silk skirts, looping her slender fingers through the blue ribbon trimming, fingering the embroidered roses that encrusted the padded petticoat of her sumptuous going-away gown. Following the now fashionable custom, instead of spending the next day "at home," the young couple left for the country immediately after the wedding reception.

Humphrey Millbank's Bloomsbury Square residence had been thronged with wellwishers. When people congratulated them, saying what a charming couple they made, Catrin's heart ached. During the reception her ailing stepfather had reclined on a sofa, beaming with pride and happiness. To show his appreciation for her obedience to his wishes he had promised Catrin a spanking new wardrobe, the like of which had not been seen this season. And she thanked him, inwardly wanting to decline his generosity. Noting the sorrow in her gray eyes, he had sought to cheer her. Poor Papa. Had he but known the actual cause of her pain. He thought he had already guessed the reason behind her sadness—her aversion to this marriage was of long standing. She also had the added burden of Ness's imprisonment to add to her pain. It was no use. When she tried to tell him she was in love with another man, Humphrey Millbank had shouted her down in an emotional tirade which she feared would bring about a second stroke. Those months "up north," as he referred to them, spent in the company of friends—

she had not dared tell him the whole truth—were not a subject he chose to discuss.

To Catrin's great surprise Bryce had substantiated her story. At first she thought it was to silence the tongues—which had never ceased wagging since Booth Merriam's masquerade ball— that he pretended he had rescued her from danger in a nation virtually under siege. His inventiveness knew no bounds. Bryce gave Crannock House, their Appin billet, as the address of Catrin's "friends," telling her stepfather she had been invited there before the hostilities broke out and was unable to leave. Privately she wondered if Bryce's story had been to protect them both. To have his wife pointed out as a Jacobite could be decidedly uncomfortable for a staunch Whig of his social standing, and for him to have married a woman whom he suspected of living with another man would make him a laughingstock.

By now Bryce nodded, his full mouth slack. After the reception he had changed from his uniform into a beautifully cut coat of swallow blue satin lavish with gold lace. Lace frothed at the neck and sleeves of his fine cambric shirt; his scarlet velvet waistcoat was embroidered in gold.

Catrin studied her husband in repose, never having been granted such a searching examination, and she again saw his resemblance to Cumberland. Bryce was a year younger than the royal duke, but his likeness to the hated Butcher earned Catrin's contempt. Whenever she thought about Cumberland she was reminded of the bloodshed and horror carried out in his name. He also was responsible for destroying her life, for robbing her of her beloved...

The coach lurched. Bryce jerked partially awake, snorting and smacking his lips before he slid even lower in his seat. His legs, encased in silk stockings with fashionable red-embroidered clocks, sprawled across her full skirts. Catrin tugged her dress free, pushing away his red-heeled silver buckled shoes, distressed to find the silk now marked with filth from London's streets. When she compared the man before her to David she could not hold back her tears. For some time she had striven to keep his image at bay, his name off her lips. It had been hard, yet with supreme effort she had managed it. Now all the pain of her lost love surged back until she gasped with the severity of her emotion. Turning her face to the window she glanced at a passing pear orchard where red admiral butterflies hovered over the fallen fruit. And she wept. Silent, relieving tears obliterated the neat rows of green-leaved fruit trees, the passing fields stained scarlet with sorrel. David's handsome face haunted her as he sprang vividly to life in the wavering mist; his name was a penance on her lips.

It was late afternoon before they reached Hursthampton. Autumn chill seeped keenly from the woods as they skirted the rolling parkland and clopped along Hursthampton's impressive rhododendron-lined drive.

The house was built of limestone at the end of the last century by Bryce's grandfather. Hursthampton's impressive façade with its tall columns was reminiscent of ancient Rome. A giant cupola was flanked by urns set atop the central pillars. The house was fronted by a colonnade that gave the impression of great height. The west, east, and north aspects were supported by giant pilasters surmounted by a frieze depicting coats of arms and figures from mythology. Leading up from a beautifully landscaped garden was a flight of broad shallow steps. Facing the house's eastern exposure were French windows opening onto a terrace, which led down to a two-acre lake where moored boats bobbed in the freshening breeze and pink waterlilies closed their petals against the oncoming night.

"Well, dearest, what do you think of my home?"

"It's quite splendid, Bryce. Much larger than I'd expected," Catrin mumbled uncomfortably, wondering if she could feel at home in a house that reminded her of a municipal building.

"I've added a walled garden, a temple of the four winds, new stables and kennels. In fact, my love, we've pulled down most of the village of Kinghampton to make our estate even more beautiful. That collection of rundown hovels will never be missed, I assure you."

Catrin doubted the villagers had viewed the loss of their homes in the same light, but she did not mention that. Bryce was being his most charming; at the moment she could not afford to rouse that other, less pleasant side of his character.

An army of liveried servants appeared at the mansion's impressive entrance, ranging themselves on the steps to greet their master and his bride. Bryce repositioned his wig and set his cocked hat squarely on his head; then, reaching for his silver-handled cane, he assumed his most benevolent smile as he prepared to greet his household.

The coach door was opened and footmen in dark livery handed Catrin out of the coach. Her legs were stiff after the long journey and she walked unsteadily over the gravel drive toward the shallow flight of steps. Bryce was ahead of her, already greeting the servants, his voice unnaturally jovial. Suddenly she heard someone calling her name, the voice cutting through the obsequious greetings.

"Catrin."

Turning around Catrin faced the brazen light of the setting sun. Shielding her eyes with her gloved hand, she saw a man detach himself from the shrubbery on the far side of the drive and limp toward her. Her heart froze, then began a frenzied beat. Could it be David? He wore a plaid waistcoat and leather riding boots; there were bandages around his head...

"Sister dearest... and my beloved brother-in-law."

It was Ness!

"Oh, they said I couldn't see you. Oh, Ness! Ness!" Catrin exclaimed in delight, racing toward him with arms outstretched. Bryce snapped a sharp command for her to stop but she ignored him. Appalled by Ness's changed appearance, Catrin checked her headlong rush when she drew close enough to see there was no welcoming smile on his face.

"Ness," she repeated unsurely, her voice husky with tears, "Oh, my dear, how wonderful to see you at last. Are you well? They never told me you were wounded."

"I wonder if you even bothered to ask. Nay, I'm sure you were far too busy with your marriage plans to worry about me."

"Ness! That's so unfair. You know the story behind this..."

"What the devil do you mean coming here, Blair? You're supposed to be crossing the Channel," Bryce thundered as he reached his wife's side. "By God, I've a mind to have you thrown back in gaol. The effrontery of it!"

"Have no fear, Cavendish, I'll be gone within the hour. I just wanted to bid my dear, loyal sister goodbye. Surely you won't deny me that after all I've suffered."

Bryce tried to compose his lips in a smile and failed. "Very well, I suppose it's not much to ask. Unexpected, but it can't be helped. Damned unfortunate, though..."

"Damned unfortunate," Ness repeated, his eyes narrowing.

Catrin stared at her brother. His gaunt, bearded face was ashen from sickness and long imprisonment. They must have given him new clothes, for though shabby, his garments were in reasonable repair. The most shocking discovery of all was the coldness in his eyes. Ness was a stranger.

"So, you went over to the victor, eh, Catrin? A friend of Butcher Cumberland at that. Can it be you don't know what atrocities were committed in his name? Is that the reason you've married one of his bosom friends? Didn't you hear about the rapes, the burnings, the murders? Didn't you know the appalling conditions we had to endure? In the Inverness jail the filth was waist high! On the transport ships wounded men lay in their filth on the ballast rocks, bleeding and dying in the holds until they had enough cargo to make the voyage profitable . . ."

"By Christ! That's enough! I'll not have you speak thus to my wife!"

Bryce took a menacing step toward Ness, who shoved away his raised arm. "Have no fear, brother-in-law, I've little wish to gaze long on either of you. Our friends were made to suffer at their hands, sister dear. Remember that well in the years to come, take comfort from it . . ."

"Ness, please, listen. Don't be so harsh. I'd no choice. I only learned about your imprisonment last week. No one told me a thing."

Ness's thin lips curled in scorn. "Pitiful lack of concern these people show, me dear. I often wondered why no one did anything when wounded men were dying around me."

"Ness, please, don't, don't. Oh, my brother, I love you, I love you so." Catrin could go no further as tears choked her voice.

"Love! My dear Lady Cavendish, I wonder what that word means to you? Once I had a sweet sister, but she died somewhere in the Scottish Highlands. I'm going now," Ness said, thrusting off Bryce's hand when he would have restrained him. "May your marriage be every bit as joyful as you deserve."

"Ness, wait, please . . ."

Bryce grabbed Catrin's arm, preventing her from following the shabby embittered man who deliberately turned his back on her, refusing to listen to her pleas as he limped toward a bare-boned nag tethered beneath an oak. Several servants sprinted after the stranger before Bryce called them back.

"Let him go! Don't soil your hands." Turning to Catrin, his full lips curled in scorn, Bryce said, "So nice to have seen your brother again, me dear. Wouldn't have missed your tender farewell for the world."

All the misery she had fought to vanquish returned in a flood of grief. Not giving her a chance to follow Ness, Bryce propelled Catrin forward to greet his waiting household. Tears blinded her as she stumbled up the first step. Muttering in anger at having his grand homecoming tarnished by the unpleasant scene, Bryce bore her up none too gently, forcing her toward the first curtsying servant.

"So very pleased to have you home, ma'am," mumbled the housekeeper, her soft heart pierced for this strange woman's pain.

"Yes, it's lovely to be here," Catrin mumbled like a mechanical doll. Her stricken face was ashen, her breath choking in her throat. The horror of her confrontation with her brother filled her mind as she toiled through the polite greetings until she finally reached the top step and was allowed to enter Hursthampton.

Inside the darkened house she was met by an unending vista of lofty-ceilinged, marble-floored rooms, adorned with columns of jasper and Siena marble. Their footsteps clattered and echoed through the hollow rooms, which were as silent as a mausoleum. As Catrin crossed the circular black and white marble-floored hall, white marble busts stared at her with sightless eyes from blue-painted niches.

"Bring some refreshments," Bryce commanded a servant who bowed and disappeared. "Damned inconvenient this, to say the least. Ruined our homecoming, demme if it didn't."

Catrin perched on the edge of a satin upholstered couch, too tense to lean against the blue tasseled pillows piled artistically at either end of the couch. Bryce paced before the hearth, having given sharp orders to a servant to light a fire.

"Never mind, me dear, don't give it a second thought. We're home now and life goes on. You'll soon forget," he soothed as he offered her a narrow crystal glass of dry sherry. Bryce poured himself a generous serving of brandy in a large snifter, then leaned against the marble mantel to survey his bride.

"I know you're trying to be kind, Bryce, but I'd rather not discuss it, if you don't mind."

He shrugged and continued to sip his brandy. "Very well, me dear, as you please. Can't expect much better, though, from these damned Jacobites. Your father's right when he says they're nothing but a lousy rabble . . ."

"Bryce, please!" she cried, so tense she felt as if she would snap.

"If you think we're going to ignore the subject, you're sadly mistaken. Though I supported you in your lies to your father, I've no intention of maintaining the lie in private."

"I didn't expect you to."

"Good, glad to get that straightened out. Now, me dear," Bryce said, his tone changing, "there's something I want you to see. Had it done specially for you . . . cost a mint getting it ready at such short notice, but then, as your dearest papa will be paying for it in the long run, he shouldn't object if it makes you happy."

Bryce set down his empty brandy snifter and motioned for her to follow him. They ascended a curving stair with a marble balustrade. Gold-edged draperies were drawn across a huge window spanning the three stories about which the stair wound. Following them at a discreet distance came half a dozen servants. It was too much for Catrin to hope she would have the opportunity to retire to the sanctuary of her room to cry for all the grief her meeting with Ness had brought. They hurried up the stair and finally stopped before a dove-gray door lavishly decorated in gilt. As he leaned across her to open the door, Bryce brushed her brow with his lips.

The door swung inward to reveal a room decorated in rose pink from the heavy velvet draperies to the floral gros point carpet beside the bed. The canopied cream bed was decorated with swags of flowers and much gesso work, not gilded in the usual fashion, but finished in silver, which was far more rare. Twin chairs upholstered in pink velvet, a bench and a small dressing table with an ornate mirror hanging above it, all matched the elaborate bed. The bed's swagged draperies were held back by huge satin bows; the bed's ceiling was of pleated satin radiating from an enameled oval depicting flowers and nymphs.

"Now, how do you like it? I had it created just for you, Lady Cavendish!"

"It's lovely! And this is so much more magnificent than I expected," Catrin gasped, genuinely pleased by the extravagant room, but still too shattered by Ness's anger to react as she knew Bryce expected. "Thank you, Bryce, it's very thoughtful of you."

"Oh, I expect to be rewarded," he said in a husky voice, his hand moving over her back in an intimate, searching caress.

His reminder brought a wave of nausea washing over her. She supposed she dared not ask to be spared her wifely obligations tonight.

"I'd hoped..." she began falteringly, her voice fading as his expression turned hostile.

"Those hopes are not going to be indulged. Demme, Catrin, haven't I been patient long enough? You made certain promises to me...or have you already forgotten?"

She had not forgotten. The servants were melting into the background, leaving them alone. And she knew it was time to start repaying Bryce for his generosity.

"We'll dispense with valets and maids tonight. Stand there, don't move. I want to undress you myself, Catrin. I've dreamed of this moment."

What to Bryce was unquestionably an erotic encounter was to Catrin an ordeal to be endured. Dutifully she stood while he fumbled to undo the lacings of her gown, trying to remove herself from this time and place. Bryce was gentle; he did not rip the fastenings as she had expected. His newfound patience was largely because this dress was far too costly to ruin and be charged to his generous father-in-law's account. Bryce's lips were wet against her neck and Catrin closed her eyes, trying not to see David, not to compare these kisses to his.

Bryce allowed her skirts to fall about her ankles; her petticoats followed. Catrin stood there in her lawn bodice, her full breasts protruding above the whalebone stays, so burstingly provocative Bryce could endure no longer. With a constricted sob he fastened his hands about her inviting flesh, finally possessing what he had so long desired.

"We were affianced, Catrin, through no choice of our own," he admitted huskily, his breath hot against her neck. "Yet had I chosen freely, I couldn't have wished for a lovelier bride. You're the most desirable woman in England...perhaps in the whole world."

Catrin allowed him to embrace her, to kiss her, shrinking inwardly when his embraces became more passionate, when his surging flesh could no longer be ignored. A hot wave of nausea came to her throat.

"You are my wife...and I'm the proudest man in the world because of it," Bryce breathed sincerely as he scooped her in his arms, surprising her by his strength as he carried her effortlessly to the pink satin coverlet. Gently he placed her amid the frothing lace and satin ribbon bows, and Catrin fought to hold back her nausea and tears. A picture of Ness, his face grimly indifferent, flashed through her mind. Tears filled her eyes and spilled down her cheeks.

"Don't be afraid of me," Bryce soothed, noting her tears as he struggled out of his clothes. Impatient now, too eager for care, he flung his gold-laced coat and waistcoat on the floor; his breeches followed. He did not seem to notice that she turned away, not anxious to view him naked. At last he was ready and he flung himself down beside her, his arms reaching out, his lips hot and eager.

He kissed her tear-wet cheeks, soothing her, trying his utmost to please this reluctant bride who lay submissive in his arms, her mind and heart elsewhere. Jealous because he had no control over that part of her, he tried to force down the emotion. Wasting no more time in preliminaries, Bryce pressed her into the satin coverlet, covering her body with his own. He did not ask her to caress him, he did not demand she kiss him in return, as, with a cry of suppressed desire, he joined their bodies in a burst of passion.

Catrin lay there staring at the pleated pink canopy overhead. Now, at last, she dared think about David. Effortlessly her tears flowed, numbing her to the reality of Bryce's lovemaking. To her surprise he gasped and cried out before flopping breathlessly against the feather pillows. It was over.

Catrin said nothing. She lay with her eyes closed, waiting for him to leave. Suddenly she felt his hand rough on her arm as he jerked her toward him. Eyes snapping open, Catrin stared at him. It was quite dark outside. Twin candles burned on the sidetable, thoughtfully placed there by a servant. In the dim candlelight it was hard for her to see his face.

"That poor performance won't do. I'll forgive you tonight . . . tomorrow you must do better," he growled, barely restraining his temper.

"I'm sorry, Bryce, so much has happened. Seeing Ness, and I . . ." The lump grew in her throat until Catrin could say no more.

"Ness—and that accursed Scottish Jacobite who warmed your nights," he snarled. "Don't think I've forgotten about him. Old man Millbank may believe your foolish tales, maybe others do too, but we both know them for the trumped-up pack of lies they are. Your lover was the fugitive David Stewart, wasn't he?"

"That's all in the past, Bryce. I've tried so hard to bury it."

He snorted in anger, seizing her and brutally devouring her mouth. "How convenient for you. Well, if you manage to live up to your bargain, perhaps I can bury it too."

This time, when he thrust his body inside her, Catrin could not ignore the pain. Unaroused as she was, she failed to accommodate him easily. Her flesh pulled and dragged until she wept not for lost loves and broken loyalties—this time her tears were of pain!

Chapter 19

By early October Catrin was the possessor of two fine bay mares, two pairs of hounds, a beribboned lapdog and a wardrobe full of beautiful garments. Her stepfather and her husband appeared to be trying to outdo each other in their generosity.

As Catrin had suspected, Bryce's debts were high and much of his lavish habits were being financed by Humphrey Millbank. Her stepfather seemed unconcerned by his new son-in-law's extravagance, considering the honor of having his daughter made Lady Cavendish to be reward enough.

The beautiful parkland surrounding Hursthampton was veiled in gold and the woods were heavy with the scent of decaying vegetation. As the month progressed the tall beeches turned brilliant shades from orange to copper, while bronze oaks and scarlet sycamores set the countryside afire. Early morning mists hung low over the tree tops until the mild October sun finally burned them away. One of Catrin's greatest joys was riding about the estate on the lovely bay hunter Bryce had given her. As she cantered beneath the autumn trees on the sleek, perfectly proportioned animal, Catrin tried to forget the price she had paid for all this.

Early one morning, when the mist still cloaked the woodland and obliterated the distant hills, Catrin rode along the path skirting the woods. That morning Bryce had not accompanied her, and she was grateful for the legal matter that had taken him to the neighboring village. Never good, as the weeks passed their personal relationship had rapidly deteriorated. Though

Bryce still lavished gifts on her in a frantic effort to buy her
love, Catrin grew ever colder toward him. Their hours alone
became an ordeal, for sooner or later the conversation shifted
to the private battle waged behind their bedchamber door. Of
late Bryce's frustration had errupted in violence. Frequent bruises
and once a black eye had made Catrin wary of crossing him.
Even his lovemaking had turned violent, and this loathsome
new aspect served only to increase the disgust she already felt
for Lord Cavendish.

A flutter of white caught her eye. Forewarned, she was able
to check Rose's fright when the mare shied at something lying
half buried in the rusting bracken beside the path.

Her heart pitched as she wondered if it was a body. She
had seen death often enough in Scotland, yet she had managed
to thrust the horror of that time to the back of her mind, successfully blocking the hideous memories until now. Panic seized
her, setting her heart thundering and constricting her throat
until she had to fight the desire to ride back as fast as she could
to Hursthampton.

"Lady, help me."

At first Catrin wondered if she had imagined the feeble cry.
With shaking hands she dismounted and looped Rose's reins
about a nearby branch. Crouching, she reached down to the
figure and parted the wet bracken to see a young woman whose
blood-matted blond hair straggled over her bruised face.

"Oh, God, what happened to you? Who are you?"

Supporting the woman's thin shoulders, Catrin helped her
to sit, cradling her battered face against the bodice of her scarlet
riding habit.

"I'm Tess Hodge, milady. Be you from the Hall?"

"Yes, I'm Lady Cavendish."

The girl's thin mouth curved slightly. "We heard his lordship
was married."

"How badly are you hurt? Were you run down or did someone beat you?"

"I was jumped on me way home," Tess mumbled, her eyes
cast down. "I hadn't a chance. There were three of 'em. Big
lads . . . gardeners by the looks of it."

"You mean our gardeners attacked you, here, in these
woods?"

Tess nodded, biting her lip. "I know I was trespassing,
milady, but we've always come to gather nuts and berries. The

old lord let the villagers pick what they wanted. They only put up the walls recently . . . and besides, last autumn we was living over yonder!"

Catrin saw the girl's face harden as she glanced in the direction of Bryce's splendid new landscaped gardens. "Let me take you home to your family," she suggested kindly.

Tess shook her head. "There's no family now. Me man was sent to prison for poaching. I'm on me own, 'cept for Ma. She's old and gone childish. Maybe I could just have a ride to the other side of the wall."

Catrin smoothed back the girl's hair, while she wondered how to help her. She appeared badly bruised, and as her skirts were also bloody, she suspected her rape had been brutal. Whoever was responsible for the crime must be made to pay!

"Stay where you are. I'll go for help."

"No! No one else . . . I'm too ashamed," Tess cried, thrusting away Catrin's soothing hand as she struggled to her feet. Her face was ashen and she leaned against a tree for support as a wave of weakness washed over her.

"You certainly can't walk home. Stay here and I'll get help. Promise not to try to leave."

Tess sank to the ground at the foot of the tree, wiping sweat from her upper lip. "All right, your ladyship, I promise. Reckon I'm not as tough as I thought."

Catrin gave the girl an encouraging smile before she ran back to her horse. Soon she was flying along the path toward Hursthampton, seething with anger when she considered the crime. Bryce must help her settle this, for the army of gardeners was under his jurisdiction.

The servants responded quickly to her request for help, concerned when they learned the victim's identity; Tess Hodge was considered a good woman, not prone to loose morals.

When they neared the place where Catrin had left the injured girl, she half expected to find Tess had gone. She was gratified to see her still leaning against the tree trunk. The manservants lifted Tess into the cart and Catrin rode beside her on the journey home.

Catrin instructed the maids to bathe Tess's wounds and allow her to rest in one of the servants' chambers until she felt better. The housekeeper, who also served as the household apothecary, brewed a soothing drink and offered her own secret ointment to help heal Tess's wounds.

It was late afternoon before Bryce returned from the magistrate's court. By now Tess was sleeping. Though reluctant to do so, the girl had finally revealed the names of her attackers, abandoning her pretense that the men were strangers. Though Catrin knew it was probably imprudent of her to do so, she was so angry over their gardeners' conduct that she immediately confronted Bryce about his employees' misdoing, barely waiting until he had exchanged polite greetings and ordered a refreshing sherry.

"Christ—a village chit taken by a few louts and you want to raise a hue and cry about it! Have sense, Catrin. There's no real crime been committed. What on earth do you expect me to do?"

"Bring the guilty men here, reprimand them at the least—dismiss them, for preference . . ."

"Dismiss! You're insane! Good gardeners are hard to find. Now don't start defending the little chit, she's probably as loose-moraled as a Drury Lane whore. You're too naive, Catrin, and these locals know it. Besides, I've had a hard day—we sentenced two poachers to transportation to the Indies. It was a damned nerve-racking ordeal, I can tell you . . . thank you, Potts." Bryce eagerly downed his sherry and sat sprawled in a chair, his stock loosened and his red camlet waistcoat unbuttoned.

"Had them transported for poaching! Oh, Bryce, surely that's too harsh a sentence. Couldn't they have been sent to prison?"

His full lips jutted belligerently. "How dare you question my actions? Demme, Catrin, sometimes I think I'll be glad to rejoin the regiment. I'm a wounded veteran of Fontenoy, a trusted officer of His Majesty, not just some damned local squire frittering away his time with his horses and hounds. I tell you, our honeymoon's been far from the joyful idyll I envisioned—damned far. Not content with trying to freeze me to death in me own bed, now you're trying to dispense justice. I won't have it! Transportation's too good for the wretches! Should've hanged, that's the punishment they should have got. Time and again I've made my position clear. Anyone'd think the land was theirs."

"Apparently your father gave the villagers free rein to pick berries and nuts. Maybe he also turned a blind eye to a little poaching. Since you pulled down their homes, some of the people are close to starvation."

Jumping to his feet, Bryce grabbed her arm, his fingers gouging her flesh. "Father never allowed any such thing! More likely it was that weakling brother of mine, coughing up his guts for nearly ten years. It's under his leadership all this nonsense got started. I won't have it! And I won't have you telling me what I should do."

"Bryce, stop it, you're hurting me," Catrin cried, trying to free her wrist.

"Hurting you!" The smile on his face turned cruel. "Oh, my dear Catrin, the hurting's not even begun yet. You can forget any idea of ruling the manor—I give the orders and you obey. Do you understand?"

She nodded, biting back tears, knowing it was useless to fight him. At Hursthampton her power was nonexistent.

"Good. At least you're learning sense. Now, where is this filthy little chit? Surely not in the house—oh, demme, Catrin, not in the house! We'll be overrun with vermin. How could you?"

"She was in pain. I didn't see any harm in it."

Bryce was not listening. He marched to the bellpull and summoned Potts, whom he commanded to throw out the wench.

Risking his anger, Catrin ran into the hallway ahead of the butler.

"There's no need to throw the girl out, Potts. I'll tell her to leave myself."

"You stay out of it!" Bryce bellowed from the drawing room.

"I'm the one who brought the girl to Hursthampton. It's my responsibility to see that she leaves."

Bryce backed off, evidently seeing some reason in her words. "Demme, Catrin, perhaps you're right at that. Tell her we'll punish the lads. Fob her off with some story. I'm not exactly viewed as Lord Bountiful in the village, no reason to stir them up any further, now, is there?"

When Catrin climbed the twisting stair to the servants' attics she discovered a decidedly different view of stately Hursthampton. Here the walls were dingy and the rooms poorly lit and ventilated. Furniture was spartan and the servants' tiny, boxlike rooms were cheerless as a prison. When Bryce rejoined his regiment, Catrin decided she would spruce up this forgotten part of the house. Once the work was done, there would be little he could do to change matters.

"Tess, how are you feeling now?" she asked as she leaned over the narrow bed. Now that her face had been washed and her hair brushed, Tess looked young and vulnerable.

"Much better, thank you, milady. You're a saint to 'ave taken me in like this. God bless you!"

Catrin swallowed, finding what she had to say even more difficult after such glowing words. "Tess," she began hesitantly, "I'm glad you're feeling better, because I'm afraid Lord Cavendish . . ."

"Wants me out. That's all right, milady, I understand. I can go home now without shame. The housekeeper even gave me a gown. Oh, it's so pretty with blue flowers and all. Look!"

Touched by Tess's delight, Catrin made an admiring comment about the cheap cotton gown. She helped the girl dress, for her multiple bruises made movement difficult.

"I've told Lord Cavendish and he said he'll speak to the men responsible."

Tess cocked an eyebrow and made no comment. She suspected that "speaking to them" meant no more mention would be made of the crime. Lady Cavendish seemed a good enough sort, too good for him, cruel, pompous creature that he was. In the past she had greatly admired young Bryce Cavendish in his striking uniform. That was before she had known what he could do, before he ordered the village pulled down and its people dispossessed.

"You must take a basket of food with you . . . no, I insist, and remember I'll be here if you ever need help. Lord Cavendish will soon be returning to his regiment."

No further exchange was necessary; they both understood what that significant statement implied. Tess gripped Catrin's hand in gratitude and she bobbed a shy curtsy.

"Thank you, milady. And you remember, if you ever need help I'll be here too."

After Tess had left, Catrin smiled as she reviewed the girl's touching offer. What possible help could a poor village girl give Lady Cavendish? Hers were ailments not mended by poppy tea and a calico gown.

During the following week Bryce resumed his habit of accompanying Catrin on her morning ride about the estate. No further mention was ever made of Tess, or of the outcome of his conversation with the guilty gardeners. When Catrin tried to reopen the subject, he gruffly silenced her, telling her the matter was closed.

Now, when they rode down the main street of the neighboring village of Sedgely, an ominous change had become apparent. No villager doffed his cap and waved, no child ran out to look at the fine horses; even the assorted village dogs who usually yapped at their heels were absent. Knots of surly villagers stood muttering in their doorways as they passed. And today an unseen hand pitched a clod of earth after them as they neared the end of the street.

"Ungrateful bastards," Bryce snarled, uncomfortably aware of the growing resentment in the village. "They want everything their way. No punishment, everything handed to them."

Catrin found the villagers' changing attitude rather alarming, and she was glad to be away from the huddle of thatched cottages. Tess had been friendly toward her, yet these people were openly hostile; at times their looks were downright mutinous.

"Can't you reconsider the men's punishment?" she ventured as they cantered past the Norman parish church.

Bryce, however, remained unbending. His chin held high, his face dark with anger, he roared, "Be damned to them! Besides, it's not I who set the punishment. There's a judicial system, me dear."

"We agreed not to lie to each other, Bryce. I'm aware you own the local magistrate and that any recommendations made by you will be followed to the letter."

He turned in the saddle, his face white with anger. "How dare you accuse me of buying the court?"

"Only because it's true," she snapped, pulling ahead. Catrin increased her speed and soon left him behind as she galloped across the rolling farmland toward the comparative safety of Hursthampton's stone walls.

Bryce galloped after her, the wild ride finally erasing his foul humor. By the time they entered the gateway to his estate, he was smiling. "Nothing like a good gallop to bring a man around—you minx, you're not as unfeeling as you pretend, after all."

Catrin grew wary of his jovial mood when she noticed that gleam in his blue eyes. He had dismounted. Reaching up, Bryce swung her from her sidesaddle into his embrace. His mouth was hot and demanding.

"I didn't mean to be artful," she explained when at last she was able to speak.

"Well then, you must be artful without knowing it. Come, let's walk past the lily pond and into the garden. You've not seen the clever pagoda and the oriental garden. Not as splendid as the temple of the four winds, but eyecatching to say the least."

His innocent suggestion did not deceive Catrin. As she expected, after a perfunctory inspection of the intricately laid-out garden filled with rocks and miniature shrubs, Bryce pulled her into his arms. After kissing her hungrily, he urged her to walk with him across the narrow red bridge over a tinkling stream, and enter the red-and-yellow painted summerhouse built in the shape of a pagoda.

A huge brass gong hung on the wall, and the building's single room was furnished with a white wicker couch and a table and dining chairs. It was to the couch Bryce drew her, his voice softly winning, his hands eagerly exploring.

"Please, Bryce, not here," she protested, turning her face aside as he kissed her passionately.

He seized her chin, his fingers biting hard. "Not here . . . not anywhere. Damn you, Catrin Blair, I keep trying to overlook your shortcomings because you're so deuced attractive. You're never going to forget that traitor Jacobite, are you! I'll bet you weren't cold to him. You likely spread your legs eager as any penny drab. Damn you! Damn him!"

Catrin screamed as he grasped her and shook her till her teeth rattled. Her plumed felt hat fell off and her piled chestnut hair tumbled about her shoulders. Her transformation only heightened his lust. Staring at her, all flushed and disheveled, Bryce's breathing quickened and his face beaded with sweat.

"Ravishing," he breathed. "Simply ravishing."

She screamed again when he reached for her tightly buttoned bodice, hooked his fleshy hands in the neckline and wrenched it open. Small black buttons and red velvet bows flew about the room and bounced across the floorboards. Catrin's efforts to defend herself were futile as he ripped open her shift and impatiently thrust aside her petticoat and the small wicker hoop under her riding habit. Eagerly baring her white thighs, Bryce fumbled for entrance. He did not bother to remove his own clothing, merely plunged inside her, bending her in an excruciatingly painful position over the arm of the wicker couch. Catrin cried out, expecting her back to snap as she fought to keep her balance under the onslaught.

At last Bryce pulled from her and threw her to the floor. Angry tears filled Catrin's eyes. She felt as violated as Tess Hodge.

"Damn you, Bryce Cavendish, don't you ever do that to me again!"

For a moment he stared speechless at her, his blue eyes starting from his head, until, gathering his wits, he fumbled to close his breeches, aware his state of undress robbed him of dignity. Bellowing in rage, Bryce leaped toward her.

Catrin scrambled to her feet, but she was not fast enough. He caught her and pinned her against the doorjamb.

"I'll do whatever I want with you, dearest, because you're me wife. In payment for becoming Lady Cavendish you sold me your body. And don't forget it. Tonight I think I'll teach you a new delight. I intend to master a part of your body denied me until now. As you needn't be hot for that, it should suit you admirably." With that he thrust her from him, sending her sprawling down the short flight of steps.

Weeping more out of anger than pain, Catrin picked herself up and limped to her waiting horse. Bryce bellowed for her to stop, but she ignored him. Scrambling into the saddle, she hung on, for without a mounting block she was at a decided disadvantage until she finally mastered her seat. Then she was off. She had a head start on Bryce as he came blundering down the steps, cursing as he tried to unloop his horse's reins from the railing.

Urging Rose to a gallop, Catrin drew closer to the house. He would not touch her now; she was safe until tonight.

Catrin sat sipping an after-dinner cordial in the plum-brocade-walled dining room. To her relief Bryce had excused himself early and she had only her silky lap dog for company. As the room grew darker she became aware of an unnatural glow suffusing the sunset sky. When Catrin first saw the crimson gash in the misty distance, she panicked. Hateful visions of Appin blazing in the night took her breath. Then she realized how foolish she was being! This was England, not Scotland. No enemy rampaged here dealing death and destruction.

"Potts, what's burning? Is it a hay rick?" she asked the butler when he entered the room to refill his master's brandy decanter.

Potts gave her a strange look. "Burning, my lady? Where?"

Going to the window, Catrin pointed to the distant glow. To her surprise the fire had shifted, coming closer to the house now, more in the direction of the stables. But no, when she looked again, she saw the fire had not shifted, merely multiplied. Twin blazes brightened the dusk, filling the crisp autumn evening with the acrid stench of flame.

His face stricken at the discovery, Potts wheeled and raced from the room, calling to the menservants to assist him as he ran. Catrin ran after him, amazed by the alarm displayed by such a normally calm individual.

"What is it? Are the stables on fire?"

"Save yourself, milady. There's going to be trouble."

"Save myself, Potts? I don't understand."

Before Potts could reply, Bryce came thundering down the stair. "What's the meaning of it? I saw it just now from my study. The buggers are insane! There's a whole army of them. Get out the firing pieces, Potts, give 'em to the men. We'll blow their fool heads off if they dare set foot on the terrace."

"Bryce, for the love of God, what is it?" Catrin demanded, seizing his arm and pulling him up short.

He viewed her with distaste. "You fool woman, what are you doing down here? Get upstairs. And don't show yourself. They're likely to try to take you hostage. They wouldn't dare touch one of His Majesty's officers . . . but you're another matter. Go on, get upstairs. What are you waiting for?"

"An answer."

He blinked, his mouth working. "The blasted villagers, that's who. Yesterday they threatened to burn the place around my ears for sending those rascals to the Indies. But, by Jove, I never expected them to carry it out. The effrontery of those creatures! Well, I'll show them. Get upstairs! Now!"

Reacting to Bryce's commanding tone in spite of herself, Catrin found herself racing upstairs before she realized what she was doing. On the second-floor landing she stopped, aware of a growing buzz she could not identify. After listening to it for a few minutes she realized it was the sound of many shouting voices. The angry villagers were coming toward the house.

Fear flashed through her. Though she had given them no reason to hate her, to them she represented the ruling class. She had not personally ill treated them, yet she was the wife of a man who had. Bryce's punishment would become hers also.

The housekeeper and the maids dithered about the landing, also sent upstairs by the master to protect themselves. The menservants stood below, armed with fowling pieces, swords, any weapon they could find to defend the house from the advancing rabble.

Bryce stood on the steps before the open door, daring the

villagers to set foot on his lawns. In a booming voice he threatened to call out the militia and have them all transported to the Indies.

"Milady, come this way. Pack some things ready to leave," urged the housekeeper, finally gathering her wits. "Tessie will help you."

So stunned was Catrin by the unexpected events, she did not relate the name Tessie to the girl she had rescued from the woods until she was confronted by her in her bedchamber. Tess had already packed several gowns and sets of underwear in a large tapestry valise. Bobbing a quick curtsy when she saw Catrin, she said, "Because you helped me, milady, I'll help you. Come on, we haven't much time."

"Surely they don't intend to enter the house—to harm us?"

"They mean to harm you all right. Riots is getting commonplace in this country nowadays. It's not just Sedgley men, they're gathered from all over. They hate his lordship for miles around for what he's done to the village lads. No man's been transported from hereabouts in over a hundred years. Now hurry, I don't want to see you hurt."

Catrin grabbed a pair of shoes, some toilet articles, and a nightgown, which she thrust inside the valise. Her lapdog whined and scrabbled at her feet and she stooped to pick her up.

"No, leave the dog 'ere. We can't risk it yapping and giving us away. Come on."

Tess grasped her arm. She was now in charge and she relished the reversal of roles.

Down the back stairs they fled. The smell of burn was far stronger here and Catrin discovered the rabble had already set fire to the outbuildings, the stables, and the kennels. The sound of shattering glass told her they were now smashing the windows.

Outside the billowing smoke was thick, searing her nose and throat until she began to cough and gag. Memories of the horror of Garth's destruction were uppermost in her mind as she fled into the night, pulling her dark hood about her face as Tess had instructed.

"Eh, Tess, who you got there?" demanded a rawboned yokel wielding a pitchfork.

"She's my friend from the kitchens. Let us by, Cobby, there's a good lad."

"A friend, eh. I'll have to 'ave a look at her, might fancy a roll in the hay with that one. Pretty she be."

"Go on with you, Cobby, she's a virgin. Scared little thing she is. Her maw's over Broomridge way. That's where I'm taking her."

Begrudgingly, Cobby let them by. At the last minute he reached for Catrin's hood. Then he turned to hear what another man was shouting to him and Tess pulled her away.

"Come on, what're you waiting for?" Tess darted into the smoke-filled darkness, dragging Catrin with her. The valise was heavy and Catrin doubted the wisdom of bringing so many clothes. Puffing and gasping, she finally had to stop to rest.

"Come on!" Tess cried, shoving her along. "If they knew it was you, I wouldn't give a farthing for your chances."

That final warning was sufficient to speed Catrin's lagging steps. They rounded the front of the house to behold a scene reminiscent of the rape of Garth; only these aggressors wore farm smocks instead of regimental uniforms. Furniture was being carried outside to be set alight, while other smaller pieces were seized and quickly vanished into the woods.

"Damn you, you worthless rabble! How dare you touch that!"

Bryce leaped down the steps, his sword flashing. He caught two men about the head, slicing off their ears and sending them screaming for cover. A third man stumbled in front of him and received the blade in his stomach. At first the villagers were afraid to confront this dervish with the gleaming blade; centuries of servitude had conditioned them to regard the gentry as inviolate. But others, from a newer breed of angry, resentful men, swept the cowards aside to challenge his lordship with their own weapons. Amid shouts and curses, wooden clubs and pitchforks descended and though some of the men received sword slashes for their pains, might finally triumphed. Bryce fell on the steps and they leaped on top of him.

Viciously stabbing the fallen nobleman with a pitchfork, a huge bear of a man roared in triumph. "The bastard's dead. Come on, lads, let's go inside. Let's show 'em we mean business!"

Catrin stood transfixed with horror as she stared at the bleeding figure lying half on, half off the steps, and at the thundering herd that leaped over him as they raced indoors to defile the symbol of his authority.

"Come on, this way."

Tess saw an opening and she darted for it, seizing Catrin's cloak and dragging her along. They stumbled into the shrubbery edging the open woodland and lay there panting, trying to catch their breath. Catrin suddenly remembered Tess's strange offer of aid, which at the time had seemed sweet and highly improbable.

"Did you know about this when you told me if I needed help you'd be there?"

"Not really—suspected's more truthful, milady. There's been talk about this for weeks. Thank God I was able to help you. Women aren't a pretty sight after a mob gets hold of them."

There was little to choose between mobs or soldiers of the King, Catrin thought bitterly as she stumbled along the woodland path in the dark, following Tess. Once again she was a homeless fugitive, and she despaired of ever knowing peace again.

Tess took Catrin inside her small hut, where her old mother was asleep on a bed of rags. The basket of food Catrin had given them yesterday hung from a beam in the center of the room.

"Safer there from the rats," Tess informed as she saw Catrin looking at the hanging basket. "Now you rest a while, milady, let me think what I'm going to do with you. They'll soon find you're gone and Cobby might gather 'is wits long enough to put two and two together."

Less than an hour later the two women were setting out again. Tess had decided it would be wiser to head for Broomridge, where Catrin could board the London mailcoach when it stopped at the Angel and Child. She doubted the villagers would dare invade the inn to search for Lady Cavendish, so it would be far safer there than for her to stay where she was.

Misty dawn was already breaking over the countryside when the weary travelers reached the Angel and Child. A slip of harvest moon was still visible in the sky as Tess banged on the inn's side door, requesting a room for her lady.

Tess spun such a tale of terror at Hursthampton, of villagers gone berserk, that the sympathetic landlord and his wife became gravely alarmed for Lady Cavendish's safety. The landlord sent a potboy to rouse the militia while his wife brought refreshment for her ladyship.

So much seemed to have happened in such a short time that when the landlord's wife woke Catrin to tell her the coach had arrived, she wondered if the night's events had been a terrible nightmare. One glance at the drawn faces about her, at her own soot-blackened clothes, and she knew she had not been dreaming. Gloom settled over her as she realized her life was shattered. She had no choice but to go home to Bloomsbury. Once again she would descend on her stepfather and beg his forbearance. Yet this time her misfortune was not of her own making.

Bidding Tess a tearful goodbye and waving to the kindly landlord and his wife, Catrin heaved a great sigh of relief when the coach finally pulled away from the Angel and Child in the mild October sunshine. Golden trees showered their leaves before them in the lane, and chattering squirrels darted up tree trunks as they passed. Catrin suddenly realized she was free. Bryce was dead! She no longer had to honor obligations to save her brother's life, or to allow David time to escape, or even to please her stepfather. At last, and perhaps for the first time in her life, she was finally her own person.

As soon as Catrin entered her stepfather's darkened house she knew something was terribly wrong. The servants did not answer her knock, so, finding the door unlatched, she opened it and let herself in.

"Where is everyone?" she called, wondering at the disorder in this household, which usually ran like clockwork.

A wan figure finally appeared; it was Jessie, clad in a nightgown. When she saw who the visitor was, the maid's face crumpled in grief. "Oh, Miss Catrin . . . Lady Cavendish," she corrected hastily. "Oh, it's terrible—poor Mr. Millbank's been taken so bad. Some of the staff's gone and I'm at me wit's end. What a godsend that you've come home."

Appalled by Jessie's news, Catrin hurried upstairs.

"When did it happen? How bad is he?" But Jessie was too rattled to answer her questions as she chatted on about unimportant details in an agitated voice. Catrin followed the maid to her stepfather's room.

"Who's there?" The feeble voice coming from behind the drawn bed curtains belonged to a stranger.

"It's me, Papa, Catrin."

"Ah, lass, come here."

Catrin clasped his hand. Her stepfather didn't look at her; it was almost as if he had already forgotten her presence.

"Why wasn't I sent for earlier?" she demanded of Jessie, who stood wringing her hands as she hovered in the background.

"He was taken sudden-like," Jessie said defensively, put out by Miss Catrin's accusing tone. "A letter was written and posted two days ago. It's a miracle you arrived when you did. I thought you must've got the letter, miss, and that's why you was here."

"All right, Jessie, it doesn't matter. I'm here now. How bad is he?"

Jessie drew her away from the bedside. "Dr. Little says there's no hope. A few days, a week . . . that's why you was sent for . . . I don't know, indeed I don't, why you didn't get the letter . . ."

"Shh, Jessie, it's all right. You may go now."

It was very quiet in the curtained room. From the hallway came the steady tick of the mahogany-cased clock, its bass voice booming out on the half hour, seeming to echo the heartbeat of the dying man, who lapsed in and out of consciousness. Catrin was thankful her stepfather was not sufficiently aware of his surroundings to notice her disheveled appearance. So far there had been no need to explain her unexpected arrival or her deplorable state. Jessie had been too distracted to care and the other servants did not appear to have noticed.

So quiet was it in her stepfather's bedroom that Catrin became aware of her thumping heart, of the pulse beating in her throat, the ache pounding in her head. How many more crises would she have to endure before she found peace? What a foolish question to ask, she thought, as tears slid down her nose. At this moment she was so vulnerable. Fate had absolved her of the need to explain the calamity at Hursthampton, or how disastrous her glorious marriage had become.

"Catrin, lass, are you still there?"

His feeble voice tugged at her heart. It was pitiful to find bombastic, aggressive Humphrey Millbank reduced to this. Tears splashed on the coverlet as she leaned over her stepfather to ask, "What is it, Papa?"

"Is Adam here yet?"

Adam? She drew back, wondering if she should remind him that his favorite nephew was dead. He must have forgotten that Adam had died in the suicidal defense of Carlisle ordered by Prince Charles on his retreat to Scotland.

"Not yet, Papa."

"He's taking his time. A real scamp is Adam. When he's grown our Isobel'll need to watch him. Now, lass, tell me how you like the pony."

Catrin racked her brain for memories of a girlhood pony. Humphrey Millbank's foggy brain traversed the comforting roads of the past. Perhaps it was as well he now dwelt in the years before Ness had disillusioned him, before she too had done her part to cause him pain . . .

"Well, 'ow's it ride? I paid a pretty penny for the little creature."

Memory came flooding back, providing Catrin with a mental image of the dainty pony he had given her on her thirteenth birthday. "She's lovely, Papa. Thank you for buying her."

"Aye, I knew you'd like her. But don't let that brother of yours ride her. Ness is a tearaway who'll come to no good, you mark my words."

His reminder of Ness's wasted life brought ready tears.

As the old man rambled on, disjointed sentences, words, laughter all mingled together, she wept for all that was gone. For her beloved brother who had turned against her. For youthful hopes turned sour, for heartache and lost love—for David! Oh, yes, her tears for David were the most bitter of all.

Chapter 20

Catrin put down her brush and stood back to survey the painting on the easel. This Scottish scene of tall mountains surrounding a loch, their sides brilliant with purple heather, created an intense longing in her to be there again. Her deepest longing of all was for the man she had left behind, whose memory this scene brought vividly to life.

Methodically she began to clean her brushes, deciding not to continue painting. Her current melancholy mood took the pleasure out of painting. During the four years since her step-father's death she had never painted a Highland scene, finding her memories too painful. This autumn she had finally felt able to confront those memories again. This purging of the heart had not been painless, yet it had proved highly therapeutic.

"Will you take tea, milady?"

"Lovely, Jessie. You timed it perfectly."

Catrin smiled at the maid, who had become her devoted companion since she had become mistress of the Bloomsbury townhouse. The delicate teaset Jessie placed on the mahogany drum table was of palest green china, lavishly adorned with gold leaf. The maid poured the amber brew and Catrin accepted a dainty cup, holding it carefully so as not to mark the china with her paint-stained fingers.

Jessie looked critically at the unfinished painting. "That's never Rome, milady, surely."

Catrin laughed. "No, Jessie, it's the Scottish Highlands."

"What with you talking about taking a painting holiday to

316

Italy and all, I thought you must be painting them foreign scenes again. Will that be all, milady?"

"Yes, thank you, Jessie, that's all."

For some time after the maid left, Catrin stared at the canvas scene, trying to accept the pain of her memories and purge herself of their sharpness. She should go to Rome—heaven knows she had talked about it for three years. She had always promised herself she would return to Italy if she were able. Yet part of her past always held her back.

She had inherited Humphrey Millbank's fortune, becoming one of London's richest heiresses. Once she was out of mourning a swarm of suitors began to call; and she was invited to dozens of parties. However, this past year both the invitations and the men's interest had begun to wane, simply because she failed to reciprocate. Not that she was a recluse—she rode frequently and a small circle of women friends joined her two afternoons a week for tea or accompanied her to the theater. On occasion Catrin even enjoyed the company of the ladies' brothers, but in all this time she had entertained no romantic thoughts about the fashionable men of her acquaintance. Unpleasant memories of Bryce, mingled with her anguish over losing David, made her immune to their attentions.

Catrin put down her cup and crossed to the window. The trees in the square below were already tinged with yellow; autumn would soon be here, followed by another dismal winter. She had grown so weary of this life. She had money in abundance, which allowed her to purchase whatever she wanted—she had completely refurnished this house to her own taste—but what did she do now? She was twenty-six years old, not an impressionable girl, yet she still ached for something that all the money in the world could not buy. She wanted David's love. Without it her newfound wealth became meaningless.

Why not go to Rome? She would avoid the gloom of a London winter. There she could immerse herself in exotic surroundings, painting to her heart's content. Yet gossip that David was sharing a villa with Brenda Carmichael in Rome's neighboring countryside kept her in London. To see him with Brenda was more than she could bear. That he even lived was a miracle for which she gave frequent thanks; yet to know he was living with Brenda was a torment too painful to accept.

"Miss Catrin, there's a gentleman to see you."

Catrin turned from the window to find her young housemaid,

Pansy, curtsying apologetically as she made her announcement.

"I'm not receiving company today, Pansy."

"No, Miss, I told him that. But he insisted . . . oh, sir, you can't go in . . ."

Pansy was thrust aside as a soberly dressed man walked inside the room. On the verge of ordering him out, Catrin gasped in joy as she recognized that face with its aggressive jaw and pronounced nose, the thick chestnut hair now heavily flecked with gray.

"Ness! Oh, Ness!"

Flying into his outstretched arms, Catrin wept as if her heart would break. Pansy, surprised to see the stranger being so well received, curtsied again and backed from the room.

"So we meet again. You've changed, you know, Catrin . . . but then, so've I," Ness remarked jovially, as he quickly took in the room's bright new furnishings. "You've changed the house too, a great improvement—never did care for old Millbank's taste."

"What are you doing in London? Oh, why didn't you let me know you were coming? Look at me! In a painting smock and my hair's a fright. Oh, Ness, how I've longed to see you. Tell me, how long will you be here?"

He patted her shoulder affectionately before sprawling in a nearby chair.

"That depends entirely on you, sister."

"On me? Why, you can stay here as long as you wish. I'm mistress of the house now Papa's gone. Will you take refreshments?"

"Brandy, if you please. Only the best stuff."

Catrin rang the bell and ordered brandy for the gentleman, albeit with some reluctance, because it was evident Ness had already drunk a considerable amount. The odor of brandy wafted about him and at times his speech was somewhat slurred. She looked at him with a heavy heart, seeing that time and suffering had aged him beyond his years, uniting with the ravages of a dissolute life to finally take their toll of his former youthful good looks.

"You've still not told me why you're in London. And even if it's all right for you to be here, considering your . . . sentence." She hesitated to refer to the unhappy past, but there was no way round it.

Pansy came and went, leaving behind a decanter of brandy and a glass.

Ness grinned and poured himself a generous bumper. Raising his glass, he drank to her health. "I can't tell you *why* I'm here, Catrin—demme, you'd have us all arrested. There are several more of us slinking about London, just like the old days."

His lighthearted explanation made her feel slightly sick; an unpleasant feeling of déjà-vu passed over her. Ness was still involved in intrigue. The past had not taught him anything.

"Oh, God, Ness, surely not another plot! Not after all you've gone through, what all of us went through. You surely can't be consider . . ."

"I'm considering just one thing, my dear sister," he snapped, leaning forward. A strange, hard expression crossed his face, reminding her of the way he had looked during that terrible confrontation at Hursthampton. "Apparently Papa left all his wealth to you. Becoming Lady Cavendish wasn't enough . . ."

"Bryce was killed four years ago, or haven't you heard?"

"Oh, yes, we heard the sad story. Such a pity, don't you think. I know how distressed you must have been."

His sarcastic tone put her on guard, and Catrin even contemplated ringing the bell for Terence. "Ness, surely after all this time we can be friends. When last we met you made terrible accusations . . . I married Bryce to ensure your release from prison. I would have done anything to save your life. For months I'd tried to find out where you were—I didn't even know if you were alive. No one could tell me anything. You can't blame me for your imprisonment. I'd nothing to do with it."

"You married one of the enemy. That's a fact you can't escape," he snarled, quaffing the last of the brandy and pouring himself another. When Catrin tried to take the bottle from him, he pushed her hand aside. "What, growing niggardly in your old age? Brandy's the staff of life, the fuel that keeps us poor disheartened Jacobites alive. Impoverished, embittered, our lives are not the most joyful. Spirits bring a little pleasure into our otherwise colorless existence."

"I think you've had enough spirits for one day."

"Do you indeed? You've not only inherited Millbank's house and his money, you seem to have inherited his attitude as well. No one tells me what to do now, Catrin. I'm well past the age of maturity. No one. Not even you."

"Why are you here?" she demanded, rising, her hand hovering over the bellpull.

"Don't ring for the servants," he rapped menacingly.

Catrin tensed, increasingly wary of this new Ness. "What do you want from me?" she repeated.

"I hear you're a very wealthy woman. Now, sister dear, it seems unfair that you should get everything. After all, he was my stepfather too. As ever, I'm somewhat short of funds."

"How much do you need?"

"Oh, no, I won't be fobbed off with a few pounds like some poor relation. I need far more than that."

"Are you seeking funds for the cause?"

"The cause?" Ness threw back his head and laughed. "Ah, yes, the glorious cause, promoted as usual by a band of tired failures. No, I don't intend to squander another penny on old men's dreams."

She stared in disbelief at him, shocked by his unexpected attitude. "But you said you were involved in a plot, just like the old days."

"Well, yes, in a roundabout fashion, I suppose I am." Ness emptied the last of the brandy decanter into his glass. "I came to England with others interested in reviving the Stuart cause, eager to investigate the newly aroused Jacobite sympathies we've been hearing about. I know you've always thought it, but I'm not a complete fool. I've far greener pastures to investigate. My visit, sister dear, is by necessity of short duration . . . I'm to sail for the colonies. And that's where you come in."

"I?"

"I want my share of the fortune to stake me across the Atlantic."

Anger tightened her jaw at his angry demand. "You've no share of any fortune. Whatever I choose to give you will be out of kindness."

Her words sat ill with him. Carefully setting down his glass, Ness lurched unsteadily to his feet. "Now listen here, Catrin, I didn't come to argue the point, merely to get what's mine. God knows, it's the least you can do, considering what I suffered. You've no idea what those hellholes were like . . . you helped put me there and you can damned well pay for it!"

"I'd nothing to do with your imprisonment. Talk sense. You were captured and shared the fate of hundreds of others."

"Ordered by the likes of Bryce Cavendish!"

"And even if he did order it, what possible blame can you place on me?"

"You married him, damn you! No one twisted your arm to leave Appin. Oh, yes, I heard the shameful story," he added with a snarl. "Don't think no one knows about your treachery. It's common knowledge. Lives were betrayed by you. And as an added bonus you took the Butcher's friend into your bed. Now, no more pleas. You're as guilty as they are. And you owe me recompense."

"I owe you nothing!"

Ness's face darkened with anger and he seized Catrin's wrist. "What did you say?"

"I said you're owed nothing!"

"Indeed. I have a right to half the estate, perhaps even more, considering I'm the sole male heir, but I'll be generous. I haven't time to be otherwise. And you, damn you, Lady Cavendish, will do as you're told. Now get the money. You're bound to keep some on hand. You can send me the rest later."

"If you need food, I'll feed you—lodging, I'll house you, but I'll give you nothing to aid your slide into the grave. I'll not support your drinking and whoring, no more than would our stepfather. Though at the time I considered him harsh, I realize now that when he cut you out of his will his judgment was sound."

Catrin caught her breath when she saw the sheer rage in Ness's face, transforming him into a stranger. Cursing violently at being thwarted, he seized her wrists and wrenched her toward him until their faces were only inches apart.

"Damn you! How dare you speak so to me after all you've made me suffer?"

Catrin struggled to free herself, wrestling against his surprising strength. The bell pull was too far away to reach. Ness glanced about the room, his gaze finally coming to rest on a heavy silver candlestick on a side table.

"Ness, let me go! Don't!" Catrin shrieked as he whirled around and grasped the candlestick.

Gone was his brotherly affection; even the family resemblance seemed to fade from his face as he looked at her with loathing, aware only that she stood in the way of his desires. Ness raised the candlestick to strike her, shifting as he tried to plant his feet more firmly on the floor.

"Be wise, Catrin, give me the money—don't make—me—"

Desperately she fought him, trying to seize the candlestick or reach the bellpull. Ness slapped her twice, hesitating to use

the weapon. He stared at his sister, swaying there, the candlestick held aloft; then suddenly he fell, thudding unconscious
on the carpet.

Catrin became aware that her breath was rasping painfully
in her throat. When she looked down at her assailant and reminded herself that he was her brother, she felt nauseated. Yet
the man who had threatened her was not the brother she had
known; he was the product of jail cells and battlefields, of
disillusion and years of drink.

Her knees began to quake and she stumbled to a chair. Catrin
was unable to control her trembling lips.

Pansy knocked on the door, alarmed by the angry voices
she had heard in the room.

"You can come in, Pansy, it's all right," Catrin assured
unsteadily as the girl peered around the door. "The gentleman's
drunk, that's all. He'll probably sleep for a while."

"Shall I get Terence, Miss Catrin?"

"I'll send for him when I'm ready. Clear away the things
if you want, then leave me alone."

After Pansy had left, Catrin managed to compose herself
sufficiently to get up and go to where Ness sprawled before
the hearth. The last hour had been a nightmare. What had
happened to the brother she loved?

She looked in his pockets, hoping to find some clue to where
he was staying. His mysterious fellow conspirators could come
and take him back to his lodgings. It would be most unwise
to allow him to stay here. She found several papers, a notebook
that appeared to be written in cipher, and an envelope bearing
an address just off the Strand in Essex Street.

Gambling that the Essex Street address was where he was
lodged, Catrin rang the bell for Terence and told him to watch
the gentleman until her return. Though the manservant suggested he go to the gentleman's lodging instead, Catrin insisted
she would go herself. She could not endanger the others' lives
because her brother was drunk. If possible she would protect
his fellow conspirators' identities.

Catrin pulled off her paint-stained smock, brushed her hair
back from her brow, and fastened it with a velvet ribbon. She
put on outdoor shoes, picked up her cloak, and set out for the
Strand.

Her mind was in turmoil as she hurried through the busy
London streets in the mild September sunshine. Ness was her
only brother. How could she cast him off? How could she

refuse to give him money? Yet she knew that whatever she gave him would be spent on dissolute living. And when that was gone, he would probably return for more. Pain for what had once been between them brought tears to her eyes, and she blinked them away as she turned the corner into Essex Street.

The address was three houses from the corner, a tall, somber dwelling with an unmistakable air of gentility. She went boldly up the flight of steps to the front door and banged on the highly polished brass door knocker. While she waited, Catrin rehearsed what she would say to the maid. It was somewhat humiliating to have to ask if friends of Mr. Blair lived here and, if so, would they please carry him home.

Footsteps sounded beyond the door. Catrin straightened her shoulders and prepared to deliver her speech.

When the door swung inward her breath stopped in a strangled sob. David stood on the threshold. While he stared at her in disbelief, his jaw tensed and a telltale pulse began to twitch in his cheek.

"Catrin! What in God's name are you doing here?"

"I might ask you the same thing. Can I come in?"

"Certainly."

He opened the door just far enough to admit her. Catrin found his manner exceedingly strange until she glimpsed another man standing well back in the shadows of the hallway. Her heart lurched in shock as she identified that unmistakable royal presence; Charles was heavier, older, his features slightly bloated beneath a corn-yellow wig, but he was unmistakably a Stuart Prince.

"Oh, Your Highness," Catrin whispered, sinking into a curtsy as he stepped forward to greet her.

"Why, Mistress Blair, what a surprise to see you again."

"Do please forgive me for my shabby appearance," Catrin began nervously, kissing the hand he extended to her.

"Haven't you heard? Shabbiness is much in vogue at the court in exile," Charles remarked somewhat bitterly. "I'll be in the other room, Stewart of Garth. Please be brief."

Stewart of Garth! Hearing David addressed thus brought painful memories surging back, until Catrin thought she would faint. Why was David here? What was the Prince doing in England?

"I suppose you came about Ness," David said, not assisting her up from the parquet floor.

"Yes. He passed out drunk in my drawing room."

"I expected as much. I'll have someone help me fetch him." He looked closely at her, hungrily taking in each detail of her appearance. Her features were finer, her manner more sedate, yet she was still so breathtakingly lovely that his heart ached as he gazed on her. There were so many questions he longed to ask, but pride forbade the inquiry.

"Thank you, that's what I hoped to hear," Catrin said stiffly, hardly knowing what she was saying, so stunned was she at meeting him again.

"There's a carriage waiting below. We can take that. I doubt Ness is in any state to return under his own power."

Catrin waited in the chill gloomy hallway while David went into the room where the Prince waited. She could hear them conversing in Italian, before David reappeared with two other men who looked vaguely familiar. Perhaps they too had come out in the '45, as it was now referred to with almost the same sense of history she had known as a girl when old men referred to the '15. David did not introduce his companions to her and Catrin did not care enough to ask their names.

The short ride back to Bloomsbury was a terrible ordeal. The others talked in Italian, and though she knew the language, Catrin felt too distressed to listen. Seeing Ness again had been ordeal enough—she had never expected to find David at the Essex Street address. She had ached to see him again, yet here he was sitting not two feet away and exchanging small talk with his companions as if she were a stranger. What was wrong? Catrin already had the answer to her question; David no longer belonged to her. The love that had been between them long ago was dead.

They alighted from the coach outside her home. The men followed Catrin indoors, apologizing profusely for their friend's having caused her such inconvenience. No one seemed aware that she and Ness were related. When they entered the drawing room they glanced at the fallen candlestick, but no one commented and she chose not to offer any explanations. They picked Ness up and carried him downstairs to the waiting carriage. Ness had still not revived by the time his friends settled him in the corner seat and bid her goodbye.

One last time Catrin gazed at her brother, relinquishing forever the emotional ties that had made him her childhood friend. Ness was a man who had chosen a very different life from his sister. Try as she might, she could help him no longer. It was a bitter fact to swallow.

"May I come inside to speak with you for a few minutes?" David asked, after telling the others to go on ahead.

Catrin knew she should refuse his request. The weakness inside her that made her love him still would not allow it. "If you wish. I've an engagement later this afternoon."

They reentered the house, finding it cool and gloomy after the bright autumn afternoon. Light coming through the stained-glass transom fell across David's face, accenting its leanness, and making his cheekbones appear far more prominent than she remembered. David's mouth was hard, as if chiseled from marble, his eyes dark. With his determined expression and plain dark cloth suit, he looked like a divinity student. His current mode of dress was a far cry from the flamboyant brocades and velvets of the past.

"Will you come into the drawing room?"

Obediently he followed, though he declined her offer of refreshment.

"Catrin, I must have your word that this will go no further. His Highness is here in complete secrecy."

"You've no need to swear me to secrecy. I'll keep your secret. No one will ever learn from me that he is in London."

"Thank you for your consideration."

"Why is he here? Surely he's not making a second bid for the throne."

David shook his head. "On that score Charles has never given up hope, but this impromptu visit is not a step in a complicated plot. True, he's sounding out English Jacobites, but I think what he really wanted was to see London—a pleasure he was denied on his last visit to England."

Catrin exchanged tight smiles with him, aware of the slowly elapsing minutes counted by the ticking clock. She could think of little to say that didn't seem strained or stilted. David did not sit, preferring instead to stand beside the window, where the breeze stirred his thick dark hair against his brow and invoked such sweet memories that Catrin's hands began to shake.

"Are you still involved in the cause?"

"Only because I've little choice. A fugitive with forfeited lands and title would be a fool not to support the Stuarts who promise to restore those rights. If you mean am I willing to lay down my life again for a dream . . . no, I'm five years older and much wiser. Our cause, such as it is, has become little more than the dream of an aging drunkard . . . oh, yes, Charles takes increasing solace from the bottle these days . . . it's no secret."

The bitterness in his voice touched her soul. For the second time this afternoon she had heard speeches from disillusioned men who had once lived and breathed the Stuart cause.

"I've shocked you, haven't I? Oh, don't deny it. I can tell by your face."

Catrin shook her head, forced a smile, and attempted more small talk.

The minutes crept by and she found this meeting an increasing strain. Again she offered David a drink and again he refused. Sensing his hostess's growing discomfort, he finally walked toward the door.

"I trust you've been well these past years? We heard in Rome about your good fortune . . . both incidents."

When he spoke all the unresolved bitterness was plain in his face. Catrin found her breath strangling in her throat. "David, from what Ness said you believe I betrayed your people. It's not true! I tried to *save* their lives. You surely didn't think I'd betray them."

"What I thought matters little. However, I did find it strange that you so eagerly greeted a man you always professed to dislike. But then, the years have taught me much . . ."

"Bryce ordered them shot! By promising to go with him . . . to be kind to him," this she found hardest of all to say, "he spared their lives. Surely you aren't foolish enough to think it was just a stroke of good fortune that the soldiers decided not to shoot them? I paid for their lives . . . yours too! By distracting Bryce from his objective I bought time to allow you to escape." Still she could see he did not wholly accept her story. "David, you must believe me, I wouldn't betray them knowingly. I'd no choice . . . they held me at gunpoint. And I also know who betrayed me to the redcoats—Brenda Carmichael! The woman you've taken so lovingly to your bed!"

Anger blazed in his face as he swung about. "You've had your say—now it's my turn. I accept that maybe on that specific afternoon your actions were selfless. Perhaps you drew the redcoats away from me, perhaps you even pretended affection for the captain to spare my people's lives—but tell me, why did you go to London with him? Why did you marry him?

No one was holding a pistol to your head then."

Catrin could not meet his gaze as pain and the desire to weep choked her voice. "I agreed to marry Bryce to save Ness—we were affianced years ago, you knew that from the beginning. Bryce promised to arrange Ness's release after our marriage. Oh, David, you surely don't think I preferred Bryce to you?"

"I don't know what I think," he snarled, moving toward the door again.

"I disliked Bryce Cavendish no less on the day I married him. You know I never had the slightest affection for him, though to give him his due he tried to be kind at first..."

"Oh, please, spare me your tender sentiments."

His scornful words were like a slap in the face. Eyes blazing, Catrin glared at him. "How dare you infer I've been unfaithful—you who took that Carmichael woman to live with you. In London we also hear stories. I know all about your shared villa. May God bless you and make you both as happy as you deserve."

"Thank you so much for your kind wishes, Lady Cavendish."

David spun on his heel and marched to the door. He had to leave; he couldn't endure more torment. Instead of quarreling with her, he longed to seize her, to kiss her, to press her against his body and declare all the love he felt for her, love he had hoarded in preparation for today. After years of empty daydreams his cherished hope had come true. Yet their wonderful reunion had gone terribly wrong...

"How dare you speak to me so sarcastically when I tried to save your life?"

"Do forgive me, but I find it hard to forget on whose side your husband fought."

"Get out!"

"I'm going... but before I leave I want to tell you your brother will be taken care of. He sets sail for the colonies tomorrow in the company of other Jacobites. They hope to make a new beginning, far from all lost hopes and faded dreams. I even contemplated taking a passage on the next voyage... have no fear, he'll come to no harm. I'll put him aboard the vessel myself."

"Thank you, Mr. Stewart. That's very kind of you."

Catrin watched him stride purposefully down the gloomy hall. David was leaner and harder than when she had seen him last, yet the years had dealt more kindly with him than they had with her brother. He still limped slightly, and she realized his ankle had never mended properly. Her heart wrenched with pain as she looked at his lean tanned hand on the door handle, and she fought a wave of emotion when she recalled the pleasure of his touch.

"Goodbye, Lady Cavendish."

"Goodbye, Mr. Stewart."

Catrin forced herself to follow him down the hallway—she must at least see him to the door. A few feet from him she stopped, searching his set face for the betrayal of his feelings for her. She could read little in that hard face, the narrowed mouth, the drawn brows.

"Will Brenda be waiting for you?"

"I doubt it. Brenda's been free to go her own way since I showed her the door last spring. Likely she'll have a ring through some Italian count's nose by now."

"Showed her the door! She's no longer sharing your bed?"

"No—though it's hardly any concern of yours. What Brenda and I shared could never be called love—more often than not it was mutual aggravation. But I won't bore you with my personal life."

David opened the door and a warm breeze swept inside the hallway. Catrin longed to reach for him, to tell him how much she still loved him. In a few minutes he would walk out of her life forever and she would never have another chance. Her heart lurched as she remembered that he had considered sailing to the colonies with his fellow exiles. The Atlantic would be a far more formidable barrier between them than the Channel had ever been...

"David, please, wait."

He stopped, almost as if he had been waiting to hear those words.

"Yes?"

"Don't... go. Not like this."

"How should I go? You've left me in no uncertainty about your feelings for me."

Tears robbed her of speech. Catrin looked at him through a shimmer of moisture. Their eyes met and her heart twisted with pain. "Surely you're not fool enough to believe such lies?" she whispered, licking the tears from her lips.

His head came up and he searched her face, his green eyes

troubled as pride waged a war between them. They both stood unmoving, longing to embrace each other. Tears spilled down her cheeks. Finally David put out his hand to her.

At first Catrin ignored his placating gesture, standing frozen to the spot as hurt coursed through her. Because of this man she had experienced four years of pain. Despite what he now said about his feelings for Brenda Carmichael, he had lived with her since he left Scotland. "Did you mean it when you said you've never loved Brenda?"

"Yes."

She searched his face shimmering through a veil of tears. "Stay. I thought we'd never see each other again. Please, don't let's spoil it now. Don't let pride stand in the way. Oh, David, I want you so . . ."

His arm went about her and with a sob she went limp against his strong body, finding the pleasure of his embrace excruciatingly painful.

"Catrin, love, for years I've dreamed of this moment," he breathed huskily. "I'd all but given up hope of ever seeing you again."

"David, oh, David, hold me, love me. Brenda was right when she gambled that I'd never willingly let them take you!"

"Hush." He placed his fingers gently on her lips, silencing her tearful words. "That's all in the past. I've never wanted anyone but you. Say you'll come back to Rome with me. At the moment I daren't stay in England, nor am I really sure I want to. I've made tentative arrangements to follow our friends to the colonies—they tell me parts of the land are much like Appin. Yet I don't really know if that is what I truly want. Today all I'm sure of is that I want to be with you."

"Sweetheart, hold me close, kiss me and make me forget," she whispered, clinging to his neck. The marvelous scent of his body, hot, fragrant, and highly masculine, filled her nostrils as she lost herself in the heavenly warmth of his embrace. "Love me as if nothing had ever gone wrong between us. We can go anywhere you wish, do anything you wish. We can even go to the colonies together, if you like. Maybe there at last we will both find peace. You can be laird of your own land, for I've gold enough for both of us."

David smiled as he buried his face against her perfumed hair. All the pain of infidelity and broken dreams he gladly thrust behind him. He rested his head against hers, drinking in the marvelous scent of her silky hair. Already seeds of adventure germinated in his blood. The colonies offered fresh hope to one who had thought all hope was dead. To have her there beside him, helping him build a new future in that vast land across the sea, was the answer to his prayers.

"From the ashes of the past we will rise again. Oh, Catrin, sweetheart, together we've something far more precious than gold," he breathed, holding her close, wanting this moment to last forever. "We've found love, and that's the most lasting treasure of all."

Sweeping Stories of Captivating Romance

☐20548-8 **THE EMPEROR'S LADY** Diana Summers $3.50

☐69659-7 **QUEEN OF PARIS** Christina Nicholson $3.95

☐86072-9 **THE VELVET HART** Felicia Andrews $3.95

☐05321-1 **BELOVED CAPTIVE** Iris Gower $2.95

Prices may be slightly higher in Canada.

Available wherever paperbacks are sold or use this coupon.

 CHARTER BOOKS
Book Mailing Service
P.O. Box 690, Rockville Centre, NY 11571

Please send me the titles checked above. I enclose _____ include 75¢ for postage
and handling if one book is ordered; 25¢ per book for two or more not to exceed
$1.75. California, Illinois, New York and Tennessee residents please add sales tax.

NAME_____

ADDRESS_____

CITY_____STATE/ZIP_____

(allow six weeks for delivery)